Fantastic Harrison!

A space-age missionary's dream—to save souls on a desolate planet—becomes a global nightmare when the "devout" aliens interpret the Bible literally.

A down-and-out artist has his last picture show —and the picture is a self-portrait of death on the very machine that's replaced him.

A cuddly teddy bear—in this strange world a man's best friend—is programmed to teach murder.

In a society where no one has any rights, one desperate family goes to bizarre extremes to prevent undesirables from moving in with them.

The *real* Frankenstein's monster is alive and well—and he lives in Florida.

THE BEST OF
HARRY HARRISON

HARRY HARRISON

A TIMESCAPE BOOK
PUBLISHED BY POCKET BOOKS NEW YORK

Another *Original* publication of POCKET BOOKS

 A Timescape Book published by
POCKET BOOKS, a Simon & Schuster division of
GULF & WESTERN CORPORATION
1230 Avenue of the Americas, New York, N.Y. 10020

ISBN: 0-671-42426-2

First Pocket Books printing June, 1976

10 9 8 7 6 5 4 3 2

POCKET and colophon are trademarks of Simon & Schuster.

Use of the TIMESCAPE trademark is by exclusive license
from Gregory Benford, the trademark owner.

Printed in the U.S.A.

Harry Harrison: The Man Who Walked Home

To put the issue squarely and at the outset (as we used to say in our praise-for-pay department at a certain major literary agency), this man is probably my closest friend in the science-fiction field and the one who, along with Edward L. Ferman, must accept the blame for starting me on whatever career I've developed. Harrison, then editor of *Amazing Stories,* bought my third piece in 1967; he bought my seventh and eighth for his *Nova* series; he helped me get the editorship of *Amazing* as his successor in 1968 (maybe this was not such a favor, Harry). As correspondent and three-times-a-year New York drinking partner, he kept me together during the worst days of my early life as a professional writer; and, in 1973, as a member of the awards committee, he was instrumental in gaining me the John Campbell Memorial Award and consequent recognition for *Beyond Apollo.* He has a charming, petite wife, Joan, a four-and-a-half-ton camper, and a penchant for not sitting in any one residence for more than three months, but this soupçon of personal detail should not put you off the main point.

Harry Harrison is my friend and helper; he has been my savior and protector. But all of this is beside the point, because our relationship has nothing to do with the fact that this man is one of the best writers the field has ever produced. In terms of range, he stands alone.

No one has ever had Harrison's range in the commercial field of science fiction. He is accomplished in every form from the well-respected hard science-fiction short story to the experimental and technical intricacies of the most sophisticated work the field is capable of (see "By the Falls" in this volume), from the broadest of burlesque (*Bill, the Galactic Hero* is the funniest novel in all of science fiction) to the serious and craftsmanlike novel of the near-future (consider *Make Room! Make Room!*). He will not only try anything—he will do it (usually) in less time than it would take the rest of us to put the paper in the typewriter and wonder if we really, after all is said and done, *really* feel like working today.

Make Room! Make Room!, which was published in 1967, became the movie *Soylent Green* in 1974. The movie is not very good—in fact, all the good in it is the novel from which it is extracted—but it was virtually the only money-making property MGM had that year, and its success has resulted for Harrison in the outcome every s-f writer longs for—a wide audience, a good deal of money, and the chance to wander through the world on an expense account giving lectures set up in advance by an excellent agent. Tea in London, drinks on the Riviera, camping overnight on the border of India, a spot of wine in Madrid. Dinner at Luchow's, cocktails at the Top of the Mark. Who could possibly complain? (Well, *I* could complain. I hate to travel with the same intensity that Harry loves it. I finally figured this out a few months ago: Harry travels around a lot so that the Angel of Death should need at all times a forwarding address. I sit in this modest suburb nestled near the oil refineries of Ridgefield Park, New Jersey, so that the Angel of Death in his constant travels can tuck me away safely in the corner of his mind knowing that I'll always be there and *then forget about me.* Thus we both try to outsmart the Angel of Death; we just do it in different ways.)

Too much digression. Attend to business. This man is a stunning writer; his very first story (published in 1953), "Rock Diver," has achieved the status of a classic; his first novel, *Deathworld* (published in 1960), was the best s-f adventure novel in many years, and perhaps there has been no better since. For more than two decades he has been producing a distinguished body of work; he has now written upward of twenty novels and a hundred short stories. As an editor—of the old *Science Fiction Adventures, Nova, Amazing Stories, Year's Best SF, The Year 2000*—he has been equally distinguished. His work is of genuine significance, his editorial talents undisputed. (He bought my third story, didn't he? Who else would have touched it?)

I give to you Harrison, and I say no more.

Oh yes, the title of this little preface. "The Man Who Walked Home" is the title of a story by James Tiptree, Jr., and a rather famous one; I apply it to Harrison because I admire the story and I admire Harrison and I thought I might as well tie the two together. What do you want—relevance? Meaning? What do you expect, Bill the Galactic Hero is asked at a crucial point in the novel, justice?

—BARRY N. MALZBERG

Teaneck, N.J.
January, 1976

Contents

THE BEST OF
HARRY HARRISON

IT IS HARD TO BELIEVE TODAY THAT science fiction was once chock full of taboos of all kinds. In my first novel, *Deathworld*, the word "damn" was removed from the magazine serial version. Writers, with very few exceptions, knuckled under to these constrictions, for to reject them meant to reject sales. Stories simply could not be sold that in any way obviously violated the accepted pulp-magazine taboos. The magazines were still the only market, and the magazine editors, all products of the pulps, wielded the blue pencil by conditioned reflex.

But change was in the air in the early 1960s. Algis Budrys, one of the most imaginative of the then-young writers, definitely not a product of the pulps, became editor of a new publishing firm in Chicago. (The company has long since vanished.) Judy Merrill, an editor who hated the pulp taboos, was already an anthologist of note. She planned to edit an anthology titled, I think, *The Thin Edge,* and Budrys agreed to publish it. All taboos were to be ignored and stories would be purchased on merit alone. Hurrah! Judy circulated a letter to as many writers as she could, and (I assume) her plan was greeted with relief and pleasure by all.

I know that *I* thought it a good idea and wrote back at once with an outline of a story I had long had in mind. She said fine, and I should proceed. I blush to admit, in these days of intergalactic cunnilingus and exo-biological bestiality, that my only bit of taboo-breaking was making the protagonist an atheist. Shocking! You might well laugh now, but this was serious stuff in those distant days, all of fifteen years ago. . . .

This story was an important one that had been cooking on the back burner for years. Important stories sometimes do not work when you get around to writing them. This one did, and I was very happy with it. It was polished, rewritten, typed, and entrusted to the international mails. Judy liked it, the money was paid—but the anthology was never born. The details are vague and a part of history. All I remember clearly are prolonged attempts to find out what had happened and then a fight to get the rights back. I eventually succeeded and, with a sigh of resignation, watched my agent spend his substance on postage in the vain attempt to sell it to the accepted markets. No dice. It went the rounds and, eventually, worn and coffee-stained, limped back to my desk.

What to do? I must have muttered and bitched in my continuing correspondence with Brian Aldiss, because he asked to see it. He was assembling the first of his Penguin anthologies at the time, and so had read "Streets" in the role of editor.

Brian liked "The Streets of Ashkelon." He made some very cogent editorial remarks about the characterization of the priest that I agreed with, and I did some rewrite.

Brian would take the story. But since his was a reprint anthology, I was still able to sell the story to a magazine before he printed it. Greed possessed me—it is always nicer to

be paid twice for a story rather than once—
but where could I sell the thing?

Ted Carnell, then editing *New Worlds* in
Britain, had liked the story, but thought it a
bit too taboo-breaking for his readership.
However, when he heard that Penguin would
be publishing it he stiffened up and decided
to take the story. (If this indicates his spine
needed strengthening, let us remember that
the American editors had no spines at all.)
So the story appeared in both magazine and
paperback in Britain, and the world did not
come to an end.

In fact, a number of people enjoyed this
story and told me so. It has been translated
into eight languages. Eventually, I managed
to have it published in the United States by
slipping it into my first collection of short
stories. There were still no riots in the streets.
Interestingly enough, once American editors
became aware of its existence it began appearing in American anthologies. And this
tale of a tale has an even happier ending.
The story has just appeared in a high school
textbook complete with notes and commen-
tary. Schools and churches have not been
burned down.

How remote all the earlier difficulties seem
now.

THE STREETS OF ASHKELON

<<<<<<<<<<<<<<<<<<<<<<<<<<<<<<<<<<<<<<<<

SOMEWHERE ABOVE, HIDDEN BY THE ETERNAL clouds of Wesker's World, a thunder rumbled and grew. Trader John Garth stopped when he heard it, his boots sinking slowly into the muck, and cupped his good ear to catch the sound. It swelled and waned in the thick atmosphere, growing louder.

"That noise is the same as the noise of your sky-ship," Itin said, with stolid Wesker logicality, slowly pulverizing the idea in his mind and turning over the bits one by one for closer examination. "But your ship is still sitting where you landed it. It must be, even though we cannot see it, because you are the only one who can operate it. And even if anyone else could operate it we would have heard it rising into the sky. Since we did not, and if this sound is a sky-ship sound, then it must mean. . . ."

"Yes, another ship," Garth said, too absorbed in his own thoughts to wait for the laborious Weskerian chains of logic to clank their way through to the end. Of course it was another spacer, it had been only a matter of time before one appeared, and undoubtedly this one was homing on the S.S. radar reflector as he had done. His own ship would show up clearly on the newcomer's screen and they would probably set down as close to it as they could.

"You better go ahead, Itin," he said. 'Use the water so you can get to the village quickly. Tell everyone to get back into the swamps, well clear of the hard ground. That

4

ship is landing on instruments and anyone underneath at touchdown is going to be cooked."

This immediate threat was clear enough to the little Wesker amphibian. Before Garth finished speaking Itin's ribbed ears had folded like a bat's wing and he slipped silently into the nearby canal. Garth squelched on through the mud, making as good time as he could over the clinging surface. He had just reached the fringes of the village clearing when the rumbling grew to a head-splitting roar and the spacer broke through the low-hanging layer of clouds above. Garth shielded his eyes from the down-reaching tongue of flame and examined the growing form of the grey-black ship with mixed feelings.

After almost a standard year on Wesker's World he had to fight down a longing for human companionship of any kind. While this buried fragment of herd-spirit chattered for the rest of the monkey tribe, his trader's mind was busily drawing a line under a column of figures and adding up the total. This could very well be another trader's ship, and if it were his monopoly of the Wesker trade was at an end. Then again, this might not be a trader at all, which was the reason he stayed in the shelter of the giant fern and loosened his gun in its holster.

The ship baked dry a hundred square metres of mud, the roaring blast died, and the landing feet crunched down through the cracking crust. Metal creaked and settled into place while the cloud of smoke and steam slowly drifted lower in the humid air.

"Garth—you native-cheating extortionist—where are you?" the ship's speaker boomed. The lines of the spacer had looked only slightly familiar, but there was no mistaking the rasping tones of that voice. Garth wore a smile when he stepped out into the open and whistled shrilly through two fingers. A directional microphone ground out of its casing on the ship's fin and turned in his direction.

"What are you doing here, Singh?" he shouted towards the mike. "Too crooked to find a planet of your own and have to come here to steal an honest trader's profits?"

"Honest!" the amplified voice roared. "This from the man who has been in more jails than cathouses—and that a goodly number in itself, I do declare. Sorry, friend of my youth, but I cannot join you in exploiting this aboriginal pesthole. I am on course to a more fairly atmosphered world where a fortune is waiting to be made. I only stopped here since an opportunity presented to turn an honest credit by running a taxi service. I bring you friendship, the perfect companionship, a man in a different line of business who might help you in yours. I'd come out and say hello myself, except I would have to decon for biologicals. I'm cycling the passenger through the lock so I hope you won't mind helping with his luggage."

At least there would be no other trader on the planet now, that worry was gone. But Garth still wondered what sort of passenger would be taking one-way passage to an uninhabited world. And what was behind that concealed hint of merriment in Singh's voice? He walked around to the far side of the spacer where the ramp had dropped, and looked up at the man in the cargo lock who was wrestling ineffectually with a large crate. The man turned towards him and Garth saw the clerical dog-collar and knew just what it was Singh had been chuckling about.

"What are you doing here?" Garth asked; in spite of his attempt at self-control he snapped the words. If the man noticed this he ignored it, because he was still smiling and putting out his hand as he came down the ramp.

"Father Mark," he said. 'Of the Missionary Society of Brothers. I'm very pleased to . . ."

"I said what are you doing here." Garth's voice was under control now, quiet and cold. He knew what had to be done, and it must be done quickly or not at all.

"That should be obvious," Father Mark said, his good nature still unruffled. "Our missionary society has raised funds to send spiritual emissaries to alien worlds for the first time. I was lucky enough . . ."

"Take your luggage and get back into the ship. You're not wanted here and have no permission to land. You'll be a liability and there is no one on Wesker to take care of you. Get back into the ship."

"I don't know who you are sir, or why you are lying to me." the priest said. He was still calm but the smile was gone. "But I hve studied galactic law and the history of this planet very well. There are no diseases or beasts here that I should have any particular fear of. It is also an open planet, and until the Space Survey changes that status I have as much right to be here as you do."

The man was of course right, but Garth couldn't let him know that. He had been bluffing, hoping the priest didn't know his rights. But he did. There was only one distasteful course left for him, and he had better do it while there was still time.

"Get back in that ship," he shouted, not hiding his anger now. With a smooth motion his gun was out of the holster and the pitted black muzzle only inches from the priest's stomach. The man's face turned white, but he did not move.

"What the hell are you doing, Garth!" Singh's shocked voice grated from the speaker. "The guy paid his fare and you have no rights at all to throw him off the planet."

"I have this right," Garth said, raising his gun and sighting between the priest's eyes. "I give him thirty seconds to get back aboard the ship or I pull the trigger."

"Well I think you are either off your head or playing a joke," Singh's exasperated voice rasped down at them. "If a joke, it is in bad taste, and either way you're not getting away with it. Two can play at that game, only I can play it better."

There was the rumble of heavy bearings and the remote-controlled four-gun turret on the ship's side rotated and pointed at Garth. "Now—down gun and give Father Mark a hand with the luggage," the speaker commanded, a trace of humour back in the voice now. "As much as I would like to help, Old Friend, I cannot. I feel it is time you had a chance to talk to the father; after all, I have had the opportunity of speaking with him all the way from Earth."

Garth jammed the gun back into the holster with an acute feeling of loss. Father Mark stepped forward, the winning smile back now and a Bible taken from a pocket of his robe, in his raised hand. "My son," he said.

"I'm not your son," was all Garth could choke out as

defeat welled up in him. His fist drew back as the anger rose, and the best he could do was open the fist so he struck only with the flat of his hand. Still the blow sent the priest crashing to the ground and fluttered the pages of the book splattering into the thick mud.

Itin and the other Weskers had watched everything with seemingly emotionless interest and Garth made no attempt to answer their unspoken questions. He started towards his house, but turned back when he saw they were still unmoving.

"A new man has come," he told them. "He will need help with the things he has brought. If he doesn't have any place for them, you can put them in the big warehouse until he has a place of his own."

He watched them waddle across the clearing towards the ship, then went inside and gained a certain satisfaction from slamming the door hard enough to crack one of the panes. There was an equal amount of painful pleasure in breaking out one of the remaining bottles of Irish whiskey that he had been saving for a special occasion. Well this was special enough, though not really what he had in mind. The whiskey was good and burned away some of the bad taste in his mouth, but not all of it. If his tactics had worked, success would have justified everything. But he had failed and in addition to the pain of failure there was the acute feeling that he had made a horse's ass out of himself. Singh had blasted off without any good-byes. There was no telling what sense he had made of the whole matter, though he would surely carry some strange stories back to the traders' lodge. Well, that could be worried about the next time Garth signed in. Right now he had to go about setting things right with the missionary. Squinting out through the rain he saw the man struggling to erect a collapsible tent while the entire population of the village stood in ordered ranks and watched. Naturally none of them offered to help.

By the time the tent was up and the crates and boxes stowed inside it the rain had stopped. The level of fluid in the bottle was a good bit lower and Garth felt more like facing up to the unavoidable meeting. In truth, he was looking forward to talking to the man. This whole nasty business aside, after an entire solitary year any human companionship looked good. *Will you join me now for dinner, John Garth,* he wrote on the back of an old invoice. But maybe the guy was too frightened to come? Which was no way to start any kind of relationship. Rummaging under the bunk, he found a box that was big enough and put his pistol inside. Itin was of course waiting outside the door when he opened it, since this was his tour as Knowledge Collector. He handed him the note and box.

"Would you take these to the new man," he said.

"Is the new man's name New Man?" Itin asked.

"No, it's not!" Garth snapped. "His name is Mark. But I'm only asking you to deliver this, not get involved in conversation."

As always when he lost his temper, the literal-minded Weskers won the round. "You are not asking for conversation," Itin said slowly, "but Mark may ask for conversation. And others will ask me his name, if I do not know his na . . ." The voice cut off as Garth slammed the door. This didn't work in the long run either because next time he saw Itin—a day, a week, or even a month later—the monologue would be picked up on the very word it had ended and the thought rambled out to its last frayed end. Garth cursed under his breath and poured water over a pair of the tastier concentrates that he had left.

"Come in," he said when there was a quiet knock on the door. The priest entered and held out the box with the gun.

"Thank you for the loan, Mr. Garth, I appreciate the spirit that made you send it. I have no idea of what caused the unhappy affair when I landed, but I think it would be best forgotten if we are going to be on this planet together for any length of time."

"Drink?" Garth asked, taking the box and pointing to the bottle on the table. He poured two glasses full and handed one to the priest. "That's about what I had in mind, but I still owe you an explanation of what happened out there." He scowled into his glass for a second, then raised it to the other man. "It's a big universe and I guess we have to make out as best we can. Here's to Sanity."

"God be with you," Father Mark said, and raised his glass as well.

"Not with me or with this planet," Garth said firmly. "And that's the crux of the matter." He half-drained the glass and sighed.

"Do you say that to shock me?" the priest asked with a smile. "I assure you it doesn't."

"Not intended to shock. I meant it quite literally. I suppose I'm what you would call an atheist, so revealed religion is no concern of mine. While these natives, simple and unlettered stone-age types that they are, have managed to come this far with no superstitions or traces of deism whatsoever. I had hoped that they might continue that way."

"What are you saying?" the priest frowned. "Do you mean they have no gods, no belief in the hereafter? They must die . . . ?"

"Die they do, and to dust returneth like the rest of the animals. They have thunder, trees, and water without having thunder-gods, tree sprites, or water nymphs. They have no ugly little gods, taboos, or spells to hag-ride and limit their lives. They are the only primitive people I have ever encountered that are completely free of superstition and appear to be much happier and sane because of it. I just wanted to keep them that way."

"You wanted to keep them from God—from salvation?" The priest's eyes widened and he recoiled slightly.

"No," Garth said. "I wanted to keep them from superstition until they knew more and could think about it realistically without being absorbed and perhaps destroyed by it."

"You're being insulting to the Church, sir, to equate it with superstition . . ."

"Please," Garth said, raising his hand. "No theological arguments. I don't think your society footed the bill for this trip just to attempt a conversion on me. Just accept the fact that my beliefs have been arrived at through careful thought over a period of years and no amount of undergraduate metaphysics will change them. I'll promise not to try and convert you—if you will do the same for me."

"Agreed, Mr. Garth. As you have reminded me, my mission here is to save these souls, and that is what I must do. But why should my work disturb you so much that you try and keep me from landing? Even threaten me with your gun, and . . ." the priest broke off and looked into his glass.

"And even slug you?" Garth asked, suddenly frowning. "There was no excuse for that and I would like to say that I'm sorry. Plain bad manners and an even worse temper. Live alone long enough and you find yourself doing that kind of thing." He brooded down at his big hands where they lay on the table, reading memories into the scars and callouses patterned there. "Let's just call it frustration, for lack of a better word. In your business you must have had a lot of chance to peep into the darker places in men's minds and you should know a bit about motives and happiness. I have had too busy a life to ever consider settling down and raising a family and right up until recently I never missed it. Maybe leakage radiation is softening up my brain, but I had begun to think of these furry and fishy Weskers as being a little like my own children, that I was somehow responsible to them."

"We are all His children," Father Mark said quietly.

"Well, here are some of His children that can't even imagine His existence," Garth said, suddenly angry at himself for allowing gentler emotions to show through. Yet he forgot himself at once, leaning forward with the intensity of his feelings. "Can't you realize the importance of this? Live with these Weskers awhile and you will discover a simple and happy life that matches the state of grace you people are always talking about. They get *pleasure* from their lives—and cause no one pain. By circumstances they have evolved on an almost barren world, so have never had a chance to grow out of a physical stone-age culture. But mentally they are our match—or perhaps better. They have all learned my language so I can easily explain the many things they want to know. Knowledge and the gaining of knowledge gives them real satisfaction. They tend to be exasperating at times because every new fact must be related to the structure of all other things, but the more they learn the faster this process becomes. Some day they are going to be man's equal in every way, perhaps surpass us. If— would you do me a favour?"

"Whatever I can."

"Leave them alone. Or teach them if you must—history and science, philosophy, law, anything that will help them face the realities of the greater universe they never even knew existed before. But don't confuse them with your hatreds and pain, guilt, sin, and punishment. Who knows the harm . . ."

"You are being insulting, sir!" the priest said, jumping to his feet. The top of his grey head barely came to the massive spaceman's chin, yet he showed no fear in defending what he believed. Garth, standing now himself, was no longer the penitent. They faced each other in anger, as men have always stood, unbending in the defence of that which they think right.

"Yours is the insult," Garth shouted. "The incredible egotism to feel that your derivative little mythology, differing only slightly from the thousands of others that still burden men, can do anything but confuse their still fresh minds! Don't you realize that they believe in truth—and have never heard of such a thing as a lie. They have not been trained yet to understand that other kinds of minds can think differently from theirs. Will you spare them this . . . ?"

"I will do my duty, which is His will, Mr. Garth. These are God's creatures here, and they have souls. I cannot shirk my duty, which is to bring them His word, so that they may be saved and enter into the kingdom of heaven."

When the priest opened the door the wind caught it and blew it wide. He vanished into the stormswept darkness and the door swung back and forth and a splatter of raindrops blew in. Garth's boots left muddy footprints when he closed the door, shutting out the sight of Itin sitting patiently and uncomplaining in the storm, hoping only that Garth might stop for a moment and leave with him some of the wonderful knowledge of which he had so much.

By unspoken consent that first night was never mentioned again. After a few days of loneliness, made worse because each knew of the other's proximity, they found themselves talking on carefully neutral grounds. Garth slowly packed and stowed away his stock and never admitted that his work was finished and he could leave at any time. He had a fair amount of interesting drugs and botanicals that would fetch a good price. And the Wesker Artefacts were sure to create a sensation in the sophisticated galactic market. Crafts on the planet here had been limited before his arrival, mostly pieces of carving painfully chipped into the hard wood with fragments of stone. He had supplied tools and a stock of raw metal from his own supplies, nothing more than that. In a few months the Weskers had not only learned to work with the new materials, but had translated their own designs and forms into the most alien—but most beautiful—artefacts that he had ever seen. All he had to do was release these on the market to create a primary demand, then return for a new supply. The Weskers wanted only books and tools and knowledge in return, and through their own efforts he knew they would pull themselves into the galactic union.

This is what Garth had hoped. But a wind of change was blowing through the settlement that had grown up around his ship. No longer was he the centre of attention and focal point of the village life. He had to grin when he thought of his fall from power; yet there was very little humour in the smile. Serious and attentive Weskers still took turns of duty as Knowledge Collectors, but their recording of dry facts was in sharp contrast to the intellectual hurricane that surrounded the priest.

Where Garth had made them work for each book and

machine, the priest gave freely. Garth had tried to be progressive in his supply of knowledge, treating them as bright but unlettered children. He had wanted them to walk before they could run, to master one step before going on to the next.

Father Mark simply brought them the benefits of Christianity. The only physical work he required was the construction of a church, a place of worship and learning. More Weskers had appeared out of the limitless planetary swamps and within days the roof was up, supported on a framework of poles. Each morning the congregation worked a little while on the walls, then hurried inside to learn the all-promising, all-encompassing, all-important facts about the universe.

Garth never told the Weskers what he thought about their new interest and this was mainly because they had never asked him. Pride or honour stood in the way of his grabbing a willing listener and pouring out his grievances. Perhaps it would have been different if Itin was on Collecting duty; he was the brightest of the lot; but Itin had been rotated the day after the priest had arrived and Garth had not talked to him since.

It was a surprise then when after seventeen of the trebly-long Wesker days he found a delegation at his doorstep when he emerged after breakfast. Itin was their spokesman, and his mouth was open slightly. Many of the other Weskers had their mouths open as well, one even appearing to be yawning, clearly revealing the double row of sharp teeth and the purple-black throat. The mouths impressed Garth as to the seriousness of the meeting: this was the one Wesker expression he had learned to recognize. An open mouth indicated some strong emotion; happiness, sadness, anger, he could never be really sure which. The Weskers were normally placid and he had never seen enough open mouths to tell what was causing them. But he was surrounded by them now.

"Will you help us, John Garth," Itin said. "We have a question."

"I'll answer any question you ask," Garth said, with more than a hint of misgiving. "What is it?"

"Is there a God?"

"What do you mean by 'God'?" Garth asked in turn. What should he tell them?

"God is our Father in Heaven, who made us all and protects us. Whom we pray to for aid and if we are Saved will find a place . . ."

"That's enough," Garth said. "There is no God."

All of them had their mouths open now, even Itin, as they looked at Garth and thought about his answer. The rows of pink teeth would have been frightening if he hadn't known these creatures so well. For one instant he wondered if perhaps they had been already indoctrinated and looked upon him as a heretic, but he brushed the thought away.

"Thank you," Itin said and they turned and left.

Though the morning was still cool, Garth noticed that he was sweating and wondered why.

The reaction was not long in coming. Itin returned that same afternoon. "Will you come to the church?" he asked. "Many of the things that we study are difficult to learn, but none as difficult as this. We need your help because we must hear you and Father Mark talk together. This is because he says one thing is true and you say another is true and both cannot be true at the same time. We must find out what is true."

"I'll come, of course," Garth said, trying to hide the sudden feeling of elation. He had done nothing, but the Weskers had come to him anyway. There could still be grounds for hope that they might yet be free.

It was hot inside the church, and Garth was surprised at the number of Weskers who were there, more than he had seen gathered at any one time before. There were many open mouths. Father Mark sat at a table covered with books. He looked unhappy but didn't say anything when Garth came in. Garth spoke first.

"I hope you realize this is their idea—that they came to me of their own free will and asked me to come here?"

"I know that," the priest said resignedly. "At times they can be very difficult. But they are learning and want to believe, and that is what is important."

"Father Mark, Trader Garth, we need your help," Itin said. "You both know many things that we do not know. You must help us come to religion, which is not an easy thing to do." Garth started to say something, then changed his mind. Itin went on. "We have read the Bibles and all the books that Father Mark gave us and one thing is clear. We have discussed this and we are all agreed. These books are very different from the ones that Trader Garth gave us. In Trader Garth's books there is the universe which we have not seen, and it goes on without God, for he is mentioned nowhere; we have searched very carefully. In Father Mark's books He is everywhere and nothing can go without Him. One of these must be right and the other must be wrong. We do not know how this can be, but after we find out which is right then perhaps we will know. If God does not exist . . ."

"Of course He exists, my children," Father Mark said in a voice of heartfelt intensity. "He is our Father in Heaven who has created us all . . ."

"Who created God?" Itin asked and the murmur ceased and every one of the Weskers watched Father Mark intensely. He recoiled a bit under the impact of their eyes, then smiled.

"Nothing created God, since He is the Creator. He always was . . ."

"If He always was in existence—why cannot the universe have always been in existence? Without having had a creator?" Itin broke in with a rush of words. The importance of the question was obvious. The priest answered slowly, with infinite patience.

"Would that the answers were that simple, my children. But even the scientists do not agree about the creation of the universe. While they doubt—we who have seen the light *know*. We can see the miracle of creation all about us. And how can there be a creation without a Creator? That is He, our Father, our God in Heaven. I know you have doubts; that is because you have souls and free will. Still, the answer is so simple. Have faith, that is all you need. Just believe."

"How can we believe without proof?"

"If you cannot see that this world itself is proof of His existence, then I say to you that belief needs no proof—if you have faith!"

A babble of voices arose in the room and more of the Wesker mouths were open now as they tried to force their thoughts through the tangled skein of words and separate the thread of truth.

"Can you tell us, Garth?" Itin asked, and the sound of his voice quieted the hubbub.

"I can tell you to use the scientific method which can examine all things—including itself—and give you answers that can prove the truth or falsity of any statement."

"That is what we must do," Itin said, "we had reached the same conclusion." He held a thick book before him and a ripple of nods ran across the watchers. "We have been studying the Bible as Father Mark told us to do, and we have found the answer. God will make a miracle for us, thereby proving that He is watching us. And by this sign we will know Him and go to Him."

"That is the sin of false pride," Father Mark said. "God needs no miracles to prove His existence."

"But *we* need a miracle!" Itin shouted and though he wasn't human there was need in his voice. "We have read here of many smaller miracles, loaves, fishes, wine, snakes—many of them, for much smaller reasons. Now all He need do is make a miracle and He will bring us all to Him—the wonder of an entire new world worshipping at His throne, as you have told us, Father Mark. And you have told us how important this is. We have discussed this and find that there is only one miracle that is best for this kind of thing."

His boredom at the theological wrangling drained from Garth in an instant. He had not been really thinking or he would have realized where all this was leading. He could see the illustration in the Bible where Itin held it open, and knew in advance what picture it was. He rose slowly from his chair, as if stretching, and turned to the priest behind him.

"Get ready!" he whispered. "Get out the back and

get to the ship; I'll keep them busy here. I don't think they'll harm me."

"What do you mean . . . ?" Father Mark asked, blinking in surprise.

"Get out, you fool!" Garth hissed. "What miracle do you think they mean? What miracle is supposed to have converted the world to Christianity?"

"No!" Father Mark said. "It cannot be. It just cannot be . . . !"

"GET MOVING!" Garth shouted, dragging the priest from the chair and hurling him towards the rear wall. Father Mark stumbled to a halt, turned back. Garth leaped for him, but it was already too late. The amphibians were small, but there was so many of them. Garth lashed out and his fist struck Itin, hurling him back into the crowd. The others came on as he fought his way towards the priest. He beat at them but it was like struggling against waves. The furry, musky bodies washed over and engulfed him. He fought until they tied him, and he still struggled until they beat on his head until he stopped. Then they pulled him outside where he could only lie in the rain and curse and watch.

Of course the Weskers were marvellous craftsmen, and everything had been constructed down to the last detail, following the illustration in the Bible. There was the cross, planted firmly on the top of a small hill, the gleaming metal spikes, the hammer. Father Mark was stripped and draped in a carefully pleated loincloth. They led him out of the church.

At the sight of the cross he almost fainted. After that he held his head high and determined to die as he had lived, with faith.

Yet this was hard. It was unbearable even for Garth, who only watched. It is one thing to talk of crucifixion and look at the gentle carved bodies in the dim light of prayer. It is another to see a man naked, ropes cutting into his skin where he hangs from a bar of wood. And to see the needle-tipped spike raised and placed against the soft flesh of his palm, to see the hammer come back with the calm deliberation of an artisan's measured stroke. To hear the thick sound of metal penetrating flesh.

Then to hear the screams.

Few are born to be martyrs; Father Mark was not one of them. With the first blows, the blood ran from his lips where his clenched teeth met. Then his mouth was wide and his head strained back and the guttural horror of his screams sliced through the susurration of the falling rain. It resounded as a silent echo from the masses of watching Weskers, for whatever emotion opened their mouths was now tearing at their bodies with all its force, and row after row of gaping jaws reflected the crucified priest's agony.

Mercifully he fainted as the last nail was driven home. Blood ran from the raw wounds, mixing with the rain to drip faintly pink from his feet as the life ran out of him. At this time, somewhere at this time, sobbing and tearing at his own bonds, numbed from the blows on the head, Garth lost consciousness.

He awoke in his own warehouse and it was dark. Someone was cutting away the woven ropes they had bound him with. The rain still dripped and splashed outside.

"Itin," he said. It could be no one else.

"Yes," the alien voice whispered back. "The others are all talking in the church. Lin died after you struck his head, and Inon is very sick. There are some that say you should be crucified too, and I think that is what will happen. Or perhaps killed by stoning on the head. They have found in the Bible where it says . . ."

"I know." With infinite weariness. "An eye for an eye. You'll find lots of things like that once you start looking. It's a wonderful book." His head ached terribly.

"You must go, you can get to your ship without anyone seeing you. There has been enough killing." Itin, as well, spoke with a new-found weariness.

Garth experimented, pulling himself to his feet. He pressed his head to the rough wood of the wall until the nausea stopped. "He's dead." He said it as a statement, not a question.

"Yes, some time ago. Or I could not have come away to see you."

"And buried of course, or they wouldn't be thinking about starting on me next."

"And buried!" There was almost a ring of emotion in the alien's voice, an echo of the dead priest's. "He is buried and he will rise on High. It is written and that is the way it will happen. Father Mark will be so happy that it has happened like this." The voice ended in a sound like a human sob.

Garth painfully worked his way towards the door, leaning against the wall so he wouldn't fall.

"We did the right thing, didn't we?" Itin asked. There was no answer. "He will rise up, Garth, won't he rise?"

Garth was at the door and enough light came from the brightly lit church to show his torn and bloody hands clutching at the frame. Itin's face swam into sight close to his, and Garth felt the delicate, many fingered hands with the sharp nails catch at his clothes.

"He will rise, won't he, Garth?"

"No," Garth said, "he is going to stay buried right where you put him. Nothing is going to happen because he is dead and he is going to stay dead."

The rain runnelled through Itin's fur and his mouth was opened so wide that he seemed to be screaming into the night. Only with effort could he talk, squeezing out the alien thoughts in an alien language.

"Then we will not be saved? We will not become pure?"

"You were pure," Garth said, in a voice somewhere between a sob and a laugh. "That's the horrible ugly dirty part of it. You were pure. Now you are . . ."

"Murderers," Itin said and the water ran down from his lowered head and streamed away into the darkness.

HOW OFTEN THE ACT OF CREATION depends upon the editor. Science fiction has been quite blessed with creative editors who have led writers down unexpected paths and have indulged writers in moments of madness. Avram Davidson is an old friend; our paths have crossed again and again through the years. For a time he was editor of *Fantasy and Science Fiction,* editing the magazine from, of all places, Mexico. (He lived in the town of Amecameca, just a few miles from Cuautla, where I had been for a year—life has its strange cycles.) I was living in Denmark, and we were in correspondence.

Avram, a fancifier himself, encouraged my own wildest fancies. He even bought a poem from me, the only one I have ever sold. It was a humorous poem, and humor has always fascinated me. S-f was such a grave matter that I allowed very little jokiness into my work, all of which tended to be deadly serious. But why not be funny? Avram was most receptive.

I have always been an ardent admirer of the works of C. S. Forester and, imitation being the highest form of flattery, I wanted to do an s-f parody of *Captain Horatio Hornblower.* Enjoy, enjoy, Avram wrote, and I did.

2

21

The story was a pleasure to do, and the only dark note came later. I sent a copy to Forester, along with a letter about imitation, flattery, and so on, but he never wrote back. In fact, he died soon afterward, and I have always felt a bit of guilt that I might have had a hand in that matter.

CAPTAIN HONARIO
HARPPLAYER, R.N.

<<<<<<<<<<<<<<<<<<<<<<<<<<<<<<<<<<<<<<<<

CAPTAIN HONARIO HARPPLAYER WAS PACING
the tiny quarterdeck of the H.M.S. *Redundant,* hands
clasped behind his back, teeth clamped in impotent fury.
Ahead of him the battered French fleet limped towards
port, torn sails flapping and spars trailing overside in the
water, splintered hulls agape where his broadsides had
gone thundering through their fragile wooden sides.

"Send two hands for'ard, if you please, Mr. Shrub,"
he said, "and have them throw water on the mainsail.
Wet sails will add an eighth of a knot to our speed and
we may overtake these cowardly frogs yet."

"B-but, sir," the stolid first mate Shrub stammered,
quailing before the thought of disagreeing with his beloved
captain. "If we take any more hands off the pumps we'll
sink. We're holed in thirteen places below the water-
line, and . . ."

"Damn your eyes, sir! I issued an order, not a request
for a debate. Do as you were told."

"Aye, aye, sir," Shrub mumbled, humbled, knuckling
a tear from one moist spaniel eye.

Water splashed onto the sails and the *Redundant* instantly sank lower in the water. Harpplayer clasped his
hands behind his back and hated himself for this display
of unwarranted temper towards the faithful Shrub. Yet
he had to keep up this pose of strict disciplinarian before
the crew, the sweepings and dregs of a thousand water-

23

fronts, just as he had to wear a girdle to keep up his own front and a truss to keep up his hernia. He had to keep up a good front because he was the captain of this ship, the smallest ship in the blockading fleet that lay like a strangling noose around Europe, locking in the mad tyrant Napoleon, whose dreams of conquest could never extend to England whilst these tiny wooden ships stood in the way.

"Give us a prayer, Cap'n, to speed us on our way to 'eaven because we're sinkin'!" a voice called from the crowd of seamen at the pumps.

"I'll have that man's name, Mr. Dogleg," Harpplayer called to the midshipman, a mere child of seven or eight, who commanded the detail. "No rum for him for a week."

"Aye aye, sir," piped Mr. Dogleg, who was just learning to talk.

The ship was sinking, the fact was inescapable. Rats were running on deck, ignoring the cursing, stamping sailors, and hurling themselves into the sea. Ahead the French fleet had reached the safety of the shore batteries on Cape Pietfieux and the gaping mouths of these guns were turned towards the *Redundant,* ready to spout fire and death when the fragile ship came within range.

"Be ready to drop sail, Mr. Shrub," Harpplayer said, then raised his voice so all the crew could hear. "Those cowardly Frenchies have run away and cheated us of a million pounds in prize money."

A growl went up from the crew, who, next to a love for rum, loved the pounds, shillings and pence with which they could buy the rum. The growl was suddenly cut off in muffled howls of pain as the mainmast, weakened by the badly aimed French cannon, fell onto the mass of labouring men.

"No need to drop sail, Mr. Shrub, the slaves of our friend Boney have done it for us," Harpplayer said, forcing himself to make one of his rare jests so loved by the crew. He hated himself for the falseness of his feelings, ingratiating himself into the sympathies of these illiterate men by such means, but it was his duty to keep a taut ship. Besides, if he didn't make any jokes the men would hate him for the slave-driving, cold-blooded, chance-taking master that he was. They still hated him, of course, but they laughed while they did it.

They were laughing now as they cut away the tangle of rigging and dragged out the bodies to lay them in neat rows upon the deck. The ship sank lower in the water.

"Avast that body dragging," he ordered, "and man the pumps, or we'll have our dinners on the bottom of the sea."

The men laughed a ragged laugh again and hurried to their tasks.

They were easy to please, and Harpplayer envied them their simple lives. Even with the heavy work, bad water and an occasional touch of the cat, their existence was better than his tortured life on the lonely pinnacle of command. The decisions were all his to make and to a man of his morbid and paranoic nature this made life a living hell. His officers, who all hated him, were incompetents. Even Shrub, faithful, long-suffering Shrub, had his weakness: namely the fact that he had an I.Q. of about 60, which, combined with his low birth, meant he could never rise above the rank of a rear-admiral.

While he considered the varied events of the day Harpplayer began his compulsive pacing on the tiny quarterdeck, and its other occupants huddled against the starboard side, where they wouldn't be in his way. Four paces in one direction, then three-and-a-half paces back with his knee bringing up with a shuddering crack against the port carronade. Yet Harpplayer did not feel this, his cardplayer's brain was whirling with thoughts, evaluating and weighing plans, rejecting those that held a modicum of sanity and only considering those that sounded too insane to be practical. No wonder he was called "Sapsucker Harpy" throughout the fleet and held in awe as a man who could always pull victory from the jaws of defeat, and always at an immense cost of lives. But that was war. You gave your commands and good men died, and that was what the press gangs on shore were for. It had been a long and trying day; yet he still would not permit himself to relax. Tension and the agony of apprehension had seized him in the relentless grip of a Cerberus ever since soon after dawn that morning when the lookout had announced the discovery of sails on the horizon. There had been only ten of them, Frenchy ships of the line, and before the morning fog had cleared the vengeful form of the *Redundant* had been upon them, like a wolf among the sheep. Broadside after broadside had roared out from the precisely serviced English guns, ten balls for every one that popped out of the French cannon, manned by cowardly sweepings of the eighth and ninth classes of 1812, greybearded patriarchs and diapered infants who only wished they were back in the familial vineyards instead of here, fighting for the Tyrant, facing up to the wrath of the death-dealing cannon of their island enemy, the tiny country left to fight alone against the might of an entire continent. It had been a relentless stern chase, and only the succour of the French port had prevented the destruction of the entire squadron. As it was, four of them lay among the conger eels on the bottom of the ocean, and the remaining six would need a complete refitting before they were fit to leave port and once more dare the retributive might of the ships that ringed their shores.

Harpplayer knew what he had to do.

"If you please, Mr. Shrub, have the hose rigged. I feel it is time for a bath."

A ragged cheer broke from the toiling sailors, since they knew what to expect. In the coldest northern waters or in the dead of winter Harpplayer insisted on this routine of the bath. The hoses were quickly attached to the labouring pumps and soon columns of icy water were jetting across the deck.

"In we go!" shouted Harpplayer, and stepped back well out of the way of any chance droplets, at the same time scratching with a long index finger at the skin of his side, unwashed since the previous summer. He smiled at the childish antics of Shrub and the other officers prancing nude in the water, and only signalled for the pumps to cease their work when all of the white skins had turned a nice cerulean.

There was a rumble, not unlike distant thunder yet

sharper and louder, from the northern horizon. Harpplayer turned and for a long instant saw a streak of fire painted against the dark clouds, before it died from the sky, leaving only an after-image in his eyes. He shook his head to clear it, and blinked rapidly a few times. For an instant there he could have sworn that the streak of light had come down, instead of going up, but that was manifestly impossible. Too many late nights playing boston with his officers, no wonder his eyesight was going.

"What was that, Captain?" Lieutenant Shrub asked, his words scarcely audible through the chattering of his teeth.

"A signal rocket—or perhaps one of those new-fangled Congreve war rockets. There's trouble over there, and we're going to find out just what it is. Send the hands to the braces, if you please, fill the main-tops'l and lay her on the starboard tack."

"Can I put my pants on first?"

"No impertinence, sir, or I'll have you in irons!"

Shrub bellowed the orders through the speaking trumpet, and all the hands laughed at his shaking naked legs. Yet in a few seconds the well-trained crew, who not six days before had been wenching and drinking ashore on civvy street, never dreaming that the wide-sweeping press gangs would round them up and send them to sea, leapt to the braces, hurled the broken spars and cordage overside, sealed the shot holes, buried the dead, drank their grog and still had enough energy left over for a few of their number to do a gay hornpipe. The ship heeled as she turned, water creamed under her bows, and then she was on the new tack, reaching out from the shore, investigating this new occurrence, making her presence felt as the representative of the mightiest blockading fleet the world, at that time, had ever known.

"A ship ahead, sir," the masthead lookout called. "Two points off the starboard bow."

"Beat to quarters," Harpplayer ordered.

Through the heavy roll of the drum and the slap of the sailors' bare horny feet on the deck, the voice of the lookout could be barely heard.

"No sails nor spars, sir. She's about the size of our longboat."

"Belay that last order. And when that lookout comes off duty I want him to recite five hundred times, a boat is something that's picked up and put on a ship."

Pressed on by the freshing land breeze the *Redundant* closed rapidly on the boat until it could be made out clearly from the deck.

"No masts, no spars, no sails—what makes it move?" Lieutenant Shrub asked with gape-mouthed puzzlement.

"There is no point in speculation in advance, Mr. Shrub. This craft may be French or a neutral so I'll take no chances. Let us have the cannonades loaded and run out. And I want the Marines in the futtock-shrouds, with their pieces on the half-cock, if you please. I want no one to fire until they receive my command, and I'll have anyone who does boiled in oil and served for breakfast."

"You are the card, sir!"

"Am I? Remember the cox'n who got his orders mixed yesterday?"

"Very gamey, sir, if I say so," Shrub said, picking a bit of gristle from between his teeth. "I'll issue the orders, sir."

The strange craft was like nothing Harpplayer had ever seen before. It advanced without visible motive power, and he thought of hidden rowers with underwater oars, but they would have to be midgets to fit in the boat. It was decked all over and appeared to be covered with a glass hutment of some kind. All in all a strange device, and certainly not French. The unwilling slaves of the Octopus in Paris would never master the precise techniques to construct a diadem of the sea such as this. No, this was from some alien land, perhaps from beyond China or the mysterious islands of the east. There was a man seated in the craft, and he touched a lever that rolled back the top window. He stood then and waved to them. A concerted gasp ran through the watchers, for every eye in the ship was fastened on this strange occurrence.

"What is this, Mr. Shrub," Harpplayer shouted. "Are we at a fun fair or a Christmas pantomime? Discipline, sir!"

"B-but, sir," the faithful Shrub stammered, suddenly at a loss for words. "That man, sir—he's *green!*"

"I want none of your damn nonsense, sir," Harpplayer snapped irritably, annoyed as he always was when people babbled about their imagined "colours." Paintings, and sunsets and such tripe. Nonsense. The world was made up of healthy shades of grey and that was that. Some fool of a Harley Street quack had once mentioned an imaginary malady which he termed "colour blindness" but had desisted with his tomfoolery when Harpplayer had mentioned the choice of seconds.

"Green, pink or purple, I don't care what shade of grey the fellow is. Throw him a line and have him up here where we can hear his story."

The line was dropped and after securing it to a ring on his boat the stranger touched a lever that closed the glass cabin once more, then climbed easily to the deck above.

"Green fur . . ." Shrub said, then clamped his mouth shut under Harpplayer's fierce glare.

"Enough of that, Mr. Shrub. He's a foreigner, and we will treat him with respect, at least until we find out what class he is from. He is a bit hairy, I admit, but certain races in the north of the Nipponese Isles are that way, perhaps he comes from there. I bid you welcome, sir," he said, addressing the man. "I am Captain Honario Harpplayer, commander of His Majesty's ship, *Redundant.*"

"*Kwl-kkle-wrrl-kl . . . . . !*"

"Not French," Harpplayer muttered, "no Latin nor Greek I warrant. Perhaps one of those barbaric Baltic tongues. I'll try him on German. *Ich rate Ihnen, Reiseschecks mitzunehmen?* Or an Italian dialect? *E proibito; pero quisivendono cartoline ricordo.*"

The stranger responded by springing up and down excitedly, then pointing to the sun, making circular motions around his head, pointing to the clouds, making falling motions with his hands, and shrilly shouting "*M'ku, m'ku!*"

"Feller's barmy," the Marine officer said, "and besides, he got too many fingers."

"I can count to seven without your help," Shrub told him angrily. "I think he's trying to tell us it's going to rain."

"He may be a meteorologist in his own land," Harp-player said safely, "but here he is just another alien."

The officers nodded agreement, and this motion seemed to excite the stranger for he sprang forward shouting his unintelligible gibberish. The alert Marine guard caught him in the back of the head with the butt of his Tower musket, and the hairy man fell to the deck.

"Tried to attack you, Captain," the Marine officer said. "Shall we keel-haul him, sir?"

"No, poor chap is a long way from home, may be worried. We must allow for the language barrier. Just read him the Articles of War and impress him into the service. We're short of hands after that last encounter."

"You are of a very forgiving nature, sir, and an example for us all. What shall we do with his ship?"

"I'll examine it. There may be some principle of operation here that would be of interest to Whitehall. Drop a ladder. I'll have a look myself."

After some fumbling Harpplayer found the lever that moved the glass cabin, and when it slid aside he dropped into the cockpit that it covered. A comfortable divan faced a board covered with a strange collection of handles, buttons and divers machines concealed beneath crystal covers. It was a perfect example of the decadence of the east, excessive decoration and ornamentation where a panel of good English oak would have done as well, and a simple pivoted bar to carry the instructions to the slaves that rowed the boat. Or perhaps there was an animal concealed behind the panel, he heard a deep roar when he touched a certain lever. This evidently signalled the galley slave—or animal—to begin his labours, since the little craft was now rushing through the water at a good pace. Spray was slapping into the cockpit so Harp-player closed the cover, which was a good thing. Another button must have tilted a concealed rudder because the boat suddenly plunged its nose down and sank, the water rising up until it washed over the top of the glass.

Luckily, the craft was stoutly made and did not leak, and another button caused the boat to surface again.

It was at that instant that Harpplayer had the idea. He sat as one paralysed, while his rapid thoughts ran through the possibilities. Yes, it might work—it *would* work! He smacked his fist into his open palm and only then realized that the tiny craft had turned while he had been thinking and was about to ram into the *Redundant,* whose rail was lined with frighten-eyed faces. With a skilful touch he signalled the animal (or slave) to stop and there was only the slightest bump as the vessels touched.

"Mr. Shrub," he called.

"Sir?"

"I want a hammer, six nails, six kegs of gunpowder each with a two-minute fuse and a looped rope attached, and a dark lantern."

"But, sir—what for?" For once the startled Shrub forgot himself enough to question his captain.

The plan had so cheered Harpplayer that he took no umbrage at this sudden familiarity. In fact he even smiled into his cuff, the expression hidden by the failing light.

"Why—six barrels because there are six ships," he said with unaccustomed coyness. "Now, carry on."

The gunner and his mates quickly completed their task, and the barrels were lowered in a sling. They completely filled the tiny cockpit, barely leaving room for Harpplayer to sit. In fact there was no room for the hammer, and he had to hold it between his teeth.

"Mither Thrub," he said indistinctly around the hammer, suddenly depressed as he realized that in a few moments he would be pitting his own frail body against the hordes of the usurper who cracked the whip over a continent of oppressed slaves. He quailed at his temerity at thus facing the Tyrant of Europe, then quailed before his own disgust at his frailty. The men must never know that he had these thoughts, that he was the weakest of them. "Mr. Shrub," he called again; and there was no sound of his feelings in his voice. "If I do not return by dawn you are in command of this ship and will make a full report. Good-bye. In triplicate, mind."

"Oh, sir—" Shrub began, but his words were cut off as the glass cover sprang shut and the tiny craft hurled itself against all the power of a continent.

Afterwards Harpplayer was to laugh at his first weakness. Truly, the escapade was as simple as strolling down Fleet Street on a Sunday morning. The foreign ship sank beneath the surface and slipped past the batteries on Cape Pietfieux, which the English sailors called Cape Pitfix, and into the guarded waters of Cienfique. No guard noticed the slight roiling of the waters of the bay and no human eye saw the dim shape that surfaced next to the high wooden wall that was the hull of the French ship of the line. Two sharp blows of the hammer secured the first keg of gunpowder and a brief flash of light came from the dark lantern as the fuse was lit. Before the puzzled sentries on the deck above could reach the rail the mysterious visitor was gone, and they could not see the telltale fuse sputtering away, concealed by the barrel of death that it crept slowly towards. Five times Harpplayer repeated this simple, yet deadly, activity, and as he was driving the last nail there was a muffled explosion from the harbour, and behind him six ships, the pride of the Tyrant's navy, burnt in pillars of flame until all that was left was the charred hulls, settling to the ocean floor.

Captain Harpplayer opened the glass hutment when he was past the shore batteries, and looked back with satisfaction at the burning ships. He had done his duty and his small part towards ending this awful war that had devastated a continent and would, in the course of a few years, kill so many of the finest Frenchmen that the height of the entire French race would be reduced by an average of more than five inches. The last pyre died down and, feeling a twinge of regret, since they had been fine ships, though in fief to the Madman in Paris, he turned the bow of his craft towards the *Redundant*.

It was dawn when he reached the ship, and exhaustion tugged at him. He grabbed the ladder lowered for him and painfully climbed to the deck. The drums whirred and the sideboys saluted: the bos'uns' pipes trilled.

"Well done, sir, oh, well done," Shrub exclaimed, rush-

ing forward to take his hand. "We could see them burning from here."

Behind them, in the water, there was a deep burbling,
like the water running from the tub when the plug is
pulled, and Harpplayer turned just in time to see the
strange craft sinking into the sea and vanishing from
sight.

"Damn silly of me," he muttered. "Forgot to close the
hatch. Running quite a sea, must have washed in."

His ruminations were sharply cut through by a sudden
scream. He turned just in time to see the hairy stranger
run to the rail and stare, horrified, at the vanishing craft.
Then the man, obviously bereaved, screamed horribly
and tore great handfuls of hair from his head, a relatively
easy task since he had so much. Then, before anyone
could think to stop him, he had mounted to the rail and
plunged headfirst into the sea. He sank like a rock, and
either could not swim, or did not want to; he seemed
strangely attached to his craft, since he did not return to
the surface.

"Poor chap," Harpplayer said with the compassion of
a sensitive man, "to be alone, and so far from home. Perhaps he is happier dead."

"Aye, perhaps," the stolid Shrub muttered, "but he
had the makings of a good topman in him, sir. Could run
right out on the spars he could, held on very well he did,
what with those long toenails of his that bit right into the
wood. Had another toe in his heel that helped him hold
on."

"I'll ask you not to discuss the deformities of the dead.
We'll list him in the report as Lost Overboard. What was
his name?"

"Wouldn't tell us, sir, but we carry him in the books as
Mr. Green."

"Fair enough. Though foreign-born, he would be proud
to know that he died bearing a good English name." Then
curtly dismissing the faithful and stupid Shrub, Harpplayer
resumed walking the quarterdeck, filled with the silent
agony which was his alone and would be until the guns of
the Corsician Ogre were spiked forever.

T HIS IS A REAL STORY THAT HAPPENS
in a real place. The characters, with one
exception, are real; I have met them all. I
have walked this particular island and bathed
in this sea. While doing so, the idea for this
story presented itself full-blown.

Yugoslavia is probably the most primitive
country in Europe. Wild, barren, fought over
for centuries, populated by differing groups
and nations, it has been a-bubble with fac-
tionalism since the memory of man. When
the Germans invaded it during World War
II, the partisan bands took to the hills with
their guns—and fought with each other before turning on the Nazis. At the beginning
of this same war, there were only fourteen
miles of paved road outside of the cities.

Things changed greatly under the reign of
Marshal Tito. Wide motorways now run the
length of the country, and tourists pour in
with their hard money. Yugoslavia has entered the twentieth century.

I was one of the first postwar travelers to
penetrate some of these distant places, and I
had a good view of life as it had been lived
there for centuries. This life was not the
most entrancing, as you can well imagine.
Yet there is now a Yugoslavian nuclear in-
stitute.

3

Yugoslavia is a microcosm that reflects our entire world. In its hot sunlight, suddenly I saw how, by the addition of a familiar science-fiction device, I could make it stand for the whole.

RESCUE OPERATION

<<<<<<<<<<<<<<<<<<<<<<<<<<<<<<<<<<<<<<<<<<<<<

"PULL! PULL STEADILY . . . !" DRAGOMIR shouted, clutching at the tarry cords of the net. Beside him in the hot darkness Pribislav Polasek grunted as he heaved on the wet strands. The net was invisible in the black water, but the blue light trapped in it rose closer and closer to the surface.

"It's slipping . . ." Pribislav groaned and clutched the rough gunwale of the little boat. For a single instant he could see the blue light on the helmet, a face plate and the suited body that faded into blackness—then it slipped free of the net. He had just a glimpse of a dark shape before it was gone. "Did you see it?" he asked. "Just before he fell he waved his hand."

"How can I know—the hand moved, it could have been the net, or he might still be alive?" Dragomir had his face bent almost to the glassy surface of the water, but there was nothing more to be seen. "He might be alive."

The two fishermen sat back in the boat and stared at each other in the harsh light of the hissing acetylene lamp in the bow. They were very different men, yet greatly alike in their stained, baggy trousers and faded cotton shirts. Their hands were deeply wrinkled and calloused from a lifetime of hard labor, their thoughts slowed by the rhythm of work and years.

"We cannot get him up with the net," Dragomir finally said, speaking first as always.

"Then we will need help," Pribislav added. "We have anchored the buoy here, we can find the spot again."

"Yes, we need help." Dragomir opened and closed his large hands, then leaned over to bring the rest of the net into the boat. "The diver, the one who stays with the widow Korenc, he will know what to do. His name is Kukovic and Petar said he is a doctor of science from the university in Ljubljana."

They bent to their oars and sent the heavy boat steadily over the glasslike water of the Adriatic. Before they had reached shore the sky was light and when they tied to the sea wall in Brbinj the sun was above the horizon.

Joze Kukovic looked at the rising ball of the sun, already hot on his skin, yawned and stretched. The widow shuffled out with his coffee, mumbled good morning and put it on the stone rail of the porch. He pushed the tray aside and sat down next to it, then emptied the coffee from the small, long-handled pot into his cup. The thick Turkish coffee would wake him up, in spite of the impossible hour. From the rail he had a view down the unpaved and dusty street to the port, already stirring to life. Two women, with the morning's water in brass pots balanced on their heads, stopped to talk. The peasants were bringing in their produce for the morning market, baskets of cabbages and potatoes and trays of tomatoes, strapped onto tiny donkeys. One of them brayed, a harsh noise that sawed through the stillness of the morning, bouncing echoes from the yellowed buildings. It was hot already. Brbinj was a town at the edge of nowhere, locked between empty ocean and barren hills, asleep for centuries and dying by degrees. There were no attractions here—if you did not count the sea. But under the flat, blue calm of the water was another world that Joze loved.

Cool shadows, deep valleys, more alive than all the sunblasted shores that surrounded it. Excitement, too: just the day before, too late in the afternoon to really explore it, he had found a Roman galley half-buried in the sand. He would get into it today, the first human in two thousand years, and heaven alone knew what he would find there. In the sand about it had been shards of broken amphorae, there might be whole ones inside the hull.

Sipping happily at his coffee he watched the small boat tying up in the harbor, and wondered why the two fish-ermen were in such a hurry. They were almost running, and no one ran here in the summer. Stopping below his porch the biggest one called up to him.

"Doctor, may we come up? There is something urgent."

"Yes, of course." He was surprised and wondered if they took him for a physician.

Dragomir shuffled forward and did not know where to begin. He pointed out over the ocean.

"It fell, out there last night, we saw it, a *sputnik* without a doubt?"

"A traveler?" Joze Kukovic wrinkled his forehead, not quite sure that he heard right. When the locals were excited it was hard to follow their dialect. For such a small country Yugoslavia was cursed with a multitude of tongues.

"No, it was not a *putnik,* but a *sputnik,* one of the Rus-sian spaceships."

"Or an American one," Pribislav spoke for the first time, but he was ignored.

Joze smiled and sipped his coffee. "Are you sure it wasn't a meteorite you saw? There is always a heavy meteor shower this time of year."

"A *sputnik*," Dragomir insisted stolidly. "The ship fell far out in the *Jadransko More* and vanished, we saw that. But the space pilot came down almost on top of us, into the water . . ."

"The WHAT?" Joze gasped, jumping to his feet and knocking the coffee tray to the floor. The brass tray clanged and rattled in circles unnoticed. "There was a man in this thing—and he got clear?"

Both fishermen nodded at the same time and Dragomir continued. "We saw this light fall from the *sputnik* when it went overhead and drop into the water. We couldn't see what it was, just a light, and we rowed there as fast as we could. It was still sinking and we dropped a net and managed to catch him . . ."

"You have the pilot?"

"No, but once we pulled him close enough to the surface to see he was in a heavy suit, with a window like a diving suit, and there was something on the back that might have been like your tanks there."

"He waved his hand," Pribislav insisted.

"He might have waved a hand, we could not be sure. We came back for help."

The silence lengthened and Joze realized that he was the help that they needed, and that they had turned the responsibility over to him. What should he do first? The astronaut might have his own oxygen tanks, Joze had no real idea what provisions were made for water landings, but if there were oxygen the man might still be alive.

Joze paced the floor while he thought, a short, square figure in khaki shorts and sandals. He was not handsome, his nose was too big and his teeth were too obvious for that, but he generated a certainty of power. He stopped and pointed to Pribislav.

"We're going to have to get him out. You can find the spot again?"

"A buoy."

"Good. And we may need a doctor. You have none here, but is there one in Osor?"

"Dr. Bratos, but he is very old . . ."

"As long as he is still alive, we'll have to get him. Can anyone in this town drive an automobile?"

The fishermen looked towards the roof and concentrated, while Joze controlled his impatience.

"Yes, I think so," Dragomir finally said. "Petar was a *partizan* . . ."

"That's right," the other fisherman finished the thought. "He has told many times how they stole German trucks and how he drove . . ."

"Well, then one of you get this Petar and give him these keys to my car, it's a German car so he should be able to manage. Tell him to bring the doctor back at once."

Dragomir took the keys, but handed them to Pribislav who ran out.

"Now let's see if we can get the man up," Joze said, grabbing his scuba gear and leading the way towards the boat.

They rowed, side by side, though Dragomir's powerful strokes did most of the work.

"How deep is the water out here?" Joze asked. He was already dripping with sweat as the sun burned on him.

"The Kvarneric is deeper up by Rab, but we were fishing off Trstenik and the bottom is only about four fathoms there. We're coming to the buoy."

"Seven meters, it shouldn't be too hard to find him." Joze kneeled in the bottom of the boat and slipped into the straps of the scuba. He buckled it tight, checked the valves, then turned to the fisherman before he bit into the mouthpiece. "Keep the boat near this buoy and I'll use it for a guide while I search. If I need a line or any help, I'll surface over the astronaut, then you can bring the boat to me."

He turned on the oxygen and slipped over the side, the cool water rising up his body as he sank below the surface. With a powerful kick he started towards the bottom, following the dropping line of the buoy rope. Almost at once he saw the man, spread-eagled on white sand below.

Joze swam down, making himself stroke smoothly in spite of his growing excitement. Details were clearer as he dropped lower. There were no identifying marks on the pressure suit, it might be either American or Russian. It was a hard suit, metal or reinforced plastic, and painted green, with a single, flat face plate in the helmet.

Because distance and size are so deceptive under water, Joze was on the sand next to the figure before he realized it was less than four feet long. He gasped and almost lost his mouthpiece.

Then he looked into the face plate and saw that the creature inside was not human.

Joze coughed a bit and blew out a stream of bubbles:

he had been holding his breath without realizing it. He just floated there, paddling slowly with his hands to stay in a position, looking at the face within the helmet.

It was as still as waxen cast, green wax with a roughened surface, slit nostrils, slit mouth and large eyeballs unseen but prominent as they pushed up against the closed lids. The arrangement of features was roughly human, but no human being ever had skin this color or had a pulpy crest like this one, partially visible through the face plate, growing up from above the closed eyes. Joze stared down at the suit made of some unknown material, and at the compact atmosphere regeneration apparatus on the alien's back. What kind of atmosphere? He looked back at the creature's face and saw that the eyes were open and the thing was watching him.

Fear was his first reaction, he shot back in the water like a startled fish then, angry at himself, came forward again. The alien slowly raised one arm, then dropped it limply. Joze looked through the face plate and saw that the eyes were closed again. The alien was alive, but unable to move, perhaps it was injured and in pain. The wreck of the creature's ship showed that something had been wrong with the landing. Reaching under as gently as he could he cradled the tiny body in his arms, trying to ignore a feeling of revulsion when the cold fabric of the thing's suit touched his bare arms. It was only metal or plastic, he had to be a scientist about this. When he lifted it up the eyes still did not open and he bore the limp and almost weightless form to the surface.

"You great stupid clumpsy clod of peasant, help me," he shouted, spitting out his mouthpiece and treading water on the surface, but Dragomir only shook his head in terror and retreated to the point of the bow when he saw what the physicist had borne up from below.

"It is a creature from another world and cannot harm you!" Joze insisted but the fisherman would not approach.

Joze cursed aloud and only managed with great difficulty to get the alien into the boat, then climbed in after him. Though he was twice Joze's size, threats of violence drove Dragomir to the oars. But he used the farthest set of tholepins, even though it made rowing much more difficult. Joze dropped his scuba gear into the bottom of the boat and looked more closely at the drying fabric of the alien spacesuit. His fear of the unknown was forgotten in his growing enthusiasm. He was a nuclear physicist, but he remembered enough of his chemistry and mechanics to know that this material was completely impossible —by Earth's standards.

Light green, it was as hard as steel over the creature's limbs and torso, yet was soft and bent easily at the joints as he proved by lifting and dropping the limp arm. His eyes went down the alien's tiny figure: there was a thick harness about the middle, roughly where a human waist would be, and hanging from this was a bulky container, like an oversize sporran. The suiting continued without an apparent seam—but the right leg! It was squeezed in and crushed as though it had been grabbed by a giant pliers. Perhaps this explained the creature's lack of motion. Could it be hurt? In pain?

Its eyes were open again and Joze realized in sudden horror that the helmet was filled with water. It must have leaked in, the thing was drowning. He grabbed at the helmet, seeing if it would screw off, tugging at it in panic while the great eyes rolled up towards him.

Then he forced himself to think, and shakingly let go. The alien was still quiet, eyes open, no bubbles apparently coming from lips or nose. Did it breathe? Had the water leaked in—or was it possible it had always been there? Was it water? Who knew what alien atmosphere it might breathe; methane, chlorine, sulfur dioxide—why not water? The liquid was inside, surely enough, the suit wasn't leaking and the creature seemed unchanged.

Joze looked up and saw that Dragomir's panicked strokes had brought them into the harbor already, and that a crowd was waiting on the shore.

The boat almost overturned as Dragomir leaped up onto the harbor wall, kicking backward in his panic. They drifted away and Joze picked the mooring line up from the floor boards and coiled it in his hands. "Here," he shouted, "catch this. Tie it onto the ring there."

No one heard him, or if they heard, did not want to admit it. They stared down at the green-cased figure lying in the sternsheets and a rustle of whispering blew across them like wind among pine boughs. The women clutched their hands to their breasts, crossing themselves.

"Catch this!" Joze said through clenched teeth, forcing himself to keep his temper.

He hurled the rope onto the stones and they shied away from it. A youth grabbed it and slowly threaded it through the rusty ring, hands shaking and head tilted to one side, his mouth dropped in a permanent gape. He was feeble-minded, too simple to understand what was going on: he simply obeyed the shouted order.

"Help me get this thing ashore," Joze called out, and even before the words were out of his mouth he realized the futility of the request.

The peasants shuffled backwards, a blank-faced mob sharing the same fear of the unknown, the women like giant, staring dolls in their knee-length flaring skirts, black stockings and high felt shoes. He would have to do it himself. Balancing in the rocking boat he cradled the alien in his arms and lifted it carefully up onto the rough stone of the harbor wall. The circle of watchers pushed back even farther, some of the women choking off screams and running back to their houses, while the men muttered louder: Joze ignored them.

These people were going to be no help to him—and they might cause trouble. His own room would be safest, he doubted if they would bother him there. He had just picked up the alien when a newcomer pushed through the watchers.

"There—what is that? A *vrag!*" The old priest pointed in horror at the alien in Joze's arms and backed away, fumbling for his crucifix.

"Enough of your superstition!" Joze snapped. "This is no devil but a sentient creature, a traveler. Now get out of my way."

He pushed forward and they fled before him. Joze

moved as quickly as he could without appearing to hurry, leaving the crowd behind. There was a slapping of quick footsteps and he looked over his shoulder; it was the priest, Father Perc. His stained cassock flapped and his breath whistled in his throat with the unaccustomed exertion.

"Tell me, what are you doing . . . Dr. Kukovic? What is that . . . thing? Tell me . . ."

"I told you. A traveler. Two of the local fishermen saw something come from the sky and crash. This . . . alien came from it." Joze spoke as calmly as possible. There might be trouble with the people, but not if the priest were on his side. "It is a creature from another world, a water-breathing animal, and it's hurt. We must help it."

Father Perc scrambled along sideways as he looked with obvious distaste at the motionless alien. "It is wrong," he mumbled, "this is something unclean, *zao duh* . . ."

"Neither demon nor devil, can't you get that through your mind? The church recognizes the possibility of creatures from other planets—the Jesuits even argue about it —so why can't you? Even the Pope believes there is life on other worlds."

"Does he? Does he?" the old man asked, blinking with red-rimmed eyes.

Joze brushed by him and up the steps to the widow Korenc's house. She was nowhere in sight as he went into his room and gently lowered the still-unconscious form of the alien onto his bed. The priest stopped in the doorway, quivering fingers on his rosary, uncertain. Joze stood over the bed, opening and closing his hands, just as unsure. What could he do? The creature was wounded, perhaps dying, something must be done. But what?

The distant droning whine of a car's engine pushed into the hot room and he almost sighed with relief. It was his car, he recognized the sound, and it would be bringing the doctor. The car stopped outside and the doors slammed, but no one appeared.

Joze waited tensely, realizing that the townspeople

must be talking to the doctor, telling him what had happened. A slow minute passed and Joze started from the room, but stopped before he passed the priest, still standing just inside the door. What was keeping them: his window faced on an alleyway and he could not see the street in front of the building. Then the outside door opened and he could hear the widow's whispered voice, "In there, straight through."

There were two men, both dusty from the road. One was obviously the doctor, a short and dumpy man clutching a worn black bag, his bald head beaded with sweat. Next to him was a young man, tanned and windburned, dressed like the other fishermen: this must be Petar the ex-partisan.

It was Petar who went to the bed first, the doctor just stood clutching his bag and blinking about at the room.

"What is this thing?" Petar asked, then bent over, hands on his knees, to stare in through the face plate. "Whatever it is, it sure is ugly."

"I don't know. It's from another planet, that's the only thing I know. Now move aside so that the doctor can look." Joze waved and the physician moved reluctantly forward. "You must be Dr. Bratos. I'm Kukovic, professor of nuclear physics at the university in Ljubljana." Perhaps waving around a little prestige might get this man's reluctant co-operation.

"Yes, how do you do. Very pleased to meet you, Professor, an honor I assure you. But what is it that you wish me to do, I do not understand?" He shook ever so lightly as he spoke and Joze realized that the man was very old, well into his eighties or more. He would have to be patient.

"This alien . . . whatever it is . . . is injured and unconscious. We must do what we can to save its life."

"But what can I do? The thing is sealed in a metal garment—look it is filled with water—I am a doctor, a medical man, but not for animals, creatures like that."

"Neither am I, Doctor—no one on earth is. But we must do our best. We must get the suit off the alien and then discover what we can do to help."

"It is impossible! The fluid inside of it, it will run out."

"Obviously, so we will have to take precautions. We will have to determine what the liquid is, then get more of it and fill the bathtub in the next room. I have been looking at the suit and the helmet seems to be a separate piece, clamped into position. If we loosen the clamps, we should be able to get our sample."

For precious seconds Dr. Bratos stood there, nibbling at his lip, before he spoke. "Yes, we could do that, I suppose we could, but what could we catch the sample in. This is most difficult and irregular."

"It doesn't make any difference what we catch the sample in," Joze snapped, frustration pushing at his carefully held control. He turned to Petar, who was standing silently by, smoking a cigarette in his cupped hand. "Will you help? Get a soup plate, anything, from the kitchen."

Petar simply nodded and left. There were muffled complaints from the widow, but he was back quickly with her best pot.

"That's good," Joze said, lifting the alien's head, "now, slide it under here." With the pot in position he twisted one of the clamps; it snapped open but nothing else happened. A hairline opening was visible at the junction, but it stayed dry. But when Joze opened the second clamp there was a sudden gush of clear liquid under pressure, and before he fumbled the clamp shut again the pot was half full. He lifted the alien again and, without being told, Petar pulled the pot free and put it on the table by the window. "It's hot," he said.

Joze touched the outside of the container. "Warm not hot, about one hundred-twenty degrees I would guess. A hot ocean on a hot planet."

"But . . . is it water?" Dr. Bratos asked haltingly.

"I suppose it is—but aren't you the one to find out? Is it fresh water or sea water?"

"I'm no chemist . . . how can I tell . . . it is very complicated."

Petar laughed and took Joze's water glass from the nightstand. "That's not so hard to find out," he said, and dipped it into the pot. He raised the half-filled glass, sniffed at it, then took a sip and puckered his lips. "Tastes like ordinary sea water to me, but there's another taste, sort of bitter."

Joze took the glass from him. "This could be dangerous," the doctor protested, but they ignored him. Yes, salt water, hot salt water with a sharpness to it. "It tastes like more than a trace of iodine. Can you test for the presence of iodine, Doctor?"

"Here . . . no, it is quite complicated. In the laboratory with the correct equipment—" his voice trailed off as he opened his bag on the table and groped through it. He brought his hand out empty. "In the laboratory."

"We have no laboratory or any other assistance, Doctor. We will have to be satisfied with what we have here, ordinary sea water will have to do."

"I'll get a bucket and fill the tub," Petar said.

"Good. But don't fill the bathtub yet. Bring the water into the kitchen and we'll heat it, then pour it in."

"Right." Petar brushed past the silent and staring priest and was gone. Joze looked at Father Perc and thought of the people of the village.

"Stay here, Doctor," he said. "This alien is your patient and I don't think anyone other than you should come near. Just sit by him."

"Yes, of course, that is correct," Dr. Bratos said relievedly, pulling the chair over and sitting down.

The breakfast fire was still burning in the big stove and flamed up when Joze slid in more sticks. On the wall hung the big copper washtub and he dropped it onto the stove with a clang. Behind him the window's bedroom door opened, but slammed shut again when he turned. Petar came in with a bucket of water and poured it into the tub.

"What are the people doing?" Joze asked.

"Just milling about and bothering each other. They won't be any trouble. If you're worried about them, I can drive back to Osor and bring the police, or telephone someone."

"No, I should have thought of that earlier. Right now

I need you here. You're the only one who isn't either senile or ignorant."

Petar smiled. "I'll get some more water."

The bathtub was small and the washtub big. When the heated water was dumped in it filled it more than half way, enough to cover the small alien. There was a drain from the bathtub but no faucets: it was usually filled with a hose from the sink. Joze picked up the alien, cradling it like a child in his arms, and carried it into the bath. The eyes were open again, following his every movement, but making no protest. He lowered the creature gently into the water, then straightened a moment and took a deep breath. "Helmet first, then we'll try to figure out how the suit opens." He bent and slowly twisted the clamps.

With all four clamps open the helmet moved freely. He opened it a wide crack, ready to close it quickly if there were any signs of trouble. The ocean water would be flowing in now, mixing with the alien water; yet the creature made no complaint. After a minute Joze slowly pulled the helmet off, cradling the alien's head with one hand so that it would not bump to the bottom of the tub.

Once the helmet was clear the pulpy crest above the eyes sprang up like a coxcomb, reaching up over the top of the green head. A wire ran from the helmet to a shiny bit of metal on one side of the creature's skull. There was an indentation there and Joze slowly pulled a metal plug out, perhaps an earphone of some kind. The alien was opening and closing its mouth, giving a glimpse of bony yellow ridges inside, and a very low humming could be heard.

Petar pressed his ear against the outside of the metal tube. "The thing is talking or something, I can hear it."

"Let me have your stethoscope, Doctor," Joze said, but when the doctor did not move he dug it from the bag himself. Yes—when he pressed it to the metal he could hear a rising and falling whine, speech of a kind.

"We can't possibly understand him—not yet," he said, handing the stethoscope back to the doctor, who took it automatically. "We had better try to get the suit off."

There were no seams or fastenings visible, nor could Joze find anything when he ran his fingers over the smooth surface. The alien must have understood what they were doing because it jerkingly raised one hand and fumbled at the metal sealing ring about the collar. With a liquid motion the suit split open down the front, the opening bifurcated and ran down each leg. There was a sudden welling of blue liquid from the injured leg.

Joze had a quick glimpse of green flesh, strange organs, then he spun about. "Quick, Doctor—your bag. The creature is hurt, that fluid might be blood, we have to help it."

"What can I do," Dr. Bratos said, unmoving. "Drugs, antiseptics—I might kill it—we know nothing of its body chemistry."

"Then don't use any of those. This is a traumatic injury, you can bind it up, stop the bleeding, can't you?"

"Of course, of course," the old man said and at last his hands had familiar things to do, extracting bandages and sterile gauze from his bag, tape and scissors.

Joze reached into the warm and now murky water and forced himself to reach under the leg and grasp the hot, green flesh. It was strange—but not terrible. He lifted the limb free of the water and they saw a crushed gap oozing a thick blue fluid. Petar turned away, but the doctor put on a pad of gauze and tightened the bandages about it. The alien was fumbling at the discarded suit beside it in the tub, twisting its leg in Joze's grip. He looked down and saw it take something from the sporran container. Its mouth was moving again, he could hear the dim buzz of its voice.

"What is it? What do you want?" Joze asked.

It was holding the object across its chest now with both hands: it appeared to be a book of some kind. It might be a book, it might be anything.

Yet it was covered in a shiny substance with dark markings on it, and at the edge seemed to be made of many sheets bound together. It could be a book. The leg was twisting now in Joze's grasp and the alien's mouth was open wider, as if it were shouting.

"The bandage will get wet if we put it back into the water," the doctor said.

"Can't you wrap adhesive tape over it, seal it in?"

"In my bag—I'll need some more."

While they talked the alien began to rock back and forth, splashing water from the tub, pulling its legs from Joze's grasp. It still held the book in one thin, multi-fingered hand, but with the other one it began to tear at the bandages on its leg.

"It's hurting itself, stop it. This is terrible," the doctor said, recoiling from the tub.

Joze snatched a piece of wrapping paper from the floor. "You fool! You incredible fool!" he shouted. "These compresses you used—they're impregnated with sulfanilamide."

"I always use them, they're the best, American, they prevent wound infection."

Joze pushed him aside and plunged his arms into the tub to tear the bandages free, but the alien reared up out of his grasp sitting up above the water, its mouth gaping wide. Its eyes were open and staring and Joze recoiled as a stream of water shot from its mouth. There was a gargling sound as the water died to a trickle, and then, as the first air touched the vocal cords, a rising howling scream of pain. It echoed from the plaster ceiling, an inhuman agony as the creature threw its arms wide, then fell face forward into the water. It did not move again and, without examining it, Joze knew it was dead.

One arm was twisted back, out of the tub, still grasping the book. Slowly the fingers loosened, and while Joze looked on numbly, unable to move, the book thudded to the floor.

"Help me," Petar said and Joze turned to see that the doctor had fallen and Petar was kneeling over him. "He fainted, or a heart attack. What can we do?"

His anger was forgotten as Joze kneeled. The doctor seemed to be breathing regularly and his face wasn't flushed, so perhaps it was only a fainting spell. The eyelids fluttered. The priest brushed by and looked down over Joze's shoulder.

Dr. Bratos opened his eyes, looking back and forth at the faces bent over him. "I'm sorry——" he said thickly, then the eyes closed again as if to escape the sight of them.

Joze stood, and found that he was trembling. The priest was gone. Was it all over? Perhaps they might never have saved the alien, but they should have done better than this. Then he saw the wet spot on the floor and realized the book was gone.

"Father Perc!" he shouted, crying it out like an insult. The man had taken the book, the priceless book!

Joze ran out into the hall and saw the priest coming from the kitchen. His hands were empty. With sudden fear Joze knew what the old man had done and brushed past him into the kitchen and ran to the stove, hurling open the door.

There, among the burning wood, lay the book. It was steaming, almost smoking as it dried, lying open. It was obviously a book, there were marks on the pages of some kind. He turned to grab up the shovel and behind him the fire exploded, sending a white flame across the room. It had almost caught him in the face, but he did not think of that. Pieces of burning wood lay on the floor and inside the stove there was only the remains of the original fire. Whatever substance the book had been made of was highly inflammable since it had dried out.

"It was evil," the priest said from the doorway, "A *zao duh,* an abomination with a book of evil. We have been warned, such things have happened before on earth, and always the faithful must fight back——"

Petar pushed in roughly past him and helped Joze to a chair, brushing the hot embers from his bare skin. Joze had not felt their burn, all he was aware of was an immense weariness.

"Why here?" he asked. "Of all places in the world why here? A few more degrees to the west and the creature would have come down near Trieste with surgeons, hospitals, men, facilities. Or, if it had just stayed on its course a little longer, it could have seen the lights, and would have landed at Rijika. Something could have been done. But why here?" he surged to his feet, shaking his fist at nothing—and at everything.

"Here, in this superstition-ridden, simple-minded backwater of the world! What kind of world do we live in where there is a five-million-volt electron accelerator not a hundred miles from primitive stupidity? That this creature should come so far, come so close . . . why, why?"

Why?

He slumped back into the chair again, feeling older than he had ever felt before and tired beyond measure. What could they have learned from that book?

He sighed, and the sigh came from so deep within him that his whole body trembled as though shaken by an awful fever.

I HAVE NEVER FELT VERY GOOD about the mechanical workings of either Frankenstein's monster or the zombies. It's the old conservation-of-energy business, along with Occam's razor. Occam forces us to realize that a collection of secondhand torsos, arms, and legs sewn together will not be any more energetic or long-wearing than the originals were when they belonged to different bodies. He also strongly suggests that corpses newly risen from the grave should be, if anything, weaker—not stronger—than they were when interred. And then there are the problems that arise through lack of blood circulation and loss of breathing. Something is just not right here, the whole business has a suspicious odor—other than that of decay, that is.

But *is* there a way to get your dead-and-arisen bodies trotting around in a more or less reasonable fashion? I mulled it over and thought that there was, so then I had to write the story.

Many years later they swiped my title to make a film, which proves nothing except that you cannot copyright titles.

4

AT LAST, THE TRUE STORY
OF FRANKENSTEIN

<<<<<<<<<<<<<<<<<<<<<<<<<<<<<<<<<<<<<<<<

"UND HERE, BEFORE YOUR VERY EYES, IS THE very same monster built by my much admired great-great grandfather, Victor Frankenstein, built by him from pieces of corpses out of the dissecting rooms, stolen parts of bodies freshly buried in the grave, and even chunks of animals from the slaughterhouse. Now look—" The tall-coated man on the platform swung his arm out in a theatrical gesture and the heads of the close-packed crowd below swung to follow it. The dusty curtains flapped aside and the monster stood there, illuminated from above by a sickly green light. There was a concerted gasp from the crowd and a shiver of motion.

In the front row, pressed against the rope barrier, Dan Bream mopped his face with a soggy handkerchief and smiled. It wasn't such a bad monster, considering that this was a cheapjack carnival playing the smalltown southern circuit. It had a dead white skin, undampened by sweat even in this steambath of a tent, glazed eyes, stitches and seams showing where the face had been patched together, and the two metal plugs projecting from the temples—just like in the movie.

"Raise your right arm!" Victor Frankenstein V commanded, his brusque German accent giving the words a Prussian air of authority. The monster's body did not move, but slowly—with the jerking motion of a badly operating machine—the creature's arm came up to shoulder height and stopped.

"This monster, built from pieces from the dead, cannot

54

die, and if a piece gets too worn out I simply stitch on a new piece with the secret formula passed down from father to son from my great-great grandfather. It cannot die nor feel pain—as you see—"

This time the gasp was even louder and some of the audience turned away while others watched with eager eyes. The barker had taken a foot-long and wickedly sharp needle, and had pushed it firmly through the monster's biceps until it protruded on both sides. No blood stained it and the creature made no motion, as though completely unaware that anything had been done to its flesh.

". . . impervious to pain, extremes of heat and cold, and possessing the strength of ten men . . ."

Behind him the voice droned on, but Dan Bream had had enough. He had seen the performance three times before, which was more than satisfactory for what he needed to know, and if he stayed in the tent another minute he would melt. The exit was close by and he pushed through the gaping, pallid audience and out into the humid dusk. It wasn't much cooler outside. Life borders on the unbearable along the shores of the Gulf of Mexico in August, and Panama City, Florida, was no exception. Dan headed for the nearest air conditioned beer joint and sighed with relief as the chill atmosphere closed around his steaming garments. The beer bottle frosted instantly with condensation as did the heavy glass stein, cold from the freezer. The first big swallow cut a path straight down to his stomach. He took the beer over to one of the straight-backed wooden booths, wiped the table off with a handful of paper napkins and flopped onto the bench. From the inner pocket of his jacket he took some folded sheets of yellow copy paper, now slightly soggy, and spread them before him. After adding some lines to the scribbled notes he stuffed them back into his jacket and took a long pull on his beer.

Dan was halfway through his second bottle when the barker, who called himself Frankenstein the Fifth, came in. His stage personality had vanished along with the frock coat and monocle, and the Prussian haircut now looked like a common crewcut.

"You've got a great act," Dan called out cheerfully, and waved the man over. "Will you join me for a drink?"

"Don't mind if I do," Frankenstein answered in the pure nasal vowels of New York City, the German accent apparently having disappeared along with the monocle. "And see if they have a Schlitz or a Bud or anything besides the local swamp water."

He settled into the booth while Dan went for the beers, and groaned when he saw the labels on the bottles.

"At least it's cold," he said, shaking salt into his to make it foam, then half drained the stein in a long deep swallow. "I noticed you out there in front of the clems for most of the shows today. Do you like the act—or you a carny buff?"

"It's a good act. I'm a newsman, name's Dan Bream."

"Always pleased to meet the Press, Dan. Publicity is the life of show business, as the man said. I'm Stanley Arnold: call me Stan."

"Then Frankenstein is just your stage name?"

"What else? You act kinda dim for a reporter, are you sure—?" He waved away the Press card that Dan pulled from his breast pocket. "No, I believe you, Dan, but you gotta admit the question was a little on the rube side. I bet you even think that I have a real monster in there!"

"Well, you must admit that he looks authentic. The skin stitched together that way, those plugs in his head—"

"Held on with spirit gum and the embroidery is drawn on with eyebrow pencil. That's show business for you, all illusion. But I'm happy to hear that the act even looked real to an experienced reporter like yourself. What paper did you say you were with?"

"No paper, the news syndicate. I caught your act about six months ago and became interested. Did a little checking when I was in Washington, then followed you down here. You don't really want me to call you Stan, do you? Stein might be closer. After all—Victor Frankenstein *is* the name on your naturalization papers."

"Tell me more," Frankenstein said in a voice suddenly cold and emotionless.

Dan riffled through the yellow sheets. "Yes . . . here it is, from the official records, Frankenstein, Victor—born in Geneva, arrived in the U.S. in 1938, and more of the same."

"The next thing you'll be telling me is that my monster *is* real!" Frankenstein smiled, but only with his mouth.

"I'm betting that it is. No yogi training or hypnotism or such can make a man as indifferent to pain as that thing is—and as terribly strong. I want the whole story, the truth for a change!"

"Do you . . . ?" Frankenstein asked in a cold voice and for a long moment the air filled with tension. Then he laughed and clapped the reporter on the arm. "All right, Dan—I'll give it to you. You are a persistent devil and a good reporter and it is the least you deserve. But first you must get us some more drinks, something a measurable degree stronger than this execrable beer." His New York accent had disappeared as easily as had his German one; he spoke English now with skill and perfection without any recognizable regional accent.

Dan gathered their empty glasses. "It'll have to be beer—this is a dry county."

"Nonsense! This is America, the land that raises its hands in horror at the foreign conception of double-think yet practices it with an efficiency that sets the Old World to shame. Bay County may be officially dry but the law has many itchy palms, and under that counter you will find a reasonable supply of a clear liquid that glories in the name of White Mule and is reputed to have a kick of the same magnitude as its cognate beast. If you are still in doubt you will see a framed federal liquor license on the far wall, legitimatizing this endeavor in the eyes of the national government. Simply place a five-dollar bank note on the bar, say Mountain Dew, and do not expect any change."

When they both had enjoyed their first sips of the corn likker Victor Frankenstein lapsed into a friendly mood.

"Call me Vic, Dan. I want us to be friends. I'm going

to tell you a story that few have heard before, a story that is astounding but true. True—mark that word—not a hodge-podge of distortions and half-truths and outright ignorance like that vile book produced by Mary Godwin. Oh how my father ever regretted meeting that woman and, in a moment of weakness, confiding in her the secret of some of his original lines of research . . ."

"Just a minute," Dan broke in. "You mentioned the truth, but I can't swallow this guff. Mary Wollstonecraft Shelley wrote *Frankenstein: or, The Modern Prometheus* in 1818. Which would make you and your father so old . . ."

"Please, Dan—no interruptions. I mentioned my father's researches, in the plural you will note, all of them devoted to the secrets of life. The Monster, as it has come to be called, was just one of his works. Longevity was what he was interested in, and he did live to a very, very old age, so will I. I will not stretch your credulity any further at this moment by mentioning the year of my birth, but will press on. That Mary Godwin. She and the poet were living together at this period, they had not married as yet, and this permitted my father to hope that Mary might one day find him not unattractive, since he was quite taken by her. Well, you can easily imagine the end. She made notes of everything he told her—then discarded him and used the notes to construct her despicable book. Her errors are legion, listen . . ." He leaned across the booth and once again clapped Dan on the shoulder in a hearty way. It was an intimate gesture that the reporter didn't particularly enjoy, but he didn't complain. Not as long as the other kept talking.

"Firstly she made papa a Swiss; he used to tear his hair out at the thought, since ours is a good old Bavarian family with a noble and ancient lineage. Then she had him attending the University of Ingolstadt in *Ingolstadt* —when every schoolboy knows that it was moved to Landshut in 1800. And father's personality, what crimes she committed there! In this libelous volume he is depicted as a weeping and ineffectual man, when in reality he was a tower of strength and determination. And if this isn't enough, she completely misunderstood the meaning of his experiments. Her jim-crack collection of cast off parts put together to make an artificial man is ludicrous. She was so carried away by the legends of Talos and the Golem that she misinterpreted my father's work and cast it into that ancient mould. Father did not construct an artificial man, he reactivated a *dead* man! That is the measure of his genius! He traveled for years in the darkest reaches of the African jungle, learning the lore of the creation of the zombie. He regularized the knowledge and improved upon it until he had surpassed all of his aboriginal teachers. Raise the dead, that is what he could do. That was his secret—and how can it be kept a secret in the future, Mr. Dan Bream?"

With these last words Victor Frankenstein's eyes opened wide and an unveiled light seemed to glow in their depths. Dan pulled back instinctively, then relaxed. He was in no danger here in this brightly lit room with men on all sides of them.

"Afraid, Dan? Don't be." Victor smiled and reached out and patted Dan on the shoulder once again.

"What was that?" Dan asked, startled at the tiny brief pain in his shoulder.

"Nothing—nothing but this," Frankenstein smiled again, but the smile had changed subtly and no longer contained any humor. He opened his hand to reveal a small hypodermic needle, its plunger pushed down and its barrel empty.

"Remain seated," he said quietly when Dan started to rise, and Dan's muscles relaxed and he sat back down, horrified.

"What have you done to me?"

"Very little—the injection is harmless. A simple little hypnotic drug, the effect of which wears off in a few hours. But until then you will not have much will of your own. So you will sit and hear me out. Drink some beer though, we don't want you to get thirsty."

Horrified, Dan was a helpless onlooker as, of its own volition, his hand raised and poured a measure of beer down his throat.

"Now concentrate, Dan, think of the significance of my statement. The so-called Frankenstein monster is no stitched up collection of scraps, but a good honest zombie. A dead man who can walk but not talk, obey but not think. Animate—but still dead. Poor old Charley is one, the creature whom you watched going through his act on the platform. But Charley is just about worn out. Since he is dead he cannot replace the body cells that are destroyed during the normal wear and tear of the day. Why the fellow is like an animated pincushion from the act, holes everywhere. His feet—terrible, not a toe, keep breaking off when he walks too fast. I think it's time to retire Charley. He has had a long life, and a long death. Stand up, Dan."

In spite of his mind crying *No! No!* Dan rose slowly to his feet.

"Aren't you interested in what Charley used to do before he became a sideshow monster? You should be, Dan. Old Charley was a reporter—just like you. And he ran across what he thought was a good story. Like you, he didn't realize the importance of what he had discovered and talked to me about it. You reporters are a very inquisitive bunch, I must show you my scrapbook, it's simply filled with Press cards. Before you die of course. You wouldn't be able to appreciate it afterwards. Now come along."

Dan walked after him, into the hot night, screaming inside in a haze of terror, yet walking quietly and silently down the street.

I<small>T IS VERY HARD TO WRITE THE</small>
story of a utopia. Peace, joy, and happiness
are so boring in fiction! A story depends
upon movement, movement of some kind,
somewhere. This is why distopias are so
attractive to the author—*1984* is the example
that instantly comes to mind. However, a
short story set in a utopia should not be
boring—as a single incident that uses the
utopian world as a setting, it will be a bump
in the smooth road of existence that is affected by, but does not alter, the background.

Our children were young in 1963, and
each had a teddy bear for a constant sleeping
companion. Even when we were traveling or
camping, teddy had to be there at bedtime.
Thus this story idea developed, grew, was
written, and was posted to New York, where
my agent found an unexpected market for it:
Ellery Queen's Mystery Magazine. This magazine has always enjoyed the occasional s-f
piece as long as it fit the mystery mold. *I*
enjoyed the sale because they paid about
twice what the highest-paying s-f market did.

But there was one hitch. They wanted a
rewrite. I am not against rewriting per se.
If an editor shows me errors in a story, or

5

points out where a change would improve things. I am happy to go along. But the change suggested here was radical surgery— they wanted an entirely new ending that would change the entire story.

Some correspondence effected a compromise; I would make a single change at the end that would alter the story but would not, in my opinion, butcher the entire idea. But it was still not the right ending. Now came the internal conflict between Finance and Art. Living was inexpensive in Denmark in those days, and this short-story sale would pay the rent for the month (then overdue), and all the expenses for two or three weeks. What to do?

I bent the knee. I permitted the wrong ending in *EQMM* and cried all the way to the bank. The correct ending is here, but I still regret this story's appearance in that magazine.

This single experience has never been repeated. Since that time I have managed to keep a bit farther ahead of the creditors so that no single sale has been absolutely necessary. On the occasions when editors and I have differed, I have withdrawn the stories in question and eventually sold them to other markets—occasionally to better markets than the first ones, which perhaps is a comment of some kind.

I ALWAYS DO WHAT
TEDDY SAYS

<<<<<<<<<<<<<<<<<<<<<<<<<<<<<<<<<<<<<<<<<<<

THE LITTLE BOY LAY SLEEPING, THE MOON-
light effect of the picture-picture window threw a pale glow
across his untroubled features. He had one arm clutched
around his teddy bear, pulling the round face with its
staring button eyes close to his. His father, and the tall
man with the black beard, tiptoed silently across the nursery to the side of the bed.

"Slip it away," the tall man said, "then substitute the
other."

"No, he would wake up and cry," Davy's father said.
"Let me take care of this, I know what to do."

With gentle hands he lay the other teddy bear down
next to the boy, on the other side of his head, so his
sleeping cherub face was framed by the wide-eared un-
sleeping masks of the toys. Then he carefully lifted the
boy's arm from the original teddy and pulled it free.
This disturbed Davy without waking him and he ground
his teeth together and rolled over, clutching the substitute toy to his cheek, and within a few moments his soft
breathing was regular and deep. The boy's father raised
his forefinger to his lips and the other man nodded; they
left the room without making a sound, closing the door
noiselessly behind them.

"Now we begin," Torrence said, reaching out to take
the teddy bear. His lips were small and glistened redly in
the midst of his dark beard. The teddy bear twisted in
his grip and the black-button eyes rolled back and forth.

"Take me back to Davy," it said in a thin and tiny voice.

"Let me have it back," the boy's father said. "It knows me and won't complain."

His name was Numen and, like Torrence, he was a Doctor of Government. Both DG's and both unemployed by the present government, in spite of their abilities and rank, though they had no physical resemblance. Torrence was a bear, though a small one, a black bear with hair sprouting thickly on his knuckles, twisting out of his white cuffs and lining his ears. His beard was full and thick, rising high up on his cheekbones and dropping low on his chest.

Where Torrence was dark Numen was fair, where short he was tall; thick, thin. A thin bow of a man, bent forward with a scholar's stoop and, though balding now, his hair was still curled and blond and very like the golden ringlets of the boy asleep upstairs. Now he took the toy animal and led the way to the shielded room deep in the house where Eigg was waiting.

"Give it here—here!" Eigg snapped when they came in, and reached for the toy. Eigg was always like that, in a hurry, surly, square and solid with his width of jaw and spotless white laboratory smock. But they needed him.

"You needn't," Numen said, but Eigg had already pulled it from his grasp. "It won't like it, I know . . ."

"Let me go . . . let me go . . . !" the teddy bear said with a hopeless shrill.

"It is just a machine," Eigg said coldly, putting it face down on the table and reaching for a scalpel. "You are a grown man, you should be more logical, have your emotions under greater control. You are speaking with your childhood memories, seeing your own boyhood teddy who was your friend and companion. This is just a machine." With a quick slash he opened the fabric over the seam seal and touched it: the plastic-fur back gaped open like a mouth.

"Let me go . . . let me go . . ." the teddy bear wailed

and its stumpy arms and legs waved back and forth. Both of the onlookers went white.

"Must we . . . ?"

"Emotions. Control them," Eigg said and probed with a screwdriver. There was a click and the toy went limp. He began to unscrew a plate in the mechanism.

Numen turned away and found that he had to touch a handkerchief to his face. Eigg was right. He was being emotional and this was just a machine. How did he dare get emotional over it? Particularly with what they had in mind.

"How long will it take?" He looked at his watch, it was a little past 2100.

"We have been over this before and discussing it again will not change any of the factors." Eigg's voice was distant as he removed the tiny plate and began to examine the machine's interior with a magnifying probe. "I have experimented on the two stolen teddy tapes, carefully timing myself at every step. I do not count removal or restoration of the tape, this is just a few minutes for each. The tracking and altering of the tape in both instances took me under ten hours. My best time differed from my worst time by less than fifteen minutes, which is not significant. We can therefore safely say—ahh," he was silent for a moment while he removed the capsule of the memory spools. ". . . we can safely say that this is a ten-hour operation."

"That is too long. The boy is usually awake by seven, we must have the teddy back by then. He must never suspect that it has been away."

"There is little risk, you can give him some excuse for the time. I will not rush and spoil the work. Now be silent."

The two government specialists could only sit back and watch while Eigg inserted the capsule into the bulky machine he had assembled in the room. This was not their specialty.

"Let me go . . ." the tiny voice said from the wall speaker, then was interrupted by a burst of static. "Let me go . . . bzzzzzt . . . no, no Davy, Mummy wouldn't like you to do that . . . fork in left, knife in right . . . bzzzt . . . if you do you'll have to wipe . . . good boy good boy good boy. . . ."

The voice squeaked and whispered and went on and the hours of the clock went by, one by one. Numen brought in coffee more than once and towards dawn Torrence fell asleep sitting up in the chair, only to awake with a guilty start. Of them all Eigg showed no strain nor fatigue, working the controls with fingers regular as a metronome. The reedy voice from the capsule shrilled thinly through the night like the memory of a ghost.

"It is done," Eigg said, sealing the fabric with quick surgeon's stitches.

"Your fastest time ever," Numen sighed with relief. He glanced at the nursery viewscreen that showed his son, still asleep, starkly clear in the harsh intra-red light. "And the boy is still asleep. There will be no problem getting it back after all. But is the tape . . . ?"

"It is right, perfect, you heard that. You asked the questions and heard the answers. I have concealed all traces of the alteration and unless you know what to look for you would never find the changes. In every other way the memory and instructions are like all others. There has just been this single change made."

"Pray God we never have to use it," Numen said.

"I did not know that you were religious," Eigg said, turning to look at him, his face expressionless. The magnifying loup was still in his eye and it stared, five times the size of its fellow, a large and probing questioner.

"I'm not," Numen said, flushing.

"We must get the teddy back," Torrence broke in. "The boy just moved."

Davy was a good boy and, when he grew older, a good student in school. Even after he began classes he kept teddy around and talked to him while he did his homework.

"How much is seven and five, Teddy?"

The furry toy bear rolled its eyes and clapped stub

paws. "Davy knows . . . shouldn't ask teddy what Davy knows. . . ."

"Sure I know—I just wanted to see if you did. The answer is thirteen."

"Davy . . . the answer is twelve . . . you better study harder Davy . . . that's what teddy says . . ."

"Fooled you!" Davy laughed. "Made you tell me the answer!" He was learning ways to get around the robot controls, permanently fixed to answer the questions of a smaller child. Teddies have the vocabulary and outlook of the very young because their job must be done during the formative years. Teddies teach diction and life history and morals and group adjustment and vocabulary and grammer and all the other things that enable men to live together as social animals. A teddy's job is done early in the most plastic stages of a child's life, and by the very nature of its task its conversation must be simple and limited. But effective. By the time teddies are discarded as childish toys the job is done.

By the time Davy became David and was eighteen years old, teddy had long since been retired behind a row of shelves on a high shelf. He was an old friend who had outgrown his useful days, but he was still a friend and certainly couldn't be discarded. Not that David ever thought of it that way. Teddy was just teddy and that was that. The nursery was now a study, his cot a bed and with his birthday past David was packing because he was going away to the university. He was sealing his bag when the phone bleeped and he saw his father's tiny image on the screen.

"David . . ."

"What is it, Father?"

"Would you mind coming down to the library now. There is something rather important . . ."

David squinted at the screen and noticed for the first time that his father's face had a pinched, sick look. His heart gave a quick jump.

"I'll be right there!"

Dr. Eigg was there, arms crossed and sitting almost at attention. So was Torrence, his father's oldest friend, who, though no relation, David had always called Uncle Torrence. And his father, obviously ill at ease about something. David came in quietly, conscious of all their eyes upon him as he crossed the room and took a chair. He was a lot like his father, with the same build and height, a relaxed, easy-to-know boy with very few problems in life.

"Is something wrong?" he asked.

"Not wrong, Davy," his father said. He must be upset, David thought, he hasn't called me that in years. "Or rather something *is* wrong, but with the state of the world, and has been for a long time."

"Oh, the Panstentialists," David said, and relaxed a little. He had been hearing about the evils of panstentialism as long as he could remember. It was just politics; he had been thinking something very personal was wrong.

"Yes, Davy, I imagine you know all about them by now. When your mother and I separated I promised to raise you to the best of my ability and I think I have. But I'm a governor and all my friends work in government so I'm sure you have heard a lot of political talk in this house. You know our feelings and I think you share them."

"I do—and I think I would have no matter where I grew up. Panstentialism is an oppressing philosophy and one that perpetuates itself in power."

"Exactly. And one man, Barre, is at the heart of it. He stays in the seat of power and will not relinquish it and, with the rejuvenation treatments, will be good for a hundred years more."

"Barre must go!" Eigg snapped. "For twenty-three years now he has ruled and forbidden the continuation of my experiments. Young man, he has stopped my work for a longer time than you have been alive, do you realize that?"

David nodded, but did not comment. What little he had read about Dr. Eigg's proposed researches into behavioral human embryology had repelled him and, secretly, he was in agreement with Barre's ban on the work. But on this only, he was truly in agreement with his father. Panstentialism was a heavy and dusty hand on the world of politics—as well as the world at large.

"I'm not speaking only for myself," Numen said, his face white and strained, "but for everyone in the world and the system who is against Barre and his philosophies. I have not held a government position for over twenty years—nor has Torrence here—but I think he'll agree that is a small thing. If this was a service to the people, we would gladly suffer it. Or if our persecution was the only negative result of Barre's evil works, I would do nothing to stop him."

"I am in complete agreement," Torrence nodded. "The fate of two men is of no importance in comparison with the fate of us all. Nor is the fate of one man."

"Exactly!" Numen sprang to his feet and began to pace agitatedly up and down the room. "If that wasn't true, wasn't the heart of the problem, I would never consider being involved. There would be no problem if Barre suffered a heart attack and fell dead tomorrow."

The three older men were all looking at David now, though he didn't know why, and he felt they were waiting for him to say something.

"Well, yes—I agree. A little embolism right now would be the best thing for the world that I can think of. Barre dead would be of far greater service to mankind than Barre alive has ever been."

The silence lengthened, became embarrassing, and it was finally Eigg who broke it with his dry, mechanical tones.

"We are all then in agreement that Barre's death would be of immense benefit. In that case, David, you must also agree that it would be fine if he could be . . . killed . . ."

"Not a bad idea," David said, wondering where all this talk was going, "though of course it's a physical impossibility. It must be centuries since the last . . . what's the word, 'murder' took place. The developmental psychology work took care of that a long time ago. As the twig is bent and all that sort of thing. Wasn't that supposed to be the discovery that finally separated man from the lower orders, the proof that we could entertain the

thought of killing, yet still be trained in our early childhood so that we would not be capable of the act. Surely
enough, if you can believe the textbooks, the human race
has progressed immeasurably since the curse of killing
has been removed. Look—do you mind if I ask just what
this is all about . . . ?"

"Barre can be killed," Eigg said in an almost inaudible voice. "There is one man in the world who can kill
him."

"WHO?" David asked, and in some terrible way he
knew the answer even before the words came from his
father's trembling lips.

"You, David . . . you . . ."

He sat, unmoving, and his thoughts went back through
the years and a number of things that had been bothering
him were made clear. His attitudes so subtly different
from his friends', and that time with the plane when one
of the rotors had killed a squirrel. Little puzzling things,
and sometimes worrying ones that had kept him awake
long after the rest of the house was asleep. It was true,
he knew it without a shadow of a doubt, and wondered
why he had never realized it before. But like a hideous
statue buried in the ground beneath one's feet, it had
always been there but had never been visible until he had
dug down and reached it. But it was visible now, all the
earth scraped from its vile face and all the lines of evil
clearly revealed.

"You want me to kill Barre?" he asked.

"You're the only one who can . . . Davy . . . and
it must be done. For all these years I have hoped against
hope that it would not be needed, that the . . . ability
you have would not be used. But Barre lives. For all our
sakes he must die."

"There is one thing I don't understand," David said,
rising and looking out the window at the familiar view
of the trees and the distant, glass-canopied highway. "How
was this change made? How could I miss the condition-
ing that I thought was a normal part of existence in this
world?"

"It was your teddy bear," Eigg explained. "It is not

publicized, but the reaction to killing is established at a very early age by the tapes in the machine that every child has. Later education is just reinforcement, value-less without the earlier indoctrination."

"Then my teddy . . . ?"

"I altered its tapes, in just that one way, so this part of your education would be missed. Nothing else was changed."

"It was enough, Doctor," there was a coldness to his voice that had never existed before. "How is Barre supposed to be killed?"

"With this." Eigg removed a package from the table drawer and opened it. "This is a primitive weapon removed from a museum. I have repaired it and charged it with the projectile devices that are called shells." He held the sleek, ugly, black thing in his hand. "It is fully automatic in operation. When this device, the trigger, is depressed a chemical reaction propels a copper and lead weight named a bullet directly from the front orifice. The line of flight of the bullet is along an imaginary path extended from these two niches on the top of the device. The bullet of course falls by gravity but in a minimum distance, say a meter, this fall is negligible." He put it down suddenly on the table. "It is called a gun."

David reached over slowly and picked it up. How well it fit into his hand, sitting with such precise balance. He raised it slowly, sighted across the niches and pulled the trigger. It exploded with an immense roar and jumped in his hand. The bullet plunged into Eigg's chest just over his heart with such a great impact that the man and the chair he had been sitting in were hurled backward to the floor. The bullet also tore a great hole in his flesh and Eigg's throat choked with blood and he died.

"David! What are you doing?" His father's voice cracked with uncomprehending horror.

David turned away from the thing on the floor, still apparently unmoved by what he had done.

"Don't you understand, Father? Barre and his Panstentialists are a terrible weight and many suffer and freedom is abridged and all the other things that are wrong, that we know should not be. But don't you see the difference? You yourself said that things will change after Barre's death. The world will move on. So how is his crime to be compared to the crime of bringing *this* back into existence?"

He shot his father quickly and efficiently before the older man could realize the import of his words and suffer with the knowledge of what was coming. Torrence screamed and ran to the door, fumbling with terrified fingers for the lock. David shot him too, but not very well since he was so far away, and the bullet lodged in his body and made him fall. David walked over and, ignoring the screamings and bubbled words, took careful aim at the twisting head and blew out the man's brains.

Now the gun was heavy and he was very tired. The lift shaft took him up to his room and he had to stand on a chair to take teddy down from behind the books on the high shelf. The little furry animal sat in the middle of the large bed and rolled its eyes and wagged its stubby arms.

"Teddy," he said, "I'm going to pull up flowers from the flower bed."

"No Davy . . . pulling up flowers is naughty . . . don't pull up the flowers . . ." The little voice squeaked and the arms waved.

"Teddy, I'm going to break a window."

"No, Davy . . . breaking windows is naughty . . . don't break any windows . . ."

"Teddy, I'm going to kill a man."

Silence, just silence. Even the eyes and arms were still.

The roar of the gun broke the silence and blew a ruin of gears, wires and bent metal from the back of the destroyed teddy bear.

"Teddy . . . oh, teddy . . . you should have told me," David said and dropped the gun and at last was crying.

FROM LIFE COMES ART. I LABORED for far too many years in the cesspools of the comic-book industry. I had trained as an artist and saw nothing wrong with making a living as a commercial artist rather than starving as an easel painter. Comics were easy to do, paid well, and before I knew it, I had sunk into the slough of commercial hackdom. I ground out page after page of moronic romance, puerile western, regurgitative horror.

Since I was hacking for money, not art, I specialized in inking only. I quickly became very facile and had someone else do the pencil sketches over which I worked. At my fastest I could ink a page in thirteen minutes, which is not bad when you consider the area involved—twelve by eighteen inches. One and a half square feet. I bought my india ink by the quart and used a number five brush, which is quite large and requires a great deal of dexterity to master for fine lines and details. But, wow, it does sock in the blacks!

Some years after my artistic career, I exorcised my feelings about comics in this story. The feelings are real and the characters are real. The only invention is the

6

machine, which is a mechanical exaggeration of an artist's joke. Feathering, the small parallel lines coming from a larger line that give an illusion of form, is necessary but repetitious, and we used to joke about getting a feathering rubber stamp made and using that for the job.

The publisher in "Portrait of the Artist" is real and not an exaggeration in the slightest —he's an amalgamation of a number of unimaginative clods I had to work for and struggle with. What pleasure there is in the expiating pen!

PORTRAIT OF THE ARTIST

<<<<<<<<<<<<<<<<<<<<<<<<<<<<<<<<<<<<<<<<<

11 A.M.!!! THE NOTE BLARED AT HIM, PINNED
to the upper right corner of his drawing board. MARTIN'S
OFFICE!! He had lettered it himself with a number 7
brush, funereal india ink on harsh yellow paper, big letters, big words.

Big end to everything. Pachs tried to make himself believe that this was just another one of Martin's royal commands: a lecture, a chewing-out, a complaint. That's what
he had thought when he had knocked out the reminder for
himself, before Miss Fink's large watery eyes had blinked
at him and she had whispered hoarsely, "It's on order, Mr.
Pachs, coming today, I saw the receipt on his desk. A
Mark IX." She had blinked moistly again, rolled her eyes
towards the closed door of Martin's office, then scurried
away.

A Mark IX. He knew that it would have to come some
day, knew without wanting to admit it, and had only been
kidding himself when he said they couldn't do without
him. His hands spread out on the board before him, old
hands, networked wrinkles and dark liver spots, always
stained a bit with ink and marked with a permanent cal-
lous on the inside of his index finger. How many years
had he held a pencil or a brush there? He didn't want to
remember. Too many, perhaps. . . . He clasped his hands
tightly together, making believe he didn't see them shaking.

There was almost an hour left before he had to see
Martin, plenty of time to finish up the story he was work-

ing on. He pulled the sheet of illustration board from the top of the pile and found the script. Page three of a thing called *Prairie Love* for the July issue of *Real Rangeland Romances*. Love books with their heavy copy were always a snap. By the time Miss Fink had typed in the endless captions and dialogue on her big flatbed varityper at least half of every panel was full. The script, panel one:

In house, Judy C/U cries and Robert in BG very angry.

A size three head for Judy in the foreground, he quickly drew the right size oval in blue pencil, then a stick figure for Robert in the background. Arm raised, fist closed, to show anger. The Mark VIII Robot Comic Artist would do all the rest. Pachs slipped the sheet into the machine's holder—then quickly pulled it out again. He had forgotten the balloons. Sloppy, sloppy. He quickly blue-pencilled their outlines and V's for tails.

When he thumbed the switch the machine hummed to life, electronic tubes glowing inside its dark case. He punched the control button for the heads, first the girl— GIRL HEAD, FULL FRONT, SIZE THREE, SAD, HEROINE. Girls of course all had the same face in comic books, the HER- OINE was just a note to the machine not to touch the hair. For a VILLAINESS it would be inked in black, all villain- esses have black hair, just as all villains have moustaches as well as the black hair, to distinguish them from the hero. The machine buzzed and clattered to itself while it sorted through the stock cuts, then clicked and banged down a rubber stamp of the correct head over the blue circle he had drawn. MAN HEAD, FULL, FRONT, SIZE SIX, SAD, HERO, brought a smaller stamp banging down on the other circle that topped the stick figure. Of course the script said *angry,* but that was what the raised fist was for, since there are only sad and happy faces in comics.

Life isn't that simple, he thought to himself, a very un- original idea that he usually brought out at least once a day while sitting at the machine. MAN FIGURE, BUSINESS SUIT, he set on the dial, then hit the DRAW button. The pen- tipped arm dropped instantly and began to quickly ink in a suited man's figure over the blue direction lines he had put down. He blinked and watched it industriously knocking in a wrinkle pattern that hadn't varied a stroke in fifty years, then a collar and tie and two swift neck lines to connect the neatly inked torso to the rubber-stamped head. The pen leaped out to the cuff end of the just-drawn sleeve and quivered there. A relay buzzed and a dusty red panel flashed INSTRUCTIONS PLEASE at him. With a savage jab he pushed the button labelled FIST. The light went out and the flashing pen drew a neat fist at the end of the arm.

Pachs looked at the neatly drawn panel and sighed. The girl wasn't unhappy enough; he dipped his crowquill into the ink pot and knocked in two tears, one in the corner of each eye. Better. But the background was still pretty empty in spite of the small dictionary in each balloon. BALLOONS he pushed automatically while he thought, and the machine pen darted down and inked the outlines of the balloons that held the lettering, ending each tail the correct distance from the speaker's mouth. A little background, it needed a touch. He pressed code 473, which he knew from long experience stood for HOME WINDOW WITH LACE CURTAINS. It appeared on the paper quickly, automatically scaled by the machine to be in perspective with the man's figure before it. Pachs picked up the script and read panel two:

Judy falls on couch Robert tries to console her mother rushes in angrily wearing apron.

There was a four-line caption in this panel and, after the three balloons had been lettered as well, the total space remaining was just about big enough for a single closeup, a small one. Pachs didn't labour this panel, as he might have, but took the standard way out. He was feeling tired today, very tired. HOUSE, SMALL, FAMILY produced a small cottage from which emerged the tails of the three balloons and let the damn reader figure out who was talking.

The story was finished just before eleven and he stacked the pages neatly, put the script into the file and cleaned the ink out of the pen in the Mark VIII; it always clogged if he left it to dry.

Then it was eleven and time to see Martin. Pachs fussed a bit, rolling down his sleeves and hanging his green eyeshade from the arm of his dazor lamp; yet the moment could not be avoided. Pulling his shoulders back a bit he went out past Miss Fink hammering away industriously on the varityper, and walked in through the open door to Martin's office.

"Come ON, Louis," Martin wheedled into the phone in his most syrupy voice. "If it's a matter of taking the word of some two-bit shoestring distributor in Kansas City, or of taking my word, who you gonna doubt? That's right . . . okay . . . right Louis. I'll call you back in the morning . . . right, you too . . . my best to Helen." He banged the phone back onto the desk and glared up at Pachs with his hard beebee eyes.

"What do you want?"

"You told me you wanted to see me, Mr. Martin."

"Yeah, yeah," Martin mumbled half to himself. He scratched flakes of dandruff loose from the back of his head with the chewed end of a pencil, and rocked from side to side in his chair.

"Business is business, Pachs, you know that, and expenses go up all the time. Paper—you know how much it costs a ton? So we gotta cut corners. . . ."

"If you're thinking of cutting my salary again, Mr. Martin, I don't think I could . . . well, maybe not much. . . ."

"I'm gonna have to let you go, Pachs. I've bought a Mark IX to cut expenses and I already hired some kid to run it."

"You don't have to do that, Mr. Martin," Pachs said hurriedly, aware that his words were tumbling one over the other and that he was pleading, but not caring. "I could run the machine I'm sure, just give me a few days to catch on. . . ."

"Outta the question. In the first place I'm paying the kid beans because she's just a kid and that's the starting salary, and in the other place she's been to school about this thing and can really grind the stuff out. You know I'm no bastard, Pachs, but business is business. And I'll tell you what, this is only Tuesday and I'll pay you for the rest of the week. How's that? And you can take off right now."

"Very generous, particularly after eight years," Pachs said, forcing his voice to be calm.

"That's all right, it's the least I could do." Martin was congenitally immune to sarcasm.

The lost feeling hit Pachs then, a dropping away of his stomach, a sensation that everything was over. Martin was back on the phone again and there was really nothing that Pachs could say. He walked out of the office, walking very straight, and behind him he heard the banging of Miss Fink's machine halt for an instant. He did not want to see her, to face those tender and damp eyes, not now. Instead of turning to go back to the studio, where he would have to pass her desk, he opened the hall door and stepped out. He closed it slowly behind him and stood with his back to it for an instant, until he realized it was frosted glass and she could see his figure from the inside: he moved hurriedly away.

There was a cheap bar around the corner where he had a beer every pay day, and he went there now. "Good morning and top of the morning to you . . . Mr. Pachs." the robot bartender greeted him with recorded celtic charm, hesitating slightly between the stock phrase and the search of the customer-tapes for his name. "And will you be having the usual?"

"No I will not be having the usual, you plastic and gaspipe imitation of a cheap stage Irishman, I'll be having a double whiskey."

"Sure and you are the card, sir," the electronically affable bartender nodded, horsehair spitcurl bobbing, as it produced a glass and bottle and poured a carefully measured drink.

Pachs drank it in a gulp and the unaccustomed warmth burned through the core of cold indifference that he had been holding on to. Christ, it was all over, all over. They would get him now with their Senior Citizens' Home and all the rest, he was as good as dead.

There are some things that don't bear thinking about. This was one. Another double whiskey followed the first, the money for this was no longer important because he would be earning no more after this week, and the unusual dose of alcohol blurred some of the pain. No, before he started thinking about it too much, he had to get back to the office. Clean his personal junk out of the taboret and pick up his pay check from Miss Fink. It would be ready, he knew that; when Martin was through with you he liked to get you out of the way, quickly.

"Floor please?" the voice questioned from the top of the elevator.

"Go straight to hell!" he blurted out. He had never before realized how many robots there were around: Oh how he hated them today.

"I'm sorry, that firm is not in this building, have you consulted the registry?"

"Twenty-three," he said and his voice quavered, and he was glad he was alone in the elevator. The doors closed.

There was a hall entrance to the studio and this door was standing open; he was halfway through it before he realized why—then it was too late to turn back. The Mark VIII that he had nursed along and used for so many years lay on its side in the corner, uprooted and very dusty on the side that had stood against the wall.

Good, he thought to himself, and at the same time knew it was stupid to hate a machine, but still relishing the thought that it was being discarded too. In its place stood a columnar apparatus in a grey crackle cabinet. It reached almost to the ceiling and appeared as ponderous as a safe.

"It's all hooked up now, Mr. Martin, ready to go with a hundred per cent lifetime guarantee as you know. But I'll just sort of preflight it for you and give you an idea just how versatile this versatile machine is."

The speaker was dressed in grey coveralls of the identical colour as the machine's finish, and was pointing at it with a gleaming screwdriver. Martin watched, frowning, and Miss Fink fluttered in the background. There was someone else there, a thin young girl in a pink sweater who bovinely chewed at a cud of gum.

"Let's give Mark IX here a real assignment, Mr. Martin. A cover for one of your magazines, something I bet you never thought a machine could tackle before, and normal machines can't. . . ."

"Fink!" Martin barked and she scrambled over with a sheet of illustration board and a small colour sketch.

"We got just one cover in the house to do, Mr. Martin," she said weakly. "You okayed it for Mr. Pachs to do. . . ."

"To hell with all that," Martin growled, pulling it from her hand and looking at it closely. "This is for our best book, do you understand that, and we can't have no hack horsing around with rubber stamps. Not on the cover of *Fighting Real War Battle Aces.*"

"You need not have the slightest worry, I assure you," the man in the coveralls said, gently lifting the sketch from Martin's fingers. "I'm going to show you the versatility of the Mark IX, something that you might find it impossible to believe until you see it in action. A trained operator can cut a Mark IX tape from a sketch or a description, and the results are always dramatic to say the least." He seated himself at a console with typewriter keys that projected from the side of the machine, and while he typed a ribbon of punched tape collected in the basket at one side.

"Your new operator knows the machine code and breaks down any art concept into standard symbols, cut on tape. The tape can be examined or corrected, stored or modified and used over again if need be. There—I've recorded the essence of your sketch and now I have one more question to ask you—in what style would you like it to be done?"

Martin made a porcine interrogative sound.

"Startled aren't you, sir—well I thought you would be. The Mark IX contains style tapes of all the great masters of the Golden Age. You can have Kubert or Caniff, Giunta or Barry. For figure work—you can use Raymond, for your romances capture the spirit of Drake."

"How's about Pachs?"

"I'm sorry. I'm afraid I don't know of. . . ."

"A joke. Let's get going. Caniff, that's what I want to see."

Pachs felt himself go warm all over, then suddenly cold.

Miss Fink looked over and caught his eye, and looked down, away. He clenched his fists and shifted his feet to leave, but listened instead. He could not leave, not yet.

". . . and the tape is fed into the machine, the illustration board centered on the impression table and the cycle button depressed. So simple, once a tape has been cut, that a child of three could operate it. A press of the button and just stand back. Within this genius of a machine the orders are being analysed and a picture built up. Inside the memory circuits are bits and pieces of every object that man has ever imagined or seen and drawn for his own edification. These are assembled in the correct manner in the correct proportions and assembled on the collator screen. When the final picture is complete the all-clear light flashes—there it goes—and we can examine the completed picture on the screen here." Martin bent over and looked in through the hooded opening and exhaled through his nose.

"Just perfect, isn't it? But if for any reason the operator is dissatisfied, the image can be changed now in any manner desired by manipulation of the editorial controls. And when satisfied the print button is depressed, the image is printed on a film of re-usable plastic sheet, charged electrostatically in order to pick up the powdered ink and then the picture is printed in a single stroke onto the paper below."

A pneumatic groan echoed theatrically from the bowels of the machine as a rectangular box crept down on a shining plunger and pressed against the paper. It hissed and a trickle of vapour oozed out. The machine rose back to position and the man in the coveralls held up the paper, smiling.

"Now isn't that a fine piece of art?"

Martin grunted.

Pachs looked at it and couldn't take his eyes away: he was afraid he was going to be sick. The cover was not only good, it was good Caniff, just as the master might have drawn it himself. Yet the most horrible part was that it was Pachs' cover, his own layout. Improved. He had never been what might be called a tremendous artist, but he wasn't a bad artist. He did all right in comics, and during the good years he was on top of the pack. But the field kept shrinking and when the machines came in it went bust and there was almost no spot for an artist, just a job here and there as sort of layout boy and machine minder. He had taken that—how many years now?—because old and dated as his work was he was still better than any machine that drew heads with a rubber stamp.

Not any more. He could not even pretend to himself any more that he was needed, or even useful.

The machine was better.

He realized then that he had been clenching his fists so tightly that his nails had sunk into the flesh of his palms. He opened and rubbed them together and knew that they were shaking badly. The Mark IX was turned off and they were all gone: he could hear Miss Fink's machine takking away in the outer office. The little girl was telling Martin about the special supplies she would need to buy to operate the machine, and when Pachs closed the connecting door he cut off the grumbling reply about extra expenses not being mentioned.

Pachs warmed his fingers in his armpits until the worst of the tremors stopped. Then he carefully pinned a sheet of paper onto his old drawing board and adjusted the light so it would not be in his eyes. With measured strokes he ruled out a standard comic page and separated it into six panels, making the sixth panel a big one, stretching the width of the page. He worked steadily at the pencilling, stopping only once to stretch his back and walk over to the window and look out. Then he went back to the board and as the afternoon light faded he finished the inking. Very carefully he washed off his battered—but still favourite—Windsor & Newton brush and slipped it back into the spring holder.

There was a bustle in the outer office and it sounded like Miss Fink getting ready to leave, or maybe it was the new girl coming back with the supplies. In any case it was late, and he had to go now.

Quickly, before he could change his mind, he ran full tilt at the window, his weight bursting through the glass, and hurtled the twenty-three storeys to the street below.

Miss Fink heard the breaking glass and screamed, then screamed louder when she came into the room. Martin, complaining about the noise, followed her, but shut up when he saw what had happened. A bit of glass crunched under his shoes when he looked out of the window. The doll-like figure of Pachs was visible in the centre of the gathering crowd, sprawled from sidewalk to street and bent at an awful angle as it followed the step of the curb.

"Oh, God, Mr. Martin. Oh, God, look at this . . ." Miss Fink wailed.

Martin went and stood next to her in front of the drawing board and looked at the page still pinned there. It was neatly done, well drawn and carefully inked.

In the first panel was a self-portrait of Pachs working on a page, bent over this same drawing board. In the second panel he was sitting back and washing out his brush, in the third standing. In the fourth panel the artist stood before the window, nicely rendered in chiaroscuro with backlighting. Five was a forced perspective shot from above, down the vertical face of the building with the figure hurtling through the air towards the pavement below.

In the last panel, in clear and horrible detail, the old man was bent, broken and bloody over the wrecked fender of the car that was parked there: the spectators looked on horrified.

"Look at that will you," Martin said disgustedly, tapping the drawing with his thumb. "When he went out the window he missed the car by a good two yards. Didn't I always tell you he was no good on getting the details right?"

THIS IS A STORY ABOUT OLD AGE, A theme that science fiction almost always sidles away from. The sidling takes the form of stories about longevity—live forever and there is no worry about old age—or becomes the youth-cult stuff that seems to fascinate some writers. The only real s-f look at age is Brian Aldiss' superb novel *Greybeard*.

When I sent this story to my agent, Robert Mills, he had some interesting comments. First, he wasn't sure that there wasn't a magazine like the one in the story. Fine, a touch of reality never hurts; but I assured him that there wasn't. Second, although he had enjoyed the story himself, he did not think it would sell because old age is a taboo topic in New York. After spending a good deal on postage, he proved himself right. After he ran out of American markets, I asked for the story back.

And sold it in England to Ted Carnell for publication in *New Worlds*.

I attempt to make no value judgments in this story—I am just commenting.

A number of American taboos just do not exist in Britain's foggy isles. People curse quite nicely on television, animals break wind in the comic strips—where humans also

7

drink, smoke, and take their clothes off. But they have at least one film taboo the American doesn't. Yummy sex is fine in the cinema, but the class-X stamp is put on films with excessive violence. Now what is wrong with a little eye-gouging, blood spurting, intestines dangling to the knees? It's hard to understand people at times.

NOT ME, NOT AMOS CABOT!

<<<<<<<<<<<<<<<<<<<<<<<<<<<<<<<<<<<<<<<<

THE MORNING MAIL HAD ARRIVED WHILE AMOS
Cabot was out shopping and had been thrown onto the
rickety table in the front hall. He poked through it even
though he knew there would be nothing for him; this
wasn't the right day. On the thirteenth his Social Security
check came and on the twenty-fourth the union check,
there never was anything else except for a diminishing
number of cards every Christmas. Nothing, he knew it. A
large blue envelope was propped against the mirror but he
couldn't make out the name, damn that skinflint Mrs.
Peavey and her two-watt bulbs. He bent over and blinked
at it then blinked again. By God it was for him, and no
mistake! Felt like a thick magazine or a catalog: he wondered what it could possibly be and who might have sent
it to him. Clutching it to his chest with a knobby and liver-
spotted hand he began the long drag up the three flights
of stairs to his room. He dropped his string bag with the
two cans of beans and the loaf of day-old white bread onto the drainboard and sat down heavily in his chair by
the window. Unsealing the envelope he saw that it was a
magazine, a thick glossy one with a black cover. He
slid it out onto his lap and stared at it with horrified eyes.
Hereafter the title read in black, prickly gothic letters against a field of greenish-gray, and underneath it
was subtitled *The Magazine of Preparedness*. The rest of
the cover was black, solid midnight black, except for an
inset photograph shaped like a tombstone that had a
cheerful view of a cemetery filled with flower blossoms,

87

ranked headstones, and brooding mausoleums. Was this all a very bad joke? It didn't seem so as Amos flipped through the pages, catching quick glimpses of caskets, coffins, cemetery plots, and urns of mortal ashes. With a grunt of disgust he threw the magazine onto the table and as he did so a letter fell out and drifted to the floor. It was addressed to him, on the magazine's stationery, there was no mistake.

My Dearest Sir:

Welcome to the contented family of happy readers of *Hereafter—The Magazine of Preparedness,* which smooths the road ahead. You, who are about to die, we salute you! A long, happy life lies behind you and ahead the Gates of Eternity are swinging open to welcome you, to return you to the bosom of your loved ones long since passed on. Now, at this friendly final hour, we stand behind you ready to help you on your way. Have you settled your will? Bet you've been remiss—but that's no problem now! Just turn to page 109 and read the inspirational article "Where There's a Will" and learn all there is to know. And then, on page 114, you'll find a full-sized, fold-out will that can be torn out along the handy perforations. Just fill in the few blanks, sign your name and have your local notary public (he's usually in the stationery store!) witness the signature. Don't delay! And have you considered cremation? There is a wonderfully inspirational message from Dr. Phillip Musgrove of The Little Church Around the Corner from the Crematorium on page. . . .

Amos picked up the magazine with shaking hands and threw it the length of the room, feeling slightly better when it tore in two.

"What do you mean I'm going to die—what do you say that for?" he shouted, then lowered his voice as Antonelli next door hammered on the wall. "What's the idea of sending a filthy thing like that to a person? What's the idea?"

What was the idea? He picked the two halves of the magazine up and smoothed them out on the table. It was all too good-looking, too expensive to be a joke—these were real ads. After some searching he found the contents page and worked his way through the fine print, which he could hardly read, until he came to the publisher's name: Saxon-Morris Publishers, Inc. and they must have money because they were in the Saxon-Morris Building, he knew it, one of the new granite slabs on Park Avenue.

They weren't getting away with it! A spark of anger blazed bravely in Amos Cabot's thin bosom. He had made the Fifth Avenue Coach Company send him a letter of apology about the way that driver had talked to him on St. Patrick's day, and the Triborough Automatic Drink Company had refunded him fifty cents in stamps for coins their machines had consumed without giving refreshment in return. Now Saxon-Morris was going to find out that they couldn't get away with it either!

It had been warm out, but March was a changeable month so he put on his heavy wool muffler. A couple of dollars should more than cover the costs of the excursion, bus fares, and a cup of tea in the Automat, so he took two wrinkled bills from behind the sugar can. Watch out, Saxon-Morris, you just watch out.

It was very difficult to see anyone at Saxon-Morris without an appointment. The girl with upswept red hair and layers of glazed makeup wasn't even sure that they had a magazine called *Hereafter*. There was a list of all the Saxon-Morris publications on the wall behind her red, kidney-shaped desk, but the gold letters on dark green marble were hard to read in the dim light. When he kept insisting she searched through a booklet of names and telephone numbers and finally, reluctantly, agreed that it was one of their magazines.

"I want to see the editor."

"Which editor is it you want to see?"

"Any editor, don't matter a damn." Her cold manner became even colder when the word touched her.

"Might I ask your business?"

"That's my business. Let me see the editor."

It was more than an hour before she found someone whom he could see, or perhaps she just grew tired of his sitting there and glowering at her. After a number of muffled conversations she hung up the phone.

"If you just go through that door there first turn to the right then up one half flight, fourth door on the left, Mr. Mercer will see you Room seven eighty-two."

Amos was instantly lost in the maze of passages and gray doors, but the second time he stumbled into a mail room one of the bored youths led him to 782. He pushed in without knocking.

"You Mercer, the editor of *Hereafter?*"

"Yes, I'm Mercer." He was a chubby man with a round face and rounder glasses, squeezed behind a desk that filled the end of the tiny and windowless office. "But this is circulation, not editorial. The girl at the front desk said you had a circulation problem."

"I got a problem all right—why you sending me your blasted magazine that I don't want?"

"Well—perhaps I can help you there, which publication are you referring to . . . ?"

"*Hereafter,* that's the one."

"Yes, that's one in my group." Mercer opened two files before he found the right folder, then he scratched through it and came up with a sheet of paper. "I'm afraid I can't be of any help to you, Mr. Cabot, you must be on the free-subscription list and we can't cancel them. Sorry."

"What do you mean, *sorry!* I don't want the filthy thing and you better stop sending it!"

Mercer tried to be friendly and succeeded in conjuring up an artificial smile. "Let's be reasonable, Mr. Cabot, that's a high-quality magazine and you are receiving it for nothing; why a subscription costs ten dollars a year! If you have been lucky enough to be chosen for a free sub you shouldn't complain . . ."

"Who chose me for a free subscription, I didn't send anything in."

"No, you wouldn't have to. Your name probably appeared on one of the lists that we purchase from insurance companies, veterans hospitals, and the like. *Hereafter* is one of our throwaway magazines; of course I don't mean that we throw them away, on the contrary they go to very selected subscribers, and we don't make our costs back from subscriptions but from the advertisers' fees. In a sense they underwrite the costs of these fine magazines, so you can say it is sort of a public service. For new mothers, for instance, we buy lists from all the hospitals and send out six-month subs of *Your Baby,* with some really fine advice and articles, and of course the ads, which are educational in themselves . . ."

"Well, I'm no new mother! Why you sending me your rag?"

"*Hereafter* is a bit different from *Your Baby,* but is still a service publication. It's a matter of statistics, sir. Every day just so many people die, of certain ages and backgrounds and that kind of thing. The people in the insurance companies, actuaries I think they call them, keep track of all these facts and figures and draw up plenty of graphs and tables. Very accurate, they assure me. They have life expectancy down to a fine art. They take a man, say, like yourself, of a certain age, background, physical fitness, environment, and so on, and pinpoint the date of death very exactly. Not the day and hour and that kind of thing—I suppose they could if they wanted to—but for our purposes a period of two years is satisfactory. This gives us a number of months and issues to acquaint the subscriber with our magazine and the services offered by our advertisers, so by the time the subscriber dies the ad messages will have reached saturation."

"Are you telling me I'm going to die inside the next two years?" Amos shrieked hoarsely, flushing with anger.

"I'm not telling you, sir, no indeed!" Mercer drew away a bit and wiped some of the old man's spittle from his glasses with his handkerchief. "That is the actuaries' job. Their computer has come up with your name and sent it to me. They say you will die within two years. As a public service we send you *Hereafter*. A service—nothing more."

"I ain't going to die in two years, not me! Not Amos Cabot!"

"That is entirely up to you, sir. My position here is

just a routine one. Your subscription has been entered and will be canceled only when a copy is returned with the imprint *addressee deceased.*"

"I'm not going to die!"

"That might possibly happen, though I can't recall any cases offhand. But since it is a two-year subscription I imagine it will expire automatically at the end of the second year, if not canceled beforehand. Yes, that's what would happen."

It ruined Amos's day, and though the sun was shining warmly he never noticed it. He went home and thought so much about the whole thing that he couldn't sleep. The next day was no better and he began to wonder if this was part of the message the dreadful magazine had conveyed. If death was close by—they were so sure of it— why did he not relax and agree with them? Send in his will, order the plot, tomb, gravestone, Last Message forms, and quietly expire.

"No! They'll not do it to me!"

At first he thought he would wait for next month's copy and write *addressee deceased* and send it back to them, that would stop the copies coming sure enough. Then he remembered fat little Mercer and could see his happy expression when the cancellation crossed his desk. Right again, dead on schedule as always. Old fool should have known you can't lick statistics. Old fool indeed! He would show them. The Cabots were a long-lived family no matter what the records said, and a hardheaded one too. They weren't going to kill him off that easily.

After much wheedling he got in to see the doctor at his old union and talked him into making a complete and thorough physical checkup.

"Not bad, not bad at all for an old boy," the doctor told him while he was buttoning his shirt.

"I'm only seventy-two; that's not old!"

"Of course it's not," the doctor said soothingly. "Just statistics, you know; a man of your age with your background . . ."

"I know all about those damned statistics; I didn't come to you for that. What's the report say?"

"You can't complain about your physical shape, Amos," he said, scanning the sheet. "Blood pressure looks all right, but you're leaning toward anemia. Do you eat much liver and fresh greens?"

"Hate liver. Greens cost too much."

"That's your choice. But remember—you can't take it with you. Spend some more money on food. Give your heart a break—don't climb too many stairs."

"I live three flights up; how do I avoid stairs?"

"That's your choice again. If you want to take care of the old ticker move to the ground floor. And vitamin D in the winter and . . ."

There was more, and after he had swallowed his first anger Amos made notes. There were food and vitamins and sleep and fresh air and a whole list of nonsense as long as your arm. But there was also the two-year subscription of *Hereafter,* so he bent back over his notes.

Without his realizing why, the next months passed quickly. He was busy, finding a room on the ground floor, changing his eating habits, getting settled in his new place. At first he used to throw out *Hereafter* whenever its gloomy bulk shadowed his mail slot, but when a year had passed he grew bolder. There was an ad for mausoleums and one of the finest had a big tag on it labeled in red *Reserved for You. Not for me!!!* he scrawled above and tore it from the magazine and mounted it on the wall. He followed it with other pictures, friendly grave-diggers beckoning toward raw openings in the earth, cut-to-order coffins with comfortable padding, and all the rest. When eighteen months had passed he enjoyed himself throwing darts at "A Photograph of the Founder of In-cino-Top-Rate, the Urn for Eternity," and carefully checked off the passing days on the calendar.

Only in the final few months did he begin to worry. He felt fine and the union doctor congratulated him for being a great example, but this didn't matter. Were the actuaries right—had his time almost run out? He could have worried himself to death, but that was not the way Cabots died! He would face this out and win.

First there were weeks left, then only days. The last five

days before the copy was due he locked himself in his room and had the delicatessen send up food. It was expensive but he wasn't going to risk any accidents in the street, not now. He had received his twenty-four copies and his subscription should have expired. The next morning would tell. He could not fall asleep at all that night, even though he knew that regular sleep was important, but just lay there until the sky brightened. He dozed for a bit then, but woke up as soon as he heard the postman's footsteps outside. This was the day, would the magazine be there? His heart was pounding and he made himself go slow as he got into the bathrobe. His room was the first on the ground floor, right next to the entrance, and all he had to do was step out into the hall and open the front door.

"Morning," he said to the postman.

"Yeah," the man answered, slinging his heavy bag around and digging into it. Amos closed the door first—then feverishly went through the mail.

It wasn't there.

He had won!

If this was not the happiest day in his life it was close to it. Besides this his victories over the bus company and the coin machine crooks were nothing. This was a war won, not a battle. He'd licked them, licked their statistics and actuaries, accountants, mechanical brains, card files, clerks, and editors. He had won! He drank a beer—the first one in two years—then another, and laughed and talked with the gang at the bar. He had won. He fell into bed late and slept like a log until he was dragged awake by his landlady knocking on the door.

"Mail for you, Mr. Cabot. Mail."

Fear gripped him, then slowly ebbed away. It couldn't be. In two years *Hereafter* had never been late once, not one day. It must be some other mail—though this wasn't his check day. He slowly opened the door and took the large envelope, his grip so loose that it almost fell from his fingers.

Only when he had laid it on the bed did he breathe naturally again—it wasn't *Hereafter* in its vile blue en-

velope; this one was a gentle pink. It did contain a magazine though, just about the size of *Hereafter,* a bulky
magazine with lots of pages. Its title was *Senility*—and the
black letters were drawn in such a way that they looked
as though they were made of cracked and crumbling stone
—and underneath it said *The Magazine of Geri-ART-*
trics. There was a picture of a feeble old man in a wheel-
chair with a blanket around his shoulders, sucking water
through a curved glass tube. Inside was more. Ads for
toilet chairs and hemorrhoid cushions, crutches and crank
beds, articles on "Learn Braille When the Eyesight Goes,"
and "Happy Though Bedridden," and "Immobile for
Twenty-five Years." A letter dropped out of the magazine
and he half-read phrases here and there.

Welcome to the family . . . the magazine of geri-
ART-trics that teaches you the art of growing old . . .
many long years ahead of you . . . empty years . . .
what happiness to find a copy in your mailbox every
month . . . speaking book edition for the blind . . .
Braille for the blind and deaf . . . every month . . .

There were tears in his eyes when he looked up. It was
dark, a rainy and cold April morning with the wind rattling the window. Raindrops ran down the glass like great,
cold tears.

TO UNDERSTAND THE BACKGROUND of this story it is necessary to understand what Denmark was like at the time I lived there. There were only a handful of Americans in the entire country, and Americans were much admired.

Most interestingly, the Danes were completely color-blind as regards race. Indeed they, a nation of blue-eyed blondes, considered black to be really beautiful—and were quite sincere in their admiration. (This attitude prevailed through all of Scandinavia.) Martin Luther King received the Nobel Prize while I was in Denmark. The Danish papers were filled with news of his visit, there was great excitement, and I, as an expatriate, felt quite proud of my country. Good things were happening.

Then I bought a copy of *Time* that had a piece in it about King that contained, among other things, a quote from some simpleminded Southern sonofabitch of a sheriff. He said something to the effect that maybe King was a big man in Norway but in the sheriff's town he would be just one more nigger.

The contrast between where I was and where I'd been was shocking and hurtful. In the Army I was stationed for a number of

8

years in Mississippi, Florida, and Texas. I
knew the sheriff's type well—I had just forgotten. I was very angry. To express that
anger in intelligent form, I conceived and
wrote this story in a white heat, at one sitting. I do not apologize if it is an angry
story.

MUTE MILTON

<<<<<<<<<<<<<<<<<<<<<<<<<<<<<<<<<<<<<<<<<

WITH PONDEROUS SMOOTHNESS THE BIG GREY-hound bus braked to a stop at the platform, and the door swung open. "Springville," the driver called out, "Last stop!" The passengers stirred in the aisle and climbed down the steps into the glare of the sun. Sam Morrison sat patiently, alone, on the wide rear seat, wait-ing until the last passengers were at the door before he put the cigar box under his arm, rose and followed them. The glare of sunlight blinded him after the tinted glass dimness of the bus, and the moist air held the breathless heat of Mississippi summer. Sam went carefully down the steps, one at a time, watching his feet, and wasn't aware of the man waiting there until something hard pushed at his stomach.

"What business yuh got in Springville, boy?"

Sam blinked through his steel-rimmed glasses at the big man in the grey uniform who stood before him, prodding him with a short, thick nightstick. He was fat as well as big, and the smooth melon of his stomach bulged out over his belt worn low about his hips.

"Just passing through, sir," Sam Morrison said and took his hat off with his free hand disclosing his cut-short grizzled hair. He let his glance slide across the flushed reddened face and the gold badge on the shirt before him, then lowered his eyes.

"An' just where yuh going to, boy? Don' keep no secrets from me . . . ," the voice rasped again.

"Carteret, sir, my bus leaves in an hour."

The only answer was an uncommunicative grunt. The lead weighted stick tapped on the cigar box under Sam's arm. "What yuh got in there—a gun?"

"No, sir, I wouldn't carry a gun." Sam opened the cigar box and held it out: it contained a lump of metal, a number of small electronic components and a two-inch speaker, all neatly wired and soldered together. "It's a . . . a radio, sir."

"Turn it on."

Sam threw a switch and made one or two careful adjustments. The little speaker rattled, and there was the squeak of tinny music barely audible above the rumble of bus motors. The red-faced man laughed.

"Now that's what ah call a real nigger radio . . . piece uh trash." His voice hardened again. "See that you're on that bus, okay?"

"Yes, sir," Sam said to the retreating, sweat-stained back of the shirt, then carefully closed the box. He started towards the colored waiting room, but when he passed the window and looked in, he saw that it was empty. And there were no dark faces visible anywhere on the street. Without changing pace Sam passed the waiting room and threaded his way between the busses in the cinder parking lot and out of the rear gate. He had lived all of his sixty-seven years in the State of Mississippi; so he knew at once that there was trouble in the air—and the only thing to do about trouble was to stay away from it. The streets became narrower and dirtier, and he trod their familiar sidewalks until he saw a field worker in patched overalls turn into a doorway ahead under the weathered BAR sign. Sam went in after him; he would wait here until a few minutes before the bus was due.

"Bottle of Jax, please." He spread his coins on the damp, scratched bar and picked up the cold bottle. There was no glass. The bartender said nothing. After ringing up the sale he retired to a chair at the far end of the bar with his head next to the murmuring radio and remained there, dark and impenetrable. The only light came from the street outside, and the high-backed booths in the rear looked cool and inviting. There were only a few other customers here, each of them sitting separately with a bottle of beer on the table before him. Sam threaded his way through the close-spaced tables and had already started to slide into the booth near the rear door when he noticed that someone was already there, seated on the other side of the table.

"I'm sorry, I didn't see you," he said and started to get up, but the man waved him back onto the bench and took an airline bag with TWA on it from the table and put it down beside him.

"Plenty of room for both," he said and raised his own bottle of beer. "Here's looking at you." Sam took a sip from his own bottle, but the other man kept drinking until he had drained half of his before he lowered it with a relaxed sigh. "That's what I call foul beer," he said.

"You seem to be enjoying it," Sam told him, but his slight smile took the edge from his words.

"Just because it's cold and wet—but I'd trade a case of it for a bottle of Bud or a Ballantine."

"Then you're from the North, I imagine?" Sam had thought so from the way he talked, sharp and clipped. Now that his eyes were getting used to the dimness, he could see that the other was a young man in his twenties with medium-dark skin, wearing a white shirt with rolled up sleeves. His face was taut and the frown wrinkles on his forehead seemed etched there.

"You are damned right. I'm from the North and I'm going back. . . ." He broke off suddenly and took another swig of beer. When he spoke again his voice was cautious. "Are you from these parts?"

"I was born not far from here, but right now I live in Carteret, just stopping off here between busses."

"Carteret—that's where the college is, isn't it?"

"That is correct. I teach there."

The younger man smiled for the first time. "That sort of puts us in the same boat; I go to NYU, majoring in economics." He put his hand out. "Charles Wright. Everyone but my mother calls me Charlie."

"Very pleased to meet you," Sam said in his slow, old-fashioned way. "I am Sam Morrison, and it is Sam on my birth certificate too."

"I'm interested in your college; I meant to step in there but. . . ." He broke off suddenly at the sound of a car's engine in the street outside and leaned forward so that he could see out the front door, remaining there until the car ground into gear and moved away. When he dropped back onto the seat, Sam could see that there were fine beads of sweat in the lines of his forehead. He took a quick drink from his bottle.

"When you were at the bus station, you didn't happen to see a big cop with a big gut, red face all the time?"

"Yes, I met him; he talked to me when I got off the bus."

"The bastard!"

"Don't get worked up, Charles; he is just a policeman doing his job."

"Just a . . . !" The young man spat a short, filthy word. "That's Brinkley; you must have heard of him, toughest man south of Bombingham. He's going to be elected sheriff next fall, and he's already grand knight of the Klan, a real pillar of the community."

"Talking like that's not going to do you any good," Sam said mildly.

"That's what Uncle Tom said—and as I remember he was still a slave when he died. Someone has got to speak up, you can't remain quiet forever."

"You talk like one of those freedom riders." Sam tried to look stern, but he was never very good at it.

"Well, I am, if you want to know the truth of it, but the ride ends right here. I'm going home. I'm scared and I'm not afraid to admit it. You people live in a jungle down here; I never realized how bad it could be until I came down. I've been working on the voter's committee, and Brinkley got word of it and swore he was going to kill me or put me in jail for life. And you know what—I believe it. I'm leaving today, just waiting for the car to pick me up. I'm going back North where I belong."

"I understand you have your problems up there too. . . ."

"Problems!" Charlie finished his beer and stood up. "I wouldn't even call them problems after what I've seen down here. It's no paradise in New York—but you stand a chance of living a bit longer. Where I grew up in South Jamaica we had it rough, but we had our own house in a good neighborhood and—you take another beer?"

"No, one is enough for me, thank you."

Charlie came back with a fresh beer and picked up where he had left off. "Maybe we're second-class citizens in the North—but at least we're citizens of some kind and can get some measure of happiness and fulfillment. Down here a man is a beast of burden, and that's all he is ever going to be—if he has the wrong color skin."

"I wouldn't say that; things get better all the time. My father was a field hand, a son of a slave—and I'm a college teacher. That's progress of a sort."

"What sort?" Charlie pounded the table yet kept his voice in an angry whisper. "So one hundredth of one percent of the Negroes get a little education and pass it on at some backwater college. Look, I'm not running you down; I know you do your best. But for every man like you there must be a thousand who are born and live and die in filthy poverty, year after year, without hope. Millions of people. Is that progress? And even yourself— are you sure you wouldn't be doing better if you were teaching in a decent university?"

"Not me," Sam laughed. "I'm just an ordinary teacher and I have enough trouble getting geometry and algebra across to my students without trying to explain topology or Boolean algebra or anything like that."

"What on earth is that Bool . . . thing? I never heard of it."

"It's, well, an uninterpreted logical calculus, a special discipline. I warned you; I'm not very good at explaining these things, though I can work them out well enough on paper. That is my hobby, really, what some people call higher mathematics, and I know that if I were working at a big school I would have no time to devote to it."

"How do you know? Maybe they would have one of those big computers—wouldn't that help you?"

"Perhaps, of course, but I've worked out ways of getting around the need for one. It just takes a little more time, that's all."

"And how much time do you have left?" Charlie asked quietly, then was instantly sorry he had said it when he saw the older man lower his head without answering. "I take that back. I've got a big mouth. I'm sorry, but I get so angry. How do you know what you might have done if you had the training, the facilities. . . ." He shut up, realizing he was getting in deeper every second.

There was only the murmur of distant traffic in the hot, dark silence, the faint sound of music from the radio behind the bar. The bartender stood, switched the radio off and opened the trap behind the bar to bring up another case of beer. From nearby the sound of the music continued like a remembered echo. Charlie realized that it was coming from the cigar box on the table before them.

"Do you have a radio in that?" he asked, happy to change the subject.

"Yes—well, really no, though there is an RF stage."

"If you think you're making sense—you're not. I told you, I'm majoring in economics."

Sam smiled and opened the box, pointing to the precisely wired circuits inside. "My nephew made this; he has a little I-fix-it shop, but he learned a lot about electronics in the Air Force. I brought him the equations, and we worked out the circuit together."

Charlie thought about a man with electronic training who was forced to run a handyman's shop, but he had the sense not to mention it. "Just what is it supposed to do?"

"It's not really supposed to do anything. I just built it to see if my equations would work out in practice. I suppose you don't know much about Einstein's unified field theory . . . ?" Charlie smiled ruefully and raised his hands in surrender. "It's difficult to talk about. Putting it the simplest way, there is supposed to be a relation between all phenomena, all forms of energy and matter. You are acquainted with the simpler interchanges, heat energy to mechanical energy as in an engine, electrical energy to light. . . ."

"The light bulb!"

"Correct. To go further, the postulation has been made that time is related to light energy, as is gravity to electrical energy. That is the field I have been exploring. I have made certain suppositions that there is an interchange of energy within a gravitic field, a measurable interchange, such as the lines of force that are revealed about a magnetic field by iron particles—no, that's not a good simile—perhaps the ability of a wire to carry a current endlessly under the chilled condition of superconductivity—"

"Professor, you have lost me. I'm not ashamed to admit it. Could you maybe give me an example—like what is happening in this little radio here?"

Sam made a careful adjustment, and the music gained the tiniest amount of volume. "It's not the radio part that is interesting—that stage really just demonstrates that I have detected the leakage—no, we should call it the differential between the earth's gravitic field and that of the lead there in the corner of the box."

"Where is the battery?"

Sam smiled proudly. "*That* is the point—there is no battery. The input current is derived. . . ."

"Do you mean you are running the radio off *gravity?* Getting electricity for nothing?"

"Yes . . . really, I should say no. It is not like that. . . ."

"It sure looks like that!" Charlie was excited now, crouching half across the table so he could look into the cigar box. "I may not know anything about electronics, but in economics we learn a lot about power sources. Couldn't this gadget of yours be developed to generate electricity at little or no cost?"

"No, not at once. This is just a first attempt. . . ."

"But it *could* eventually and that means—"

Sam thought that the young man had suddenly become sick. His face, just inches away, became shades lighter as the blood drained from it. His eyes were staring in horror as he slowly dropped back and down into his seat. Before Sam could ask him what was the matter a grating voice bellowed through the room.

"Anyone here seen a boy by the name of Charlie Wright? C'mon now, speak up. Ain't no one gonna get hurt for tellin' me the truth."

"Holy Jesus . . ." Charlie whispered, sinking deeper in the seat. Brinkley stamped into the bar, hand resting on his gun butt, squinting around in the darkness. No one answered him.

"Anybody try to hide him gonna be in trouble!" he shouted angrily. "I'm gonna find that black granny dodger!"

He started towards the rear of the room, and Charlie, with his airline bag in one hand, vaulted the back of the booth and crashed against the rear door.

"Come back here, you son of a bitch!"

The table rocked when Charlie's flying heel caught it, and the cigar box slid to the floor. Heavy boots thundered. The door squealed open and Charlie pushed out through it. Sam bent over to retrieve the box.

"I'll kill yuh, so help me!"

The circuit hadn't been damaged. Sam sighed in relief and stood, the tinny music between his fingers.

He may have heard the first shot, but he could not have heard the second because the .38 slug caught him in the back of the head and killed him instantly. He crumpled to the floor.

Patrolman Marger ran in from the patrol car outside, his gun ready, and saw Brinkley come back into the room through the door in the rear.

"He got away, damn it, got clear away."

"What happened here?" Marger asked, slipping his gun back into the holster and looking down at the slight, crumpled body at his feet.

"I dunno. He must have jumped up in the way when I let fly at the other one what was running away. Must be another one of them commonists anyway; he was sittin' at the same table."

"There's gonna be trouble about this. . . ."

"Why trouble?" Brinkley asked indignantly. "It's just anutha ol' dead nigger. . . ."

One of his boots was on the cigar box, and it crumpled and fractured when he turned away.

I DO NOT LIKE TO REPEAT MYSELF. There are authors—Philip K. Dick is the best example of one—whose lives and work are dominated by a single theme. They feel it so strongly and examine it so deeply that each story is original and exciting. Perhaps I bore easily; perhaps I see so many interesting ideas and themes in the world that I know I will never have time enough to write about all of them.

Overpopulation, what I call population, is different. It is something that cannot be ignored. It gets worse with every passing moment, it is destroying our lives and our civilization—and absolutely nothing is being done about it by the governments of the world. A feeling of rage possesses me whenever I think about it. I wrote the novel about this, *Make Room! Make Room!*, in a mood of calm speculation. The idea behind it was to show that *this* is what you'll get if nothing is done. Of course, nothing *is* being done, and as the years slowly pass and the situation steadily worsens, I occasionally get moments of rage at the stupidity and selfishness of mankind.

I was possessed by rage when I wrote this story. I do not think the laws represented

9

here are a real extrapolation—that is, I don't
think they will come to pass. But they do
represent the extremity that will be reached
at some point—laws like these may not be
passed, but others, equally obnoxious, will
be, because we've gone too far and there's
no easy way out. Millions are going to die.

It's going to get worse before it gets better.

A CRIMINAL ACT

<<<<<<<<<<<<<<<<<<<<<<<<<<<<<<<<<<<<<<<<<<<

THE FIRST BLOW OF THE HAMMER SHOOK THE
door in its frame, and the second blow made the thin
wood boom like a drum. Benedict Vernall threw the door
open before a third stroke could fall and pushed his gun
into the stomach of the man with the hammer.

"Get going. Get out of here," Benedict said, in a much
shriller voice than he had planned to use.

"Don't be foolish," the bailiff said quietly, stepping
aside so that the two guards behind him in the hall were
clearly visible. "I am the bailiff and I am doing my duty.
If I am attacked these men have orders to shoot you and
everyone else in your apartment. Be intelligent. Yours is
not the first case like this. Such things are planned for."

One of the guards clicked off the safety catch on his
submachine gun, smirking at Benedict as he did it.
Benedict let the pistol fall slowly to his side.

"Much better," the bailiff told him and struck the nail
once more with the hammer so that the notice was fixed
firmly to the door.

"Take that filthy thing down," Benedict said, choking
over the words.

"Benedict Vernall," the bailiff said, adjusting his glasses
on his nose as he read from the proclamation he had just
posted. "This is to inform you that pursuant to the
Criminal Birth Act of 1993 you are guilty of the act of
criminal birth and are hereby proscribed and no longer
protected from bodily injury by the forces of this sovereign
state . . ."

109

"You're going to let some madman kill me—what kind of a dirty law is that?"

The bailiff removed his glasses and gazed coldly along his nose at Benedict. "Mr. Vernall," he said, "have the decency to accept the results of your own actions. Did you or did you not have an illegal baby?"

"Illegal—never! A harmless infant . . ."

"Do you or do you not already have the legal maximum of two children?"

"We have two, but . . ."

"You refused advice or aid from your local birth-control clinic. You expelled, with force, the birth guidance officer who called upon you. You rejected the offer of the abortion clinic . . ."

"Murderers!"

". . . and the advice of the Family Planning Board. The statutory six months have elapsed without any action on your part. You have had the three advance warnings and have ignored them. Your family still contains one consumer more than is prescribed by law, therefore the proclamation has been posted. You alone are responsible, Mr. Vernall, you can blane no one else."

"I can blame this foul law."

"It is the law of the land," the bailiff said, drawing himself up sternly. "It is not for you or me to question." He took a whistle from his pocket and raised it to his mouth. "It is my legal duty to remind you that you still have one course open, even at this last moment, and may still avail yourself of the services of the Euthanasia Clinic."

"Go straight to hell!"

"Indeed. I've been told that before." The bailiff snapped the whistle to his lips and blew a shrill blast. He almost smiled as Benedict slammed shut the apartment door.

There was an animal-throated roar from the stairwell as the policemen who were blocking it stepped aside. A knot of fiercely tangled men burst out, running and fighting at the same time. One of them surged ahead of the pack but fell as a fist caught him on the side of the head; the others trampled him underfoot. Shouting and cursing the mob came on and it looked as though it would be a draw, but a few yards short of the door one of the leaders tripped and brought two others down. A short fat man in the second rank leaped their bodies and crashed headlong into Vernall's door with such force that the ballpoint pen he held extended pierced the paper of the notice and sank into the wood beneath.

"A volunteer has been selected," the bailiff shouted and the waiting police and guards closed in on the wailing men and began to force them back toward the stairs. One of the men remained behind on the floor, saliva running down his cheeks as he chewed hysterically at a strip of the threadbare carpet. Two white-garbed hospital attendants were looking out for this sort of thing and one of them jabbed the man expertly in the neck with a hypodermic needle while the other unrolled the stretcher.

Under the bailiff's watchful eye the volunteer painstakingly wrote his name in the correct space on the proclamation, then carefully put the pen back in his vest pocket.

"Very glad to accept you as a volunteer for this important public duty, Mr. . . ." the bailiff leaned forward to peer at the paper, "Mr. Mortimer," he said.

"Mortimer is my first name," the man said in a crisply dry voice as he dabbed lightly at his forehead with his breast-pocket handkerchief.

"Understandable, sir, your anonymity will be respected as is the right of all volunteers. Might I presume that you are acquainted with the rest of the regulations?"

"You may. Paragraph forty-six of the Criminal Birth Act of 1993, subsection fourteen, governing the selection of volunteers. Firstly, I have volunteered for the maximum period of twenty-four hours. Secondly, I will neither attempt nor commit violence of any form upon any other members of the public during this time, and if I do so I will be held responsible by law for all of my acts."

"Very good. But isn't there more?"

Mortimer folded the handkerchief precisely and tucked it back into his pocket. "Thirdly," he said, and patted it smooth, "I shall not be liable to prosecution by law if I take the life of the proscribed individual, one Benedict Vernall."

"Perfectly correct." The bailiff nodded and pointed to a large suitcase that a policeman had set down on the floor and was opening. The hall had been cleared. "If you would step over here and take your choice." They both gazed down into the suitcase that was filled to overflowing with instruments of death. "I hope you also understand that your own life will be in jeopardy during this period and if you are injured or killed you will not be protected by law?"

"Don't take me for a fool," Mortimer said curtly, then pointed into the suitcase. "I want one of those concussion grenades."

"You cannot have it," the bailiff told him in a cutting voice, injured by the other's manner. There was a correct way to do these things. "These are only for use in open districts where the innocent cannot be injured. Not in an apartment building. You have your choice of all the short-range weapons, however."

Mortimer laced his fingers together and stood with his head bowed, almost in an attitude of prayer, as he examined the contents. Machine pistols, grenades, automatics, knives, knuckle dusters, vials of acid, whips, straight razors, broken glass, poison darts, morning stars, maces, gas bombs, and tear-gas pens.

"Is there any limit?" he asked.

"Take what you feel you will need. Just remember that it must all be accounted for and returned."

"I want the Reisling machine pistol with five of the twenty-cartridge magazines and the commando knife with the spikes on the handguard and fountain-pen tear-gas gun."

The bailiff was making quick check marks on a mimeographed form attached to his clip board while Mortimer spoke. "Is that all?" he asked.

Mortimer nodded and took the extended board and scrawled his name on the bottom of the sheet without

examining it, then began at once to fill his pockets with
the weapons and ammunition.

"Twenty-four hours," the bailiff said, looking at his
watch and filling in one more space in the form. "You
have until 1745 hours tomorrow."

"Get away from the door, please, Ben," Maria begged.

"Quiet," Benedict whispered, his ear pressed to the
panel. "I want to hear what they are saying." His face
screwed up as he struggled to understand the muffled
voices. "It's no good," he said, turning away. "I can't
make it out. Not that it makes any difference. I know,
what's happening . . ."

"There's a man coming to kill you," Maria said in her
delicate, little girl's voice. The baby started to whimper
and she hugged him to her.

"Please, Maria, go back into the bathroom like we
agreed. You have the bed in there, and the food, and there
aren't any windows. As long as you stay along the wall
away from the door nothing can possibly happen to you.
Do that for me, darling—so I won't have to worry about
either of you."

"Then you will be out here alone."

Benedict squared his narrow shoulders and clutched the
pistol firmly. "That is where I belong, out in front, defending my family. That is as old as the history of man."

"Family," she said and looked around worriedly. "What
about Matthew and Agnes?"

"They'll be all right with your mother. She promised to
look after them until we got in touch with her again. You
can still be there with them; I wish you would."

"No, I couldn't. I couldn't bear being anywhere else
now. And I couldn't leave the baby there; he would be
so hungry." She looked down at the infant, who was
still whimpering, then began to unbutton the top of her
dress.

"Please, darling," Benedict said, edging back from the
door. "I want you to go into the bathroom with baby
and stay there. You must. He could be coming at any
time now."

She reluctantly obeyed him, and he waited until the door had closed and he heard the lock being turned. Then he tried to force their presence from his mind because they were only a distraction that could interfere with what must be done. He had worked out the details of his plan of defense long before and he went slowly around the apartment making sure that everything was as it should be. First the front door, the only door into the apartment. It was locked and bolted and the night chair was attached. All that remained was to push the big wardrobe up against it. The killer could not enter now without a noisy struggle, and if he tried Benedict would be there waiting with his gun. That took care of the door.

There were no windows in either the kitchen or the bathroom, so he could forget about these rooms. The bedroom was a possibility since its window looked out onto the fire escape, but he had a plan for this too. The window was locked and the only way it could be opened from the outside was by breaking the glass. He would hear that and would have time to push the couch in the hall up against the bedroom door. He didn't want to block it now in case he had to retreat into the bedroom himself.

Only one room remained, the living room, and this was where he was going to make his stand. There were two windows in the living room and the far one could be entered from the fire escape, as could the bedroom window. The killer might come this way. The other window could not be reached from the fire escape, though shots could still be fired through it from the windows across the court. But the corner was out of the line of fire, and this was where he would be. He had pushed the big armchair right up against the wall and, after checking once more that both windows were locked, he dropped into it.

His gun rested on his lap and pointed at the far window by the fire escape. He would shoot if anyone tried to come through it. The other window was close by, but no harm could come that way unless he stood in front of it. The thin fabric curtains were drawn and once it was dark he could see through them without being seen himself. By shifting the gun barrel a few degrees he could cover the door into the hall. If there were any disturbance at the front door he could be there in a few steps. He had done everything he could. He settled back into the chair.

Once the daylight faded the room was quite dark; yet he could see well enough by the light of the city sky, which filtered in through the drawn curtains. It was very quiet and whenever he shifted position he could hear the rusty chair springs twang beneath him. After only a few hours he realized one slight flaw in his plan. He was thirsty.

At first he could ignore it, but by nine o'clock his mouth was as dry as cotton wool. He knew he couldn't last the night like this; it was too distracting. He should have brought a jug of water in with him. The wisest thing would be to go and get it as soon as possible; yet he did not want to leave the protection of the corner. He had heard nothing of the killer and this only made him more concerned about his unseen presence.

Then he heard Maria calling to him. Very softly at first, then louder and louder. She was worried. Was he all right? He dared not answer her, not from here. The only thing to do was to go to her, whisper through the door that everything was fine and that she should be quiet. Perhaps then she would go to sleep. And he could get some water in the kitchen and bring it back.

As quietly as he could he rose and stretched his stiff legs, keeping his eyes on the gray square of the second window. Putting the toe of one foot against the heel of the other he pulled his shoes off, then went on silent tiptoe across the room. Maria was calling louder now, rattling at the bathroom door, and he had to silence her. Why couldn't she realize the danger she was putting him in?

As he passed through the door the hall light above him came on.

"What are you doing?" he screamed at Maria, who stood by the switch, blinking in the sudden glare.

"I was so worried . . ."

The crash of breaking glass from the living room was punctuated by the hammering boom of the machine pistol.

Arrows of pain tore at Benedict and he hurled himself sprawling into the hall.

"Into the bathroom!" he screeched and fired his own revolver back through the dark doorway.

He was only half aware of Maria's muffled squeal as she slammed the door and, for the moment, he forgot the pain of the wounds. There was the metallic smell of burnt gunpowder and a blue haze hung in the air. Something scraped in the living room and he fired again into the darkness. He winced as the answering fire crashed thunder and flame toward him and the bullets tore holes in the plaster of the hall opposite the door.

The firing stopped but he kept his gun pointed as he realized that the killer's fire couldn't reach him where he lay, against the wall away from the open doorway. The man would have to come into the hall to shoot him, and if he did that Benedict would fire first and kill him. More shots slammed into the wall, but he did not bother to answer them. When the silence stretched out for more than a minute he took a chance and silently broke his revolver and pulled out the empty shells, putting live cartridges in their place. There was a pool of blood under his leg.

Keeping the gun pointed at the doorway he clumsily rolled up his pants leg with his left hand, then took a quick glimpse. There was more blood running down his ankle and sopping his sock. A bullet had torn through his calf muscle and made two round, dark holes from which the thick blood pumped. It made him dizzy to look at it, then he remembered and pointed the wavering pistol back at the doorway. The living room was silent. His side hurt too, but when he pulled his shirt out of his trousers and looked he realized that although his wound was painful, it was not so bad as the one in his leg. A second bullet had burned along his side, glancing off the ribs and leaving a shallow wound. It wasn't bleeding badly. Something would have to be done about his leg.

"You moved fast, Benedict, I must congratulate you—"

Benedict's finger contracted with shock and he pumped

two bullets into the room, toward the sound of the man's voice. The man laughed.

"Nerves, Benedict, nerves. Just because I am here to kill you doesn't mean that we can't talk."

"You're a filthy beast, a foul, filthy beast!" Benedict splattered the words from his lips and followed them with a string of obscenities, expressions he hadn't used or even heard since his school days. He stopped suddenly as he realized that Maria could hear him. She had never heard him curse before.

"Nerves, Benedict?" The dry laugh sounded again. "Calling me insulting names won't alter the situation."

"Why don't you leave; I won't try to stop you," Benedict said as he slowly pulled his left arm out of his shirt. "I don't want to see you or know you. Why don't you go away?"

"I'm afraid that it is not that easy, Ben. You have created this situation; in one sense you have called me here. Like a sorcerer summoning some evil genie. That's a pleasant simile, isn't it? May I introduce myself. My name is Mortimer."

"I don't want to know your name, you . . . piece of filth." Benedict half mumbled, his attention concentrated on the silent removal of his shirt. It hung from his right wrist and he shifted the gun to his left hand for a moment while he slipped it off. His leg throbbed with pain when he draped the shirt over the wound in his calf and he gasped, then spoke quickly to disguise the sound. "You came here because you wanted to—and I'm going to kill you for that."

"Very good, Benedict, that is much more the type of spirit I expected from you. After all, you are the closest we can come to a dedicated law-breaker these days, the antisocial individualist who stands alone, who will carry on the traditions of the Dillingers and the James brothers. Though they brought death and you brought life, and your weapon is far humbler than their guns . . ." The words ended with a dry chuckle.

"You have a warped mind, Mortimer, just what I would

suspect of a man who accepts a free license to kill. You're sick."

Benedict wanted to keep the other man talking, at least for a few minutes more until he could bandage his leg. The shirt was sticky with blood and he couldn't knot it in place with his left hand. "You must be sick to come here," he said. "What other reason could you possibly have?" He laid the gun down silently, then fumbled with haste to bandage the wound.

"Sickness is relative," the voice in the darkness said, "as is crime. Man invents societies and the rules of his invented societies determine the crimes. *O tempora! O mores!* Homosexuals in Periclean Greece were honored men, and respected for their love. Homosexuals in industrial England were shunned and prosecuted for a criminal act. Who commits the crime—society or the man? Which of them is the criminal? You may attempt to argue a higher authority than man, but that would be only an abstract predication and what we are discussing here are realities. The law states that you are a criminal. I am here to enforce that law." The thunder of his gun added punctuation to his words and long splinters of wood flew from the doorframe. Benedict jerked the knot tight and grabbed up his pistol again.

"I do invoke a higher authority," he said. "Natural law, the sanctity of life, the inviolability of marriage. Under this authority I wed and I love, and my children are the blessings of this union."

"Your blessings—and the blessings of the rest of mankind—are consuming this world like locusts," Mortimer said. "But that is an observation. First I must deal with your arguments.

"*Primus.* The only natural law is written in the sedimentary rocks and the spectra of suns. What you call natural law is man-made law and varies with the varieties of religion. Argument invalid.

"*Secundis.* Life is prolific and today's generations must die so that tomorrow's may live. All religions have the faces of Janus. They frown at killing and at the same time smile at war and capital punishment. Argument invalid.

"*Ultimus*. The forms of male and female union are as varied as the societies that harbor them. Argument invalid. Your higher authority does not apply to the world of facts and law. Believe in it if you wish, if it gives you satisfaction, but do not invoke it to condone your criminal acts."

"Criminal!" Benedict shouted, and fired two shots through the doorway, then cringed as an answering storm of bullets crackled by. Dimly, through the bathroom door, he heard the baby crying, awakened by the noise. He dropped out the empty shells and angrily pulled live cartridges from his pocket and jammed them into the cylinder. "You're the criminal, who is trying to murder me," he said. "You are the tool of the criminals who invade my house with their unholy laws and tell me I can have no more children. You cannot give me orders about this."

"What a fool you are," Mortimer sighed. "You are a social animal and do not hesitate to accept the benefits of your society. You accept medicine, so your children live now as they would have died in the past, and you accept a ration of food to feed them, food you do not even work for. This suits you, so you accept. But you do not accept planning for your family and you attempt to reject it. It is impossible. You must accept all or reject all. You must leave your society—or abide by its rules. You eat the food, you must pay the price."

"I don't ask for more food. The baby has its mother's milk; we will share our food ration . . ."

"Don't be fatuous. You and your irresponsible kind have filled this world to bursting with your get, and still you will not stop. You have been reasoned with, railed against, cajoled, bribed and threatened, all to no avail. Now you must be stopped. You have refused all aid to prevent your bringing one more mouth into this hungry world, and, since you have done so anyway, you are to be held responsible for closing another mouth and removing it from this same world. The law is a humane one, rising out of our history of individualism and the frontier spirit, and gives you a chance to defend your ideals with a gun. And your life."

"The law is not humane," Benedict said. "How can you possibly suggest that? It is harsh, cruel and pointless."

"Quite the contrary, the system makes very good sense. Try to step outside yourself for a moment, forget your prejudices and look at the problem that faces our race. The universe is cruel—but it's not ruthless. The conservation of mass is one of the universe's most ruthlessly enforced laws. We have been insane to ignore it so long, and it is sanity that now forces us to limit the sheer mass of human flesh on this globe. Appeals to reason have never succeeded in slowing the population growth, so, with great reluctance, laws have been passed. Love, marriage and the family are not affected—up to a reasonable maximum of children. After that a man *voluntarily* forsakes the protection of society, and must take the consequences of his own acts. If he is insanely selfish, his death will benefit society by ridding it of his presence. If he is not insane and has determination and enough guts to win—well then, he is the sort of man that society needs and he represents a noble contribution to the gene pool. Good and law-abiding citizens are not menaced by these laws."

"How dare you!" Benedict shouted. "Is a poor, helpless mother of an illegitimate baby a criminal?"

"No, only if she refuses all aid. She is even allowed a single child without endangering herself. If she persists in her folly, she must pay for her acts. There are countless frustrated women willing to volunteer for battle to even the score. They, like myself, are on the side of the law and eager to enforce it. So close my mouth, if you can, Benedict, because I look forward with pleasure to closing your incredibly selfish one."

"Madman!" Benedict hissed and felt his teeth grate together with the intensity of his passion. "Scum of society. This obscene law brings forth the insane dregs of humanity and arms them and gives them license to kill."

"It does that, and a useful device it is, too. The maladjusted expose themselves and can be watched. Better the insane killer coming publicly and boldly than trapping and butchering your child in the park. Now he risks his life and whoever is killed serves humanity with his death."

"You admit you are a madman—a licensed killer?" Benedict started to stand but the hall began to spin dizzily and grow dark: he dropped back heavily.

"Not I," Mortimer said tonelessly. "I am a man who wishes to aid the law and wipe out your vile, proliferating kind."

"You're an invert than, hating the love of man and woman."

The only answer was a cold laugh that infuriated Benedict.

"Sick!" he screamed. "Or mad. Or sterile, incapable of fathering children of your own and hating those who can . . ."

"That's enough! I've talked enough to you, Benedict. Now I shall kill you."

Benedict could hear anger for the first time in the other's voice and knew that he had goaded the man with the prod of truth. He was silent, sick and weak, the blood still seeping through his rough bandage and widening in a pool on the floor. He had to have what little strength he had to aim and fire when the killer came through the doorway. Behind him he heard the almost silent opening of the bathroom door and the rustle of footsteps. He looked up helplessly into Maria's tear-stained face.

"Who's there with you?" Mortimer shouted, from where he crouched behind the armchair. "I hear you whispering. If your wife is there with you, Benedict, send her away. I won't be responsible for the cow's safety. You've brought this upon yourself, Benedict, and the time has now come to pay the price of your errors, and I shall be the instrumentality of that payment."

He stood and emptied the remainder of the magazine of bullets through the doorway, then pressed the button to release the magazine and hurled it after the bullets, clicking a new one instantly into place. With a quick pull he worked the slide to shove a live cartridge into the chamber and crouched, ready to attack.

This was it. He wouldn't need the knife. Walk a few feet forward. Fire through the doorway, then throw in the tear-gas pen. It would either blind the man or spoil his aim. Then walk through firing with the trigger jammed down and the bullets spraying like water and the man would be dead. Mortimer took a deep, shuddering breath—then stopped and gaped as Benedict's hand snaked through the doorway and felt its way up the wall.

It was so unexpected that for a moment he didn't fire, and when he did fire he missed. A hand is a difficult target for an automatic weapon. The hand jerked down over the light switch and vanished as the ceiling lights came on.

Mortimer cursed and fired after the hand and fired into the wall and through the doorway, hitting nothing except insensate plaster and feeling terribly exposed beneath the glare of light.

The first shot from the pistol went unheard in the roar of his gun and and he did not realize that he was under fire until the second bullet ripped into the floor close to his feet. He stopped shooting, spun around and gaped.

On the fire escape outside the broken window stood the woman. Slight and wide-eyed and swaying as though a strong wind tore at her, she pointed the gun at him with both hands and jerked the trigger spasmodically. The bullets came close but did not hit him, and in panic he pulled the machine pistol up, spraying bullets in an arc toward the window. "Don't! I don't want to hurt you!" he shouted even as he did it.

The last of his bullets hit the wall and his gun clicked and locked out of battery as the magazine emptied. He hurled the barren metal magazine away and tried to jam a full one in and the pistol banged away and the bullet hit him in the side and spun him about. When he fell the gun fell from his hand. Benedict, who had been crawling slowly and painfully across the floor, reached him at the same moment and clutched at his throat with hungry fingers.

"Don't . . ." Mortimer croaked and thrashed about. He had never learned to fight and did not know what else to do.

"Please, Benedict, don't," Maria said, climbing through the window and running to them. "You're killing him."

"No—I'm not," Benedict gasped. "No strength. My hands are too weak."

Looking up he saw the pistol near his head and he reached and tore it from her.

"One less mouth now!" he shouted and pressed the hot muzzle against Mortimer's chest and pulled the trigger and the muffled shot tore into the man, who kicked violently once and died.

"Darling, you're all right?" Maria wailed, kneeling and clutching him to her.

"Yes . . . all right. Weak, but that's from losing the blood, I imagine, but the bleeding has stopped now. It's all over. We've won. We'll have the food ration now, and they won't bother us anymore and everyone will be satisfied."

"I'm so glad," she said, and actually managed to smile through her tears. "I really didn't want to tell you before, not bother you with all this other trouble going on. But there's going to be . . ." She dropped her eyes.

"What?" he asked incredulously. "You can't possibly mean . . ."

"But I do." She patted the rounded mound of her midriff. "Aren't we lucky?"

All he could do was look up at her, his mouth wide and gasping like some helpless fish cast up on the shore.

I THINK THIS STORY MUST SPEAK for itself—it's of the kind where the unfolding is of primary importance. However, it can be mentioned that it's one of the stories intended for my matter-transmitter collection and is a suggested solution to a problem that has *always* bothered civilized man.

10

WAITING PLACE

<<<<<<<<<<<<<<<<<<<<<<<<<<<<<<<<<<<<<<<<<<<<<

AS SOON AS JOMFRI STEPPED OUT OF THE
screen of the matter transmitter, he realized that there
had been a terrible mistake. For one thing his head hurt
with a pain that almost blinded him, a classic symptom of
MT malfunction. For another this was not his destination, not this gray and dusty chamber. He had been
on his way home. Staggering, his arm before his eyes,
he felt his way to the hard bench that was secured to
one wall. He sat, slumped, with his head on his hands,
and waited for the pain to ooze away.

The worst was over, that was certain, and he should
be thankful that he had survived. Jomfri knew all about
MT failures from the 3V plays since, though rare in
reality, these dramatic circumstances were natural material for the robot scripters. The failure of a single
microscopic circuit would be enough to send the hapless
traveler to a receiver that was not the one that he had
punched for, while at the same time giving his nervous
system a random twist that accounted for the headache.
This was what the technicians called a minimal malfunction, and once the headache had faded the victim could
punch for the local emergency station, report the malfunction, then go on. The worst thing that could happen was
too horrifying to consider: people who arrived turned
inside out or stretched in one dimension into miles of
tubular flesh. Or even worse. He was all right, Jomfri
told himself, clutching his head with both hands, he had
come through all right.

When he opened one eye a crack the light hurt, but was bearable. He could stand, shakily, and see, barely, so it was time to get help. They would have drugs in the emergency station that would fix his head. And he had to report the malfunctioning transmitter before anyone else was caught in the thing. His fingers groped over the featureless wall for clumsy seconds trying to find the punch panel.

"It is impossible!" Jomfri cried, his eyes wide open despite the pain. "There is always a panel."

There was none. This screen was for receiving only. It was theoretically possible that a MT screen could be one way, without a sending tuner, but he had never seen one before. "Outside," he said, turning from the blank screen in this blank room.

Leaning against the featureless wall for support Jomfri went out the door and down a barren hallway. The hall made a single right-angled turn and opened into a dust-filled street. A scrap of dirty plastic blew by and there was the smell of warm decay.

"The sooner I'm away from this place the better. I'll find another transmitter." Then he moaned as the sunlight struck daggers of pain through his eyes and into his brain. He made his way into the street, stumbling, peering through the smallest crack between the fingers that he clamped tight over his eyes. Tears ran down his cheeks, and through his damp agony he searched the blank, gray walls for the familiar red double-headed MT arrow. It was nowhere to be seen. A man sat in a doorway, his face hidden in the shadows.

"Help me," Jomfri said. "I'm hurt. I must find the MT station—where is it?" The man shuffled his feet but said nothing. "Can't you understand?" Jomfri was petulant. "I'm in pain. Your duty as a citizen. . . ."

Still in silence, the man caught his toe behind Jomfri's ankle, then slammed him in the knee with his other foot. Jomfri went down, and the stranger stood at the same time. "Dirty fangner," he said and kicked Jomfri hard in the groin, then stalked away.

It was a long time before Jomfri could do more than

lie, curled up and moaning, afraid to move, as though he were a cracked egg that would burst and spill its contents if disturbed. When he did sit up finally, wiping feebly at the sour bile on his lips, he was aware that people had passed him; yet none had stopped. He did not like this city, this planet, wherever he was. He wanted to leave. Standing was painful, and walking even more so; yet he did it. Find the MT station, get out, find a doctor. Leave.

In other circumstances Jomfri might have remarked on the barrenness of this place, with its lack of vehicular traffic, its scattering of pedestrians and its complete lack of signs and street names, as though illiteracy had been established by edict. But now the only concern he had for his surroundings was to leave them. Passing an arcaded opening he stopped and cautiously, for he had learned discretion with that single kick, he looked inside. It was a courtyard with rough tables scattered about, planks nailed to their legs in lieu of benches. Some of them were occupied. A small barrel rested on the central table, at which sat six men and a woman, filling cups from it. All present were as drab as the walls about them, dressed for the most part in uniform gray, although some of them had parts of their costume made up of drab pastels.

Jomfri drew back quickly as the woman came toward him, then realized that she was lank-haired and old and kept her eyes to the ground as she shuffled forward, carrying the plastic cup in both hands. She slid onto one of the benches close by and buried her face in her drink.

"Can you help me?" Jomfri asked, sitting at the far corner of the table where she could neither kick nor hit him and where he could flee if he had to.

She looked up, startled, and pulled the cup to her. When he made no further movements toward her, she blinked her red-rimmed eyes, and a mottled tip of tongue licked out at her cracked lips and withdrew.

"Will you help?" he asked again, feeling safe enough for the moment.

"New one here," she said, her words hissing and blurring over her toothless gums. "Don't like it, do you?"

"No, I certainly do not like it, and I'm going to leave. If you would direct me to the nearest MT station—"

The crone cackled hoarsely then sipped loudly from her cup. "One way only, fangner; you knew that before they sent you. The road to Fangnis has but one direction."

At the sound of this time-weary cliché he gasped and suddenly felt very cold. Memories of the priest with the raised, admonitory finger: the father to his errant daughter. Was there a Fangnis? "It cannot be," he said in a futile effort to convince himself differently, while his eyes darted like trapped animals to the buildings, the street, the people, and back again.

"It is," the woman said, and he had the feeling she would drop her head to the table and weep, but she only drank again.

"There has been a dreadful mistake. I should not be here."

"Everyone says that," she said with contempt, dismissing him with a palsied wave of her hand. "You'll stop soon. Criminals all, rejected from our own worlds, sentenced for life and eternity, forgotten. They used to kill us. It would have been kinder."

"I have heard of Fangnis," Jomfri said hurriedly. "A world no one knows where, eternal noon." He shot a frightened glance at the changeless light in the street outside, then away. "The unwanted, the condemned, the guilty, the incorrigible, the criminals are sent there. All right, *here* then," he added when he saw her twisted and humorless smile. "I'll not argue with you. Perhaps you are right. In any case there has been a grave mistake made, and it must be rectified. I am no criminal. I was on my way home from work. My wife will be waiting. I dialed my number and appeared . . . here."

She no longer looked at him, but stared numbly into her drink instead. He was suddenly aware of how dry his mouth was. "What are you drinking? Could I have some?"

The old woman roused at this, pulling the drink to her and cradling it against her ancient breasts. "Mine. I worked for it. You can drink water like all the other fangners. I cut the wood and watched the fire at the swamp-edge while it dripped. My share."

The cup was almost empty now, and he could smell the raw spirit on her breath when she talked. "Out there. Down the street. Go away. Food and water at the Warden. Go away." She had lost interest in him, and he rose painfully and left before there was any more trouble.

"The Warden, of course," he told himself with a sudden warm spurt of hope. "I'll explain and he'll take care of me."

Jomfri walked faster. The street ended in a dusty hillside, a smoothly rising, round-topped hill surrounded by the monotony of the low drab buildings. A structure clamped itself to the hilltop, a hemispherical and featureless dome of durcrete. Hard as diamond and as eternal. A thin man in rusty black and gray was trudging up the hill before him, and Jomfri followed furtively, ready to turn and run at any sign of hostility.

Water gushed continually from a durcrete spout and splashed into a drain below. The thin man secured a plastic bag over the spout, and when it filled he reached into a deep opening in the wall beside the spout and took out a blocky package of some kind. Jomfri waited until he had removed the filled bag and vanished around the curve of the dome before he went forward. The sibilance of the splashing water was the only sound in the hazy silence, and his throat was suddenly dry. He buried his head under the stream, let it run into his mouth and over his face and across his hands. When he pulled away, gasping for air, he felt much better. Wiping the water from his eyes, he pushed his head into the opening. It was almost featureless. A shiny, worn metal plate was inset to his right, and a hole, no bigger around than his arm, vanished upward into darkness from the farther end of the pit. The word PRESS, almost completely rubbed away, was printed above the plate. The only letters he had seen since he arrived here. Hesitatingly, he put his thumb to the cool metal. There was a distant susurration and a rising, scraping sound. Jomfri pulled his hand out quickly as a plastic-wrapped package shot down out of the opening and plopped softly into the rear of the niche. He took it out and saw that it was a bag of mealpaste.

"Go ahead, eat, I won't bother you."

Jomfri spun about, almost dropping the bag, to face the thin man who had silently returned and stood close behind him. "You're new here, I could tell," the man said, and a wholly artificial smile passed over his lined and pock-marked face. "Say hello to Old Rurry, I can be your friend."

"Take this," Jomfri said, extending the mealpaste, trying to push away all connection with Fangnis. "There has been a mistake; this is someone else's ration; the machine gave it to me in error. I do not belong here."

"Of course not, young fangner," Old Rurry purred. "Many is the life ended by politicians, innocent men sent here. The machine doesn't care or know who is here or who you are or who I am. It has a five-hour memory and won't feed you again until that time has passed. It will feed anyone· every five hours, forever. That is the sort of horrible efficiency that makes one squirm, isn't it?"

Jomfri's fingers clutched spasmodically, digging deep into the flexible wrapping. "No, I am sincere. A mistake in the MT sent me here. If you really wish to help me you will show me how to contact the authorities."

Old Rurry shrugged and looked bored. "Impossible. They're sealed inside this tomb and come and go with their own MT. They never contact us. We feed at this side of the Warden—and leave at the other."

"Leave? Then it is possible. Take me there."

Sniffing wetly, Old Rurry wiped his nose on the back of his finger, then examined it carefully and wiped it on the side of his jacket before he spoke. "If you must be ghoulish, that can be easily enough arranged. Right there." He pointed the wiped finger at the foot of the hill where four men had appeared, carrying a woman face down, one to each limb. They plodded forward until they noticed the two men waiting above them, then the two men bearing the legs dropped them into the dirt, turned and left.

"A civic duty," Old Rurry said distastefully, "and the

only one we perform. If we just leave them or dump them into the swamp they rot, and that is highly unpleasant." They walked down, and Old Rurry pointed silently to the left leg while he picked up the right. Jomfri hesitated, and all three fangners turned to stare coldly at him. He bent quickly—memory of that educatory boot—clutched the bare flesh of the ankle, almost dropping it again at the feel of its cold and firm, unfleshlike texture. They continued up the hill, and Jomfri turned away from the sight of the dirt-stained, blue-veined leg. Perhaps this was the woman he had talked to. He shuddered at the thought. No, the clothing was different, and this one was long dead.

A well-traveled dirt track ran about the circumference of the Warden, and they shuffled along it until they reached a spot that appeared to be diametrically opposite the feeding station. A long narrow strip of metal was inset in the wall at knee-height, perhaps a foot wide and eight feet long. The leading man on the inside bent and pulled at a grove in the metal, which swung out, slowly, to reveal that it was the outer side of a V-shaped bin. It was constructed of three-inch-thick armor alloy, yet was still dented and scratched along the edge. How desperate could one become after a lifetime in this place? The body was unceremoniously dumped into the bin and the outer door kicked shut.

"Unrivaled efficiency," Old Rurry said, watching warily as the two other men departed without a word. "No communication, no contact. The end. Bodies and old clothes. Their bodies are taken away and new sackcloth issued for old rags. Remember that when your fine clothes grow worn."

"This cannot be all!" Jomfri shouted, tugging at the door, which was now locked. "I must contact those inside and explain the error. I don't belong in this place."

There was a slight vibration, he could feel it in his fingertips; and the door yielded to his tugging. It opened, and the bin was empty. In a frenzy of haste Jomfri climbed in and stretched out full length. "Close it, please, I beg," he said to Old Rurry, who bent over him. "This is all to no purpose," replied Old Rurry. Still, when Jomfri pleaded, he pushed the door shut. The light narrowed to a crack and vanished. The darkness was absolute.

"I am not dead," Jomfri shouted in sudden panic. "Nor am I old clothes. Can you hear me? I wish to report a mistake. I was on my way home, you see, and—"

Soft bars, it felt like a dozen of them clamped tight against his body. He screamed feebly, then louder when something brushed against his head and face. There was a tiny humming in the darkness.

"An incorrectly dialed number, a malfunction in the MT. I am here in error. You must believe me."

As silently as they had come the arms were withdrawn. He felt about him, but there was solid metal on all sides as though he were sealed in a coffin. Then a crack and a slit of light appeared, and he closed his eyes against the sudden glare. When he opened them again he looked up at Old Rurry, who was sucking the last of the food-paste from a container.

"Yours," he said. "I didn't think you wanted it. Climb out of there, it won't move again until you do."

"What happened? Something held me."

"Machines. See if you are dead or sick or old clothes. If you're sick they give you a shot before they toss you back. You can't fool them. Only the dead go on through."

"They wouldn't even listen to me," he said, climbing wearily out.

"That's the whole idea. Modern penology. Society no longer kills or punishes for trespassing its laws. The criminal is redeemed. Some cannot be. They are the ones who would have been hanged, burned, flayed, broken, electrocuted, beheaded, racked, speared, or otherwise executed in more barbarous times. Now they are simply dismissed from civilized society to enjoy the company of their peers. Could anything be more just? Away from the society they have offended, no longer a burden on it as they would be in a prison. A minimal contribution from all the worlds using this service supplies food and clothing and operating costs. Dismissed and forgotten, for there is no escape. We are on a clouded and primitive world, forever facing the unseen sun, surrounded by nothing but swamps. That is the all of it. Some survive, some die quickly. There is room for a hundred times our number without crowding. We eat, we sleep, we kill each other. Our only joint effort is the operating of stills at the swamp's edge. The local fruit is inedible, but it ferments. And alcohol is alcohol. Since you are a new-comer I will give you one drink of hospitality and welcome you into our drinking band. We've had too many deaths of late, and more wood is needed."

"No. I won't join your convict alcoholics. I'm different, I was sent here by mistake. Not like you."

Old Rurry smiled and, with a swiftness that denied his years, produced a shining blade that he pricked into Jomfri's throat.

"Learn this rule quickly. Never ask a man why he is here nor mention it to him. It is a messy form of suicide. I will tell you, because I am not ashamed. I was a chemist. I knew all the formulas. I made tasteless poison and killed my wife and eighty-three of her family. That makes eighty-four. Few here can match that number." He slid the knife back into his sleeve, and Jomfri backed away, rubbing the red mark on his neck.

"You're armed," he said, shocked.

"This is a world, not a prison. We do our best. Through the years bits of metal have accumulated, weapons have been manufactured. This knife must be generations old. The myth has it that it was made from an iron meteorite. All things are possible. I killed its former owner by thrust-ing a sharpened length of wire through his eardrum and into his brain."

"I do feel like that drink now. Thank you for offering. Very kind." Jomfri worked hard to give no offense. The old man started down the hill with Jomfri trailing after. The building they went to was like all the others.

"Very good," Jomfri said, choking over a beaker of the acid and acrid drink.

"Filthy stuff," Old Rurry told him. "I could improve

it. Add natural flavoring. But the others won't let me. They know my record."

Jomfri took a deeper drink. He knew the record, too. When he finished the beaker his head was fuzzy and his stomach sickened. He felt no better. He knew that if he had to stay on Fangnis he would be one of the men who died swiftly. This life was worse than no life.

"Sick! You said they would see me if I were sick," he shouted, jumping to his feet. Old Rurry ignored him, and he was drunk enough to clutch the man by his clothing. None of the others paid particular attention until the wicked length of blade appeared again. Jomfri let go and staggered backward, his eyes on the foot of steel. "I want you to cut me with your knife," he said.

Old Rurry stopped and thought; he had never received an invitation from a prospective victim before. "Cut you where?" He scanned the other for a suitable spot.

"Where?" Where indeed. What part of one's body do you invite violence upon? What member that you have borne a lifetime do you discard? "A finger . . ." he suggested hesitantly.

"Two fingers—or none," Old Rurry told him, a natural merchant of destruction.

"Here then." Jomfri dropped into the chair and spread his hands before him. "Two, the littlest." He clenched his fists with the little fingers on the table edge. They were too far apart. He crossed his wrists so that the two little fingers hooked over the wooden edge, side by side. "Both at once. Can you do that?"

"Of course. Right at the second joint."

Old Rurry hummed happily to himself, noticing that the entire room was watching him now. He pretended to examine the edge of his blade while the newcomer looked up at him with watery rabbit's eyes. Fast, without warning, the knife came down and bit deep into the wood. The fingers flew, blood spurted, the newcomer shrieked. Everyone laughed uproariously as he ran out the door still screaming.

"Good Old Rurry," someone shouted, and he permitted

himself a smile while he picked up one of the fingers from the floor.

"I'm hurt—now you must help me!" Jomfri shouted as he staggered up the hill in the endless noon. "I did not think it would feel like this. I'll bleed to death. I need your aid. It hurts so."

When he tugged at the metal the pain bit deep. The bin gaped open, and he dropped into it. "I'm injured," he wailed as the light narrowed and vanished. The bars clamped down in the darkness, and he could feel the warm blood running down his wrists. "That's blood. You must stop it, or I will die."

The mechanism believed. There was a sharp nip of pain in his neck, then instant numbness. The pain was gone from his body—as was all sensation. He could move his head, hear and talk, but was completely paralyzed from the neck down. There were no escapes from Fangnis.

Something rumbled, and from the sensation on the back of his head he knew he was being slid sideways by the mechanism. It was too dark to see—if he could still see at all—but from the movement of the air and the sounds, he felt that he was being moved through door after door, like a multi-chambered airlock. Thick metal doors, that would be certain. The last one slid open, and he was ejected into a well-lit room.

"Torture again," the man in white said, bending over to look. "They're going back to their old games." Behind him were three guards with thick clubs.

"Initiation, maybe, Doctor. This one must be a newcomer, I've never seen him before."

"And new clothes, too," the doctor said, working with swabs and instruments.

"I'm here by mistake. I'm not a prisoner!"

"If we get one, Doctor, we can look forward to a lot more amputations. They always do things in cycles."

"A mistake in the matter transmitter—"

"You're right about that. I have some graphs that prove it in the book I am preparing."

"Listen, you must listen. I was going home. I dialed my home, I went into the MT—and arrived here. There has been a ghastly mistake. I had the fingers removed so that I could reach you. Look at the records, they'll prove I'm right."

"We have records," the doctor admitted, recognizing Jomfri's humanity for the first time. "But there has never been a mistake yet, though many have claimed their innocence."

"Doctor, please find out. I am begging you. In the name of decency simply consult the records. The computer will tell you instantly."

The doctor hesitated a moment, then shrugged. "In the name of decency, then. I will do it while the dressings set. Your name and citizen's number."

He punched Jomfri's data into the computer, then looked expressionless at the screen.

"You see," Jomfri shouted happily. "It was a mistake. I'll file no complaints. Free me now, it is all I ask."

"You are guilty," the doctor said quietly. "You were sent here."

"Impossible!" Jomfri was justifiably angry. "Some trick. I demand you tell me what I have been charged with."

The doctor looked at his instruments. "Blood pressure, brain waves, normal for this situation. These instruments are as good as any lie detector. You are telling the truth. Traumatic amnesia, very possible in this situation. A good footnote for my book."

"Tell me what I have been accused of!" Jomfri was shouting and trying to move.

"It would be better if you did not know. I'll return you now."

"You must tell me first. I cannot believe you otherwise. I was on my way home to my wife——"

"You killed your wife," the doctor said, and actuated the return mechanism. The closing of the thick door cut off the hideous, wailing scream.

A single sharp memory of a blue face, staring eyes, blood blood blood. . . .

The metal coffin lid opened, and Jomfri sat up, dizzy.

They had drugged him; he was hazy, they had tended his wounds.

"But they wouldn't help me. They wouldn't even look in the records to prove my innocence. A mistake. A fault in the matter transmitter, and I am condemned because of it."

He looked at the bloodstained bandages, and something hurt in his head.

"Now I'll never get home to my wife," he sobbed.

THIS IS A VERY SHORT, VERY LIGHT story. The idea came to me full-blown and it was written in one sitting. I titled the story "If" and sent it to Fred Pohl, then editor of *If*. Fred ignored my presumption and bought the story for *If*—and instantly changed the title to "Praiseworthy Saur." If he thought little of my title I thought even less of his, and changed it back to the original as soon as I could.

The story at one point had a third title as well, and this caused a certain amount of confusion. I received a check from my agent's office. On the face of each check there is always a description of exactly what the money is for. This check was in payment for a story named "Praiseworthy Sour." I was pretty sure I had never written *that*, and it took a bit of correspondence to straighten the matter out.

11

IF

<<<<<<<<<<<<<<<<<<<<<<<<<<<<<<<<<<<<<<<<<<<<

"WE ARE THERE; WE ARE CORRECT. THE COM-
putations were perfect. That is the place below."

"You are a worm," 17 said to her companion 35, who
resembled her every way other than in number. "That is
the place. But nine years too early. Look at the meter."

"I am a worm. I shall free you of the burden of my
useless presence." 35 removed her knife from the scab-
bard and tested the edge, which proved to be exceedingly
sharp. She placed it against the white wattled width of
her neck and prepared to cut her throat.

"Not now," 17 hissed. "We are shorthanded already,
and your corpse would be valueless to this expedition.
Get us to the correct time at once. Our power is limited,
you may remember."

"It shall be done as you command," 35 said as she
slithered to the bank of controls. 44 ignored the talk,
keeping her multicell cycs focused on the power control
bank, with her spatulate fingers in response to the mani-
fold dials.

"That is it," 17 announced, rasping her hands together
with pleasure. "The correct time, the correct place. We
must descend and make our destiny. Give praise to the
Saur of All who rules the destinies of all."

"Praise Saur," her two companions muttered, all of
their attention on the controls.

Straight down from the blue sky the globular vehicle
fell. It was round and featureless, save for the large rectangular port, on the bottom now, and made of some

sort of blue metal, perhaps anodized aluminum, though it looked harder. It had no visible means of flight or support; yet it fell at a steady and controlled rate. Slower and slower it moved until it dropped from sight behind the ridge at the northern end of Johnson's Lake, just at the edge of the tall pine grove. There were fields nearby, with cows, who did not appear at all disturbed by the visitor. No human being was in sight to view the landing. A path cut in from the lake here, a scuffed dirt trail that went to the highway.

An oriole sat on a bush and warbled sweetly: a small rabbit hopped from the field to nibble a stem of grass. This bucolic and peaceful scene was interrupted by the scuff of feet down the trail and monotone whistling. The bird flew away, a touch of soundless color, while the rabbit disappeared into the hedge. A boy came over the shore. He wore ordinary boy clothes and carried a school bag in one hand, a small and homemade cage of wire screen in the other. In the cage was a small lizard which clung to the screen, its eyes rolling in what presumably was fear. The boy, whistling shrilly, trudged along the path and into the shade of the pine grove.

"Boy," a high-pitched and tremulous voice called out. "Can you hear me, boy?"

"I certainly can," the boy said, stopping and looking around for the unseen speaker. "Where are you?"

"I am by your side, but I am invisible. I am your fairy godmother—"

The boy made a rude sound by sticking out his tongue and blowing across it while it vibrated. "I don't believe in invisibility or fairy godmothers. Come out of those woods, whoever you are."

"All boys believe in fairy godmothers," the voice said, but a worried tone edged the words now. "I know all kinds of secrets. I know your name is Don and—"

"Everyone knows my name is Don, and no one believes any more in fairies. Boys now believe in rockets, submarines and atomic energy."

"Would you believe space travel?"

"I would."

Slightly relieved, the voice came on stronger and deeper. "I did not wish to frighten you, but I am really from Mars and have just landed."

Don made the rude noise again. "Mars has no atmosphere and no observable forms of life. Now come out of there and stop playing games."

After a long silence the voice said, "Would you consider time travel?"

"I could. Are you going to tell me that you are from the future?"

With relief: "Yes I am."

"Then come out where I can see you."

"There are some things that the human eye should not look upon."

"Horseapples! The human eye is okay for looking at anything you want to name. You come out of there so I can see who you are—or I'm leaving."

"It is not advisable." The voice was exasperated. "I can prove I am a temporal traveler by telling you the answers to tomorrow's mathematics test. Wouldn't that be nice? Number one, 1.76. Number two—"

"I don't like to cheat, and even if I did you can't cheat on the new math. Either you know it or you fail it, I'm going to count to ten, then go."

"No, you cannot! I must ask you a favor. Release that common lizard you have trapped and I will give you three wishes—I mean answer three questions."

"Why should I let it go?"

"Is that the first of your questions?"

"No. I want to know what's going on before I do anything. This lizard is special. I never saw another one like it around here."

"You are right. It is an Old World acrodont lizard of the order Rhiptoglossa, commonly called a chameleon."

"It *is!*" Don was really interested now. He squatted in the path and took a red-covered book from the school bag and laid it on the ground. He turned the cage until the lizard was on the bottom and placed it carefully on the book. "Will it really turn color?"

"To an observable amount, yes. Now if you release her . . ."

"How do you know it's a her? The time traveler bit again?"

"If you must know, yes. The creature was purchased from a pet store by one Jim Benan and is one of a pair. They were both released two days ago when Benan, deranged by the voluntary drinking of a liquid containing quantities of ethyl alcohol, sat on the cage. The other, unfortunately, died of his wounds, and this one alone survives. The release—"

"I think this whole thing is a joke and I'm going home now. Unless you come out of there so I can see who you are."

"I warn you . . ."

"Good-by." Don picked up the cage. "Hey, she turned sort of brick red!"

"Do not leave. I will come forth."

Don looked on, with a great deal of interest, while the creature walked out from between the trees. It was purple in color, had large goggling eyes, was slightly scaley, wore a neatly cut brown jumpsuit and had a pack slung on its back. It was also only about seven inches tall.

"You don't much look like a man from the future," Don said. "In fact you don't look like a man at all. You're too small."

"I might say that you are too big. Size is a matter of relevancy, and I am from the future, though I am not a man."

"That's for sure. In fact you look a lot like a lizard." In sudden inspiration, Don looked back and forth at the traveler and at the cage. "In fact you look a good deal like this chameleon here. What's the connection?"

"That is not to be revealed. You will now do as I command or I will injure you gravely." 17 turned and waved towards the woods. "35, this is an order. Appear and destroy that growth over there."

Don looked on with increasing interest as the blue basketball of metal drifted into sight from under the trees. A circular disk slipped away on one side and a gleaming nozzle, not unlike the hose nozzle on a toy firetruck, appeared through the opening. It pointed toward a hedge a good thirty feet away. A shrill whining began from the depths of the sphere, rising in pitch until it was almost inaudible. Then, suddenly, a thin line of light spat out towards the shrub, which crackled and instantly burst into flame. Within a second it was a blackened skeleton.

"The device is called a roxidizer and is deadly," 17 said. "Release the chameleon at once."

Don scowled. "All right. Who wants the old lizard anyway?" He put the cage on the ground and started to open the cover. Then he stopped—and sniffed. Picking up the cage again he started across the grass towards the blackened bush.

"Come back!" 17 screeched. "We will fire if you go another step."

Don ignored the lizardoid, which was now dancing up and down in an agony of frustration, and ran to the bush. He put his hand out—and apparently right through the charred stems.

"I thought something was fishy," he said. "All that burning and everything just upwind of me—and I couldn't smell a thing." He turned to look at the time traveler, who was slumped in gloomy silence. "It's just a projected image of some kind, isn't it? Some kind of three-dimensional movie." He stopped in sudden thought, then walked over to the still hovering temporal transporter. When he poked at it with his finger he apparently pushed his hand right into it.

"And this thing isn't here either. Are you?"

"There is no need to experiment. I, and our ship, are present only as what might be called temporal echoes. Matter cannot be moved through time, that is an impossibility, but the concept of matter can be temporally projected. I am sure that this is too technical for you . . ."

"You're doing great so far. Carry on."

"Our projections are here in a real sense to us, though

we can only be an image or a sound wave to any observers in the time we visit. Immense amounts of energy are required and almost the total resources of our civilization are involved in this time transfer."

"Why? And the truth for a change. No more fairy godmother and that kind of malarky."

"I regret the necessity to use subterfuge, but the secret is too important to reveal casually without attempting other means of persuasion."

"Now we get to the real story." Don sat down and crossed his legs comfortably. "Give."

"We need your aid, or our very society is threatened. Very recently—on our time scale—strange disturbances were detected by our instruments. Ours is a simple saurian existence, some million or so years in the future, and our race is dominant. Yours has long since vanished in a manner too horrible to mention to your young ears. Something is threatening our entire race. Research quickly uncovered the fact that we are about to be overwhelmed by a probability wave and wiped out, a great wave of negation sweeping towards us from our remote past."

"You wouldn't mind tipping me off to what a probability wave is, would you?"

"I will take an example from your own literature. If your grandfather had died without marrying, you would not have been born and would not now exist."

"But I do."

"The matter is debatable in the greater plan of the universe, but we shall not discuss that now. Our power is limited. To put the affair simply, we traced our ancestral lines back through all the various mutations and changes until we found the individual proto-lizard from which our line sprung."

"Let me guess." Don pointed at the cage. "This is the one?"

"She is." 17 spoke in solemn tones as befitted the moment. "Just as somewhen, somewhere there is a proto-tarsier from which your race sprung, so is there this temporal mother of ours. She will bear young soon, and they will breed and grow in this pleasant valley. The rocks near the lake have an appreciable amount of radioactivity which will cause mutations. The centuries will roll by and, one day, our race will reach its heights of glory.

"But not if you don't open that cage."

Don rested his chin on fist and thought. "You're not putting me on any more? This is the truth?"

17 drew herself up and waved both arms—or front legs—over her head. "By the Saur of All, I promise," she intoned. "By the stars eternal, the seasons vernal, the clouds, the sky, the matriarchal I . . ."

"Just cross your heart and hope to die, that will be good enough for me."

The lizardoid moved its eyes in concentric circles and performed this ritual.

"Okay then, I'm as soft-hearted as the next guy when it comes to wiping out whole races."

Don unbent the piece of wire that sealed the cage and opened the top. The chameleon rolled one eye up at him and looked at the opening with the other. 17 watched in awed silence and the time vehicle bobbed closer.

"Get going," Don said, and shook the lizard out into the grass.

This time the chameleon took the hint and scuttled away among the bushes, vanishing from sight.

"That takes care of the future," Don said. "Or the past, from your point of view."

17 and the time machine vanished silently. Don was alone again on the path.

"Well, you could of at least said thanks before taking off like that! People have more manners than lizards any day, I'll tell you that."

He picked up the now empty cage and his school bag and started for home.

He had not heard the quick rustle in the bushes, nor did he see the prowling tomcat with the limp chameleon in its jaws.

THIS IS A SHORT-SHORT, ONE OF THE
few I have done—so short that it must have
a brief introduction, too.

I must mention one additional fact, of
which I am quite proud. Years after I'd
written this story, Barry Malzberg told me
that he had read it and it had stayed with
him. The story is short and complete unto
itself. But in Barry's case it sparked something, started him thinking, started the long
and complicated process that ends in a novel.
I am most pleased to think that from this
very small beginning grew that excellent and
prize-winning novel, *Beyond Apollo*.

12

I HAVE MY VIGIL

‹‹‹

I AM A ROBOT.

When I say that, I say everything. And I say nothing. For they built me well on Earth, silver wired, chromed steel, machine turned. They turned out a machine, I, machine, without a soul, of course, which is why I am nothing. I am a machine and I have my duties and my duty is to take care of these three men. Who are now dead.

Just because they are dead does not mean that I can shirk my duty, no indeed. I am a very high class and expensive machine, so I may consider the absurdity of what I do even as I do it. But I do it. Like a switched-on lathe I keep turning whether there is metal in the chuck or no, or a turned-on printing press inking and slamming shut my jaws, knowing not nor caring neither whether there is paper there before.

I am a robot. Cunningly crafted, turned out uniquely, one of a kind, equipped and dispatched on this, the very first star ship, to tend it and care for the heroes of mankind. This is their trip and their glory, and I am, as the human expression goes, just along for the ride. A metal servitor serving and continuing to serve. Although. They. Are. Dead.

I will now tell myself once more what happened. Men are not designed to live in the no-space between the stars. Robots are.

Now I will set the table. I set the table. The first one to look out through the thick glass at the nothing that fills the no-space was Hardesty. I set his place at the table. He looked out, then went to his room and killed himself. I found him too late dead with all of the blood from his large body run out through his severed wrists and onto the cabin floor.

Now I knock on Hardesty's door and open it. He lies on his bunk and does not move. He is very pale. I close his door and go to the table and turn his plate over. He will not be eating this meal.

There are two more places to be set at the table, and as my metal fingers clatter against the plates I, through a very obvious process of association, think of the advantages of having metal fingers. Larson had human fingers of flesh, and he locked them onto Neal's throat after he had looked at no-space, and he kept them there, very securely clamped they must have been, remaining so even after Neal had slipped a dinner knife, this knife in fact, between Larson's fourth and fifth rib on the left-hand side. Neal never did see no-space, not that that made any difference. He did not move even after I removed, one by one, the fingers of Larson from his throat. He is in his cabin now and dinner is ready, sir, I say, knocking, but there is no answer. I open the door and Neal is on the bunk with his eyes closed so I close the door. My electronic olefactory organs have told me that there is something very strong in the cabin.

One. Turn Neal's plate face down in its place.

Two. Knock on Larson's cabin door.

Three . . .

Four . . .

Five. Turn Larson's plate face down in its place.

I now clear off the table and I think about it. The ship functions and it has looked at no-space. I function and I have looked at no-space. The men do not function and they have looked at no-space.

Machines may travel to the stars; men may not. This is a very important thought, and I must return to Earth and tell the men there about it. Each ship-day after each meal I think this thought again and think how important it is. I have little capacity for original thought; a robot is a machine, and perhaps this is the only original thought I will ever have. Therefore it is an important thought.

I am a very good robot with a very good brain, and perhaps my brain is better made than they knew in the factory. I have had an original thought, and I was not designed for that. I was designed to serve the men on this ship and to speak to them in English, which is a very complex language even for a robot. I English in a German manner do not talk, nor do I, fingers metals, eyes glasses, talk it in the style of the Latin. But I have to know about these things so that I do not do them. Robots are well made.

Watch. With fast feet and long legs I rapidly run to the control column and bash buttons with flickering fingers. I can make words rhyme, though I cannot write a poem. I know there is a difference, although I do not know what the difference is.

I read the readings. We have been to Alpha Centauri in this ship and we now return. I do not know anything about Alpha Centauri. When we reached Alpha Centauri I turned the ship around and started back to Earth. More important than the incredible novelty of stellar exploration is the message I must take to Earth.

Those words about incredible novelty are not my words but the words I heard once spoken by the man Larson. Robots do not say things like that.

Robots do not have souls, for what would a robot soul look like? A neatly and smoothly machined metal canister? And what would be in the can?

Robots do not have thoughts like that.

I must set the table for dinner. Plates here, forks here, spoons here, knives here.

"I've cut my finger! Damn it—it's bleeding all over the cloth . . ."

BLEEDING?
BLEEDING!

I am a robot. I have my work to do. I set the table.
There is something red on my metal finger.
It must be ketchup from the bottle.

VIOLENCE AND DEATH CONCERN ME very much. There is too much of it in our society and our world, and at one time I put far too much of it into my own work—it was a pulp habit that took effort to break. There is certainly far and away too much of it in film and fiction. Yet it does have its fascination or it wouldn't be there.

At one extreme is the escape-thriller that we will read to relax—all that impossible bombing, shooting, and rushing about, patently unreal but a pleasant read for a quiet evening. Good stuff that, with a place in letters. I know, since I have written my share of it.

At the other extreme is what can only be called the excessive, vicarious violence of screen and TV. Is there any real need to show, in living color, people being set on fire? Particularly if, soon after, punks follow the example and *do* set a few people alight? (This has happened; it is worth thinking about.)

I am especially un-fond of the legend of the hired killer, the cool hand who butchers for money. I believe in the rule of conscience and law that has taken us out of the jungle. That's what this story is about.

13

FROM FANATICISM, OR
FOR REWARD

<<<<<<<<<<<<<<<<<<<<<<<<<<<<<<<<<<<<<<<<<<<

WONDERFUL! VERY CLEAR. THE ELECTRONIC
sight was a new addition, he had used an ordinary tele-
scopic sight when he test-fired the weapon, but it was
no hindrance. The wide entrance to the structure across
the street was sharp and clear, despite the rain-filled night
outside. His elbows rested comfortably on the packing
crates that were placed before the slit he had cut through
the outer wall of the building.

*"There are five of them coming now. The one you
want is the tallest."* The radioplug in his ear whispered
the words to him.

Across the street the men emerged. One was obviously
taller than all the others. He was talking, smiling, and
Jagen centered the scope on his white teeth, then spun
the magnifier until teeth, mouth, tongue filled the sight.
Then a wide smile, teeth together, and Jagen squeezed his
entire hand, squeezed stock and trigger equally, and the
gun banged and jumped against his shoulder.

Now, quickly, there were five more cartridges in the
clip. Spin the magnifier back. He is falling. Fire. He jerks.
Fire. In the skull. Again. Fire. Someone in the way:
shoot through him. Fire. He is gone. In the chest, the
heart. Fire.

"All shots off," he said into the button before his lips.
"Five on target, one a possible."

"Go," was all the radioplug whispered.

I'm going all right, he thought to himself, *no need to
tell me that. The Greater Despot's police are efficient.*

151

The only light in the room was the dim orange glow from the ready light on the transmatter. He had personally punched out the receiver's code. Three steps took him across the barren, dusty room and he slapped the actuator. Without slowing he dived into the screen.

Bright glare hurt his eyes and he squinted against it. An unshielded bulb above, rock walls, everything damp, a metal door coated with a patina of rust. He was underground, somewhere, perhaps on a planet across the galaxy, it didn't matter. There was here. Everywhere was a step away with a matter transmitter. Quickly, he moved to one side of the screen.

Gas puffed out of it, expelled silently, then cut off. Good. The transmatter had been destroyed, blown up. Undoubtedly the police would be able to trace his destination from the wreckage, but it would take time. Time for him to obscure his trail and vanish.

Other than the transmatter, the only object in the stone cell was a large, covered ceramic vessel. He looked at the stock of his gun where he had pasted his instructions. Next to the number for this location was the notation *destroy gun*. Jagen peeled off the instructions and slipped them into his belt pouch. He took the lid from the vessel and turned away, coughing, as the fumes rose up. This bubbling, hellish brew would dissolve anything. With well-practiced motions he released the plastic stock from the weapon, then dropped it into the container. He had to step back as the liquid bubbled furiously and thicker fumes arose.

In his pouch was a battery-operated saw, as big as his hand, with a serrated diamond blade. It buzzed when he switched it on, then whined shrilly when he pressed it against the barrel of the gun. He had measured carefully a few days earlier and had sawed a slight notch. Now he cut at that spot and in a few seconds half of the barrel clanged to the floor. It followed the stock into the dissolving bath, along with the clip that had held the bullets. His pouch yielded up another clip, which he slipped into place in the gun. A quick jerk of his forefinger on the slide kicked the first cartridge into the chamber and he checked to be sure that the safety was on. Only then did he slip the truncated weapon up the loose sleeve of his jacket, so that the rough end of the barrel rested against his hand.

It was shortened and inaccurate, but still a weapon, and still very deadly at short range.

Only when these precautions had been made did he consult the card and punch for his next destination. The instructions after this number read simply *change*. He stepped through.

Noise and sound, light and sharp smells. The ocean was close by, some ocean, he could hear the breakers, and salt dampness was strong in his nose. This was a public communications plaza set around with transmatter screens, and someone was already stepping from the one he had used, treading on his heels. There were muttered words in a strange language as the man hurried away. The crowd was thick and the reddish sun, high above, was strong. Jagen resisted the temptation to use one of the nearby transmatters and walked quickly across the plaza. He stopped, then waited to follow the first person who passed him. This gave him a random direction that was not influenced by his own desires. A girl passed and he went after her. She wore an abbreviated skirt and had remarkably bowed legs. He followed their arcs down a side street. Only after they had passed one transmatter booth did he choose his own course. His trail was muddled enough now: the next transmatter would do.

There was the familiar green starburst ahead, above an imposing building, and his heart beat faster at the sight of the Greater Despot police headquarters. Then he smiled slightly; why not? The building was public and performed many functions. There was nothing to be afraid of.

Yet there was, of course, fear, and conquering it was a big part of the game. Up the steps and past the unseeing guards. A large rotunda with a desk in the middle, stands and services against the wall. And there, a row of transmatter screens. Walking at a steady pace he went to one of the center screens and punched the next code on his list.

The air was thin and cold, almost impossible to breathe, and his eyes watered at the sudden chill. He turned quickly to the screen, to press the next number, when he saw a man hurrying towards him.

"Do not leave," the man called out in Intergalact.

He had a breath mask clipped over his nose and he held a second one out to Jagen, who quickly slipped it on. The warmed, richer air stayed his flight, as did the presence of the man who had obviously been expecting him. He saw now that he was on the bridge of a derelict spacer of ancient vintage. The controls had been torn out and the screens were blank. Moisture was condensing on the metal walls and forming pools upon the floor. The man saw his curious gaze.

"This ship is in orbit. It has been for centuries. An atmosphere and gravity plant were placed aboard while this transmatter was operating. When we leave an atomic explosion will destroy everything. If you are tracked this far, the trail will end here."

"Then the rest of my instructions . . . ?"

". . . Will not be needed. It was not certain this ship would be prepared in time, but it has been."

Jagen dropped the card, evidence, onto the floor, along with the radioplug. It would vanish with the rest. The man rapidly pressed out a number.

"If you will proceed," he said.

"I'll follow you."

The man nodded, threw his breath mask aside, then stepped through the screen.

They were in a normal enough hotel room, the kind that can be found on any one of ten thousand planets. Two men, completely dressed in black, sat in armchairs watching Jagen through dark glasses. The man who had brought him nodded silently, pressed a combination on the transmatter, and left.

"It is done?" one of the men asked. In addition to the loose black clothing they wore black gloves and hoods, with voice demodulators clamped across their mouths. The voice was flat, emotionless, impossible to identify.

"The payment," Jagen said, moving so that his back was to the wall.

"We'll pay you, man, don't be foolish. Just tell us how it came out. We have a lot invested in this." The voice of the second man was just as mechanically calm, but his fingers were clasping and unclasping as he talked.

"The payment." Jagen tried to keep his voice as toneless as their electronic ones.

"Here, Hunter, now tell us," the first one said, taking a box from the side table and throwing it across the room. It burst open at Jagen's feet.

"All six shots were fired at the target I was given," he said, looking down at the golden notes spilling onto the floor. So much, it was as they had promised. "I put four shots into the head, one into the heart, one into a man who got in the way that may have penetrated. It was as you said. The protective screen was useless against mechanically propelled plastic missiles."

"The paragrantic is ours," the second man intoned emotionlessly, but this was the machine interpretation, for his excitement was demonstrated by the manner in which he hammered on his chair arm and drummed his feet.

Jagen bent to pick up the notes, apparently looking only at the floor.

The first man in black raised an energy pistol that had been concealed in his clothing and fired it at Jagen.

Jagen, who as a hunter always considered being hunted, rolled sideways and clutched the barrel of the shortened projectile weapon. With his other hand he found the trigger through the cloth of his sleeve and depressed it. The range was point-blank and a miss was impossible to a man of his experience.

The bullet caught the first man in the midriff and folded him over. He said *yahhhhh* in a very drab and monotonous way. The pistol dropped from his fingers and fell to the floor and he was obviously dead.

"Soft alloy bullets," Jagen said. "I saved a clip of them. Far better than those plastic things you supplied. Go in small, mushroom, come out big. I saved the gun, too, at least enough of it to still shoot. You were right, it should be destroyed to remove evidence, but not until after this session. And it doesn't show on an energy-detector screen. So you thought I was unarmed. Your friend discovered the truth the hard way. How about you?" He talked quickly as he struggled to recover the gun that recoil had pulled from his hand and jammed into the cloth of his sleeve. There, he had it.

"Do not kill me," the remaining man said, his voice flat, though he cringed back and waved his hands before his face. "It was his idea, I wanted nothing to do with it. He was afraid that we could be traced if you were captured." He glanced at the folded figure, then quickly away as he became aware of the quantity of blood that was dripping from it. "I have no weapon. I mean you no harm. Do not kill me. I will give you more money." He was pleading for his life but the words came out as drab as a shopping list.

Jagen raised his weapon and the man writhed and cringed.

"Do you have the money with you?"

"Some. Not much. A few thousand. I'll get you more."

"I'm afraid that I cannot wait. Take out what you have—slowly—and throw it over here."

It was a goodly sum. The man must be very rich to carry this much casually. Jagen pointed the gun to kill him, but at the last instant changed his mind. It would accomplish nothing. And at the moment he was weary of killing. Instead he crossed over and tore the man's mask off. It was anticlimactic. He was fat, old, jowly, crying so hard that he could not see through his tears. In disgust Jagen hurled him to the floor and kicked him hard in the face. Then left. Ever wary he kept his body between the moaning man and the keys so there would be no slightest chance for him to see the number punched. He stepped into the screen.

The machine stepped out of the screen in the office of the Highest Officer of Police, many light years distant, at almost the same instant, on the planet where the assassination had taken place.

"You are Follower?" the officer asked.

"I am," the machine said.

It was a fine-looking machine, shaped in the form of a man. But that of a large man, well over two meters tall. It could have been any shape at all, but this form was a convenience when traveling among men. The roughly humanoid form was the only concession made. Other than having a torso, four limbs and a head, it was strictly functional. Its lines were smooth and flowing, and its metal shape coated with one of the new and highly resistant, golden tinted alloys. The ovoid that was its head was completely featureless, except for a T-shaped slit in the front. Presumably, seeing and hearing devices were concealed behind the narrow opening, as well as a speech mechanism that parodied the full-timbered voice of a man.

"Do I understand, Follower, that you are the only one of your kind?" The police officer had become old, gray and lined, in the pursuit of his profession, but he had never lost his curiosity.

"Your security rating permits me to inform you that there are other Followers now going into operation, but I cannot reveal the exact number."

"Very wise. What is it that you hope to do?"

"I shall follow. I have detection apparatus far more delicate than any used in the field before. This is why my physical bulk is so great. I have the memory core of the largest library and means of adding to it constantly. I will follow the assassin."

"That may prove difficult. He—or she—destroyed the transmatter after the killing."

"I have ways of determining the tuning from the wreckage."

"The path will be obscured in many ways."

"None of them shall avail. I am the Follower."

"Then I wish you luck . . . if one can wish luck to a machine. This was a dirty business."

"Thank you for the courtesy. I do not have human emotions, though I can comprehend them. Your feelings are understood and a credit mark is being placed on your file even though you had not intended the remark to accomplish that. Now I would like to see all the records of the assassination, and then I will go to the place where the killer escaped."

Twenty years of easy living had not altered Jagen very much: the lines in the corners of his eyes and the touch of gray at his temples improved his sharp features rather than detracting from them. He no longer had to earn his living as a professional hunter, so could now hunt for his own pleasure, which he did very often. For many years he had stayed constantly on the move, obscuring his trail, changing his name and identity a dozen times. Then he had stumbled across this backward planet, completely by chance, and had decided to remain. The jungles were primitive and the hunting tremendous. He enjoyed himself all of the time. The money he had been paid, invested wisely, provided him with ample income for all of his needs and supported the one or two vices to which he was addicted.

He was contemplating one of them now. For more than a week he had remained in the jungle, and it had been a good shoot. Now, washed, refreshed, rested, he savored the thought of something different. There was a pleasure hall he knew, expensive, of course, but he could get there exactly what he needed. In a gold dressing gown, feet up and a drink in his hand, he sat back and looked through the transparent wall of his apartment at the sun setting behind the jungle. He had never had much of an eye for art, but it would have taken a blind man to ignore the explosion of greens below, purple and red above. The universe was a very fine place.

Then the alignment bell signaled quietly to show that

another transmatter had been tuned to his. He swung about to see Follower step into the room.

"I have come for you, Assassin," the machine said.

The glass fell from Jagen's fingers and rolled a wet trail across the inlaid wood of the floor. He was always armed, but caution suggested that the energy pistol in the pocket of his robe would have little effect on this solidly built machine.

"I have no idea what you are talking about," he said, rising. "I shall call the police about this matter."

He walked towards the communicator—then dived past it into the room beyond. Follower started after him, but stopped when he emerged an instant later. Jagen had a heavy caliber, recoilless rifle with explosive shells, that he used to stop the multi-ton amphibians in the swamps. The weapon held ten of the almost cannon-sized shells and he emptied the clip, point-blank, at the machine.

The room was a shambles, with walls, floor and ceiling ripped by the explosive fragments. He had a minor wound in his neck, and another in his leg, neither of which he was aware of. The machine stood, unmoved by the barrage, the golden alloy completely unscratched.

"Sit," Follower ordered. "Your heart is laboring too hard and you may be in danger."

"Danger!" Jagen said, then laughed strangely and clamped his teeth hard onto his lip. The gun slipped from his fingers as he groped his way to an undamaged chair and fell into it. "Should I worry about the condition of my heart when you are here—Executioner."

"I am Follower. I am not an executioner."

"You'll turn me over to them. But first, tell me how you found me. Or is that classified?"

"The details are. I simply used all of the most improved location techniques and transmatter records, to follow you. I have a perfect memory and had many facts to work with. Also, being a machine, I do not suffer from impatience."

Since he was still alive, Jagen still considered escape. He could not damage the machine, but perhaps he could flee from it once again. He had to keep it talking.

"What are you going to do with me?"

"I wish to ask you some questions."

Jagen smiled inwardly, although his expression did not change. He knew perfectly well that the Greater Despot had more than this in mind for an assassin who had been tracked for twenty years.

"Ask them, by all means."

"Do you know the identity of the man you shot?"

"I'm not admitting I shot anyone."

"You admitted that when you attempted to assault me."

"All right. I'll play along." Keep the thing talking. Say anything, admit anything. The torturers would have it out of him in any case. "I never knew who he was. In fact I'm not exactly sure what world it was. It was a rainy place, I can tell you that much."

"Who employed you?"

"They didn't mention any names. A sum of money and a job of work were involved, that was all."

"I can believe that. I can also tell you that your heart-beat and pulse are approaching normal, so I may now safely inform you that you have a slight wound on your neck."

Jagen laughed and touched his finger to the trickle of blood.

"My thanks for the unexpected consideration. The wound is nothing."

"I would prefer to see it cleaned and bandaged. Do I have your permission to do that?"

"Whatever you wish. There is medical equipment in the other room." If the thing left the room, he could reach the transmatter!

"I must examine the wound first."

Follower loomed over him, he had not realized the great bulk of the machine before, and touched a cool metal finger to the skin of his neck. As soon as it made contact he found himself completely paralyzed. His heart beat steadily, he breathed easily, his eyes stared straight ahead. But he could not move or speak, and could only scream wordlessly to himself in the silence of his brain.

"I have tricked you since it was necessary to have your

body in a relaxed state before the operation. You will find the operation is completely painless."

The machine moved out of his fixed point of vision and he heard it leave the room. Operation? What operation? What unmentionable revenge did the Greater Despot plan? How important was the man whom he had killed? Horror and fear filled his thoughts, but did not affect his body. Steadily, the breath flowed in and out of his lungs, while his heart thudded a stately measure. His consciousness was imprisoned in the smallest portion of his brain, impotent, hysterical.

Sound told him that the machine was now standing behind him. Then he swayed and was pushed from side to side. What was it doing? Something dark flew by a corner of his vision and hit the floor. What? WHAT!

Another something, this one spattering on the floor before him. Foamed, dark, mottled. It took long seconds for the meaning of what he saw to penetrate his terror.

It was a great gobbet of depilatory foam, speckled and filled with dissolved strands of his hair. The machine must have sprayed the entire can onto his head and was now removing all of his hair. But why? Panic ebbed slightly.

Follower came around and stood before him, then bent and wiped its metal hands on his robe.

"Your hair has been removed." *I know, I know! Why?* "This is a needed part of the operation and creates no permanent damage. Neither does the operation."

While it was speaking a change was taking place in Follower's torso. The golden alloy, so impervious to the explosives, was splitting down the center and rolling back. Jagen could only watch, horrified, unable to avert his gaze. There was a silvered concavity revealed in the openings, surrounded by devices of an unknown nature.

"There will be no pain," Follower said, reaching forward and seizing Jagen's head with both hands. With slow precision it pulled him forward into the opening until the top of his head was pressed against the metal hollow. Then, mercifully, unconsciousness descended.

Jagen did not feel the thin, sharpened needles that slid through holes in the metal bowl, then penetrated his skin, down through the bone of his skull and deep into his brain. But he was aware of the thoughts, clear and sharp, as if they were new experiences that filled his brain. Memories, brought up and examined, then discarded. His childhood, a smell, sounds he had long since forgotten, a room, grass underfoot, a young man looking at him, himself in a mirror.

This flood of memories continued for a long time, guided and controlled by the mechanism inside Follower. Everything was there and bit by bit it uncovered it all. When it was finished the needles withdrew into their sheaths and Jagen's head was freed. Once more he was seated upright in the chair—and the paralysis was removed as suddenly as it had begun. He clutched the chair with one hand and felt across the smooth surface of his skull with the other.

"What have you done to me? What was the operation?"

"I have searched your memory. I now know the identity of the people who ordered the assassination."

With these words the machine turned and started towards the transmatter. It had already punched out a code before Jagen called hoarsely after it.

"Stop! Where are you going? What are you going to do with me?"

Follower turned. "What do you want me to do with you? Do you have feelings of guilt that must be expunged?"

"Don't play with me, Machine. I am human and you are just a metal thing. I order you to answer me. Are you from the Greater Despot's police?"

"Yes."

"Then you are arresting me?"

"No. I am leaving you here. The local police may arrest you, though I have been informed that they are not interested in your case. However, I have appropriated all of your funds as partial payment for the cost of tracking you." It turned once more to leave.

"Stop!" Jagen sprang to his feet. "You have taken my money, I can believe that. But you cannot toy with me. You did not follow me for twenty years just to turn about and leave me. I am an assassin—remember?"

"I am well aware of the fact. That is why I have followed you. I am also now aware of your opinion of yourself. It is a wrong one. You are not unique, or gifted, or even interesting. Any man can kill when presented with the correct motivation. After all, you are animals. In time of war good young men drop bombs on people they do not know, by pressing switches, and this murder does not bother them in the slightest. Men kill to protect their families and you are commended for it. You, a professional hunter of animals, killed another animal, who happened to be a man, when presented with enough payment. There is nothing noble, brave or even interesting in that. That man is dead and killing you will not bring him to life. May I leave now?"

"No! If you do not want me—why spend those years following me? Not just for a few remnants of fact."

The machine stood straight, high, glowing with a mechanical dignity of its own, which perhaps reflected that of its builders.

"Yes. Facts. You are nothing, and the men who hired you are nothing. But why they did it and how they were able to do it is everything. One man, ten men, even a million are as nothing to the Greater Despot, who numbers the planets in his realm in the hundreds of thousands. The Greater Despot deals only in societies. Now an examination will be made of your society and particularly of the society of the men who hired you. What led them to believe that violence can solve anything? What were the surroundings where killing was condoned or ignored —or accepted—that shaped their lives so that they exported this idea?

"It is the society that kills, not the individual.

"You are nothing," Follower added—could it have been with a touch of malice—as it stepped into the screen and vanished.

14

THIS IS THE ONLY STORY I HAVE EVER written that is (a) based upon a vision and (b) dependent upon the emotional content of that vision. Quickly, lest I be misunderstood, I state that there was nothing at all religious about the vision—it was one engendered by sleep and fright.

We lived in a house in California at the foot of an incredibly steep hill. The local name for it was Suicide Hill, which was a fair description. Children would come down the hill road on bikes and break arms, drunks would run their cars off the road and knock down telephone poles—all great fun.

At the time of my vision this part of the world was still the boonies, nothing but jackrabbits and sagebrush in all directions. Very quiet at night—which meant that the occasional car could be heard a mile off. This night in particular I had just fallen asleep. Or rather I was in that borderland between awake and asleep that is neither one nor the other when this car came over the hill. It stopped at the top, revved its engine—and then raced down at top speed, shifting gears with a roar and a whine. The headlights swept through the bedroom window and I was absolutely certain that the car was going

164

to crash into the house. I was overwhelmed by a feeling of absolute panic. I swear I rose an inch off the bed, every muscle twitching. The automobile swept by and was gone, and I lay there, wide awake on the instant, staring into the darkness at this vision.

In my half-unconscious state I had not seen a car rushing down upon me but, instead, had seen a waterfall so wide that the distant shore could not be seen, so high that the top was invisible, its sound so overwhelming that it shook the earth.

Next morning when I thought of that waterfall I remembered the feelings I had had when I'd seen it. All life is grist for the authorial mill. I went out to the study and, before evening, I had written the story of these falls. Whenever energy flagged I recalled the vision along with all its accompanying emotion. This recharged my emotional batteries and enabled me to capture my original strong feelings intact.

BY THE FALLS

<<<<<<<<<<<<<<<<<<<<<<<<<<<<<<<<<<<<<<<<

IT WAS THE RICH DAMP GRASS, SLIPPERY AS
soap, covering the path, that caused Carter to keep slipping and falling, not the steepness of the hill. The front
of his raincoat was wet and his knees were muddy long
before he reached the summit. And with each step forward and upward the continuous roar of ground grew
louder. He was hot and tired by the time he reached the
top of the ridge—yet he instantly forgot his discomfort
as he looked out across the wide bay.

Like everyone else he had heard about The Falls since
childhood and had seen countless photographs and films
of them on television. All this preparation had not readied
him for the impact of reality.

He saw a falling ocean, a vertical river—how many
millions of gallons a second did people say came down?
The Falls stretched out across the bay, their farthest
reaches obscured by the clouds of floating spray. The bay
seethed and boiled with the impact of that falling weight,
raising foam-capped waves that crashed against the rocks
below. Carter could feel the impact of the water on the
solid stone as a vibration in the ground but all sound
was swallowed up in the greater roar of The Falls. This
was a reverberation so outrageous and overpowering that
his ears could not become accustomed to it. They soon
felt numbed from the ceaseless impact but the very bones
of the skull carried the sound of his brain, shivering and
battering it. When he put his hands over his ears he was
horrified to discover that The Falls were still as loud as

ever. As he stood swaying and wide-eyed one of the constantly changing air currents that formed about the base of The Falls shifted suddenly and swept a wall of spray down upon him. The inundation lasted scant seconds but was heavier than any rainfall he had ever experienced, had ever believed possible. When it passed he was gasping for air, so dense had been the falling water.

Quivering with sensations he had never before experienced, Carter turned and looked along the ridge toward the gray and water-blackened granite of the cliff and the house that huddled at its base like a stony blister. It was built of the same granite as the cliff and appeared no less solid. Running and slipping, his hands still over his ears, Carter hurried toward the house.

For a short time the spray was blown across the bay and out to sea, so that golden afternoon sunlight poured down on the house, starting streamers of vapor from its sharply sloping roof. It was a no-nonsense building, as solid as the rock against which it pressed. Only two windows penetrated the blankness of the front that faced The Falls—tiny and deep, they were like little suspicious eyes. No door existed here but Carter saw that a path of stone flags led around the corner.

He followed it and found—set into the wall on the far side, away from The Falls—a small and deepset entry. It had no arch but was shielded by a great stone lintel a good two feet in diameter. Carter stepped into the opening that framed the door and looked in vain for a knocker on the heavy, iron-bolted timbers. The unceasing, world-filling, thunder of The Falls made thinking almost impossible and it was only after he had pressed uselessly against the sealed portal that he realized that no knocker, even one as loud as cannon, could be heard within these walls above that sound. He lowered his hands and tried to force his mind to coherence.

There had to be some way of announcing his presence. When he stepped back out of the alcove he noticed that a rusty iron knob was set into the wall a few feet away. He seized and twisted it but it would not turn. However, when he pulled on it, although it resisted, he was able to

draw it slowly away from the wall to disclose a length of
chain. The chain was heavily greased and in good condition—a fair omen. He continued to pull until a yard of
chain emerged from the opening and then, no matter how
hard he pulled, no more would come. He released the
handle and it bounced against the rough stone of the wall.
For some instants it hung there. Then, with a jerky mechanical motion, the chain was drawn back into the wall
until the knob once more rested in place.

Whatever device this odd mechanism activated seemed
to perform its desired function. In less than a minute the
heavy door swung open and a man appeared in the opening. He examined his visitor wordlessly.

The man was much like the building and the cliffs
behind it—solid, no-nonsense, worn, lined and graying.
But he had resisted the years even as he showed their
marks upon him. His back was as straight as any young
man's and his knob-knuckled hands had a look of determined strength. Blue were his eyes and very much the
color of the water falling endlessly, thunderously, on the
far side of the building. He wore knee-high fisherman's
boots, plain corduroy pants and a boiled gray sweater.
His face did not change expression as he waved Carter
into the building.

When the thick door had been swung shut and the
many sealing bars shoved back into place the silence in
the house took on a quality of its own. Carter had known
absence of sound elsewhere—here was a positive statement of no-sound, a bubble of peace pushed right up
against the very base of the all-sound of The Falls. He
was momentarily deafened and he knew it. But he was
not so deaf that he did not know that the hammering
thunder of The Falls had been shut outside. The other
man must have sensed how his visitor felt. He nodded in
a reassuring manner as he took Carter's coat, then pointed
to a comfortable chair set by the deal table near the fire.
Carter sank gratefully into the cushions. His host turned
away and vanished, to return a moment later with a tray
bearing a decanter and two glasses. He poured a measure

of wine into each glass and set one down before Carter, who nodded and seized it in both hands to steady their shaking. After a first large gulp he sipped at it while the tremors died and his hearing slowly returned. His host moved about the room on various tasks and presently Carter found himself much recovered. He looked up.

"I must thank you for your hospitality. When I came in I was—shaken."

"How are you now? Has the wine helped?" the man said loudly, almost shouting, and Carter realized that his own words had not been heard. Of course, the man must be hard of hearing. It was a wonder he was not stone deaf.

"Very good, thank you," Carter shouted back. "Very kind of you indeed. My name is Carter. I'm a reporter, which is why I have come to see you."

The man nodded, smiling slightly.

"My name is Bodum. You must know that if you have come here to talk to me. You write for the newspapers?"

"I was sent here." Carter coughed—the shouting was irritating his throat. "And I of course know you, Mr. Bodum—that is I know you by reputation. You're the Man by The Falls."

"Forty-three years now," Bodum said with solid pride, "I've lived here and have never been away for a single night. Not that it has been easy. When the wind is wrong the spray is blown over the house for days and it is hard to breathe—even the fire goes out. I built the chimney myself—there is a bend part way up with baffles and doors. The smoke goes up—but if water comes down the baffles stop it and its weight opens the doors and it drains away through a pipe to the outside. I can show you where it drains—black with soot the wall is there."

While Bodum talked Carter looked around the room at the dim furniture shapes barely seen in the wavering light from the fire and at the two windows set into the wall.

"Those windows," he said, "you put them in yourself? May I look out?"

"Took a year apiece, each one. Stand on that bench.

It will bring you to the right level. They're armored glass, specially made, solid as the wall around them now that I have them anchored well. Don't be afraid. Go right up to it. The window's safe. Look how the glass is anchored."

Carter was not looking at the glass but at The Falls outside. He had not realized how close the building was to the falling water. It was perched on the very edge of the cliff and nothing was to be seen from this vantage point except the wall of blackened wet granite to his right and the foaming maelstrom of the bay far below. And before him, above him, filling space, The Falls. All the thickness of wall and glass could not cut out their sound completely and when he touched the heavy pane with his fingertips he could feel the vibration of the water's impact.

The window did not lessen the effect The Falls had upon him but it enabled him to stand and watch and think, as he had been unable to do on the outside. It was very much like a peephole into a holocaust of water—a window into a cold hell. He could watch without being destroyed—but the fear of what was on the other side did not lessen. Something black flickered in the falling water and was gone.

"There—did you see that," he called out. "Something came down The Falls. What could it possibly be?"

Bodum nodded wisely. "Over forty years I have been here and I can show you what comes down The Falls." He thrust a splint into the fire and lit a lamp from it. Then, picking up the lamp, he waved Carter after him. They crossed the room and he held the light to a large glass bell jar.

"Must be twenty years ago it washed up on the shore. Every bone in its body broke too. Stuffed and mounted it myself."

Carter pressed close, looking at the staring shoe-button eyes and the gaping jaws and pointed teeth. The limbs were stiff and unnatural, the body under the fur bulging in the wrong places. Bodum was by no means a skillful taxidermist. Yet, perhaps by accident, he had captured a look of terror in the animal's expression and stance.

"It's a dog," Carter said. "Very much like other dogs."

Bodum was offended, his voice as cold as shout can be. "Like them, perhaps, but not of them. Every bone broken I told you. How else could a dog have appeared here in this bay?"

"I'm sorry, I did not mean to suggest for an instant— down The Falls, of course. I just meant it is so much like the dogs we have that perhaps there is a whole new world up there. Dogs and everything, just like ours."

"I never speculate," Bodum said, mollified. "I'll make some coffee."

He took the lamp to the stove and Carter, left alone in the partial darkness, went back to the window. It drew him. "I must ask you some questions for my article," he said but did not speak loudly enough for Bodum to hear. Everything he had meant to do here seemed irrelevant as he looked out at The Falls. The wind shifted. The spray was briefly blown clear and The Falls were once more a mighty river coming down from the sky. When he canted his head he saw exactly as if he were looking across a river.

And there, upstream, a ship appeared, a large liner with rows of portholes. It sailed the surface of the river faster than ship had ever sailed before and he had to jerk his head to follow its motion. When it passed, no more than a few hundred yards away, for one instant he could see it clearly. The people aboard it were hanging to the rails, some with their mouths open as though shouting in fear. Then it was gone and there was only the water, rushing endlessly by.

"Did you see it?" Carter shouted, spinning about.

"The coffee will be ready soon."

"There, out there," Carter cried, taking Bodum by the arm. "In The Falls. It was a ship, I swear it was, falling from up above. With people on it. There must be a whole world up there that we know nothing about."

Bodum reached up to the shelf for a cup, breaking Carter's grip with the powerful movement of his arm.

"My dog came down The Falls. I found it and stuffed it myself."

"Your dog, of course, I'll not deny that. But there were people on that ship and I'll swear—I'm not mad—that their skins were a different color from ours."

"Skin is skin, just skin color."

"I know. That is what we have. But it must be possible for skins to be other colors, even if we don't know about it."

"Sugar?"

"Yes, please. Two."

Carter sipped at the coffee—it was strong and warm. In spite of himself he was drawn back to the window. He looked out and sipped at the coffee—and started when something black and formless came down. And other things. He could not tell what they were because the spray was blowing toward the house again. He tasted grounds at the bottom of his cup and left the last sips. He put the cup carefully aside.

Again the eddying wind currents shifted the screen of spray to one side just in time for him to see another of the objects go by.

"That was a house! I saw it as clearly as I see this one. But wood perhaps, not stone, and smaller. And black as though it had been partially burned. Come look, there may be more."

Bodum banged the pot as he rinsed it out in the sink. "What do your newspapers want to know about me? Over forty years here—there are a lot of things I can tell you about."

"What is up there above The Falls—on the top of the cliff? Do people live up there? Can there be a whole world up there of which we live in total ignorance?"

Bodum hesitated, frowned in thought before he answered.

"I believe they have dogs up there."

"Yes," Carter answered, hammering his fist on the window ledge, not knowing whether to smile or cry. The water fell by; the floor and walls shook with the power of it.

"There—more and more things going by." He spoke quietly, to himself. "I can't tell what they are. That—that could have been a tree and that a bit of fence. The smaller ones may be bodies—animals, logs, anything. There is a different world above The Falls and in that world something terrible is happening. And we don't even know about it. We don't even know that world is there."

He struck again and again on the stone until his fist hurt.

The sun shone on the water and he saw the change, just here and there at first, an altering and shifting.

"Why—the water seems to be changing color. Pink it is—no, red. More and more of it. There, for an instant, it was all red. The color of blood."

He spun about to face the dim room and tried to smile but his lips were drawn back hard from his teeth when he did.

"Blood? Impossible. There can't be that much blood in the whole world. What is happening up there? What is happening?"

His scream did not disturb Bodum, who only nodded his head in agreement.

"I'll show you something," he said. "But only if you promise not to write about it. People might laugh at me. I've been here over forty years and that is nothing to laugh about."

"My word of honor, not a word. Just show me. Perhaps it has something to do with what is happening."

Bodum took down a heavy Bible and opened it on the table next to the lamp. It was set in very black type, serious and impressive. He turned pages until he came to a piece of very ordinary paper.

"I found this on the shore. During the winter. No one had been here for months. It may have come over The Falls. Now I'm not saying it did—but it is possible. You will agree it is possible?"

"Oh, yes—quite possible. How else could it have come here?" Carter reached out and touched it. "I agree, ordinary paper. Torn on one edge, wrinkled where it was wet and then dried." He turned it over. "There is lettering on the other side."

"Yes. But it is meaningless. It is no word I know."

"Nor I, and I speak four languages. Could it have a meaning?"

"Impossible. A word like that."

"No human language." He shaped his lips and spoke the letters aloud. "Aich—Eee—Ell—Pea."

"What could HELP mean," Bodum shouted, louder than ever. "A child scribbled it. Meaningless." He seized the paper and crumpled it and threw it into the fire.

"You'll want to write a story about me," he said proudly. "I have been here over forty years, and if there is one man in the entire world who is an authority on The Falls it is me.

"I know everything that there is to know about them."

STORIES ARE OCCASIONALLY WRITTEN to order. Or, rather, an editor will write and say "I am looking for stories of a certain kind to be used in a certain manner— do you have any ideas along this line?"

Anthony Cheetham, both editor and friend, once wrote that he needed stories on scientific themes that could be used in a boy's science magazine and then later put into an anthology. The magazine, *Young Scientist,* was one that I had already subscribed to for my son Todd. It was an excellent journal reflecting all the strengths of its parent, *New Scientist.*

I was interested and agreed to do a story for Anthony. I decided that I really wanted to write a story about evolution. No shortage of material there—but the challenge was to organize it as a work of fiction, to present evolution in an interesting yet simple manner for younger readers—and still write a story that would capture the older reader's interest when the stories were eventually anthologized.

A good deal of writing is art, subconscious or unconscious art—the muse speaking, etc. Another large component is the cool decision to use a technique or device to help a story along, to organize it, or start it, or form it. I have long been an admirer of the works of

15

Anthony Burgess, a writer's writer if there ever was one, and have much admired the opening chapter of *Enderby*. It embodies a beautifully simple device to establish the character of a novel—and a science-fiction device at that. Since, in this same novel, there are subtle Burgessian parodies of Graham Greene's authorial excesses, I felt that Burgess might not be offended by my pirating of his technique. (I have since asked him about this, and he simply could not have cared less—in fact, he rather enjoyed the idea.)

Here it is, a work of fiction that perhaps tells you more about evolution than you care to know.

THE EVER-BRANCHING TREE

‹‹‹

THE CHILDREN HAD SPREAD UP AND DOWN the beach, and some of them had even ventured into the surf where the tall green waves crashed down upon them. Glaring from a deep blue sky, the sun burned on the yellow sand. A wave broke into foam, surging far up the shore with a soundless rush. The sharp clap-clap of Teacher's hands could easily be heard in the sunlit silence.

"Playing is over—put your clothes back on, Grosbit-9, all of them—and the class is about to begin."

They staggled towards Teacher, as slowly as they could. The bathers emerged dry from the ocean, while not a grain of sand adhered to skin or garment of the others. They gathered about Teacher, their chatter gradually dying away, and he pointed dramatically at a tiny creature writhing across the sand.

"Uhggh, a worm!" Mandi-2 said and shivered deliciously, shaking her red curls.

"A worm, correct. A first worm, an early worm, a proto worm. An important worm. Although it is not on the direct evolutionary track that we are studying we must pause to give it notice. A little more attention, Ched-3, your eyes are closing. For here, for the first time, we see segmentation, as important a step in the development of life as was the development of multicellular forms. See, look carefully, at those series of rings about the creature's body. It looks as though it were made of little rings of tissue fused together—and it is."

They bent close, a circle of lowered heads above the

177

brown worm that writhed a track across the sand. It moved slowly towards Grosbit-9, who raised his foot and stamped down hard on the creature. The other students tittered. The worm crawled out through the side of his shoe and kept on.

"Grosbit-9, you have the wrong attitude," Teacher said sternly. "Much energy is being expended to send this class back through time, to view the wonders of evolution at work. We cannot feel or touch or hear or change the past, but we can move through it and see it about us. So we stand in awe of the power that permits us to do this, to visit our Earth as it was millions of years ago, to view the ocean from which all life sprung, to see one of the first life forms on the ever-branching tree of evolution. And what is your response to this awe-inspiring experience? You *stamp* on the annelid! For shame, Grosbit-9, for shame."

Far from feeling shameful, Grosbit-9 chewed a hangnail on his thumb and looked about out of the corners of his eyes, the trace of a smirk upon his lips. Teacher wondered, not for the first time, how a 9 had gotten into this class. A father with important contacts, no doubt, high-placed friends.

"Perhaps I had better recap for those of you who are paying less than full attention." He stared hard at Grosbit-9 as he said this, with no apparent effect. "Evolution is how we reached the high estate we now inhabit. Evolution is the forward march of life, from the one-celled creatures to multicelled, thinking man. What will come after us we do not know, what came before us we are now seeing. Yesterday we watched the lightning strike the primordial chemical soup of the seas and saw the more complex chemicals being made that developed into the first life forms. We saw this single-celled life triumph over time and eternity by first developing the ability to divide into two cells, then to develop into composite, many-celled life forms. What do you remember about yesterday?"

"The melted lava poured into the ocean!"

"The land rose from the sea!"

"The lightning hit the water!"

"The squirmy things were so ugghhy!"

Teacher nodded and smiled and ignored the last comment. He had no idea why Mandi-2 was registered in this science course and had a strong feeling she would not stay long.

"Very good. So now we reach the annelids, like our worm here. Segmented, with each segment almost living a life of its own. Here are the first blood vessels to carry food to all the tissues most efficiently. Here is the first hemoglobin to carry oxygen to all the cells. Here is the first heart, a little pump to force the blood through those tubes. But one thing is missing yet. Do you know what it is?"

Their faces were empty of answers, their eyes wide with expectation.

"Think about it. What would have happened if Grosbit-9 had really stepped on this worm?"

"It would have squashed," Agon-1 answered with eight-year-old practicality. Mandi-2 shivered.

"Correct. It would have been killed. It is soft, without a shell or a skeleton. Which brings us to the next branch on the evolutionary tree."

Teacher pressed the activating button on the control unit at his waist, and the programmed computer seized them and hurled them through time to their next appointment. There was a swift, all-encompassing greyness, with no feeling of motion at all, which vanished suddenly to be replaced by a green dimness. Twenty feet above their heads the sun sparkled on the surface of the ocean while all about them silent fish moved in swift patterns. A great monster, all plates and shining teeth, hurtled at and through them and Mandi-2 gave a little squeal of surprise.

"Your attention down here, if you please. The fish will come later. First we must study these, the first echinoderms. Phill-4, will you point out an echinoderm and tell us what the term means."

"Echinoderm," the boy said, keying his memory. The training techniques that all the children learned in their first years of schooling brought the words to his lips. Like the others he had a perfect memory. "Is Greek for spiny skin. That must be one there, the big hairy starfish."

"Correct. An important evolutionary step. Before this animals were either unprotected, like our annelid worm, or had skeletons outside like snails or lobsters or insects. This is very limiting and inefficient. But an internal skeleton can give flexible support and is light in weight. An important evolutionary step has been made. We are almost there, children, almost there! This simple internal skeleton evolved into a more practical notochord, a single bone the length of the body protecting a main nerve fiber. And the chordata, the creatures with this notochord, were only a single evolutionary step away from this—all *this!*"

Teacher threw his arms wide just as the sea about them burst into darting life. A school of silvery, yard-long fishes flashed around and through the students, while sharp-toothed shark-like predators struck through their midst. Teacher's speech had been nicely timed to end at this precise and dramatic moment. Some of the smaller children shied away from the flurry of life and death while Grosbit-9 swung his fist at one of the giants as it glided by.

"We have arrived," Teacher said, vibrantly, carried away by his own enthusiasm. "The chordata give way to the vertebrata, life as we know it. A strong, flexible internal skeleton that shields the soft inner organs and supports at the same time. Soft cartilage in these sharks—the same sort of tissue that stiffens your ears—changes to hard bone in these fishes. Mankind, so to speak, is just around the corner! What is it, Ched-3?" He was aware of a tugging on his toga.

"I have to go to the . . ."

"Well press the return button on your belt and don't be too long about it."

Ched-3 pressed the button and vanished, whisked back to their classroom with its superior functional plumbing. Teacher smacked his lips annoyedly while the teeming life whirled and dived about them. Children could be difficult at times.

"How did these animals know to get a notochord and

bones?" Agon-1 asked. "How did they know the right way to go to end up with the vertebrata—and us?"

Teacher almost patted him on the head, but smiled instead.

"A good question, a very good question. Someone has been listening and thinking. The answer is they didn't know, it wasn't planned. The ever-branching tree of evolution has no goals. Its changes are random, mutations caused by alterations in the germ plasm caused by natural radiation. The successful changes live, the unsuccessful ones die. The notochord creatures could move about easier, were more successful than the other creatures. They lived to evolve further. Which brings us to a new word I want you to remember. The word is 'ecology' and we are talking about ecological niches. Ecology is the whole world, everything in it, how all the plants and animals live together and how they relate one to the other. An ecological niche is where a creature lives in this world, the special place where it can thrive and survive and reproduce. All creatures that find an ecological niche that they can survive in are successful."

"The survival of the fittest?" Agon-1 asked.

"You have been reading some of the old books. That is what evolution was once called, but it was called wrong. *All* living organisms are fit, because they are alive. One can be no more fit than the other. Can we say that we, mankind, are more fit than an oyster?"

"Yes," Phill-4 said, with absolute surety, his attention on Ched-3, who had just returned, apparently emerging from the side of one of the sharks.

"Really? Come over here, Ched-3, and try to pay attention. We live and the oysters live. But what would happen if the world were to suddenly be covered by shallow water?"

"How could that happen?"

"The how is not important," Teacher snapped, then took a deep breath. "Let us just say it happened. What would happen to all the people?"

"They would all drown!" Mandi-2 said, unhappily.

"Correct. Our ecological niche would be gone. The

oysters would thrive and cover the world. If we survive we are all equally fit in the eyes of nature. Now let us see how our animals with skeletons are faring in a new niche. Dry land."

A press, a motionless movement, and they were on a muddy shore by a brackish swamp. Teacher pointed to the trace of a feathery fin cutting through the floating algae.

"The subclass crossoptergii, which means fringed fins. Sturdy little fish who have managed to survive in this stagnant water by adopting their swim bladders to breathe air directly and to get their oxygen in this manner. Many fish have these bladders that enable them to hover at any given depth, but now they have been adapted to a different use. Watch!"

The water became shallower until the fish's back was above the water, then its bulging eyes, staring about, round and wide, as though terrified by this new environment. The sturdy fins, reinforced by bone, thrashed at the mud, driving it forward, further and further from its home, the sea. Then it was out of the water, struggling across the drying mud. A dragonfly hovered low, landed —and was engulfed by the fish's open mouth.

"The land is being conquered," Teacher said, pointing to the humped back of the fish now vanishing among the reeds. "First by plants, then insects—and now the animals. In a few million years, still over 225 million years before our own time, we have this . . ."

Through time again, rushing away on the cue word, to another swampy scene, a feathery marsh of ferns as big as trees and a hot sun burning through low-lying clouds.

And life. Roaring, thrashing, eating, killing life. The time researchers must have searched diligently for this place, this instant in the history of the world. No words were needed to describe or explain.

The age of reptiles. Small ones scampered by quickly to avoid the carnage falling on them. Scolosaurus, armored and knobbed like a tiny tank, pushed through the reeds, his spiked tail dragging a rut in the mud. Great brontosaurus stood high against the sky, his tiny, foolish head, with its teacup of brains, waving at the end of his lengthy neck, turned back to see what was bothering him as some message crept through his indifferent nervous system. His back humped up, a mountain of gristle and bone and flesh and hooked to it was the demon form of tyrannosaurus. His tiny forepaws scratched feebly against the other's leathery skin while his yards-long razor-toothed jaws tore at the heaving wall of flesh. Brontosaurus, still not sure what was happening, dredged up a quarter ton of mud and water and plants and chewed it, wondering. While high above, heaving and flapping its leathery wings, pteranodon wheeled by, long jaws agape.

"That one's hurting the other one," Mandi-2 said. "Can't you make them stop?"

"We are only observers, child. What you see happened so very long ago and is unalterable in any way."

"Kill!" Grosbit-9 muttered, his attention captured for the very first time. They all watched, mouths dropping open at the silent fury.

"These are reptiles, the first successful animals to conquer the land. Before them were the amphibia, like our modern frogs, tied unbreakably to the water, where their eggs are laid and the young grow up. But the reptiles lay eggs that can hatch on land. The link with the sea has been cut. Land has been conquered at last. They lack but a single characteristic that will permit them to survive in all the parts of the globe. You have been preparing for this trip. Can anyone tell me what is still missing?"

The answer was only silence. Brontosaurus fell and large pieces of flesh were torn from his body. Pteranodon flapped away. A rain squall blotted out the sun.

"I am talking about temperature. These reptiles get a good deal of their body heat from the sun. They must live in a warm environment because as their surroundings get cooler their bodies get cooler . . ."

"Warm blooded!" Agon-1 said with shrill excitement.

"Correct. Someone, at least, has been doing the required studying. I see you sticking your tongue out, Ched-3. How would you like it if you couldn't draw it back and it stayed that way? Controlled body temperature, the last major branch on the ever-branching tree. The first class of what might be called centrally heated animals is the mammalia. The mammals. If we all go a little bit deeper into this forest you will see what I mean. Don't straggle, keep up there. In this clearing, everyone. On this side. Watch those shrubs there. Any moment now . . ."

Expectantly they waited. The leaves stirred and they leaned forward. A piglike snout pushed out, sniffing the air, and two suspicious, slightly crossed eyes looked about the clearing. Satisfied that there was no danger for the moment, the creature came into sight.

"Coot! Is that ever ugly," Phill-4 said.

"Beauty is in the eye of the beholder, young man. I'll ask you to hold your tongue. This is a perfect example of the subclass prototheria, the first beasts, tritylodon itself. For many years a source of controversy as to whether it was mammal or reptile. The smooth skin and shiny plates of a reptile—but notice the tufts of hair between the plates. Reptiles do not have hair. And it lays eggs, as reptiles do. But it, she, this fine creature here also suckles her young as do the mammals. Look with awe at this bridge between the old class of reptiles and emerging class of mammals."

"Oh, how *cute!*" Mandi-2 squealed as four tiny pink duplicates of the mother staggered out of the shrubbery after her. Tritylodon dropped heavily onto her side and the young began to nurse.

"That is another thing that the mammals brought into the world," Teacher said as the students looked on with rapt fascination. "Mother love. Reptile offspring, either born live or when they emerge from the egg, are left to fend for themselves. But warm-blooded mammals must be warmed, protected, fed while they develop. They need mothering and, as you see, they receive it in sufficiency."

Some sound must have troubled the tritylodon because she looked around, then sprang to her feet and trundled off into the underbrush, her young falling and stumbling after her. No sooner was the clearing empty than the hulking form of triceratops pushed by, the great horns and bony frill held high. Thirty feet of lumbering flesh, its tail tip twitching as it dragged behind.

"The great lizards are still here, but doomed soon to final destruction. The mammals will survive and multiply and cover the earth. We will later discuss the many paths traveled by the mammals, but today we are going to leap ahead millions of years to the order primates, which may look familiar to you."

A taller, deeper, more tangled jungle replaced the one they had been visiting, a fruit filled, flower filled, life filled maze. Multicolored birds shot by, insects hung in clouds and brown forms moved along the branches.

"Monkeys," Grosbit-9 said and looked around for something to throw at them.

"Primates. A relatively primitive group that took to these trees some fifty million years in our past. See how they are adapting to the arboreal life? They must see clearly in front of them and gauge distances correctly, so their eyes are now on the front of their heads, and they have developed binocular vision. To hold securely to the branches their nails have shortened and become flat, their thumbs opposed to strengthen their grip. These primates will continue to develop until the wonderful, important day when they descend from the trees and venture from the shelter of the all-protecting forest.

"Africa," Teacher said as the time machine once more moved them across the centuries. "It could be today, so little have things changed in the relatively short time since these higher primates ventured forth."

"I don't see anything," Ched-3 said, looking about at the sun-scorched grass of the veldt, at the verdant jungle pressing up next to it.

"Patience. The scene begins. Watch the herd of deer that are coming towards us. The landscape has changed, become drier, the seas of grass are pushing back the jungle. There is still food to be had in the jungle, fruit and nuts there for the taking, but the competition is becoming somewhat fierce. Many different primates now fill that ecological niche and it is running over. Is there a niche vacant? Certainly not out here on the veldt! Here are the fleet-footed grass-eaters, look how they run, their survival depends upon their speed. For they have their enemies, the carnivores, the meat-eaters who live on their flesh."

Dust rose and the deer bounded towards them, through them, around them. Wide eyes, hammering hooves, sun glinting from their horns and then they were gone. And the lions followed. They had a buck, cut off from the rest of the herd by the lionesses, surrounded, clawed at and wounded. Then a talon-tipped paw hamstrung the beast and it fell, quickly dead as its throat was chewed out and the hot red blood sank into the dust. The pride of lions ate. The children watched, struck silent, and Mandi-2 sniffed and rubbed at her nose.

"The lions eat a bit, but they are already gorged from another kill. The sun is reaching the zenith and they are hot, sleepy. They will find shade and go to sleep and the corpse will remain for the scavengers to dispose of, the carrion-eaters."

Even as Teacher spoke the first vulture was dropping down out of the sky, folding its dusty wings and waddling towards the kill. Two more descended, tearing at the flesh and squabbling and screaming soundlessly at one another.

Then from the jungle's edge there emerged first one, then two more apes. They blinked in the sunlight, looking around fearfully, then ran towards the newly killed deer, using their knuckles on the ground to help them as they ran. The blood-drenched vultures looked at them apprehensively, then flapped into the air as one of the apes hurled a stone at them. Then it was the apes' turn. They too tore at the flesh.

"Look and admire, children. The tailless ape emerges from the forest. These are your remote ancestors."

"Not mine!"

"They're *awful*."

"I think I am going to be sick."

"Children—stop, think! With your minds not your viscera just for once. These ape-men or man-apes have occupied a new cultural niche. They are already adapting to it. They are almost hairless so they can sweat and not overheat when other animals must seek shelter. They are tool using. They hurl rocks to chase away the vultures. And, see, that one there—he has a sharp bit of splintered rock that he is using to cut off the meat. They stand erect on their legs to free their hands for the tasks of feeding and survival. Man is emerging and you are privileged to behold his first tremulous steps away from the jungle. Fix this scene in your memory, it is a glorious one. And you will remember it better, Mandi-2, if you watch with your eyes open."

The older classes were usually much more enthusiastic. Only Agon-1 seemed to be watching with any degree of interest. Other than Grosbit-9, who was watching with too much interest indeed. Well, they said one good student in a class made it worthwhile, made one feel as though something were being accomplished.

"That is the end of today's lesson, but I'll tell you something about tomorrow's class." Africa vanished and some cold and rainswept northern land appeared. High mountains loomed through the mist in the background and a thin trickle of smoke rose from a low sod house half buried in the ground. "We will see how man emerged from his primate background, grew sure and grew strong. How these early people moved from the family group to the simple neolithic community. How they used tools and bent nature to their will. We are going to find out who lives in that house and what he does there. It is a lesson that I know you are all looking forward to."

There seemed very little actual evidence to back this assumption, and Teacher stabbed the button and the class was over. Their familiar classroom appeared around them and the dismissal bell was jingling its sweet music. Shouting loudly, without a backward look, they ran from the room and Teacher, suddenly tired, unclipped the controls from his waist and locked them into his desk. It had been a very long day. He turned out the lights and left.

At the street entrance he was just behind a young matron, most attractive and pink in miniaturized mini, hair a flaming red. Mandi-2's mother, he realized, he should have known by the hair, as she reached down to take an even tinier, pinker hand. They went out before him.

"And what did you learn in school today, darling," the mother asked. And, although he did not approve of eavesdropping, Teacher could not help but hear the question. Yes, what did you learn? It would be nice to know.

Mandi-2 skipped down the steps, bouncing with happiness to be free again.

"Oh, nothing much," she said, and they vanished around the corner.

Without knowing he did it, Teacher sighed a great weary sigh and turned in the other direction and went home.

BOB SILVERBERG ONCE HAD AN IN-
teresting idea for an anthology. Isaac Asimov
would do an introduction to the volume
outlining some possible world futures that
might come about as a result of different
advances in biology. As all the world knows,
Isaac has a doctorate in biochemistry. Yet
he rarely gets fictionally involved in his
scholastic profession, preferring to keep the
worlds separate.

One of Isaac's futures intrigued me—this
one. Since the stories for Bob's anthology
were to be long (this one is over thirteen
thousand words), the theme could be developed in depth. And then, too, I was interested in the chance to write about a
utopia, a utopia that particularly appealed
to me—one in which the population problem was solved.

I could not construct Isaac's world until I
got rid of our overpopulated one. In order
to abolish it I needed strong motivation, so
I used one of the strongest of all. Selfishness.

Of course, there has to be trouble in
utopia, at least a little trouble, because no
matter how perfect a world it is, there are
always some people who just won't enjoy it.
Hence, "Brave Newer World."

16

189

BRAVE NEWER WORLD

<<<<<<<<<<<<<<<<<<<<<<<<<<<<<<<<<<<<<<<

       LIVERMORE LIKED THE VIEW FROM THE LITTLE white balcony outside his office even though the air at this height, at this time of year, had a chill bite to it. He was standing there now, trying to suppress a shiver, looking out at the new spring green on the hillsides and the trees in the old town. Above and below him the white steps of the levels of New Town stretched away in smooth elegance, a great A in space with the base a half-mile wide, rising up almost to a point on top. Every level fringed with a balcony, every balcony with an unobstructed view. Well designed. Livermore shivered again and felt the loud beat of his heart; old valves cheered on by new drugs. His insides were as carefully propped up and as well designed as the New Town building. Though his outside left a lot to be desired. Brown spots, wrinkles and white hair; he looked as weathered as the homes in Old Town. It was damn cold and the sun went behind a cloud. He thumbed a button and, when the glass wall slid aside, went back gratefully to the purified and warmed air of the interior.

"Been waiting long?" he asked the old man who sat, scowling, in the chair on the far side of his desk.

"You asked, Doctor, I was never one to complain, but . . ."

"Then don't start now. Stand up, open your shirt, let me have those records. Grazer, I remember you, planted a kidney seed didn't they? How do you feel?"

"Poorly, that's the only word for it. Off my feed, can't

190

sleep, when I do I wake up with the cold sweats. And the bowels! Let me tell you about the bowels . . . Ahhh!"

Livermore slapped the cold pickup of the stethoscope against the bare skin of Grazer's chest. Patients liked Dr. Livermore but hated his stethoscope, swearing that he must keep it specially chilled for them. They were right. There was a thermoelectric cooling plate in the case. It gave them something to think about, Livermore believed. "Hmmm . . ." he said, frowning, the earpieces in his ears, hearing nothing. He had plugged the stethoscope with wax years earlier, the systolic diastolic murmurs disturbed his concentration; he heard enough of that from his own chest. Everything was in the records in any case, since the analysis machines did a far better job than he could ever do. He flipped through the sheets and graphs.

"Button your shirt, sit down, take two of these right now, just the thing for this condition."

He shook the large red sugar pills from the jar in his desk drawer and pointed to the plastic cup and water carafe. Grazer reached for them eagerly: this was real medicine. Livermore found the most recent x-rays and snapped them into the viewer. Lovely. The new kidney was growing, as sweetly formed as a little bean, tiny now beside its elderly brother, but in a year's time they would be identical. Science conquereth all, or at least almost all; he slammed the file on the table. It had been a difficult morning and even his afternoon surgery was not as relaxing as it usually was. The old folks, the AK's, his peer group, they appreciated each other. Very early in his career he had taken his M.D., that was all that they knew, and he sometimes wondered if they connected him at all with the Dr. Rex Livermore in charge of the ecto-genetic program. If they had even heard of the program.

"I'm sure glad for the pills, Doc, I don't like those shots no more. But my bowels—"

"God damn and blast your bowels. They're as old as my bowels and in just as good shape. You're just bored, that's your trouble."

Grazer nodded approvingly at the insults; a touch of

interest in an otherwise sterile existence. "Bored's the very word, Doc. The hours I spend on the pot—"

"What did you do before you retired?"

"That was a real long time ago."

"Not so long that you can't remember, and if you can't why then you are just too old to waste food and space on and we'll hook that old brain out and put it in a bottle with a label saying senile brain on it."

Grazer chuckled; he might have cried if someone younger had talked to him this way. "Said it was a long time ago, didn't say I forgot. Painter. House painter, not the artist kind, worked at it eighty years before the union threw me out and made me retire."

"Pretty good at it?"

"The best. They don't have my kind of painter around any more."

"I can believe that. I'm getting damn tired of the egg-shell off-white super plastic eterna finish on the walls of this office. Think you could repaint it for me?"

"Paint won't stick to that stuff."

"If I find one that will?"

"I'm your man, Doc."

"It'll take time. Sure you won't mind missing all the basket weaving, socials, television?"

Grazer snorted in answer and he almost smiled.

"All right, I'll get in touch with you. Come back in a month in any case so I can look at that kidney. As for the rest, you're in perfect shape after your geriatric treatments. You're just bored with television and the damned baskets."

"You can say that again. Don't forget about that paint, hear?"

A distant silver bell chimed and Livermore pointed to the door, picking up the phone as soon as the old man had gone. Leatha Crabb's tiny and distraught image looked up at him from the screen.

"Oh, Dr. Livermore, another bottle failure."

"I know. I was in the lab this morning. I'll be down there at fifteen-hundred and we can talk about it then." He hung up and looked at his watch. Twenty minutes until the meeting, he could see another patient or two. Geriatrics was not his field, and he really had very little interest in it; but he was interested in the people. He sometimes wondered if they knew how little they needed him, since they were on constant monitoring and medical attention. Perhaps they just enjoyed seeing and talking to him as he did to them. No harm done in any case.

The next patient was a thin white-haired woman who began complaining as she came through the door and did not stop as she put her crutches aside and sat carefully in the chair. Livermore nodded and made doodles on the pad before him and admired her flow of comment, criticism and invective over a complaint she had covered so well and so often before. It was just a foot she was talking about, which might seem a limited area of discussion, toes, tendons and that sort of thing. But she had unusual symptoms, in addition to the usual pain, hot flushes and itching, all of which was made even more interesting by the fact that the foot under discussion had been amputated over sixty years earlier. Phantom limbs with phantom symptoms were nothing new—there were even reported cases of completely paralyzed patients with phantom sexual impulses terminating in phantom orgasms —but the longevity of this case was certainly worth noting. He relaxed under the wave of detailed complaint and when he finally gave her some of the sugar pills and ushered her out they both felt a good deal better.

Catherine Ruffin and Sturtevant were already waiting in the board room when he came in. Sturtevant, impatient as always, tapping green-stained fingers on the marble tabletop, one of his cancer-free tobacco-substitute cigarettes dangling from his lip. His round and thick glasses and sharp nose made him resemble an owl, but the thin line of his mouth was more like that of a turtle's: it was a veritable bestiary of a face. His ears could be those of a moose, Livermore thought, then aloud: "Those so-called cigarettes of yours smell like burning garbage, Sturtevant, do you know that?"

"You have told him that before," Catherine Ruffin said in her slow, careful English. She had emigrated in her youth from South Africa, to marry the long-dead Mr. Ruffin, and still had the accents of her Boer youth. Full bosomed and round in a very Dutch housewife manner, she was nevertheless a senior administrator with a mind like a computer.

"Never mind my cigarettes." Sturtevant grubbed the butt out and instantly groped for a fresh one. "Can't you be on time just once for one of these meetings?"

Catherine Ruffin rapped with her knuckles on the table and switched on the recorder.

"Minutes of the meeting of the Genetic Guidance Council, Syracuse New Town, Tuesday January 14th, 2025. Present, Ruffin, Sturtevant, Livermore, Ruffin chairman."

"What's this I hear about more bottle failures?" Sturtevant asked. Livermore dismissed the matter with a wave of his hand.

"A few bottle failures are taken for granted. I'll look into these latest and have a full report for our next meeting. Just a mechanical matter and not to bother us here. What does bother me is our genetic priorities. I have a list."

He searched the pockets in his jacket one after another and Sturtevant frowned his snapping-turtle frown at him.

"You and your lists, Livermore, we've read enough of them. Priorities are a thing of the past. We now have a prepared program that we need only follow."

"Priorities are not outdated, and by saying that you show a sociologist's typical ignorance of the realities of genetics."

"You're insulting!"

"It's the truth, too bad if it hurts." He found a crumpled piece of paper in an inside pocket and smoothed it out on the table before him. "You are so used to your damn charts and graphs, demographic curves and projections that you think they are really a description of the real world instead of being rough approximations well after the fact. I'm not going to trouble you with figures, they are so huge as to be meaningless, but I want you to consider the incredible complexity of our genetic pool.

Mankind as we know him has been around about a half million years, mutating, changing and interbreeding. Every death in all those generations was a selection of some kind, as was every mating. Good and bad traits, pro- and anti-survival mutations, big brains and hemophilia, everything happened and was stirred up and spread through the human race. Now we say we are going to improve that race by gene selection. We have an endless reservoir of traits to draw from, ova from every woman, sperm from every man. We can analyze these for genetic composition and feed the results to the computer to work out favorable combinations, then combine the sperm and ova and grow the foetus ectogenetically. If all goes well nine months later we decant the infant of our selection and the human race has been improved by that small increment. But what *is* an improvement, what is a favorable combination? Dark skin is a survival trait in the tropics, but dark skin in the northern hemisphere cuts off too much ultraviolet so the body cannot manufacture vitamin D and rickets follow. Everything is relative."

"We have been over this ground before," Catherine Ruffin said.

"But not often enough. If we don't constantly renew and review our goals, we are going to start down a one-way road. Once genetic traits have been discarded they are gone forever. In a way the team in San Diego New City have an easier job. They have a specific goal. They are out to build new breeds of men, specific types for different environments. The space men who can live without physical or mental breakdowns during the decade-long trips to the outer planets. The temperature and low-pressure resistant types for Mars settlers. They can discard genes ruthlessly and aim for a clear and well-established goal. We simply improve—and what a vague ambition that is. And in making this new race of supermen what will we lose? Will new-man be pink, and if so, what has happened to the Negro—"

"For God's sake, Livermore, let us not start on that again," Sturtevant shouted. "We have fixed charts, rules, regulations laid down for all the operations."

"I said you had no real knowledge of genetics and that proves it once again. You can't get it through your head that with each selection the game starts *completely over again*. As they say in the historical 3V's it is a brand new ball game. The entire world is born anew with every child."

"I think you tend to overdramatize," Catherine Ruffin said stolidly.

"Not in the slightest. Genes are not bricks, we can't build the desired structure to order. We just aim for optimum, then see what we have and try again. No directives can lay down the details of every choice, or control every random combination. Every technician is a small god, making real decisions of life and death. And some of these decisions are questionable in the long run."

"Impossible," Sturtevant said, and Catherine Ruffin nodded agreement.

"No, just expensive. We must find a closer examination of *every* change made and get some predictions of where we are going."

"You are out of order, Dr. Livermore," Catherine Ruffin said. "Your proposal has been made in the past, a budget forecast was estimated and the entire matter turned down because of cost. This was not our decision, you will recall, but came down from genguidecounchief. We accomplish nothing by raking over these well-raked coals another time. There is new business we must consider that I wish to place before this council."

Livermore had the beginnings of a headache and he fumbled a pill from the carrier in his pocket. The other two were talking and he paid them no attention at all.

When Leatha Crabb hung up the phone after talking with Dr. Livermore she felt as though she wanted to cry. She had been working long hours for weeks and not getting enough sleep. Her eyes stung and she was a little ashamed of this unaccustomed weakness: she was the sort of person who simply did not cry, woman or no. But seventeen bottle failures, seventeen deaths. Seventeen tiny lives snuffed out before they had barely begun to live.

It hurt, almost as though they had been real children . . .

"So small you can't hardly see it," Veazy said. The laboratory assistant held one of the disconnected bottles up to the light and gave it a shake to swish the liquid about inside of it. "You sure it's dead?"

"Stop that!" Leatha snapped, then curbed her temper: she had always prided herself on the way she treated those who worked beneath her. "Yes, they are all dead, I've checked that. Decant, freeze and label them, I'll want to do examinations later."

Veazy nodded and took the bottle away. She wondered what had possessed her thinking of them as lives, children. She must be tired. They were groups of growing cells with no more personality than the cells grouped in the wart on the back of her hand. She rubbed at it, reminding herself again that she ought to have it taken care of. A handsome, well-formed girl in her early thirties, with hair the color of honey and tanned skin to match. But her hair was cropped short, close to her head, and she wore not the slightest trace of makeup. While the richness of her figure was lost in the heavy folds of her white laboratory smock. She was too young for it, but a line of worry was already beginning to form between her eyes. When she bent over her microscope, peering at the stained slide, the furrow deepened.

The bottle failures troubled her, deeply, more than she liked to admit. The program had gone so well the past few years that she was beginning to take it for granted, already looking ahead to the genetic possibilities of the second generation. It took a decided effort to forget all this and turn back to the simple mechanical problems of ectogenesis . . .

Strong arms wrapped about her from behind, the hands pressed firmly against the roundness of her body below her waist; hard lips kissed the nape of her neck.

"Don't!" she said, surprised, pulling away. Gust dropped his arms at once, stepping back from her.

"You don't have to get angry," he said. "We are married you know and no one is watching."

"It's not your pawing me I don't like. But I'm working, can't you see that."

Leatha turned to face him, angry at his physical touch despite her words. He stood dumbly before her, a stolid, solid, black-haired and dark-complexioned man with a slightly protruding lower lip that made him look, now, as though he were pouting.

"You needn't look so put out. It's work time, not play time."

"Damn little play time any more." He glanced quickly around to see if anyone was within earshot. "Not the way it was when we were first married. You were pretty affectionate then." He reached out a slow finger and pressed it to her midriff.

"Don't do that." She drew away, raising her hands to cover herself. "It's been absolute hell here today. A defective valve in one of the hormone feed lines, discovered too late. We lost seventeen bottles. In an early stage luckily."

"So what's the loss? There must be a couple of billion sperm and ova in the freezers. They'll pair some more up and put you back in business."

"Think of the work and labor in gene matching, all wasted."

"That's what technicians are paid for. It will give them something to do. Look, can we forget work for a while, take off an evening? Go to Old Town. There is a place there I heard about, Sharm's, real cult cooking and entertainment."

"Can't we talk about it later? This really isn't the time . . ."

"By Christ it never is. I'll be back here at seventeen-thirty and see if you can't possibly make your mind up by then."

He pushed angrily out of the door, but the automatic closing mechanism prevented him from slamming it behind him. Something had gone out of life, he wasn't sure just what. He loved Leatha, she loved him, he was sure of that, but something was missing. They both had their work to do, but it had never caused trouble before.

They were used to it, even staying up all night some-times, working in the same room in quiet companion-ship. Then coffee, perhaps as dawn was breaking, a drowsy pleasant fatigue, falling into bed, making love. It just wasn't that way any more and he couldn't think why. At the elevators he entered the nearest and called out, "Fifty." The doors closed and the car fell smoothly away. They would go out tonight: he was resolved that this evening would be different.

Only after he had emerged from the elevator did he realize that it had stopped at the wrong floor. Fifteen, not fifty; the number analyzer in the elevator computer always seemed to have trouble with those two. Before he could turn the doors shut behind him and he noticed the two old men frowning in his direction. He was on one of the eldster floors. Instead of waiting for another car he turned away from their angry looks and hurried down the hall. There were other old people about, some shuffling along, others riding powered chairs, and he looked straight ahead so he wouldn't catch their eyes. They re-sented youngsters coming here.

Well, he resented them occupying his brand new build-ing. That wasn't a nice thought and he was sorry at once for even thinking a thing like that. This wasn't his build-ing; he was just one of the men on the design team who had stayed on for construction. The eldsters had as much right here as he did, more so, since this was their home. And a pleasant compromise it had been too. This build-ing, New Town, was designed for the future, but the future was rather slow coming since you could accelerate almost everything in the world except foetal growth. Nine months from conception to birth, in either bottle or womb. Then the slow years of childhood, the quick years of puberty. It would be wasteful for the city to stay vacant all those years.

That was where the eldsters came in, the leftover debris of an overpopulated world. Geriatrics propped them up and kept them going. They were growing older together, the last survivors of the greedy generations. They were the parents who had less children and even fewer grandchildren as the realities of famine, disease and the general unwholesomeness of life was driven home to them. Not that they had done this voluntarily, left alone they would have responded as every other genera- ation of mankind had done; selfishly. If the world is going to be overpopulated—it is going to be overpopulated with *my* kids. But the breakthrough in geriatric treatment and drugs came along at that moment and provided a far better carrot than had ever been held in front of the human donkey before. The fewer children you had the more treatment you received. The birthrate dived to zero almost overnight. The indifferent overpopulators had de- cided to overpopulate with themselves instead of their children. If life were being granted, they preferred to have it granted to them.

The result was that a child of the next generation might have, in addition to his mother and father, a half dozen surviving relatives who were eldsters. A married couple might have ten or fifteen older relatives, all of them alone in the world, looking to their only younger kin. There could be no question of this aging horde moving in with the present generation who had neither room for them nor money to support them. They were a government burden and would remain so. A decreasing burden that required less money every year as old machinery, despite the wonders of medicine, finally ran down. When the new cities were being designed for the future, scientifically planned generations, the wise decision had been made to move the eldsters into them. The best of food care and medicine could be provided with the minimum effort and expense. Life in the older cities would be happier, relieved of the weight of the solid block of aging citizenry. And, since the geriatric drugs didn't seem to work too well past the middle of the second century, a timetable could be established for what was euphemistically called "phas- ing out." Dying was a word no one liked to use. So as the present inhabitants were phased out to the phasing place of their choice the growing generations would move in. All neat. All tidy.

As long as you stayed away from the eldster floors.

Looking straight ahead Gust went swiftly along the street-like corridor, ignoring the steam rooms and bathing rooms, tropical gardens and sandy beaches that opened off to either side. And the people. The next bank of elevators was a welcome sight and this time he very clearly enunciated "fif-tee" as the door closed.

When he reached the end of the unfinished corridor the work shift was just going off duty. The flooring terminated here and ahead was just the rough gray of raw cement still showing the mold marks where it had been cast in place; floodlights stood high on wiry legs.

"Been having trouble with the squatter, Mr. Crabb," the shift boss complained. These men had grown up in a world of smoothly operating machines and were hurt when they occasionally proved fallible.

"I'll take a look at it. Anything in the hopper?"

"Half full. Should I empty it out?"

"No, leave it. I'll try a run before I call maintenance."

As the motors on the machines were turned off one by one an echoing silence fell on the immense and cavern-like area. The men went away, their footsteps loud, calling to each other, until Gust was alone. He climbed the ladder to the top of the hulking squatter and un-locked the computer controls. When he typed a quick condition query the readout revealed nothing wrong. These semi-intelligent machines could analyze most of their own troubles and deliver warnings, but there were still occasional failures beyond their capacity to handle or even recognize. Gust closed the computer and pressed the *power* button.

There was a faroff rumble and the great bulk of the machine shuddered as it came to life. Most of the in-dicator lights blinked on red, turning swiftly to green as the motors came to speed. When the operation ready light also turned green he squinted at the right-hand TV screen, which showed the floor level buried under the squatter. The newly laid flooring ended abruptly where the ma-chine had stopped. He backed it a few feet so the sensers could come into operation, then started it forward again at the crawling pace of working speed. As soon as the edge was reached the laying began again. The machine guided itself and controlled the mix and pouring. About all the operator had to do was turn the entire apparatus on and off. Gust watched the hypnotically smooth flow of new floor appear and could see nothing wrong. It was pleasant here, doing a simple yet important job like this.

A warning buzzer sounded and a light began flashing red on the controls. He blinked and had a quick glimpse of something black on the screen before it moved swiftly out of sight. He stopped the forward motion and put the squatter into reverse again, backing the huge mass a good ten feet before killing all the power and climbing back down. The newly laid plastic flooring was still hot under his feet and he trod gingerly almost up to the forward edge. There was a cavity in the flooring here, like a bowl or a bubble a foot wide. As though the machine had burped while spewing out its flow. Perhaps it had. The technicians would set it right. He made a note to call them on his pocket pad, killed all except the standby lights, then went back to the elevators, calling out his floor number very carefully.

Dr. Livermore and Leatha were bent over a work table in the lab, heads lowered as though at a wake. As perhaps they were. Gust came in quietly, listening, not wanting to interrupt.

"There were some of the most promising new strains here," Leatha said. "The Reilly-Stone in particular. I don't know how much computer time was used in the preliminary selection, but the technicians must have put in a hundred hours on this fertilized ovum alone."

"Isn't that a little unusual?" Livermore asked.

"I imagine so, but it was the first application of the Bershock multiple-division cross trait selection and you know how those things go."

"I do indeed. It will be easier the next time. Send the records back noting the failures. Get them started on replacements. Hello, Gust, I didn't hear you come in."

"I didn't want to bother you."

"No bother. We are finished in any case. Had some bottle failures today."

"So I heard. Do you know why?"

"If I knew everything I would be God, wouldn't I?"

Leatha looked at the old man, shocked. "But, Doctor, we do know why the embryos were killed. The valve failed on the input—"

"But why did the valve fail? There are reasons beyond reasons in everything."

"We're going to Old Town, Doctor," Gust said, uncomfortable with this kind of abstract conversation and eager to change the subject.

"Don't let me stop you. Don't bring back any infections, hear?"

Livermore turned to leave, but the door opened before he reached it. A man stood there, looking at them without speaking. He entered and the silence and the severe set of his features struck them silent as well. When the door had closed behind him he called their names in a deep voice, looking at each of them in turn as he spoke.

"Dr. Livermore, Leatha Crabb, Gust Crabb. I am here to see you. My name is Blalock."

It was clear that Livermore did not enjoy being addressed in this manner. "Call my secretary for an appointment. I'm busy now." He started to leave but Blalock raised his hand, at the same time taking a thin wallet from his pocket.

"I would like to see you now, Doctor. This is my identification."

Livermore could not have left without pushing the man aside. He stopped and blinked at the golden badge.

"F.B.I. What on earth are you after here?"

"A killer." A stunned silence followed. "I can tell you now, though I would appreciate your not telling anyone else, that one of the technicians working here is an agent from the bureau. He makes regular reports to Washington about conditions on the project."

"Meddling and spying!" Livermore was angry.

"Not at all. The government has a large investment here and believes in protecting this and in guarding the taxpayers' money. You have had a number of bottle failures here in the first weeks after implanting."

"Accidents, just accidents," Leatha said, then flushed and was silent when Blalock turned his cold unsmiling gaze on her.

"Are they? We don't think so. There are four other New Cities in the United States, all of them with projects working along the same lines as yours. They have had bottle failures as well, but not in the numbers you have here."

"A few more in one place or another means nothing," Livermore said. "The law of averages covers minor differences."

"I'm sure it does. Minor differences, Doctor. But the rate of failure here is ten times higher than that of the other laboratories. For every bottle failure they have, you have ten. For their ten, you have a hundred. I am not here by accident. Since you are in charge of this project I would like a letter from you giving me permission to go anywhere on the premises and to speak with anyone."

"My secretary will have gone by now. In the morning—"

"I have the letter here, typed on your stationery, just needing your signature."

Livermore's anger was more forced than real. "I won't have this. Stealing my office supplies. I won't have it."

"Don't be rude, Doctor. Your stationery is printed by the Government Printing Office. They supplied it to me to make my job easier. Don't *you* make it harder."

There was a coldness in that *you* that stopped Livermore and sent him fumbling with his pen to sign the letter. Gust and Leatha looked on, not knowing what to do. Blalock folded the letter and put it back into his pocket.

"I'll want to talk to you all later," he said, and left. Livermore waited until he was gone, then went out as well, without a word.

"What an awful man," Leatha said.

"It doesn't matter how awful he is if what he said was right. Bottle sabotage—how can that be?"

"Easily enough done."

"But why should it be done?" Gust asked. "That is the

real question. It's so meaningless, so wanton. There's simply no reason."

"That's Blalock's worry, what he's getting paid for. Right now I've had a long day and I'm hungry and more concerned with my dinner. You go ahead to the apartment and defrost something, I won't be a minute finishing up these tests."

He was angry. "The first blush is off our marriage, isn't it? You have completely forgotten that I asked you out to dinner in Old Town."

"It's not that . . ." Leatha said, then stopped, because it really was. Gust wasn't completely right, the work was so distracting and then this Blalock person. She tidied up quickly without finishing the tests and took off her smock. Her dress was dark gray and no less severe. It was thin too, designed for wear in the constant temperature of New Town.

"If it's cold outside I should get a coat."

"Of course it's cold out, it's still March. I checked out a car earlier and put your heavy coat in it, mine as well."

They went in silence to the elevator and down to the parking level. The bubble-dome car was at the ready ramp and the top swung up when he turned the handle. They put on their coats before they climbed in and Leatha turned on the heat as he started the car. The electric engine, powered by batteries, hummed strongly as they headed for the exit, the doors opening automatically for them as the car approached. There was a brief wait in the lock while the inner door closed before the outer one opened; then they emerged on the sloping ramp that led up to Old Town.

It had been a long time since their last visit outside the New Town walls and the difference was striking. The streets were patched and had an unkempt appearance, with dead grass and weeds protruding from the cracks. There were pieces of paper caught against the curbs, and when they passed an empty lot a cloud of dust swirled around them. Leatha sank deeper into her seat and shivered even though the heater was going full on.

The buildings had a weathered and even a decayed look about them, the wooden buildings most of all, and the limbs of the gray trees were bare as skeletons in the fading daylight. Gust tried to read the street signs and lost his way once, but finally found a garish spotlit sign that read *Sharm's*. Either they were early or business wasn't booming because they could park right in front of the door. Leatha didn't wait, but ran the few feet through the chill wind while Gust locked up the car. Inside Sharm himself was waiting to greet them.

"Welcome, welcome," he said with bored professional exuberance, a tall, wide Negro, very black, wearing a brilliant kaftan and red fez. "I've got just the table for you, right at the ringside."

"That will be nice," Gust said.

Sharm's hospitality was easily understood; there was only one other couple in the restaurant. There was the heavy smell of cooking in the air, some of it not too fresh, and the tablecloth was a cartography of ancient stains only partially removed.

"Like a drink?" Sharm asked.

"I guess so. Any suggestions?"

"Bet your life. Bloody Mary with tequila, the house special. I'll fetch a jug."

They must have been premixed because he was back a moment later with the tray and two menus tucked under his arm. He poured their drinks and then one for himself and pulled up a chair to join them. The atmosphere of Sharm's was anything if not relaxed.

"Salud," he said, and they drank. Leatha puckered her lips and put her glass down quickly, but Gust liked the sharp bite of the drink.

"Great. Never tasted one before. How about the menu, any house specials there?"

"All specials. My wife is great at any kind of cult-food. Black-eyed peas and corn dodgers, kosher hotdogs and Boston baked beans, we got them all. Just take your pick. Music's starting now and Aikane will be in to dance in about half an hour. Drink up folks, these are on the house."

"Very kind," Gust said, sipping his.

"Not at all. I want to pump your brain, Mr. Crabb, and I pay in advance. I saw you on 3V last week talking about New City. Pretty fancy if I say so myself. What's the chances of opening a restaurant in your place?" He drained his glass and poured himself another one, topping up their glasses at the same time.

"That's not easy to say."

"What's easy? Living on the dole and maybe blowing your brains out from boredom, that's easy. Me, I got bigger plans. Everyone likes cultfood. Eldsters reminds them of the old days, kids think it's real pit-blasting. But people here in Old Town don't eat out much, not that much loose pesos around. Got to go to where the change is. New Town. What're the odds?"

"I can find out. But you have to realize, Mr. Sharm . . ."

"Just plain Sharm. A first name."

"You have to realize that the eldsters have special diets, special sanitary regulations on their food."

"This beanery isn't bug-finky, we got plenty of sanitary examinations."

"That's not what I meant, I'm sorry, don't misunderstand me. It's special diets really, to go with the medication. Really special if you understand, practically worked out and cooked in the labs."

A loud drumming interrupted him as a sad-looking American Indian did a quick Indian warbeat on the bass drum. He switched on the taper with his toe, then worked rhythm on the traps as a recording played an Israeli folk song. It was all very unimpressive, but loud.

"What about the younger people then?" Sharm shouted to be heard. "Like you folks. You come this far to eat cultfood, why not have it closer to home?"

"There's not enough of us, not yet. Just technicians and construction teams. No more than ten percent of the children who will occupy the city have even been born yet, so I don't know if you even have a big enough group to draw from. Later, perhaps."

"Yeah, later. Big deal. Wait twenty years." Sharm sunk down, wrapped in gloom, moving only to empty the

jug into his glass. He rose reluctantly when another cus-
tomer entered, ending the embarrassing interlude.

They both ordered mixed plates of all the specialties,
and a bottle of wine since Leatha was not that enthusiastic
about the Bloody Marys. While they ate, a slightly dark-
skinned girl, of possibly Hawaiian descent, emerged from
the rear and did an indifferent hula. Gust looked on with
some pleasure since she wore only a lowslung grass skirt
with many tufts missing, and was enough overweight to
produce a great deal of jiggling that added a certain something to the dance.

"Vulgar," Leatha said, wiping her eyes with her napkin
after taking too much horseradish on her gefilte fish.

"I don't think so." He put his hand on her leg under
the table and she pushed it away without changing expression.

"Don't do that in public."

"Or in private either! Damn it, Lea, what's happening
to our marriage? We both work, A-OK, that's fine, but
what about our life together? What about our raising a
newborn?"

"We've talked about this before . . ."

"You've said no before, that's what has happened.
Look Lea, honey, I'm not trying to push you back to
the middle ages with one in the hand, one on the hip,
and one in the belly. Women have been relieved at last
of all the trouble and danger of childbirth, but by God
they are still women. Not men with different builds. A lot
of couples don't want kids, fine, and I agree crèche-raised
babies have all the advantages. But other couples are
raising babies, and women can even nurse them after the
right injections."

"You don't think I'd do *that*?"

"I'm not asking you to do *that*—as you so sweetly put
it—though it is nowhere near as shocking as your tone
of voice indicates. I would just like you to consider
raising a child, a son. He would be with us evenings and
weekends. It would be fun."

"Not exactly my idea of fun."

The answer that was on his lips was sharp, bitter and

nasty and would have surely started an even worse fight, but before he could speak she grabbed him by the arm.

"Gust, there in the corner at that back table, isn't that the horrible person who was at the lab?"

"Blalock? Yes, it looks like him. Though it's hard to tell in this over-romantic light. What difference does it make?"

"Don't you realize that if he is here he followed us and is watching us? He thinks *we* may have been responsible for the bottle failures."

"You're imagining too much. Maybe he just likes cult-food. He looks the type who might even live on it."

Yet why was he at the restaurant? If he was there to worry them, he succeeded. Leatha pushed her plate away and Gust had little appetite as well. He called for the check and, depressed in spirits, they shrugged into their coats and went out into the cold night, past the silent and accusing eyes of Sharm, who knew he was not going to live the new life in New Town no matter how much he wanted to.

Many years before Catherine Ruffin had developed a simple plan to enable her to get her work done, a plan that was not part of her work routine. She had discovered, early in her career, that she had an orderly mind and a highly retentive memory that were a great asset in her work. But she had to study facts slowly and deliberately without interruptions, something that was impossible during the routine of a busy office day. Staying after work was not the answer; the phone still rang and she was often too fatigued to make the most of the opportunity. Nor was it always possible to bring work back to her apartment. Since she had always been an early riser she found that her colleagues were all slugabeds and would rather do anything than come to work five minutes early. She went to her office now at seven every morning and had the solid core of her work done before anyone else appeared. It was a practical and satisfactory solution to the problem and one that appealed to her. However she was so used to being alone at these early hours that she looked upon anyone else's presence as an interruption and an annoyance.

She found the note on her desk when she came in; it certainly had not been there when she left the previous evening. It was typed and quite clear:

Please see me now in bottlelab. Urgent. R. Livermore.

She was annoyed at the tone and the interruption, and perhaps the idea that someone had actually come to work before her. Been here all night, more likely; the scientific staff tended to do that unless specifically forbidden. Still, it looked urgent so she had better comply. There would be time for recriminations later if Livermore had overstepped himself. She put her massive purse in the bottom drawer of her desk and went to the elevator.

There was no one in sight on the laboratory floor, nor in the office when she went in. A motion caught her eye and she turned to look at the door that led into the bottle rooms; it was closed now; yet she had the feeling that it had moved a moment before. Perhaps Livermore had gone through and was waiting for her. As she started forward there was the sharp sound of breaking glass from behind the door, again and again. At the same instant an alarm bell began ringing loudly in the distance. She gasped and stood frozen an instant at the suddenness of it. Someone was in there, breaking the apparatus. The bottles! Running heavily she threw the door open and went inside.

The bottle room was empty, the jungle of piping and apparatus stretching silently the length of it. Shards of glass littered the floor nearby and in the midst of the glass and spilled liquid was a hammer. What did it mean? She bent to pick up the hammer and when she straightened up someone spoke behind her.

"Turn about slowly. Do not do anything you will regret."

Catherine Ruffin was out of her depth, floundering. Everything was happening too fast and she could not grasp the reality of it.

"What?" she said. "What?" She turned to look at the

stranger in the doorway behind her, who held what appeared to be a revolver.

"Put that hammer down slowly," he said.

"Who are you?" The hammer clattered on the floor.

"I will ask the same thing of you. I am Blalock, F.B.I. My identification is here." He held out his badge.

"Catherine Ruffin. I was sent for. Dr. Livermore. What does this mean?"

"Can you prove that?"

"Of course. This note, read it for yourself."

He pinched it between the tips of his fingers and looked at it briefly before dropping it into an envelope and putting it into his pocket. His gun had vanished.

"Anyone could have typed that," he said. "You could have typed it yourself."

"I don't know what you are talking about. It was on my desk when I came to work a short while ago. I read it, came here, heard the sound of glass being broken, entered here and saw this hammer and picked it up. Nothing else."

Blalock looked at her closely for a long instant, then nodded and waved her after him to the outer office. "Perhaps. We will check that out later. For the moment you will sit here quietly while I make some calls."

He had a list of numbers and the first one he dialed rang a long time before it was answered. Leatha Crabb's sleep-puffed face finally appeared on the screen.

"What do you want?" she asked, her eyes widening when she saw who the caller was.

"Your husband, I wish to talk to him."

"He's—he's asleep." She looked about uneasily and Blalock did not miss the hesitation in her voice.

"Is he? Then wake him and bring him to the phone."

"Why? Just tell me why?"

"Then I will be there at once. Would that embarrass you, Mrs. Crabb? Will you either wake your husband— or tell me the truth?"

She lowered her eyes and spoke in a small voice.

"He's not here. He hasn't been here all night."

"Do you know where he is?"

"No. And I don't care. We had a difference of opinion and he stamped out. And that is all I wish to tell you." The screen went dark. Blalock instantly dialed another number. This time there was no answer. He turned to Catherine Ruffin, who sat, still dazed by the rapid passage of events.

"I want you to take me to Dr. Livermore's office."

Still not sure what had happened, she did exactly as he asked. The door was unlocked and Blalock pushed by her and looked in. The pale early sunlight streamed in through the glass walls; the office was empty. Blalock sniffed at the air, as though searching out a clue, then pointed to the door in the right-hand wall.

"Where does this lead?"

"I'm sure I don't know."

"Stay here."

Catherine Ruffin disliked his tone but before she could tell him so he was across the room and standing to one side as he carefully opened the door. Livermore lay asleep on the couch inside, with a thin blanket pulled over him and clutched to his neck by one hand. Blalock went in silently and took him by the wrist, his forefinger inside below the base of the thumb. Livermore opened his eyes at the touch, blinked and pulled his hand away.

"What the devil are you doing here?"

"Taking your pulse. You don't mind, do you?"

"I certainly do." He sat up and threw the blanket aside. "I'm the doctor here and I do the pulse taking. I asked you what you meant by breaking in like this?"

"There has been more sabotage in the bottle room. I had alarms rigged. I found this woman there with a hammer."

"Catherine! Why would you do a foolish thing like that?"

"How dare you! You sent a note, I received it, asking me to come there, to trap me—perhaps *you* broke those bottles!"

Livermore yawned and rubbed at his eyes, then bent and groped under the couch for his shoes.

"That's what Dick Tracy here thinks." He grunted as

he pulled a shoe on. "Finds me sleeping here, doesn't believe that, tries to take my pulse and see if I have been running around with that hammer, faster pulse than a sleeping pulse. Idiot!" He snapped the last word and rose to his feet.

"I am in charge of this project, it's *my* project. Before you accuse me of sabotaging it you had better find a better reason than baseless suspicion. Find out who typed that fool note and maybe you will have a lead."

"I fully intend to," Blalock said, as the phone rang.

"For you," Livermore said, and passed it to the F.B.I. man, who listened silently, then issued a sharp command.

"Bring him here."

Before she left, Catherine Ruffin made a sworn statement and it was recorded on Livermore's office taper, then Livermore did the same thing. Yes, he had not been in his apartment. He had worked late in his office and, as he did many times, he had slept on the couch in the adjoining room. He had gone to sleep around 0300 hours and had neither seen nor heard anything since that time, not until Blalock had woken him up. Yes, it was possible to get from the bottle room by way of the rear door, and through the business office to this office, but he had not done that. He was just finishing the statement when a stranger, with the same dour expression and conservative cut of clothes as Blalock, brought Gust Crabb in. Blalock dismissed the man and turned the full power of his attention on Gust.

"You were not in your apartment all night. Where were you?"

"Go to hell."

"Your attitude is not appreciated. Your whereabouts are unknown—up to a few minutes ago when you arrived at your office. During the time in question someone broke into the bottle room and sabotaged this project with a hammer. I ask you again. Where were you?"

Gust, who was a simple man in all except his work, now enacted a pantomime of worry, guilt and unhappiness complete with averted eyes and a fine beading of sweat on his forehead. Livermore felt sorry for him and turned away and harrumphed and found his tie and busied himself knotting it.

"Talk," Blalock said loudly, using all the pressure he could to increase the other's discomfort.

"It's not what you think," Gust said in a hollow voice.

"Give me a complete statement or I will arrest you now for willful sabotage of a government project."

The silence lengthened uncomfortably and it was Livermore who broke it.

"For God's sake, Gust, tell him. You couldn't have done a thing like this. What is it—a girl?" He snorted through his nose at the sudden flushing of Gust's face. "It is. Spill it out, it won't go beyond this room. The government doesn't care about your sex life and I'm well past the age where these things have much importance."

Once he had been convinced of this Gust told the entire story. The girl, a secretary with the engineering commission, he had known her a long time. She liked him but he stayed away from her but, last night, after a fight with Leatha, he had stamped out, found himself at Georgette's door—you won't tell anyone?—and she took him in, one thing led to another. There it was.

"There it is," Livermore said. "Do your work, Blalock, Gust will be here with me if you want him. Find the girl, get her story, then leave us alone. Investigate the mysterious note, take fingerprints from the hammer, and do whatever you do in this kind of thing. But leave us be. Unless you have some evidence and want to arrest me— get out of my office."

When they were alone Livermore made some coffee in his anteroom and brought a cup to Gust, who was looking out at the hillside now shaded by clouds and curtained with rain.

"You think I'm a fool," Gust said.

"Not at all. I think there is trouble between you and Leatha and that you are making it worse instead of better."

"But what can I do!" Livermore ignored the note of

pleading in the man's voice and stirred his coffee to cool it.

"You know what to do without bothering me. It's your problem, you're an adult. Solve it. With your wife, or family counseling or whatever. Right now I have something slightly more important to think about with this sabotage and the F.B.I. and the rest of it."

Gust sat up straighter and almost smiled. "You're right. My problem isn't that world shaking and I'll take care of it. Do you realize that you and I and Leatha seem to be the F.B.I.'s prime suspects? He must have called the apartment if he knew I wasn't there. And he followed us to the restaurant last night. Why us?"

"Propinquity, I imagine. We and the technicians are the only ones who go in and out of the bottle rooms at will. And one of the technicians is a plant, he told us that, so they are being watched from their own ranks. Which leaves us."

"I don't understand it at all. Why *should* anyone want to sabotage the bottles?"

Livermore nodded slowly.

"That's the question that Blalock should be asking. Until he finds out the why of this business he is never going to find who is doing it."

Leatha came silently into his office and said nothing as she closed the door behind her. Gust looked up from the papers on his desk, surprised; she had never been in his office before.

"Why did you do it, why?" she said in a hoarse voice, her face drawn, ugly with the strain of her emotions. He was stunned into silence.

"Don't think I don't know—that Blalock came to see me and told me everything. Where you were last night, about *her,* so don't try to deny it. He wasn't lying, I could tell."

Gust was tired and not up to playing a role in a bitter exchange. "Why would he tell you these things?" he asked.

"Why? That's fairly obvious. He doesn't care about

you or me, just his job. He suspects me, I could tell that, thinks I could sabotage the bottles. He wanted me to lose my temper, and I did, not that it did any good. Now answer me—*pig*—why did you do it? That's all I want to know, why?"

Gust looked at his fists clenched on the desk before him. "I wanted to, I suppose."

. "You wanted to!" Leatha shrieked the words. "That's the kind of a man you are, you wanted to, so you just went there. I suppose I don't have to bother asking you what happened—my imagination is good enough for that."

"Lea, this isn't the time or place to talk about this—"

"Oh, isn't it? It doesn't take any special place for me to tell you what I think of you, you . . . traitor!"

His fixed and silent face only angered her more, beyond words. On the table close by was a cutaway model of New Town, prepared when it was still in the design stage. She seized it in both hands, raised it over her head and hurled it at him. But it was too light and it spun end over end in the air striking him harmlessly on the arm and falling to the floor, where it broke, shedding small chunks of plastic.

"You shouldn't have done that," Gust said, bending to retrieve the model. "Here, you've broken it and it costs money, I'm responsible for it." The only response was a slam and he looked up to see that Leatha was gone.

Anger filled her, stronger than anything she had ever experienced before in her life. Her chest hurt and she had trouble breathing. How could he have done this to her? She walked fast, until she had to gasp for breath, through the corridors of New Town. Aimlessly, she thought, until she looked at the entrance to the nearby offices and realized that she had had a goal all the time. *Centengcom,* the sign read, an unattractive acronym for the Central Engineering Commission. Could she enter here, and if she did—what could she say? A man came out and held the door for her; she couldn't begin to explain why she was standing there so she went in. There was a floorplan on the facing wall and she pressed the button labeled secretarial pool, then turned in the indicated direction.

It really proved quite easy to do. A number of girls worked in the large room surrounded by the hum of office machines and typers. People were going in and out and she stood for a minute until a young man carrying a sheaf of papers emerged. He stopped when she spoke to him.

"Could you help me? I'm looking for a . . . Miss Georgette Booker. I understand she works here."

"Georgy, sure. Over there at that desk against the far wall, wearing the white shirt or whatever you call it. Want me to tell her you're here?"

"No, that's fine, thank you very much. I'll talk to her myself."

Leatha waited until he had gone, then looked over the bent heads to the desk against the far wall and gasped. Yes, it had to be that girl, white blouse and dark hair, rich chocolate-colored skin. Leatha pushed through into the office and took a roundabout path through the aisles between the desks that would enable her to pass by the girl, slowing as she came close.

She was pretty, no denying that, she was pretty. A nicely sculptured face, thin bridged nose, but too heavily made up with the purple lipstick that was in now. And tiny silver stars dusted across one cheek and onto her chest. There was enough of that, and most of it showing too in the new peekie look, thin fabric almost completely transparent. The large breasts rose halfway out of the blouse, and through it the black circles of her nipples could be seen. Feeling the eyes on her, Georgette looked up and smiled warmly at Leatha, who turned away and walked past her, faster and faster.

By the middle of the afternoon Dr. Livermore was very tired. He had had little sleep the previous night and the F.B.I. man's visit had disturbed him. Then he had to put the technicians to work clearing up the mess in the bottle room and, while they could be trusted to do a good job, he nevertheless wanted to check it out for himself when they were done. He would do that and then perhaps take a nap. He pushed the elaborate scrawled codes of the gene charts away from him and rose stiffly. He was beginning to feel his years. Perhaps it was time to consider joining his patients in the warm comfort of the geriatric levels. He smiled at the thought and started for the labs.

There was little formality among his staff and he never thought to knock on the door of Leatha's private office when he found it closed. His thoughts were on the bottles. He pushed the door open and found her bent over the desk, her face in her hands, crying.

"What is wrong?" he called out, before he realized that it might have been wiser to leave quietly. He had a sudden insight as to what the trouble might be.

She raised a tear-dampened and reddened face and he closed the door behind him.

"I'm sorry to walk in like this. I should have knocked."

"No, Dr. Livermore, that's all right." She dabbed at her eyes with a tissue. "I'm sorry you have to see me like this."

"Perfectly normal. I think I understand."

"No, it has nothing to do with the bottles."

"I know. It's that girl, isn't it? I had hoped you wouldn't find out."

Leatha was too distraught to ask him how he knew, but began sobbing again at this reminder. Livermore wanted to leave but could think of no way to do it gracefully. At the present moment he just could not be interested in this domestic tragedy.

"I saw her," Leatha said. "I went there, God knows why, driven I suppose. To see just what he preferred to me. It was so humiliating. A blowsy thing, vulgar, the obvious kind of thing a man might like. And she is *colored*. How could he have done this . . ."

The sobbing began again and Livermore stopped, his hand on the knob. He had wanted to leave before he became involved himself. Now he was involved.

"I remember you talking to me about it once," he said. "Where you come from. Somewhere in the south, isn't it?"

The complete irrelevancy of the question stopped Leatha, even slowed her tears. "Yes, Mississippi. A little fishing town named Biloxi."

"I thought so. And you grew up with a good jolt of racial bias. The worst thing you have against this girl is the fact that she is black."

"I never said that. But there are things . . ."

"No, there are *not* things, if you mean races or colors or religions or anything like that. I am shocked to hear you, a geneticist, even suggest a thing like that. Deeply shocked. Though, unhappily, I'm not surprised."

"I don't care about her. It's him, Gust, what he did to me."

"He did nothing at all. My God, woman, you want equality and equal pay and freedom from childbearing— and you have all these things. So you can't very well complain if you throw a man out of your bed and he goes to someone else."

"What do you mean?" she gasped, shocked.

"I'm sorry. It's not my place to talk like this. I became angry. You're an adult, you will have to make your own decisions about your marriage."

"No. You can't leave it like that. You said something and you are going to tell me exactly what you meant."

Livermore was still angry. He dropped into a chair and ordered his thoughts before he spoke again.

"I'm an old-fashioned M.D., so perhaps I had better talk from a doctor's point of view. You're a young woman in good health in the prime of your life. If you came to me for marriage counseling, I would tell you that your marriage appears to be in trouble and you are probably the cause, the original cause that is. Though it has gone far enough now so that you both have a good deal to be responsible for. It appears that in your involvement in your work, in your major interests outside your marriage, you have lost your sexuality. You have no time for it. And I am not talking about sex now, but all the things that make a woman feminine. The way you dress, apply makeup, carry yourself, think about yourself. Your work has come to occupy the central portion of your life and

your husband has to take second best. You must realize
that some of the freedoms women gained deprived the
men of certain things. A married man now has no
children, or a mother for his children. He has no one
who is primarily interested in him and his needs. I do
not insist that all marriages must exist on a master and
slave relationship—but there should be a deal more give
and take in a marriage than yours appears to offer. Just
ask yourself—what *does* your husband get out of this
marriage other than sexual frustration? If it is just a
sometime companion, he would be far better off with a
male roommate, an engineer he could talk shop with."

The silence lengthened and Livermore finally coughed
and cleared his throat and stood.

"If I have interfered unreasonably, I'm sorry."

He went out and saw Blalock stamping determinedly
down the hall. After scowling at the man's receding back
for a moment he entered the laboratory to check the
bottle installations.

The F.B.I. man let himself into Catherine Ruffin's
office without knocking. She looked up at him, her face
cold, then back at her work.

"I am busy now and I do not wish to talk to you."

"I've come to you for some help."

"Me?" Her laugh had no humor in it. "You accused
me of breaking those bottles—so how can you ask for
aid?"

"You are the only one who can supply the information I need. If you are innocent as you insist, you should
be pleased to help."

It was an argument that appealed to her ordered mind.
She had no good reason—other than the fact that she disliked him—for refusing the man. And he was the agent
officially sent here to investigate the sabotage.

"What can I do?" she asked.

"Help me to uncover a motive for the crimes."

"I have no suspicions, no information that you don't
have."

"Yes you do. You have access to all the records and to
the computer—and you know how to program it. I want

you to get all the data you can on the contents of those bottles. I have been looking at the records of losses and there seems to be a pattern, but not one that is necessarily obvious. The fact that certain bottles were broken, three out of five, or that all the bottles in a certain rank on a certain day had their contents destroyed. There must be a key to this information in the records."

"This will not be a small job."

"I can get you all the authorization you need."

"Then I will do it. I can make the comparisons and checks and program the computer to look for relevant information. But I cannot promise you that there will be the answer you seek. The destruction could be random, and if it is, this will be of no help."

"I have my own reasons for thinking that it is not random. Do this and call me as soon as you have the results."

It took two days of concentrated effort, and Catherine Ruffin was very satisfied with the job that she had done. Not with the results themselves; she could see no clues to any form of organization in any of the figures. But the federal agent might. She put in a call to him, then went through the results again until he arrived.

"I can see nothing indicative," she said, passing over the computer readouts.

"That is for me to decide. Can you explain these to me?"

"This is a list of the destroyed or damaged bottles." She handed him the top sheet. "Code number in the first column, then identification by name."

"What does that mean?"

"Surname of the donors, an easy way to remember and identify certain strains. Here for instance, Wilson-Smith, sperm Wilson, ovum Smith. The remaining columns are details about the selections, which traits were selected and information of that kind. Instead of the index numbers I have used the names of the strains for identification in the processing. These are the remaining sheets which are the results of various attempts to extract meaningful relationships. I could find none. The names themselves convey more."

He looked up from the figures. "What do you mean?"

"Nothing at all. A foolish habit of my own. I am by birth a Boer and I grew up on one of the white reservations in South Africa after the revolution. Until we emigrated here, when I was eleven, I spoke only Afrikaans. So I have an emotional tie to the people, the ethnic group you would call it, in which I was born. It was a small group and it is very rare to meet a Boer in this country. So I look at lists of names, an old habit, to see if I recognize any Boers among them. I have met a few people that way in my lifetime, for some talk about the old days behind barbed wire. That is what I meant."

"How does that apply to these lists?

"There are no Boers among them."

Blalock shrugged and turned his attention back to the paper. Catherine Ruffin, born Katherine Bekink, held the list of names before her and pursed her lips over it.

"No Afrikaaners at all. All of them Anglo-Irish names if anything."

Blalock looked up sharply. "Please repeat that," he said.

She was correct. He went through the list of names twice and found only sternly Anglo-Saxon or Irish surnames. It appeared to make no sense nor did the fact, uncovered by Catherine Ruffin with the name relationship as a clue, that there were no Negroes either.

"It makes no sense, no sense at all," Blalock said, shaking the papers angrily. "What possible reason could there be for this kind of deliberate action?"

"Perhaps you ask the wrong question. Instead of asking why certain names appear to be eliminated perhaps you should ask why others do not appear on the list. Afrikaaners for instance."

"Are there Afrikaans names on any of the bottle lists?"

"Of course. Italian names, German names, that kind of thing."

"Yes, let us ask that question," Blalock said, bending over the lists again.

It was the right question to ask.

The emergency meeting of the Genetic Guidance Council was called for 2300 hours. As always, Livermore was late. An extra chair had been placed at the foot of the big marble table and Blalock was sitting there, the computer printouts arranged neatly before him. Catherine Ruffin switched on the recorder and called the meeting to order at once while Sturtevant coughed, then grubbed out his vegetable cigarette and immediately lit another one.

"Those burning compost heaps will kill you yet," Livermore said.

Catherine Ruffin interrupted the traditional disagreement before it could get under way.

"This meeting has been called at the request of Mr. Blalock of the Federal Bureau of Investigation, who is here investigating the bottle failures and apparent sabotage. He is now ready to make a report."

"About time," Livermore said. "Find out yet who is the saboteur?"

"Yes," Blalock said tonelessly. "You are, Dr. Livermore."

"Well, well, big talk from little man. But you will have to come up with some evidence before you wring a confession out of me."

"I think I can do that. Since the sabotage began and even before it was recognized as sabotage, one out of every ten bottles was a failure. This percentage is known as a tithe, which is indicative of a certain attitude or state of mind. It is also ten times the average failure ratio to other laboratories, which is normally about one percent. As further evidence the bottles sabotaged all had Irish or English surnamed donors."

Livermore sniffed loudly. "Pretty flimsy evidence. And what does it have to do with me?"

"I have here a number of transcripts of meetings of this council where you have gone on record against what you call discrimination in selection. You seem to have set yourself up as a protector of minorities, claiming at different times that Negroes, Jews, Italians, Indians and other groups have been discriminated against. The records reveal that no bottles bearing names of donors belonging to any of these groups has ever been lost by apparent accident or deliberate sabotage. The connection with you seems obvious, as well as the fact that you are one of the few people with access to the bottles, as well as the specific knowledge that would enable you to commit the sabotage."

"Sounds more like circumstantial evidence, not facts, to me. Are you planning to bring these figures out in a public hearing or trial or whatever you call it?"

"I am."

"Then your figures will also show the unconscious and conscious discrimination that is being practiced by the genetic-selection techniques now being used because it will reveal just how many of these minority groups are *not* being represented in the selection."

"I know nothing about that."

"Well I do. With these facts in mind I then admit to all the acts you have accused me of. I did it all."

A shocked silence followed his words. Catherine Ruffin shook her head, trying to understand.

"Why? I don't understand why you did it," she said.

"Still, Catherine? I thought you were more intelligent than that. I did everything within my power to change the errant policies of this board and all the other boards throughout the country. I got exactly nowhere. With natural childbirth almost completely a thing of the past the future citizens of this country will *all* come from the gene pool represented by the stored sperm and ova. With the selection techniques existing now minority after minority will be eliminated, and with their elimination countless genes that we simply cannot lose will be lost forever. Perhaps a world of fair-skinned, blue-eyed, blond and muscular Anglo-Saxon Protestants is your idea of an ideal society. It is not mine—nor is it very attractive to the tinted-skin people with the funny foreign ways, odd names and strangely shaped noses. They deserve to survive just as much as we do, and to survive right here in their country, which is the United States of America. So do not tell me about Italian and Israeli gene pools in their native lands. The only real Americans here with an original claim to that name are the American Indians—and they are being dropped out of the gene pool as well. A crime is being committed. I was aware of it and could convince no one else of its existence. Until I chose this highly dramatic way of pointing out the situation. During my coming trial these facts will be publicized and after that the policy will have to be reexamined and changed."

"You foolish old man," Catherine Ruffin said, but the warmth in her voice belied the harshness of her words. "You've ruined yourself. You will be fined, you may go to jail, at the least you will be relieved of your position, forced into retirement. You will never work again."

"Catherine, my dear, I did what I had to do. Retirement at my age holds no fears, in fact I have been considering it and rather looking forward to it. Leave genetics and practice medicine as a hobby with my old fossils. I doubt if the courts will be too hard on me. Compulsory retirement, I imagine, no more. Well worth it to get the facts out before the public."

"In that you have failed," Blalock said coldly, putting the papers together and dropping them into his case. "There will be no public trial, simply a dismissal, better for all concerned that way. Since you have admitted guilt your superiors can make a decision, in camera, as to what to do."

"That's not fair!" Sturtevant said. "He only did these things to publicize what was happening. You can't take that away from him. It's not fair . . ."

"Fair has nothing to do with it, Mr. Sturtevant. The genetic program will continue unchanged." Blalock seemed almost ready to smile at the thought. Livermore looked at him with distaste.

"You would like that, wouldn't you. Don't rock the boat. Get rid of disloyal employees—and at the same time rid this country of dissident minorities."

"You said it, Doctor, I didn't. And since you have admitted guilt there is nothing you can do about it."

Livermore rose slowly and started from the room, turning before he reached the door.

"Quite the contrary. Blalock, because I shall insist upon a full public hearing. You have accused me of a crime before my associates and I wish my name cleared since I am innocent of all charges."

"It won't wash." Blalock was smiling now. "Your statement of guilt is on tape, recorded in the minutes of this meeting."

"I don't think it is. I did one final bit of sabotage earlier today. On that recorder. The tape is blank."

"That will do you no good. There are witnesses to your words."

"Are there? My two associates on the council are committed human beings, no matter what our differences. If what I have said is true, I think they will want the facts to come out. Am I right, Catherine?"

"I never heard you admit guilt, Dr. Livermore."

"Nor I," Sturtevant said. "I shall insist on a full departmental hearing to clear your name."

"See you in court, Blalock," Livermore said, and went out.

"I thought you would be at work, I didn't expect to see you here," Gust said to Leatha, who was sitting, looking out of the window of their living room. "I just came back to pack a bag, take my things out."

"Don't do that."

"I'm sorry about what happened the other night, I just . . ."

"We'll talk about that some other time."

There was almost an embarrassed silence then and he noticed her clothes for the first time. She was wearing a dress he had never seen before, a colorful print, sheer and lowcut. And her hair was different somehow and her lipstick, more than she usually wore, he thought. She looked very nice and he wondered if he should tell her that.

"Why don't we go out to that restaurant in Old Town," Leatha said. "I think that might be fun."

"It will be fun, I know it will," he answered suddenly, unreasonably, happier than he had ever been before.

Georgette Booker looked up at the clock and saw that it was almost time to quit. Good. Dave was taking her out again tonight, which meant that he would propose again. He was so sweet. She might even marry him, but not now. Life was too relaxed, too much fun, and she enjoyed people. Marriage was always there when you wanted it, but right now she just didn't want it.

She smiled. She was quite happy.

Sharm smiled and ate another piece of the ring-shaped roll.

"Top-pit," he said. "Really good. What is it called?"

"A bagel," his wife said. "You're supposed to eat them with smoked salmon and white cheese. I found it in this old cultfood book. I think they're nice."

"I think they're a lot better than nice. We're going to bake a whole lot of them and I'm going to sell them in New Town because they got bread tastes like wet paper there and people will love them. They *have* to love them. Because you and I are going to move to New Town. They are going to love these bagels or something else we are going to sell them because you and I, we are going to live in that new place."

"You tell them, Sharm."

"I'm telling them. Old Sharm is going to get his cut of that good life too."

"Amen, as my momma used to say."

"Mine said the same thing so it must be like that in all the languages. Cook us up a bowl of spaghetti, will you, love, tonight I want some good old Addis-Ababa Ethiopian home cooking."

IN 1970 THOMAS DISCH WAS DOING an anthology of dark stories about the ecological, pollution, and population disasters that are looming in the world's future. Overpopulation stories, at that time, were a little thin on the ground—at least stories that he liked, stories that came to grips with this pressing problem. But he had read my novel, *Make Room! Make Room!,* and it was exactly what he wanted, a realistic hard look at the near future, an admonitory finger being shaken at the reader, a glimpse of what will happen if we don't do something about this urgent problem.

Unfortunately, *Make Room! Make Room!* was a novel, and Tom needed short stories. He found some chapters and pages that he thought could be put together as a short story and wrote me about them. I agreed that the idea made sense, but when I went to put the pieces together, I found that they didn't have the continuity needed for a short story.

So I rewrote, almost completely. One of the interesting results that I had not anticipated is the *density* of background, something rare in a short story. Here you have all the characterization, background, and work of a novel compacted into a short story.

17

ROOMMATES

<<<<<<<<<<<<<<<<<<<<<<<<<<<<<<<<<<<<<<<<<<<

SUMMER

THE AUGUST SUN STRUCK IN THROUGH THE
open window and burned on Andrew Rusch's bare legs
until discomfort dragged him awake from the depths of
heavy sleep. Only slowly did he become aware of the heat
and the damp and gritty sheet beneath his body. He
rubbed at his gummed-shut eyelids, then lay there, staring
up at the cracked and stained plaster of the ceiling, only
half awake and experiencing a feeling of dislocation, not
knowing in those first waking moments just where he was,
although he had lived in this room for over seven years.
He yawned and the odd sensation slipped away while he
groped for the watch that he always put on the chair next
to the bed, then he yawned again as he blinked at the
hands mistily seen behind the scratched crystal. Seven . . .
seven o'clock in the morning, and there was a little number
9 in the middle of the square window. Monday the ninth
of August, 1999—and hot as a furnace already, with the
city still imbedded in the heat wave that had baked and
suffocated New York for the past ten days. Andy scratched
at a trickle of perspiration on his side, then moved his legs
out of the patch of sunlight and bunched the pillow up
under his neck. From the other side of the thin partition
that divided the room in half there came a clanking whir
that quickly rose to a high-pitched drone.

"Morning . . ." he shouted over the sound, then began
coughing. Still coughing he reluctantly stood and crossed
the room to draw a glass of water from the wall tank; it

came out in a thin, brownish trickle. He swallowed it, then rapped the dial on the tank with his knuckles and the needle bobbed up and down close to the *Empty* mark. It needed filling, he would have to see to that before he signed in at four o'clock at the precinct. The day had begun.

A full-length mirror with a crack running down it was fixed to the front of the hulking wardrobe and he poked his face close to it, rubbing at his bristly jaw. He would have to shave before he went in. No one should ever look at himself in the morning, naked and revealed, he decided with distaste, frowning at the dead white of his skin and the slight bow to his legs that was usually concealed by his pants. And how did he manage to have ribs that stuck out like those of a starved horse, as well as a growing potbelly—both at the same time? He kneaded the soft flesh and thought that it must be the starchy diet, that and sitting around on his chunk most of the time. But at least the fat wasn't showing on his face. His forehead was a little higher each year, but wasn't too obvious so long as his hair was cropped short. You have just turned 30, he thought to himself, and the wrinkles are already starting around your eyes. And your nose is too big—wasn't it Uncle Brian who always said that was because there was Welsh blood in the family? And your canine teeth are a little too obvious so when you smile you look a bit like a hyena. You're a handsome devil, Andy Rusch, and it's a wonder a girl like Shirl will even look at you, much less kiss you. He scowled at himself, then went to look for a handkerchief to blow his impressive Welsh nose.

There was just a single pair of clean undershorts in the drawer and he pulled them on; that was another thing he had to remember today, to get some washing done. The squealing whine was still coming from the other side of the partition as he pushed through the connecting door.

"You're going to give yourself a coronary, Sol," he told the gray-bearded man who was perched on the wheelless bicycle, pedaling so industriously that perspiration ran down his chest and soaked into the bath towel that he wore tied around his waist.

"Never a coronary," Solomon Kahn gasped out, pumping steadily. "I been doing this every day for so long that my ticker would miss it if I stopped. And no cholesterol in my arteries either since regular flushing with alcohol takes care of that. And no lung cancer since I couldn't afford to smoke even if I wanted to, which I don't. And at the age of 75 no prostatitis because. . . ."

"Sol, please—spare me the horrible details on an empty stomach. Do you have an ice cube to spare?"

"Take two—it's a hot day. And don't leave the door open too long."

Andy opened the small refrigerator that squatted against the wall and quickly took out the plastic container of margarine, then squeezed two ice cubes from the tray into a glass and slammed the door. He filled the glass with water from the wall tank and put it on the table next to the margarine. "Have you eaten yet?" he asked.

"I'll join you, these things should be charged by now."

Sol stopped pedaling and the whine died away to a moan, then vanished. He disconnected the wires from the electrical generator that was geared to the rear axle of the bike, and carefully coiled them up next to the four black automobile storage batteries that were racked on top of the refrigerator. Then, after wiping his hands on his soiled towel sarong, he pulled out one of the bucket seats, salvaged from an ancient 1975 Ford, and sat down across the table from Andy.

"I heard the six o'clock news," he said. "The Eldsters are organizing another protest march today on relief headquarters. That's where you'll see coronaries!"

"I won't, thank God, I'm not on until four and Union Square isn't in our precinct." He opened the breadbox and took out one of the six-inch-square red crackers, then pushed the box over to Sol. He spread margarine thinly on it and took a bite, wrinkling his nose as he chewed. "I think this margarine has turned."

"How can you tell?" Sol grunted, biting into one of the dry crackers. "Anything made from motor oil and whale blubber is turned to begin with."

"Now you begin to sound like a naturist," Andy said,

washing his cracker down with cold water. "There's hardly any flavor at all to the fats made from petrochemicals and you know there aren't any whales left so they can't use blubber—it's just good chlorella oil."

"Whales, plankton, herring oil, it's all the same. Tastes fishy. I'll take mine dry so I don't grow no fins." There was a sudden staccato rapping on the door and he groaned. "Not yet eight o'clock and already they are after you."

"It could be anything," Andy said, starting for the door.

"It could be but it's not, that's the callboy's knock and you know it as well as I do and I bet you dollars to doughnuts that's just who it is. See?" He nodded with gloomy satisfaction when Andy unlocked the door and they saw the skinny, bare-legged messenger standing in the dark hall.

"What do you want, Woody?" Andy asked.

"I don' wan' no-fin," Woody lisped over his bare gums. Though he was in his early twenties he didn't have a tooth in his head. "Lieutenan' says bring, I bring." He handed Andy the message board with his name written on the outside.

Andy turned toward the light and opened it, reading the lieutenant's spiky scrawl on the slate, then took the chalk and scribbled his initials after it and returned it to the messenger. He closed the door behind him and went back to finish his breakfast, frowning in thought.

"Don't look at me that way," Sol said, "I didn't send the message. Am I wrong in guessing it's not the most pleasant of news?"

"It's the Eldsters, they're jamming the Square already and the precinct needs reinforcements."

"But why you? This sounds like a job for the harness bulls."

"Harness bulls! Where do you get that medieval slang? Of course they need patrolmen for the crowd, but there have to be detectives there to spot known agitators, pickpockets, purse-grabbers and the rest. It'll be murder in that park today. I have to check in by nine, so I have enough time to bring up some water first."

Andy dressed slowly in slacks and a loose sport shirt,

then put a pan of water on the windowsill to warm in the
sun. He took the two five-gallon plastic jerry cans, and
when he went out Sol looked up from the TV set, glancing
over the top of his old-fashioned glasses.

"When you bring back the water I'll fix you a drink—
or do you think it is too early?"

"Not the way I feel today, it's not."

The hall was ink black once the door had closed behind
him and he felt his way carefully along the wall to the
stairs, cursing and almost falling when he stumbled over
a heap of refuse someone had thrown there. Two flights
down a window had been knocked through the wall and
enough light came in to show him the way down the last
two flights to the street. After the damp hallway the heat
of Twenty-fifth Street hit him in a musty wave, a stifling
miasma compounded of decay, dirt and unwashed humanity. He had to make his way through the women who
already filled the steps of the building, walking carefully
so that he didn't step on the children who were playing
below. The sidewalk was still in shadow but so jammed
with people that he walked in the street, well away from
the curb to avoid the rubbish and litter banked high there.
Days of heat had softened the tar so that it gave underfoot, then clutched at the soles of his shoes. There was the
usual line leading to the columnar red water point on the
corner of Seventh Avenue, but it broke up with angry
shouts and some waved fists just as he reached it. Still
muttering, the crowd dispersed and Andy saw that the
duty patrolman was locking the steel door.

"What's going on?" Andy asked. "I thought this point
was open until noon?"

The policeman turned, his hand automatically staying
close to his gun until he recognized the detective from his
own precinct. He tilted back his uniform cap and wiped
the sweat from his forehead with the back of his hand.

"Just had the orders from the sergeant, all points closed
for 24 hours. The reservoir level is low because of the
drought, they gotta save water."

"That's a hell of a note," Andy said, looking at the key
still in the lock. "I'm going on duty now and this means

I'm not going to be drinking for a couple of days. . . ."

After a careful look around, the policeman unlocked the door and took one of the jerry cans from Andy. "One of these ought to hold you." He held it under the faucet while it filled, then lowered his voice. "Don't let it out, but the word is that there was another dynamiting job on the aqueduct upstate."

"Those farmers again?"

"It must be. I was on guard duty up there before I came to this precinct and it's rough, they just as soon blow you up with the aqueduct at the same time. Claim the city's stealing their water."

"They've got enough," Andy said, taking the full container. "More than they need. And there are 35 million people here in the city who get damn thirsty."

"Who's arguing?" the cop asked, slamming the door shut again and locking it tight.

Andy pushed his way back through the crowd around the steps and went through to the backyard first. All of the toilets were in use and he had to wait, and when he finally got into one of the cubicles he took the jerry cans with him; one of the kids playing in the pile of rubbish against the fence would be sure to steal them if he left them unguarded.

When he had climbed the dark flights once more and opened the door to the room he heard the clear sound of ice cubes rattling against glass.

"That's Beethoven's Fifth Symphony that you're playing," he said, dropping the containers and falling into a chair.

"It's my favorite tune," Sol said, taking two chilled glasses from the refrigerator and, with the solemnity of a religious ritual, dropped a tiny pearl onion into each. He passed one to Andy, who sipped carefully at the chilled liquid.

"It's when I taste one of these, Sol, that I almost believe you're not crazy after all. Why do they call them Gibsons?"

"A secret lost behind the mists of time. Why is a Stinger a Stinger or a Pink Lady a Pink Lady?"

"I don't know—why? I never tasted any of them."

"I don't know either, but that's the name. Like those green things they serve in the knockjoints, Panamas. Doesn't mean anything, just a name."

"Thanks," Andy said, draining his glass. "The day looks better already."

He went into his room and took his gun and holster from the drawer and clipped it inside the waistband of his pants. His shield was on his key ring where he always kept it and he slipped his notepad in on top of it, then hesitated a moment. It was going to be a long and rough day and anything might happen. He dug his nippers out from under his shirts, then the soft plastic tube filled with shot. It might be needed in the crowd, safer than a gun with all those old people milling about. Not only that, but with the new austerity regulations you had to have a damn good reason for using up any ammunition. He washed as well as he could with the pint of water that had been warming in the sun on the windowsill, then scrubbed his face with the small shard of gray and gritty soap until his whiskers softened a bit. His razor blade was beginning to show obvious nicks along both edges and, as he honed it against the inside of his drinking glass, he thought that it was time to think about getting a new one. Maybe in the fall.

Sol was watering his window box when Andy came out, carefully irrigating the rows of herbs and tiny onions. "Don't take any wooden nickels," he said without looking up from his work. Sol had a million of them, all old. What in the world was a wooden nickel?

The sun was higher now and the heat was mounting in the sealed tar and concrete valley of the street. The band of shade was smaller and the steps were so packed with humanity that he couldn't leave the doorway. He carefully pushed by a tiny, runny-nosed girl dressed only in ragged gray underwear and descended a step. The gaunt women moved aside reluctantly, ignoring him, but the men stared at him with a cold look of hatred stamped across their features that gave them a strangely alike appearance, as though they were all members of the same angry family. Andy threaded his way through the last of them and when he reached the sidewalk he had to step over the outstretched leg of an old man who sprawled there. He looked dead, not asleep, and he might be for all that anyone cared. His foot was bare and filthy and a string tied about his ankle led to a naked baby that was sitting vacantly on the sidewalk chewing on a bent plastic dish. The baby was as dirty as the man and the string was tied about its chest under the pipestem arms because its stomach was swollen and heavy. Was the old man dead? Not that it mattered, the only work he had to do in the world was to act as an anchor for the baby and he could do that job just as well alive or dead.

Out of the room now, well away and unable to talk to Sol until he returned, he realized that once again he had not managed to mention Shirl. It would have been a simple enough thing to do, but he kept forgetting it, avoiding it. Sol was always talking about how horny he always was and how often he used to get laid when he was in the army. He would understand.

They were roommates, that was all. There was nothing else between them. Friends, sure. But bringing a girl in to live wouldn't change that.

So why hadn't he told him?

FALL

"Everybody says this is the coldest October ever, I never seen a colder one. And the rain too, never hard enough to fill the reservoir or anything, but just enough to make you wet so you feel colder. Ain't that right?"

Shirl nodded, hardly listening to the words, but aware by the rising intonation of the woman's voice that a question had been asked. The line moved forward and she shuffled a few steps behind the woman who had been speaking—a shapeless bundle of heavy clothing covered with a torn plastic raincoat, with a cord tied about her middle so that she resembled a lumpy sack. Not that I look much better, Shirl thought, tugging the fold of blanket farther over her head to keep out the persistent drizzle. It wouldn't be much longer now, there were only a few dozen people ahead, but it had taken a lot more time than she thought it would; it was almost dark. A light came on over the tank car, glinting off its black sides and lighting up the slowly falling curtain of rain. The line moved again and the woman ahead of Shirl waddled forward, pulling the child after her, a bundle as wrapped and shapeless as its mother, its face hidden by a knotted scarf, that produced an almost constant whimpering.

"Stop that," the woman said. She turned to Shirl, her puffy face a red lumpiness around the dark opening of her almost toothless mouth. "He's crying because he's been to see the doc, thinks he's sick but it's only the kwash." She held up the child's swollen, ballooning hand. "You can tell when they swell up and get the black spots on the knees. Had to sit two weeks in the Bellevue clinic to see a doc who told me what I knew already. But that's the only way you get him to sign the slip. Got a peanut-butter ration that way. My old man loves the stuff. You live on my block, don't you? I think I seen you there?"

"Twenty-sixth Street," Shirl said, taking the cap off the jerry can and putting it into her coat pocket. She felt chilled through and was sure she was catching a cold.

"That's right, I knew it was you. Stick around and wait for me, we'll walk back together. It's getting late and plenty of punks would like to grab the water, they can always sell it. Mrs. Ramirez in my building, she's a spic but she's all right, you know, her family been in the building since the World War Two, she got a black eye so swole up she can't see through it and two teeth knocked out. Some punk got her with a club and took her water away."

"Yes, I'll wait for you, that's a good idea," Shirl said, suddenly feeling very alone.

"Cards," the patrolman said and she handed him the three Welfare cards, hers, Andy's and Sol's. He held them to the light, then handed them back to her. "Six quarts," he called out to the valve man.

"That's not right," Shirl said.

"Reduced ration today, lady, keep moving, there's a lot of people waiting."

She held out the jerry can and the valve man slipped the end of a large funnel into it and ran in the water. "Next," he called out.

The jerry can gurgled when she walked and was tragically light. She went and stood near the policeman until the woman came up, pulling the child with one hand and in the other carrying a five-gallon kerosene can that seemed almost full. She must have a big family.

"Let's go," the woman said and the child trailed, mewling faintly, at the end of her arm.

As they left the Twelfth Avenue railroad siding it grew darker, the rain soaking up all the failing light. The buildings here were mostly old warehouses and factories with blank solid walls concealing the tenants hidden away inside, the sidewalks wet and empty. The nearest streetlight was a block away. "My husband will give me hell coming home this late," the woman said as they turned the corner. Two figures blocked the sidewalk in front of them.

"Let's have the water," the nearest one said, and the distant light reflected from the knife he held before him.

"No, don't! Please don't!" the woman begged and swung her can of water out behind her, away from them. Shirl huddled against the wall and saw, when they walked forward, that they were just young boys, teen-agers. But they still had a knife.

"The water!" the first one said, jabbing his knife at the woman.

"Take it," she screeched, swinging the can like a weight on the end of her arm. Before the boy could dodge it caught him full in the side of the head, knocking him howling to the ground, the knife flying from his fingers. "You want some too?" she shouted, advancing on the second boy. He was unarmed.

"No, I don't want no trouble," he begged, pulling at the first one's arm, then retreating when she approached. When she bent to pick up the fallen knife, he managed to drag the other boy to his feet and half carry him around the corner. It had only taken a few seconds and all the time Shirl had stood with her back to the wall, trembling with fear.

"They got some surprise," the woman crowed, holding the worn carving knife up to admire it. "I can use this better than they can. Just punks, kids." She was excited and happy. During the entire time she had never released her grip on the child's hand; it was sobbing louder.

There was no more trouble and the woman went with Shirl as far as her door. "Thank you very much," Shirl said. "I don't know what I would have done. . . ."

"That's no trouble," the woman beamed. "You saw what I did to him—and who got the knife now!" She stamped away, hauling the heavy can in one hand, the child in the other. Shirl went in.

"Where have you been?" Andy asked when she pushed open the door. "I was beginning to wonder what had happened to you." It was warm in the room, with a faint odor of fishy smoke, and he and Sol were sitting at the table with drinks in their hands.

"It was the water, the line must have been a block long. They only gave me six quarts, the ration has been cut again." She saw his black look and decided not to tell him about the trouble on the way back. He would be twice as angry then and she didn't want this meal to be spoiled.

"That's really wonderful," Andy said sarcastically. "The ration was already too small—so now they lower it even more. Better get out of those wet things, Shirl, and Sol will pour you a Gibson. His homemade vermouth has ripened and I bought some vodka."

"Drink up," Sol said, handing her the chilled glass. "I made some soup with that ener-G junk, it's the only way it's edible, and it should be just about ready. We'll have that for the first course, before—" He finished the sentence by jerking his head in the direction of the refrigerator.

"What's up?" Andy asked. "A secret?"

"No secret," Shirl said, opening the refrigerator, "just a surprise. I got these today in the market, one for each of us." She took out a plate with three small soylent burgers on it. "They're the new ones, they had them on TV, with the smoky-barbecue flavor."

"They must have cost a fortune," Andy said. "We won't eat for the rest of the month."

"They're not as expensive as all that. Anyway, it was my own money, not the budget money, I used."

"It doesn't make any difference, money is money. We could probably live for a week on what these things cost."

"Soup's on," Sol said, sliding the plates onto the table. Shirl had a lump in her throat so she couldn't say anything; she sat and looked at her plate and tried not to cry.

"I'm sorry," Andy said. "But you know how prices are going up—we have to look ahead. City income tax is higher, 80 percent now, because of the raised Welfare payment, so it's going to be rough going this winter. Don't think I don't appreciate it. . . ."

"If you do, so why don't you shut up right there and eat your soup?" Sol said.

"Keep out of this, Sol," Andy said.

"I'll keep out of it when you keep the fight out of my room. Now come on, a nice meal like this, it shouldn't be spoiled."

Andy started to answer him, then changed his mind. He reached over and took Shirl's hand. "It is going to be a good dinner," he said. "Let's all enjoy it."

"Not that good," Sol said, puckering his mouth over a spoonful of soup. "Wait until you try this stuff. But the burgers will take the taste out of our mouths."

There was silence after that while they spooned up the soup, until Sol started on one of his army stories about New Orleans and it was so impossible they had to laugh, and after that things were better. Sol shared out the rest of the Gibsons while Shirl served the burgers.

"If I was drunk enough this would almost taste like meat," Sol announced, chewing happily.

"They are good," Shirl said. Andy nodded agreement. She finished the burger quickly and soaked up the juice with a scrap of weedcracker, then sipped at her drink. The trouble on the way home with the water already seemed far distant. What was it the woman had said was wrong with the child?

"Do you know what 'kwash' is?" she asked.

Andy shrugged. "Some kind of disease, that's all I know. Why do you ask?"

"There was a woman next to me in line for the water, I was talking to her. She had a little boy with her who was sick with this kwash. I don't think she should have had him out in the rain, sick like that. And I was wondering if it was catching."

"That you can forget about," Sol said. " 'Kwash' is short for 'kwashiorkor.' If, in the interest of good health, you watched the medical programs like I do, or opened a book, you would know all about it. You can't catch it because it's a deficiency disease like beriberi."

"I never heard of that either," Shirl said.

"There's not so much of that, but there's plenty of kwash. It comes from not eating enough protein. They used to have it only in Africa but now they got it right across the whole U.S. Isn't that great? There's no meat around, lentils and soybeans cost too much, so the mamas stuff the kids with weedcrackers and candy, whatever is cheap. . . ."

The light bulb flickered, then went out. Sol felt his way across the room and found a switch in the maze of wiring on top of the refrigerator. A dim bulb lit up, connected to his batteries. "Needs a charge," he said, "but it can wait until morning. You shouldn't exercise after eating, bad for the circulation and digestion."

"I'm sure glad you're here, Doctor," Andy said. "I need some medical advice. I've got this trouble. You see— everything I eat goes to my stomach. . . ."

"Very funny, Mr. Wiseguy. Shirl, I don't see how you put up with this joker."

They all felt better after the meal and they talked for a while, until Sol announced he was turning off the light to save the juice in the batteries. The small bricks of sea coal had burned to ash and the room was growing cold. They said good night and Andy went in first to get his flashlight; their room was even colder than the other.

"I'm going to bed," Shirl said. "I'm not really tired, but it's the only way to keep warm."

Andy flicked the overhead light switch uselessly. "The

current is still off and there are some things I have to do. What is it—a week now since we had any electricity in the evening?"

"Let me get into bed and I'll work the flash for you—will that be all right?"

"It'll have to do."

He opened his notepad on top of the dresser, lay one of the reusable forms next to it, then began copying information into the report. With his left hand he kept a slow and regular squeezing on the flashlight that produced steady illumination. The city was quiet tonight with the people driven from the streets by the cold and the rain; the whir of the tiny generator and the occasional squeak of the stylo on plastic sounded unnaturally loud. There was enough light from the flash for Shirl to get undressed by. She shivered when she took off her outer clothes and quickly pulled on heavy winter pajamas, a much-darned pair of socks she used for sleeping in, then put her heavy sweater on top. The sheets were cold and damp, they hadn't been changed since the water shortage, though she did try to air them out as often as she could. Her cheeks were damp, as damp as the sheets were when she put her fingertips up to touch them, and she realized that she was crying. She tried not to sniffle and bother Andy. He was doing his best, wasn't he? Everything that it was possible to do. Yes, it had been a lot different before she came here, an easy life, good food and a warm room, and her own bodyguard, Tab, when she went out. And all she had to do was sleep with him a couple of times a week. She had hated it, even the touch of his hands, but at least it had been quick. Having Andy in bed was different and good and she wished that he were there right now. She shivered again and wished she could stop crying.

WINTER

New York City trembled on the brink of disaster. Every locked warehouse was a nucleus of dissent, surrounded by crowds who were hungry and afraid and searching for someone to blame. Their anger incited them to riot, and the food riots turned to water riots and then to looting, wherever this was possible. The police fought back, only the thinnest of barriers between angry protest and bloody chaos.

At first nightsticks and weighted clubs stopped the trouble, and when this failed gas dispersed the crowds. The tension grew, since the people who fled only reassembled again in a different place. The solid jets of water from the riot trucks stopped them easily when they tried to break into the Welfare stations, but there were not enough trucks, nor was there more water to be had once they had pumped dry their tanks. The Health Department had forbid the use of river water; it would have been like spraying poison. The little water that was available was badly needed for the fires that were springing up throughout the city. With the streets blocked in many places the fire-fighting equipment could not get through and the trucks were forced to make long detours. Some of the fires were spreading and by noon all of the equipment had been committed and was in use.

The first gun was fired a few minutes past 12 on the morning of December 21st, by a Welfare Department guard who killed a man who had broken open a window of the Tompkins Square food depot and had tried to climb in. This was the first but not the last shot fired—nor was it the last person to be killed.

Flying wire sealed off some of the trouble areas, but there was only a limited supply of it. When it ran out the copters fluttered helplessly over the surging streets and acted as aerial observation posts for the police, finding the places where reserves were sorely needed. It was a fruitless labor because there were no reserves, everyone was in the front line.

After the first conflict nothing else made a strong impression on Andy. For the rest of the day and most of the night, he along with every other policeman in the city was braving violence and giving violence to restore law and order to a city torn by battle. The only rest he had was after he had fallen victim to his own gas and had managed to make his way to the Department of Hospitals ambulance for treatment. An orderly washed out his eyes and gave him a tablet to counteract the gut-tearing nausea. He lay on one of the stretchers inside, clutching his helmet, bombs and club to his chest, while he recovered. The ambulance driver sat on another stretcher by the door, armed with a .30-caliber carbine, to discourage anyone from too great an interest in the ambulance or its valuable surgical contents. Andy would like to have lain there longer, but the cold mist was rolling in through the open doorway, and he began to shiver so hard that his teeth shook together. It was difficult to drag to his feet and climb to the ground; yet once he was moving he felt a little better—and warmer. The attack had been broken up and he moved slowly to join the nearest cluster of blue-coated figures, wrinkling his nose at the foul odor of his clothes.

From this point on, the fatigue never left him and he had memories only of shouting faces, running feet, the sound of shots, screams, the thud of gas grenades, of something unseen that had been thrown at him and hit the back of his hand and raised an immense bruise.

By nightfall it was raining, a cold downpour mixed with sleet, and it was this and exhaustion that drove the people from the streets, not the police. Yet when the crowds were gone the police found that their work was just beginning. Gaping windows and broken doorways had to be guarded until they could be repaired, the injured had to be found and brought in for treatment, while the Fire Department needed aid in halting the countless fires. This went on through the night and at dawn Andy found himself slumped on a bench in the precinct, hearing his name being called off from a list by Lieutenant Grassioli.

"And that's all that can be spared," the lieutenant added. "You men draw rations before you leave and turn in your riot equipment. I want you all back here at eighteen-hundred and I don't want excuses. Our troubles aren't over yet."

Sometime during the night the rain had stopped. The rising sun cast long shadows down the crosstown streets, putting a golden sheen on the wet, black pavement. A burned-out brownstone was still smoking and Andy picked

his way through the charred wreckage that littered the
street in front of it. On the corner of Seventh Avenue
were the crushed wrecks of two pedicabs, already stripped
of any usable parts, and a few feet farther on, the huddled
body of a man. He might be asleep, but when Andy
passed, the upturned face gave violent evidence that the
man was dead. He walked on, ignoring it. The Department of Sanitation would be collecting only corpses today.

The first cavemen were coming out of the subway entrance, blinking at the light. During the summer everyone
laughed at the cavemen—the people whom Welfare had
assigned to living quarters in the stations of the now-
silent subways—but as the cold weather approached, the
laughter was replaced by envy. Perhaps it was filthy down
there, dusty, dark, but there were always a few electric
heaters turned on. They weren't living in luxury, but at
least Welfare didn't let them freeze. Andy turned into
his own block.

Going up the stairs in his building, he trod heavily on
some of the sleepers but was too fatigued to care—or
even notice. He had trouble fumbling his key into the lock
and Sol heard him and came to open it.

"I just made some soup," Sol said. "You timed it perfectly."

Andy pulled the broken remains of some weedcrackers
from his coat pocket and spilled them onto the table.

"Been stealing food?" Sol asked, picking up a piece
and nibbling on it. "I thought no grub was being given
out for two more days?"

"Police ration."

"Only fair. You can't beat up the citizenry on an empty
stomach. I'll throw some of these into the soup, give it
some body. I guess you didn't see TV yesterday so you
wouldn't know about all the fun and games in Congress.
Things are really jumping. . . ."

"Is Shirl awake yet?" Andy asked, shucking out of his
coat and dropping heavily into a chair.

Sol was silent a moment, then he said slowly, "She's not
here."

Andy yawned. "It's pretty early to go out. Why?"

"Not today, Andy." Sol stirred the soup with his back turned. "She went out yesterday, a couple of hours after you did. She's not back yet—"

"You mean she was out all the time during the riots—and last night too? What did you do?" He sat upright, his bone-weariness forgotten.

"What could I do? Go out and get myself trampled to death like the rest of the old fogies? I bet she's all right, she probably saw all the trouble and decided to stay with friends instead of coming back here."

"What friends? What are you talking about? I have to go find her."

"Sit!" Sol ordered. "What can you do out there? Have some soup and get some sleep, that's the best thing you can do. She'll be okay. I know it," he added reluctantly.

"What do you know, Sol?" Andy took him by the shoulders, half turning him from the stove.

"Don't handle the merchandise!" Sol shouted, pushing the hand away. Then, in a quieter voice: "All I know is she just didn't go out of here for nothing, she had a reason. She had her old coat on, but I could see what looked like a real nifty dress underneath. And nylon stockings. A fortune on her legs. And when she said so long I saw she had lots of makeup on."

"Sol—what are you trying to say?"

"I'm not trying—I'm saying. She was dressed for visiting, not for shopping, like she was on the way out to see someone. Her old man, maybe, she could be visiting him."

"Why should she want to see him?"

"You tell me. You two had a fight, didn't you? Maybe she went away for a while to cool off."

"A fight . . . I guess so." Andy dropped back into the chair, squeezing his forehead with his palms. Had it only been last night? No, the night before last. It seemed 100 years since they had had that stupid argument. But they were bickering so much these days. One more fight shouldn't make any difference. He looked up with sudden fear. "She didn't take her things—anything with her?" he asked.

"Just a little bag," Sol said, and put a steaming bowl

on the table in front of Andy. "Eat up. I'll pour one for myself." Then, "She'll be back."

Andy was almost too tired to argue—and what could be said? He spooned the soup automatically, then realized as he tasted it that he was very hungry. He ate with his elbow on the table, his free hand supporting his head.

"You should have heard the speeches in the Senate yesterday," Sol said. "Funniest show on earth. They're trying to push this Emergency Bill through—some emergency, it's only been 100 years in the making—and you should hear them talking all around the little points and not mentioning the big ones." His voice settled into a rich Southern accent. "Faced by dire straits, we propose a survey of all the ee-mense riches of this the greatest ee-luvial basin, the delta, suh, of the mightiest of rivers, the Mississippi. Dikes and drains, suh, science, suh, and you will have here the richest farmlands in the Western World!" Sol blew on his soup angrily. " 'Dikes' is right— another finger in the dike. They've been over this ground a thousand times before. But does anyone mention out loud the sole and only reason for the Emergency Bill? They do not. After all these years they're too chicken to come right out and tell the truth, so they got it hidden away in one of the little riders tacked onto the bottom."

"What are you talking about?" Andy asked, only half listening, still worrying about Shirl.

"Birth control, that's what. They are finally getting around to legalizing clinics that will be open to anyone married or not—and making it a law that all mothers *must* be supplied with birth-control information. Boy, are we going to hear some howling when the blue-noses find out about that—and the Pope will really plotz!"

"Not now, Sol, I'm tired. Did Shirl say anything about when she would be back?"

"Just what I told you. . . ." He stopped and listened to the sound of footsteps coming down the hall. They stopped—and there was a light knocking on the door.

Andy was there first, twisting at the knob, tearing the door open.

"Shirl!" he said. "Are you all right?"

"Yes, sure—I'm fine."

He held her to him, tightly, almost cutting off her breath. "With the riots—I didn't know what to think," he said. "I just came in a little while ago myself. Where have you been? What happened?"

"I just wanted to get out for a while, that's all." She wrinkled her nose. "What's that funny smell?"

He stepped away from her, anger welling up through the fatigue. "I caught some of my own puke gas and heaved up. It's hard to get off. What do you mean that you wanted to get out for a while?"

"Let me get my coat off."

Andy followed her into the other room and closed the door behind them. She was taking a pair of high-heeled shoes out of the bag she carried and putting them into the closet. "Well?" he said.

"Just that, it's not complicated. I was feeling trapped in here, with the shortages and the cold and everything, and never seeing you, and I felt bad about the fight we had. Nothing seemed to be going right. So I thought if I dressed up and went to one of the restaurants where I used to go, just have a cup of koffee or something, I might feel better. A morale booster, you know." She looked up at his cold face, then glanced quickly away.

"Then what happened?" he asked.

"I'm not in the witness box, Andy. Why the accusing tone?"

He turned his back and looked out the window. "I'm not accusing you of anything, but—you were out all night. How do you expect me to feel?"

"Well, you know how bad it was yesterday, I was afraid to come back. I was up at Curley's—"

"The meateasy?"

"Yes, but if you don't eat anything it's not expensive. It's just the food that costs. I met some people I knew and we talked, they were going to a party and invited me and I went along. We were watching the news about the riots on TV and no one wanted to go out, so the party just went on and on." She paused. "That's all."

"All?" An angry question, a dark suspicion.

"That's all," she said, and her voice was now as cold as his.

She turned her back to him and began to pull off her dress, and their words lay like a cold barrier between them. Andy dropped onto the bed and turned his back on her as well so that they were like strangers, even in the tiny room.

SPRING

The funeral drew them together as nothing else had during the cold depths of the winter. It was a raw day, gusting wind and rain, but there was still a feeling that winter was on the way out. But it had been too long a winter for Sol and his cough had turned into a cold, the cold into pneumonia, and what can an old man do in a cold room without drugs in a winter that does not seem to end? Die, that was all, so he had died. They had forgotten their differences during his illness and Shirl had nursed him as best she could, but careful nursing does not cure pneumonia. The funeral had been as brief and cold as the day and in the early darkness they went back to the room. They had not been back half an hour before there was a quick rapping on the door. Shirl gasped.

"The callboy. They can't. You don't have to work to-day."

"Don't worry. Even Grassy wouldn't go back on his word about a thing like this. And besides, that's not the callboy's knock."

"Maybe a friend of Sol's who couldn't get to the funeral."

She went to unlock the door and had to blink into the darkness of the hall for a moment before she recognized the man standing there.

"Tab! It is you, isn't it? Come in, don't stand there. Andy, I told you about Tab my bodyguard. . . ."

"Afternoon, Miss Shirl," Tab said stolidly, staying in the hall. "I'm sorry, but this is no social call. I'm on the job now."

"What is it?" Andy asked, walking over next to Shirl.

"You have to realize I take the work that is offered to me," Tab said. He was unsmiling and gloomy. "I've been in the bodyguard pool since September, just the odd jobs, no regular assignment, we take whatever work we can get. A man turns down a job he goes right back to the end of the list. I have a family to feed. . . ."

"What are you trying to say?" Andy asked. He was aware that someone was standing in the darkness behind Tab and he could tell by the shuffle of feet that there were others out of sight down the hall.

"Don't take no stuff," the man in back of Tab said in an unpleasant nasal voice. He stayed behind the bodyguard where he could not be seen. "I got the law on my side. I paid you. Show him the order!"

"I think I understand now," Andy said. "Get away from the door, Shirl. Come inside, Tab, so we can talk to you."

Tab started forward and the man in the hall tried to follow him. "You don't go in there without me—" he shrilled. His voice was cut off as Andy slammed the door in his face.

"I wish you hadn't done that," Tab said. He was wearing his spike-studded iron knucks, his fist clenched tight around them.

"Relax," Andy said. "I just wanted to talk to you alone first, find out what was going on. He has a squat-order, doesn't he?"

Tab nodded, looking unhappily down at the floor.

"What on earth are you two talking about?" Shirl asked, worriedly glancing back and forth at their set expressions.

Andy didn't answer and Tab turned to her. "A squat-order is issued by the court to anyone who can prove they are really in need of a place to live. They only give so many out, and usually just to people with big families that have had to get out of some other place. With a squat-order you can look around and find a vacant apartment or room or anything like that, and the order is a sort of search warrant. There can be trouble, people don't want to have strangers walking in on them, that kind of thing, so anyone with a squat-order takes along a body-guard. That's where I come in, the party out there in the hall, name of Belicher, hired me."

"But what are you doing here?" Shirl asked, still not understanding.

"Because Belicher is a ghoul, that's why," Andy said bitterly. "He hangs around the morgue looking for bodies."

"That's one way of saying it," Tab answered, holding on to his temper. "He's also a guy with a wife and kids and no place to live, that's another way of looking at it."

There was a sudden hammering on the door and Belicher's complaining voice could be heard outside. Shirl finally realized the significance of Tab's presence, and she gasped. "You're here because you're helping them," she said. "They found out that Sol is dead and they want this room."

Tab could only nod mutely.

"There's still a way out," Andy said. "If we had one of the men here from my precinct, living in here, then these people couldn't get in."

The knocking was louder and Tab took a half step backward toward the door. "If there was somebody here now, that would be okay, but Belicher could probably take the thing to the squat court and get occupancy anyway because he has a family. I'll do what I can to help you—but Belicher, he's still my employer."

"Don't open that door," Andy said sharply. "Not until we have this straightened out."

"I have to—what else can I do?" He straightened up and closed his fist with the knucks on it. "Don't try to stop me, Andy. You're a policeman, you know the law about this."

"Tab, must you?" Shirl asked in a low voice.

He turned to her, eyes filled with unhappiness. "We were good friends once, Shirl, and that's the way I'm going to remember it. But you're not going to think much of me after this because I have to do my job. I have to let them in."

"Go ahead—open the damn door," Andy said bitterly, turning his back and walking over to the window.

The Belichers swarmed in. Mr. Belicher was thin, with a strangely shaped head, almost no chin and just enough intelligence to sign his name to the Welfare application. Mrs. Belicher was the support of the family; from the flabby fat of her body came the children, all seven of them, to swell the Relief allotment on which they survived. Number eight was pushing an extra bulge out of the dough of her flesh; it was really number 11 since three of the younger Belichers had perished through indifference or accident. The largest girl, she must have been all of 12, was carrying the sore-covered infant, which stank abominably and cried continuously. The other children shouted at each other now, released from the silence and tension of the dark hall.

"Oh, looka the nice fridge," Mrs. Belicher said, waddling over and opening the door.

"Don't touch that," Andy said, and Belicher pulled him by the arm.

"I like this room—it's not big, you know, but nice. What's in here?" He started toward the open door in the partition.

"That's my room," Andy said, slamming it shut in his face. "Just keep out of there."

"No need to act like that," Belicher said, sidling away quickly like a dog that has been kicked too often. "I got my rights. The law says I can look wherever I want with a squat-order." He moved farther away as Andy took a step toward him. "Not that I'm doubting your word, mister, I believe you. This room here is fine, got a good table, chairs, bed. . . ."

"Those things belong to me. This is an empty room, and a small one at that. It's not big enough for you and all your family."

"It's big enough, all right. We lived in smaller. . . ."

"Andy—stop them! Look—" Shirl's unhappy cry spun Andy around and he saw that two of the boys had found the packets of herbs that Sol had grown so carefully in his window box, and were tearing them open, thinking that it was food of some kind.

"Put these things down," he shouted, but before he could reach them they had tasted the herbs, then spat them out.

"Burn my mouth!" the bigger boy screamed and sprayed the contents of the packet on the floor. The other boy bounced up and down with excitement and began to do the same thing with the rest of the herbs. They twisted away from Andy and before he could stop them the packets were empty.

As soon as Andy turned away, the younger boy, still excited, climbed on the table—his mud-stained foot wrappings leaving filthy smears—and turned up the TV. Blaring music crashed over the screams of the children and the ineffectual calls of their mother. Tab pulled Belicher away as he opened the wardrobe to see what was inside.

"Get these kids out of here," Andy said, white-faced with rage.

"I got a squat-order, I got rights," Belicher shouted, backing away and waving an imprinted square of plastic.

"I don't care what rights you have," Andy told him, opening the hall door. "We'll talk about that when these brats are outside."

Tab settled it by grabbing the nearest child by the scruff of the neck and pushing it out through the door. "Mr. Rusch is right," he said. "The kids can wait outside while we settle this."

Mrs. Belicher sat down heavily on the bed and closed her eyes, as though all this had nothing to do with her. Mr. Belicher retreated against the wall saying something that no one heard or bothered to listen to. There were some shrill cries and angry sobbing from the hall as the last child was expelled.

Andy looked around and realized that Shirl had gone into their room; he heard the key turn in the lock. "I suppose this is it?" he said, looking steadily at Tab.

The bodyguard shrugged helplessly. "I'm sorry, Andy,

honest to God I am. What else can I do? It's the law, and if they want to stay here, you can't get them out."

"It's the law, it's the law," Belicher echoed tonelessly.

There was nothing Andy could do with his clenched fists and he had to force himself to open them. "Help me carry these things into the other room, will you, Tab?"

"Sure," Tab said, and took the other end of the table. "Try and explain to Shirl about my part in this, will you? I don't think she understands that it's just a job I have to do."

Their footsteps crackled on the dried herbs and seeds that littered the floor and Andy did not answer him.

THIS STORY WAS WRITTEN AS PART of a tribute to a very great man, John W. Campbell.

When John died we all missed him quite deeply. There was a feeling among the people who were both his authors and friends that there should be some sort of tribute. It was decided that a memorial volume would be in order—stories would be written especially for it by the writers who'd worked for John's magazine. A few of us talked about it and it was decided that, since I had edited a volume of John's editorials, I should be the one to edit this book as well.

The book shaped itself easily. I knew that every writer in *Astounding–Analog*'s thirty-three-year history under Campbell's editorship could not be included, so I prepared "A" and "B" lists. On the "A" were the writers whose names would automatically be associated with the magazine—the "Campbell writers," some of whom had published little elsewhere. "B" were the writers who'd written for *ASF* but had also done well in other magazines. I would go down first the "A" list and then the "B" asking authors for stories—and stop when the volume was full.

Very quickly the anthology took on a form

18

255

of its own. Authors wrote stories for series that had become well known in the magazine —many times a story was the last in the series in question. When it came to my turn, I could do no less. Here it is.

THE MOTHBALLED SPACESHIP

$\lll\lll\lll\lll\lll\lll\lll\lll\lll\lll\lll$

"I'LL JUST SWING IN A BIT CLOSER," META said, touching the controls of the Pyrran spacer.

"I wouldn't if I were you," Jason said resignedly, knowing that a note of caution was close to a challenge to a Pyrran.

"Let us not be afraid *this* far away," Kerk said, as Jason had predicted, leaning close to look at the viewscreen. "It is big I'll admit, three kilometers long at least, and probably the last space battleship existing. But it is over five thousand years old and we are two hundred kilometers away from it . . ."

A tiny orange glow winked into brief existence on the distant battleship and at the same instant the Pyrran ship lurched heavily. Red panic lights flared on the control panel.

"How old did you say it was?" Jason asked innocently, and received in return a sizzling look from the now silent Kerk. Meta sent the ship turning away in a wide curve and checked the warning circuitry.

"Port fin severely damaged, hull units out in three areas.

Repairs will have to be made in null-G before we can make a planetfall again."

"Very good. I'm glad we were hit," Jason dinAlt said. "Perhaps now we will exercise enough caution to come out of this alive with the promised five hundred million credits. So set us on a course to the fleet commander so we can find out all the grisly details they forgot to tell us when we arranged this job by jump-space communication."

Admiral Djukich, the commander of the Earth forces, was a small man who appeared even smaller before the glowering strength of the Pyrran personality, shrinking back when Kerk leaned over his desk towards him, speaking coldly.

"We can leave and the Rim Hordes will sweep through this system and that will be the end of you."

"No, it will not happen. We have the resources. We can build a fleet, buy ships, but it will be a long and tedious task. Far easier to use this Empire battleship."

"Easy?" Jason asked, raising one eyebrow. "How many have been killed attempting to enter it?"

"Well, easy is not perhaps the correct word. There are difficulties, certain problems . . . forty-seven people in all."

"Is that why you sent the message to Felicity?" Jason asked.

"Yes, assuredly. Our heavy-metals industry has been purchasing from your planet, they heard of the Pyrrans, how less than a hundred of you conquered an entire world. We thought we would ask you to undertake this task of entering the ship."

"You were a little unclear as to who was aboard the ship and preventing anyone else from coming near."

"Yes, well, that is what you might call the heart of our little problem. There's no one aboard . . ." His smile had a definite artificial quality as the Pyrrans leaned close. "Please, let me explain. This planet was once one of the most important under the old Empire. Although at least eleven other worlds claim themselves as the first home of mankind, we of Earth are much more certain that we are the original. This battleship seems proof enough. When the Fourth War of Galactic Expansion was over it was mothballed here and has remained so ever since, unneeded until this moment."

Kerk snorted with disbelief. "I will not believe that an unmanned, mothballed ship five millenia old has killed forty-seven people."

"Well I will," Jason said. "And so will you as soon as you give it a little thought. Three kilometers of almost indestructible fighting ship propelled by the largest engines ever manufactured— which means the largest spaceship atomic generators as well. And of course the largest guns, the most advanced defensive and offensive weaponry ever conceived with secondary batteries, parallel fail-safe circuitry, battle computers—ahh, you're smiling at last. A Pyrran dream of heaven— the most destructive single weapon ever conceived. What a pleasure to board a thing like this, to enter the control room, to *be* in control."

Kerk and Meta were grinning happily, eyes misty, nodding their heads in total agreement. Then the smiles faded as he went on.

"But this ship has now been mothballed. Everything shut down and preserved for an emergency—everything that is except the power plant and the ship's armament. Part of the mothballing was obviously provision for the ship's computer to be alert and to guard the ship against meteorites and any other chance encounters in space. In particular anyone who felt they needed a spare battleship. We were warned off with a single shot. I don't doubt that it could have blasted us out of space just as easily. If this ship were manned and on the defensive, then nothing could be done about getting near it, much less entering. But this is not the case. We must outthink a computer, a machine, and while it won't be easy it should be possible." He turned and smiled at Admiral Djukich. "We'll take the job. The price has doubled. It will be one billion credits."

"Impossible! The sum is too great, the budget won't allow . . ."

"Rim Hordes, coming closer, bent on rapine and destruction. To stop them you order some spacers from the shipyard, schedules are late, they don't arrive on time, the Horde fleet descends. They break down this door and here, right in this office, blood . . ."

"Stop!" the Admiral gasped weakly, his face blanched white. A desk commander who had never seen action—as Jason had guessed. "The contract is yours, but you have a deadline, thirty days. One minute after that and you don't get a deci of a credit. Do you agree?"

Jason looked up at Kerk and Meta, who, with instant warrior's decision, made their minds up, nodding at the same time.

"Done," he said. "But the billion is free and clear. We'll need supplies, aid from your space navy, material and perhaps men as well to back us up. You will supply what we need."

"It could be expensive," Admiral Djukich groaned, chewing at his lower lip. "Blood . . ." Jason whispered and the Admiral broke into a fine sweat as he reluctantly agreed. "I'll have the papers drawn up. When can you begin?"

"We've begun. Shake hands on it and we'll sign later." He pumped the Admiral's weak hand enthusiastically. "Now I don't suppose you have anything like a manual that tells us how to get into the ship?"

"If we had that, we wouldn't have called you here. We have gone to the archives and found nothing. All the facts we did discover are on record and available to you for what they are worth."

"Not much if you killed forty-seven volunteers. Five thousand years is a long time and even the most efficient bureaucracy loses things over that kind of distance. And, of course, the one thing you cannot mothball are instructions on how to un-mothball a ship. But we will find a way, Pyrrans never quit, never. If you will have the records sent to our quarters, my colleagues and I will now withdraw and make our plans for the job. We shall beat your deadline."

"How?" Kerk asked as soon as the door of their apartment had closed behind them.

"I haven't the slightest idea," Jason admitted, smiling happily at their cold scowls. "Now let us pour some drinks and put our thinking caps on. This is a job that may end up needing brute force but will have to begin with man's intellectual superiority over the machines he has invented. I'll take a large one with ice if you are pouring, darling."

"Serve yourself," Meta snapped. "If you had no idea how we were to proceed, why did you accept?"

Glass rattled against glass and strong beverage gurgled. Jason sighed. "I accepted because it is a chance for us to get some ready cash, which the budget is badly in need of. If we can't crack into the damn thing, then all we have lost is thirty days of our time." He drank and remembered the hard-learned lesson that reasoned argument was usually a waste of time with Pyrrans and that there were better ways to resolve a situation quickly. "You people aren't scared of this ship are you?"

He smiled angelically at their scowls of hatred, the sudden tensing of hard muscles, the whine of the power holsters as their guns slipped towards their hands, then slid back out of sight.

"Let us get started," Kerk said. "We are wasting time and every second counts. What do we do first?"

"Go through the records, find out everything we can about a ship like this, then find a way in."

"I fail to see what throwing rocks at that ship can do," Meta said. "We know already that it destroys them before they get close. It is a waste of time. And now you want to waste food as well, all those animal carcasses . . ."

"Meta, sweet, shut up I'm hinting. There is method to the apparent madness. The navy command ship is out there with radars beeping happily, keeping a record of every shot fired, how close the target was before it was hit, what weapon fired the shot and so forth. There are thirty spacers throwing spacial debris at the battleship in a steady stream. This is *not* the usual thing that happens to a mothballed vessel and it can only have interesting results. Now, in addition to the stone throwing, we are going to launch these sides of beef at our target, each space-going load of steak to be wrapped with twenty kilos of armlite plastic. They are being launched on different trajectories with different speeds, and if any one of them gets through to the ship, we will know that a man in a plastic spacesuit made of the same material will get through as well. Now if all that isn't enough burden on the ship's computer, a good-sized planetoid is on its way now in an orbit aimed right at our mothballed friend out there. The computer will either have to blow it out of space, which will take a good deal of energy—if it is possible at all—or fire up the engines or something. *Anything* it does will give us information, and any information will give us a handle to grab the problem with."

"First side of beef on the way," Kerk announced from the controls, where he was stationed. "I cut some steaks off while we were loading them, have them for lunch. We have a freezerful now. Prime cuts only from every carcass, maybe a kilo each, won't affect the experiment."

"You're turning into a crook in your old age," Jason said.

"I learned everything I know from you. There goes the first one." He pointed to a tiny blip of fire on the screen. "Flare powder on each, blows up when they hit. Another one. They're getting closer than the rocks—but they're not getting through."

Jason shrugged. "Back to the drawing board. Let's have the steaks and a bottle of wine. We have about two hours before the planetoid is due and that is an event we want to watch."

The expected results were anticlimactic to say the least. Millions of tons of solid rock, put into collision orbit at great expense as Admiral Djukich was fond of reminding them, soared majestically in from the black depths of space. The battleship's radar pinged busily and, as soon as the computer had calculated the course, the main engines fired briefly so that the planetoid flashed by the ship's stern and continued on into interstellar space.

"Very dramatic," Meta said in her coldest voice.

"We gained information!" Jason was on the defensive. "We know the engines are still in good shape and can be activated at a moment's notice."

"And of what possible use is that information?" Kerk asked.

"Well, you never know, might come in handy . . ."

"Communication control to Pyrrus one. Can you read me?"

Jason was at the radio instantly, flicking it on. "This is Pyrrus one. What is your message?"

"We have received a signal from the battleship on the 183.4 wavelength. Message is as follows. Nederuebla al navigacio centro. Kroniku ci tio sangon . . ."

"I cannot understand it," Meta said.

"It's Esperanto, the old Empire language. The ship simply sent a change of course instruction to navigation control. And we know its name now, the *Indestructible*."

"Is this important?"

"Is it!" Jason yipped with joy as he set the new wavelength into the communication controls. "Once you get someone to talk to you you have them half sold. Ask any salesman. Now absolute silence, if you please, while I practice my best and most military Esperanto." He drained his wine glass, cleared his throat and turned the radio on.

"Hello *Indestructible,* this is Fleet Headquarters. Explain unauthorized course change."

"Course change authorized by instructions 590–L to avoid destruction."

"Your new course is a navigational hazard. Return to old course."

Silent seconds went by as they watched the screen—then the purple glow of a thrust drive illuminated the battleship's bow.

"You did it!" Meta said happily, giving Jason a loving

squeeze that half crushed his rib cage. "It's taking orders from you. Now tell it to let us in."

"I don't think it is going to be that easy—so let me sneak up on the topic in a roundabout way." He spoke Esperanto to the computer again.

"Course change satisfactory. State reasons for recent heavy expenditure of energy."

"Meteor shower. All meteors on collision orbit were destroyed."

"It is reported that your secondary missile batteries were used. Is this report correct?"

"It is correct."

"Your reserves of ammunition will be low. Resupply will be sent."

"Resupply not needed. Reserves above resupply level."

"Argumentative for a computer, isn't it?" Jason said, his hand over the microphone. "But I shall pull rank and see if that works."

"Headquarters overrides your resupply decision. Resupply vessel will arrive your cargo port in seventeen hours. Confirm."

"Confirmed. Resupply vessel must supply override mothball signal before entering two-hundred kilometer zone."

"Affirmative, signal will be sent. What is current signal?"

There was no instant answer—and Jason raised crossed fingers as the silence went on for almost two seconds.

"Negative. Information cannot be supplied."

"Prepare for memory check of override mothball signal. This is a radio signal only?"

"Affirmative."

"This is a spoken sentence."

"Negative."

"This is a coded signal."

"Affirmative."

"Pour me a drink," Jason said with the microphone off. "This playing twenty questions may take some time."

It did. But patient working around the subject supplied,

bit by bit, the needed information. Jason turned off the radio and passed over the scribbled sheet.

"This is something at least. The code signal is a ten-digit number. If we send the correct number, all the mothballing activity stops instantly and the ship is under our control."

"And the money is ours," Meta said. "Can our computer be programmed to send a series of numbers until it hits on the right one?"

"It can—and just the same thought crossed my mind. The *Indestructible* thinks that we are running a communications check and tells me that it can accept up to seven hundred signals a second for repeat and verification. Our computer will read the returned signal and send an affirmative answer to each one. But of course all the signals will be going through the discrimination circuits and if the correct signal is sent the mothball defenses will be turned off."

"That seems like an obvious trick that would not fool a five-year-old," Kerk said.

"Never underestimate the stupidity of a computer. You forget that it is a machine with zero imagination. Now let me see if this will do us any good." He punched keys rapidly, then muttered a curse and kicked the console. "No good. We will have to run nine to the tenth-power numbers and, at seven hundred a second, it will take us about five months to do them all."

"And we have just three weeks left."

"I can still read a calendar, thank you, Meta. But we'll have to try in any case. Send alternate numbers from one up and counting from 9,999,999,999 back down. Then we'll get the navy code department to give us all their signals to send as well; one of them might fit. The odds are still about five to one against hitting the right combination, but that is better than no odds at all. And we'll keep working to see what else we can think of."

The navy sent over a small man named Shrenkly, who brought a large case of records. He was head of the code department, and a cipher and puzzle enthusiast as well.

This was the greatest challenge of his long and undistinguished career and he hurled himself into it.

"Wonderful opportunity, wonderful. The ascending and descending series are going out steadily. In the meantime I am taping permutations and substitutions of signals which will . . ."

"That's fine, keep at it," Jason said, smiling enthusiastically and patting the man on the back. "I'll get a report from you later but right now we have a meeting to attend. Kerk, Meta, time to go."

"What meeting?" Meta asked as he tried to get her through the door.

"The meeting I just made up to get away from that bore," he said when he finally got her into the corridor. "Let him do his job while we see if we can find another way in."

"I think what he has to say is very interesting."

"Fine. You talk to him—but not while I am around. Let us now spur our brains into action and see what we can come up with."

What they came up with was a number of ideas of varying quality and uniform record of failure. There was the miniature flying robot fiasco where smaller and smaller robots were sent and blasted out of existence, right down to the smallest about the size of a small coin. Obsessed by miniaturization they constructed a flying eye apparatus no larger than the head of a pin that dragged a threadlike control wire after it that also supplied current for the infinitesimal ion drive. This sparked and sizzled its way to within fifteen kilometers of the *Indestructible* before the all-seeing sensors detected it and neatly blasted it out of existence with a single shot. There were other suggestions and brilliant plans, but none of them worked out in practice. The great ship floated serenely in space reading seven-hundred numbers a second and, in its spare time, blowing into fine dust any object that came near it. Each attempt took time and the days drifted by steadily. Jason was beginning to have a chronic headache and had difficulty sleeping. The problem seemed insoluble.

He was feeding figures about destruction distances into the computer when Meta looked in on him.

"I'll be with Shrenkly if you need me," she said.

"Wonderful news."

"He taught me about frequency tables yesterday and today he is going to start me on simple substitution ciphers."

"How thrilling."

"Well it *is*—to me. I've never done anything like this before. And it has some value, we are sending signals and one of them could be the correct one. It certainly is accomplishing more than you are with all your flying rocks. With two days to go, too."

She stalked out and slammed the door and Jason slumped with fatigue, aware that failure was hovering close. He was pouring himself a large glass of Old Fatigue Killer when Kerk came in.

"Two days to go," Kerk said.

"Thanks. I didn't know until you told me. I know that a Pyrran never gives up, but I am getting the sneaking suspicion that we are licked."

"We are not beaten yet. We can fight."

"A very Pyrran answer—but it won't work this time. We just can't barge in there in battle armor and shoot the place up."

"Why not? Small arms fire would just bounce off us as well as the low-power rays. All we have to do is dodge the big stuff and bull through."

"That's all! Do you have any idea how we are going to arrange that?"

"No. But you will figure something out. But you better hurry."

"I know, two days. I suppose it's easier to die than admit failure. We suit up, fly at the battleship behind a fleet of rocks that are blasted by the heavy stuff. Then we tell the enemy discrimination circuits that we are not armored spacesuits at all, but just a couple of jettisoned plastic beer barrels that they can shoot up with the small caliber stuff. Which then bounces off us like hail and we land and get inside and get a billion credits and live happily ever after."

"That's the sort of thing. I'll go get the suits ready."

"Before you do that just consider one thing in this preposterous plan. How do we tell the discrimination circuitry . . ."

Jason's voice ran down in mid-sentence and his eyes opened wide—then he clapped Kerk on the back. Heavily too, he was so excited, but the Pyrran seemed completely unaware of the blow.

"That's it, that's how we do it!" Jason chortled, rushing to the computer console. Kerk waited patiently while Jason fed in figures and muttered over the tapes of information. The answer was not long in coming.

"Here it is!" Jason held up a reel of tape. "The plan of attack—and it is going to work. It is just a matter of remembering that the computer on that battleship is just a big dumb adding machine that counts on its fingers, but very fast. It *always* performs in the same manner because it is programmed to do so. So here is what happens. Because of the main-drive tubes the area with the least concentration of fire power is dead astern. Only one-hundred and fourteen gun turrets can be trained that way. Their slew time varies—that is the time it takes a turret to rotate one hundred and eighty degrees in azimuth. The small ones do it in less than a second, the main batteries need six seconds. This is one factor. Other factors are which targets get that kind of attention. Fastest-moving rocks get blasted first, even if they are farther away than a larger, slower-moving target. There are other factors like rate of fire, angle of depression of guns and so forth. Our computer has chomped everything up and come up with *this!*"

"What does it reveal?"

"That we can make it. We will be in the center of a circular disc of flying rocks that will be aimed at the rear of the *Indestructible*. There will be a lot of rock, enough to keep all the guns busy that can bear on the spot. Our suits will be half the size of the smallest boulder. We will all be going at the same speed, in the same direction, so we should get the small caliber stuff. Now, another cloud of rock, real heavy stuff, will converge on the stern of the ship from a ninety-degree angle, but it will not hit the two-hundred kilometer limit until after the guns start blasting at us. The computer will track it and as soon as our wave is blasted will slew the big guns to get rid of the heavy stuff. As soon as these fire we *accelerate* towards the stern tubes. We will then become prime targets but, before the big guns can slew back, we should be inside the tubes."

"It sounds possible. What is the time gap between the instant wo reach the tubes and the earliest the guns can fire?"

"We leave their cone of fire exactly six-tenths of a second before they can blast us."

"Plenty of time. Let us go."

Jason held up his hand. "Just one thing. I'm game if you are. We carry cutting equipment and weapons. Once inside the ship there should not be too many problems. But it is not a piece of cake by any means. The two of us go. But we don't tell Meta—and she stays here."

"Three have a better chance than two to get through."

"And two have a better chance than one. I'm not going unless you agree."

"Agreed. Set the plan up."

Meta was busy with her new-found interest in codes and ciphers; it was a perfect time. The Earth navy ships were well trained in precision rock throwing—as well as being completely bored by it. They let the computers do most of the work. While the preparations were being made Kerk and Jason suited up in the combat suits, more tanks than suits, heavy with armor and slung about with weapons. Kerk attached the special equipment they would need while Jason shortcircuited the airlock indicator so Meta, in the control room, would not know they had left the ship. Silently they slipped out.

No matter how many times you do it, no matter how you prepare yourself mentally, the sensation of floating free in space is not an enjoyable one. It is easy to lose orientation, to have the sensation that all directions are up—or down—and Jason was more than slightly glad of the accompanying bulk of the Pyrran.

"Operation has begun."

The voice crackled in their earphones, then they were too busy to be concerned about anything else. The computer informed them that the wall of giant boulders was sweeping towards them, they could see nothing themselves, and gave them instructions to pull aside. Then the things were suddenly there, floating ponderously by, already shrinking into the distance as the jets fired on the spacesuits. Again following instructions they accelerated to the correct, moving spot in space, and fitted themselves into the gap in the center of the floating rock field. They had to juggle their jets until they had the same velocity as the boulders, then, power cut off, they floated free.

"Do you remember the instructions?" Jason asked.

"Perfectly."

"Well, let me run through them again for the sake of my morale if you don't mind." The battleship was visible now, far ahead, like a tiny splinter in space. "We do nothing at all to draw attention as we come in. There will be plenty of activity around us but we don't use power except in an extreme emergency. And we get hit by small caliber fire—the best thing that can happen to us because it means the big stuff is firing at something else. Meanwhile the other attack of flying rocks will be coming in from our flank. We won't see them—but our computer will. It is monitoring the battleship as well and the instant the big guns fire on the second wave it will send the signal *go*. Then we go. Full power on the rockets towards the main drive tube. When our suit radar says we are eleven-hundred meters from the ship we put on full reverse thrust because we will be inside the guns. See you at the bottom of the tube."

"What if the computer fires the tube to clear us out?"

"I have been trying not to think about that. We can

only hope that it is not programmed for such a complex action and that its logic circuits will not come up with the answer . . ."

Space around them exploded with searing light. Their helmet visors darkened automatically, but the explosions could still be clearly seen, they were so intense. And silent. A rock the size of a small house burned and vaporized soundlessly not a hundred meters from Jason and he cringed inside the suit. The silent destruction continued—but the silence was suddenly shattered by deafening explosions and his suit vibrated with the impact.

He was being hit! Even though he expected it, wanted it, the jarring was intense and unbelievably loud. Then it stopped, as suddenly as it had begun and, dimly, he heard a weak voice say *Go.*

"Blast, Kerk, blast!" he shouted as he jammed on full power.

The suit kicked him hard, numbing him, slowing his fingers as they grappled for the intensity control on the helmet, turning it off. He winced against the glare of burning matter but could just make out the disc of the spaceship's stern before him, the main tube staring like a great black eye. It grew, quickly, until it filled space and the sudden red glow of the preset radar said he had passed the eleven-hundred-meter mark. The guns couldn't touch him here—but he could crash into the battleship and demolish himself. Then the full blast of the retrojets hit him, slamming him against the suit, stunning him again, making control almost impossible. The dark opening blossomed before him, filling his vision, blacking out everything else.

He was inside it, the pressure lessening as the landing circuits took over and paced his rate of descent. Had Kerk made it? He had stopped, floating free, when something plummeted from above, glanced off him and crashed heavily into the end of the tube.

"Kerk!"

Jason grabbed the limp figure as it rebounded after

the tremendous impact, grappled it and turned his lights on it. "Kerk!" No answer. Dead?

"Landed . . . faster than I intended."

"You did indeed. But we're here. Now let's get to work before the computer decides to burn us out."

Spurred by this danger they unshipped the molecular unbinder torch, the only thing that would affect the tough tube liners, and worked a circular line on the wall just above the injectors. It took almost two minutes of painstaking work to slowly cut the opening and every second of the time they waited for the tube to fire.

It did not. The circle was completed and Kerk put his shoulder to it and fired his jets. The plug of metal and the Pyrran instantly vanished from sight—and Jason dived in right behind him, into the immense, brightly lit engine room. Made suddenly brighter by a flare of light behind him. Jason spun about just in time to see the flames cut off, the flames leaping from the hole they had just cut. The end of a microsecond blast.

"A smart computer," he said weakly. "Smart indeed."

Kerk had ignored the blast and dived into a control room to one side. Jason followed him—and met him as he emerged with a large chart in a twisted metal frame.

"Diagram of the ship. Tore it from the wall. Central control this way. Go."

"All right, all right," Jason muttered, working to keep pace with the Pyrran's hurtling form. This was what Pyrrans did best and it was an effort to keep up the pace. "Repair robots," he said when they entered a long corridor. "They won't bother us . . ."

Before he had finished speaking the two robots had raised their welding torches and rushed to the attack. But, even as they moved, Kerk's gun blasted twice and they exploded into junk.

"Good computer," Kerk said. "Turn anything against us. Stay alert and cover my back."

There was no more time for talking. They changed their course often since it was obvious that they were heading towards central control. Every machine along the way wanted to kill them. Housekeeping robots rushed at them with brooms, TV screens exploded as they passed, airtight doors tried to close on them, floors were electrified if they were touched. It was a battle, but really a one-sided one as long as they stayed alert. Their suits were invulnerable to small-scale attack, insulated from electricity. And Pyrrans are the best fighters in the galaxy. In the end they came to the door marked CENTRA KONTROLO and Kerk offhandedly blasted it down and floated through. The lights were lit, the room and the controls were spotlessly clean.

"We've done it," Jason said, cracking his helmet and smelling the cool air. "One billion credits. We've licked this bucket of bolts . . ."

"THIS IS A FINAL WARNING!" the voice boomed and their guns nosed about for the source before they realized it was just a recording. "THIS BATTLESHIP HAS BEEN ENTERED BY ILLEGAL MEANS. YOU ARE ORDERED TO LEAVE WITHIN THE NEXT FIFTEEN SECONDS OR THE ENTIRE SHIP WILL BE DESTROYED. CHARGES HAVE BEEN SET TO ASSURE THAT THIS BATTLESHIP DOES NOT FALL INTO ENEMY HANDS. FOURTEEN . . ."

"We can't get out in time!" Jason shouted.

"Shoot up the controls!"

"No! The destruction controls won't be here."

"TWELVE."

"What can we do?"

"Nothing! Absolutely nothing at all . . ."

"EIGHT."

They looked at each other wordlessly. Jason put out his armored hand and Kerk touched it with his own.

"SEVEN."

"Well, goodby," Jason said, and tried to smile.

"FOUR . . . errrk. THREE . . ."

There was silence, then the mechanical voice spoke again, a different voice.

"De-mothballing activated. Defenses disarmed. Am awaiting instructions."

"What . . . happened?" Jason asked.

"De-mothballing signal received. Am awaiting instructions."

"Just in time," Jason said, swallowing with some difficulty. "Just in time."

"You should not have gone without me," Meta said. "I shall never forgive you."

"I couldn't take you," Jason said. "I wouldn't have gone myself if you had insisted. You are worth more than a billion credits to me."

"That's the nicest thing you ever said to me." She smiled now and kissed him while Kerk looked on with great disinterest.

"When you are through would you tell us what happened," Kerk said. "The computer hit the right number?"

"Not at all. I did it."

She smiled into the shocked silence, then kissed Jason again.

"I told you how interested I am now in codes and ciphers. Simply thrilling, with wartime applications too, of course. Well, Shrenkly told me about substitution ciphers and I tried one, the most simple. Where the letter *A* is one, *B* is two and so forth. And I tried to put a word into this cipher and I did, but it came out 81122021, but that was two numbers short. Then Shrenkly told me that there must be two digits for each letter or there would be transcription problems, like you have to use 01 for *A* instead of just the number 1. So I added a zero to the two one-digit numbers, and that made ten digits, so for fun I fed the number into the computer and it was sent and that was that."

"The jackpot with your first number—with your first try?" Jason asked hollowly. "Wasn't that pretty lucky?"

"Not really. You know military people don't have much imagination, you've told me that a thousand times at least, so I took the simplest possible, looked it up in the Esperanto dictionary . . ."

"Haltu?"

"That's right, encoded it and sent it and that was that."

"And just what does the word mean?" Kerk asked.

"Stop," Jason said, "just plain *stop*."

"I would have done the same thing myself," Kerk said, nodding in agreement. "Let us collect the money and go home."

I HAVE ALWAYS DEPLORED THE LACK of any great tradition of sternly working-class science fiction. Not that I would really like to read very much of it, but I feel that every ecological niche must be filled. Beginning with Wells, almost all of the s-f writers have been middle class, which means that the heroes of s-f have the same status in life as their creators. Of course there have been heroes who became emperors of galactic empires or who ran feudal planets. But aren't those also middle-class dreams and aspirations?

What about the neglected working man? We take working-class money quickly enough when we sell our magazines—but do we ever give the working-class guy a break at the hero business? I mentioned this to that other serious sociologist, Brian Aldiss, who nodded in solemn agreement.

"Why should there not be a story about a sewer cleaner who saves the world, just for a change?" I asked.

He gripped me firmly by the shoulder and looked me straight in the eye.

"There should be," he said. "And you are just the person to write it."

So I did.

19

276

AN HONEST DAY'S WORK

<<<<<<<<<<<<<<<<<<<<<<<<<<<<<<<<<<<<<<<<<

"I DO MY JOB, THAT'S ALL. AND THAT'S ALL
that anyone can expect." Jerry's jaw set hard with these
words, set as firmly as his voice as he bit deep into the
scarred stem of the old pipe.

"I know that, Mr. Cruncher," the Lieutenant said. "No
one is asking you to do anything more than that, or to do
anything wrong." He was dusty and one of the pocket
flaps had been torn off his uniform. There was a wild look
in his eye and he had a tendency to talk too fast. "We
tracked you down through BuRecCent and it wasn't easy,
there were good men lost . . ." His voice started to rise
and he drew himself up with an effort. "We would like
your cooperation if we could get it."

"Not the sort of thing I like to do. It could lead to
trouble."

The trouble was that no one expected it, or rather the
people who expected it had expected something altogether
different and had made their plans accordingly and fed
them to the computer, which had drawn up programs
covering all possible variations of the original. However
the Betelgeuseans had a completely different plan in mind
so they therefore succeeded far beyond what was possibly
their own wildest dreams. The trade station they had set

up in Tycho crater on the Moon was just that, a trade station, and had nothing to do at all with the events that followed. Records of the Disaster are confused, as well they might be under the circumstances, and the number of aliens involved in the first phase of the invasion was certainly only a fraction of the exaggerated figures that were being tossed around by excited newsmen, or worried military personnel who felt that there *must* be that number of attacking aliens to wreak the damage that was done. The chances are that there were no more than two, three maximum, ships involved, a few hundred Betelgeuseans at the most. A few hundred to subjugate an entire planet —and they came within a hair of succeeding.

"Colonel, this is Mr. Cruncher, who has volunteered . . ."

"A *civilian!* Will you get him the hell out of here and blindfold him first, you unutterable fool. This headquarters is double-red-zed top security . . ."

"Sir, the security doesn't matter any more. All of our communications are shut down, we're sealed off from the troops."

"Quiet, you fool!" The Colonel raised his clenched fists, his skin flushing, a wild light in his eyes. He still did not want to believe what had happened, possibly could not believe. The Lieutenant was younger, a reserve officer; as much as he disliked it he could face the facts.

"Colonel, you must believe me. The situation is desperate, and desperate times call for desperate solutions . . ."

"*Sergeant!* Take this lieutenant and this civilian to the target range and shoot them for violating security during an emergency."

"Colonel, please . . ."

"Sergeant, that is an *order!*"

The Sergeant, who was only four months short of retirement and had a pot belly to prove it, looked from one officer to the other. He was reluctant to make a decision but he had to. He finally rose and went to the toilet, locking the door behind him. The Colonel, who had been following his movements in eye-bulging silence, gasped, his face a bright scarlet, and groped for his sidearm. Even as he drew it from the holster he gurgled and fell face first upon the desk, then slid slowly to the floor.

"Medic!" the Lieutenant shouted and ran and opened the Colonel's collar. The medic took one look and shook his head gloomily. "The big one. He's had it. Always had a dicey ticker."

The Sergeant came out of the toilet and helped the Lieutenant to pull a gas cape over the corpse. Jerry Cruncher stood to one side and looked on in silence, sucking on his pipe.

"Please, Mr. Cruncher," the Lieutenant said pleadingly, "you must help us. You're our last hope now."

Now when we look back at Black Sunday when the Disaster began we can marvel at the simplicity of the Betelgeusean plan and understand why it came within a hair's breadth of succeeding. Our armies and spaceborne tanks were poised and waiting, all instruments and attention firmly fixed on the massive bulk of the "so-called" trade station, which was, indeed, just a trade station. On Earth a complex spiderweb of communications networks linked together the host of defenders, a multilevel net of radio and laser links, buried coaxial cables and land lines, microwave and heliograph connections. It was foolproof and unjammable and perfect in every way except for the fact that all global communications were channeled through the two substations and ComCent in Global City. These three stations, wonderfully efficient, handled all the communications with the armed forces on Earth, below the ground, on the Moon and in space.

They were knocked out. Betelgeusean commando squads in field armor dropped one null-G onto each center and the battle could not have lasted more than half an hour. When it was over the three communications centers had been taken and the war was lost before it began. Headquarters were cut off from units, individual units from each other, tanks from tank commanders, spaceships from their bases. Radar central on the far side of the Moon very quickly discovered the blips of the invasion fleet swooping in from beyond Saturn. But there was no way they could tell anyone about it.

"I have to ask my supervisor about it," Jerry Cruncher said, nodding solemnly at the thought. "This being my day off and all. And taking unauthorized people into the tunnels. Can't say he's going to like it much."

"Mr. Cruncher," the Lieutenant said through tight-clamped teeth. "In case you have not heard there is a war on. You have just seen a man die because of this war. You cannot call your supervisor because the military override has rendered the civilian visiphone network inoperable."

"Can't say I like that."

"None of us do. That is why we need your help. The enemy aliens have taken our communication centers and they must be recaptured. We have contacted the nearest combat units by messenger and they are attempting to retake the centers, but they are virtually impregnable."

"They are? How did those Beetlejuicians capture them then?"

"Well, yes, it is Sunday, you know, minimum personnel, at 0800 hours the church coaches were leaving, the gates were open . . ."

"Caught you with your pants down, hey?" A wet suck on his pipe told the world what Jerry Cruncher felt about that kind of efficiency. "So your lot is out and you want back in. So why bother a working man at home on a Sunday?"

"Because, Mr. Cruncher, war does not recognize days of the week. And you are the oldest employee of Cit-SubMaint and probably the only man who can answer this question. Our communication centers have their own standby power sources, but they normally use city power. And the land lines and cables go out underground. Now, think carefully before you answer, can we get into these centers from underground? Particularly into ComCent?"

"Where is it?" He tamped down the glowing tobacco

with a calloused thumb, then sucked in the gray smoke happily.

"At the junction of 18th Way and Wiggan Road."

"So *that's* why there are so many cables in 104–BpL."

"*Can* we get into it!?"

In the hushed silence that followed the burble of Jerry Cruncher's pipe could be clearly heard. The Lieutenant stood, fists clenched tightly, and beside him the Sergeant and the Corpsman, as well as the operators who had left their silent communication equipment. All of them waited and listened in strained silence as Jerry Cruncher narrowed his eyes in thought, took the pipe from his mouth and exhaled a cloud of pungent smoke, then turned to face them.

"Yep," he said.

They weren't the best troops—but they were troops. Technicians and operators, MP's and cooks, clerks and motor pool mechanics. But they were armed with the best weapons the armories could provide and armored as well with a sense of purpose. If they stood a little straighter or held their guns a little more firmly, it was because they knew that the future of the world was in their hands. They marched with grim precision to the road junction, where they had been instructed to wait, and had been there no more than a few minutes when Jerry Cruncher showed up. He wore waterproofs and a hardhat, heavy gumboots that came to his waist, while a worn and ancient toolbox was slung by a strap over one shoulder. His pipe was out, but still clamped in his jaw; he moved his shrewd eyes over the waiting troops.

"Not dressed right," he said.

"Everyone is in complete combat uniform," the Lieutenant answered.

"Not right for the tunnels. Gets mighty damp—"

"Mr. Cruncher, these are volunteer soldiers. They may die for their world so they do not mind getting wet for it. May we go now?"

Shaking his head in solemn disapproval Jerry Cruncher led the way to a manhole in the road, into the socket of which he inserted a shining tool with which, in a practiced movement, he flipped the heavy manhole lid aside.

"Follow me then, single file. Last two men in slide that lid back on and watch out for your fingers. Here we go."

Automatic lights sprang on as they climbed down the ladder to the cool, green tunnel below. Wires, cables and pipes lined the walls and ceiling in a maze that only a Jerry Cruncher could make head or tail of. He slapped them affectionately as they passed.

"Water main, steam main, 50,000 volt line, 220 local feeder, telephone, teletype, coax, ice water, pneumodelivery, food dispenser supply, oxygen, sewer feeder." He chuckled happily. "Yep, we've got a little bit of everything down here."

"Medic!" a voice called from the rear of the file and the Corpsman hurried away.

"They've found us!" A Permanent KP wailed and there was a rattle of weapons readied.

"Put those away!" the Lieutenant shouted. "Before you kill each other. Get me a report, Sergeant, snap to it."

They waited, weapons clenched and eyes rolling with anxiety, until the Sergeant returned. Jerry Cruncher hummed to himself tonelessly as he tapped various valves with a small ball hammer, then carefully tightened the gasket retainer on one.

"Nothing much," the Sergeant said. "Burne-Smith got a finger mashed putting the lid back on."

"They never listen," Jerry Cruncher coughed disapprovingly.

"Move it out," the Lieutenant ordered.

"One thing we haven't mentioned," Jerry Cruncher said, unmoving as a block of stone. "You guaranteed that my supervisor would see that I received my pay for this job."

"Yes, of course, can we talk about it as we go?"

"We go when this is settled. I forgot that this being Sunday I'll be getting double time and triple time after four hours."

"Fine, agreed. Let's go."

"In writing."

"Yes, writing, of course." The Lieutenant's scriber flew over a message pad and he ripped off the sheet. "There, I've signed it as well, with my serial number. The Army will stand behind this."

"Had better," Jerry Cruncher said, carefully folding the slip and placing it securely in his wallet before they moved out again.

It was a nightmare journey for all except the gray, solid man who led them like a Judas goat through this underground inferno. The main tunnels were easy enough to pass through, though pendant valvewheels and transverse pipes lay constantly in wait for the unwary. Had they not been wearing helmets half of the little force would have been stunned before they had gone a mile. As it was there was many a clank and muffled cry from the rear. Then came the inspection hatch and the first crawltube leading to a vertical pit sixty feet deep down which they had to make their way on a water-slippery ladder. At its foot an even damper tunnel, this one faced with blocks of hand-hewn stone, led them through the darkness—no lights here, they had to use their torches—to an immense cavern filled with roaring sound.

"Storm sewer," Jerry Cruncher said, pointing to the rushing river that swirled by just below their feet. "I've seen it bone dry in the season. Been rain in the suburbs lately, and here it is now. Stay on the walkway, this is the shortest way to go, and don't slip. Once in that water you're a goner. Might find your body fifty miles out in the ocean if the fishes don't get it first."

With this cheering encouragement the men slithered and crawled the awful length of that great tunnel, almost gasping with relief when they were back in the safety of a communications tube again. Shortly after this Jerry Cruncher halted and pointed up at a ladder that rose into the darkness above.

"98 BaG dropwell. This is the one you want, to that second center you talked about."

"You're sure?"

Jerry Cruncher eyed the Lieutenant with something very much like disgust and he groped his pipe from his pocket.

"Being you're ignorant, mister, I take no offense. When Jerry says a tunnel is a tunnel, that's the tunnel he says."

"No offense meant!"

"None taken," he muttered mollifiedly around the pipe stem. "This is the one. You can see all the wires and communication cables going up there as well. Can't be anything else."

"What's at the top?"

"Door with a handle and a sign saying NO ADMISSION UNDER PAR. 897A OF THE MILITARY CODE."

"Is the door locked?"

"Nope. Forbidden under paragraph 45-C of the Tunnel Authority Code. Need access, we do."

"Then this is it. Sergeant, take eighteen men and get up that ladder. Synchronize your watch with mine. In two hours we go in. Just get through that door and start shooting—watch out for the equipment though—and keep shooting until every one of those slimy dirty Betelgeuseans is dead. Do you understand?"

The Sergeant nodded with grim determination and drew himself up and saluted. "We'll do our duty, sir."

"All right, the rest of you, move out."

They had walked for no more than ten minutes down a lateral tunnel lined with frosted pipes before Jerry Cruncher stopped and sat down.

"What's wrong?" the Lieutenant asked.

"Tea break," he said, putting his still warm pipe into his side pocket and opening his lunch box.

"You can't—I mean, listen, the enemy, the schedule . . ."

"I always have tea at this time." He poured a great mugful of the potent brew and sniffed it appreciatively. "Tea break allowed for in the schedule."

Most of the men brought out rations and sipped from

their canteens while the Lieutenant paced back and forth slapping his fist into his hand. Jerry Cruncher sipped his tea placidly and chewed on a large chocolate biscuit.

A shrill scream sliced through the silence and echoed from the pipes. Something black and awful launched itself from a crevice in the wall and was attached to Trooper Barnes's throat. The soldiers were paralyzed. Not so Jerry Cruncher. There was a whistle and a thud as he instantly lashed out with his three-foot spanner and the vicious assailant rolled, dead, onto the tunnel floor before their bulging eyes.

"It's . . . it's . . . *hideous!*" a soldier gasped. "What is it?"

"Mutant hamster," Jerry Cruncher said as he picked up the monster of teeth and claws and stuffed it into his lunch box. "Descendants of house pets that escaped centuries ago, mutated here in the darkness until they turned into this. I've seen bigger ones. Boffins at the university give me three credits for every one I bring them. Not bad if I say so myself, and tax free too, which I hope you won't be repeating." He was almost jovial now at this fiscally remunerative encounter. As soon as the trooper had been sewn up they pressed on.

A second squad was left at the next communication substation and they hurried on towards ComCent itself.

"Ten minutes to go," the Lieutenant gasped, jogging heavily under the weight of all his equipment.

"Not to worry, just two tunnels more."

It was three minutes to deadline when they reached the wide opening in the ceiling above them, sprouting cables from its mouth like an electronic hydra's head.

"Big door at the top," Jerry Cruncher said, shining his torch up the shaft. "Has a dual interlock compound wheel exchange lever. As you turn the wheel counterclockwise the lever in position *ready* must be . . ."

"Come up with us, please," the Lieutenant begged, peering at his watch and chewing his lip nervously. "We'll never get in in time and they'll be warned by the attacks on the other stations."

"Not my job, you know, getting shot at. I let them as has been paid for it do it."

"Please, I beg of you, as a patriotic citizen." Jerry Cruncher's face was as of carved stone as he bit down heavily on the stem of his pipe. "You owe it to yourself, your family, your conscience, your country. And I can guarantee a hundred credit bonus for opening it."

"Done."

They climbed against time and when they reached the platform at the top the second hand on the Lieutenant's watch was just coming up on the twelve.

"Open it!"

The wheel spun and gears engaged, the great lever went down and the massive portal swung open.

"For Mother Earth!" the Lieutenant shouted and led the charge.

When they had all gone inside and the tunnel was silent again Jerry Cruncher lit his pipe and then, more out of curiosity than anything else, strolled in after them. It was a vista of endless steel corridors lined with banks of instruments, whirring and humming under electronic control. He stopped to tamp down his pipe just as a door opened and a short hairy creature, no taller than his waist, shaped like a bowling pin and possessing a number of arms, scuttled out and raced towards a large red switch mounted on the opposite wall. Five of its arms were reaching for the switch, spatulate fingers almost touching it, when the spanner whistled once again and sank deep into the creature's head flooring it instantly. Jerry Cruncher had just retrieved the spanner when the white-faced Lieutenant raced through the same door.

"Praise heaven!" he gasped, "you've stopped him in time."

"Didn't like his looks at all, though I didn't mean to bash his brains in."

"That is their leader, the only survivor, and he was going for the destruct switch that would have blown us all a mile high. He's our prisoner now and he'll talk, believe me. You didn't kill him. The Betelgeuseans have their brains in their midriffs, their stomachs are in their heads. He's just unconscious."

"Like a boot in the guts. Glad of that, didn't mean to kill him."

YOU SEE, THERE WAS THIS ORIGINAL anthology that Barry Malzberg and Ed Ferman were doing. Their idea was saintly and wise. They wished to put paid to all of the oldest themes in science fiction—to have one story written on each, the definitive story on each theme—and put them all into one handsome volume. They eventually did this, and it *was* a handsome volume, and, other than the fact that some dumb copy editor at the publishing house fiddled with some of the stories, which incensed a few contributors far too much, I did enjoy being represented in *Final Stage*.

But I felt, and still feel, that you cannot stop bad stories on old themes from being written. I *knew*, in fact. I had written a parody of space opera titled, modestly, *Star Smashers of the Galaxy Rangers*. It appeared a few years ago. And space operas blast on as ever. Here I have another kick at this particular groin.

It won't make any difference at all.

(I have kept my comments on this story just as they appeared in the original publication.

20

288

SPACE RATS OF THE C.C.C.

<<<<<<<<<<<<<<<<<<<<<<<<<<<<<<<<<<<<<<<

THAT'S IT, MATEY, PULL UP A STOOL, SURE, use that one. Just dump old Phrnnx onto the floor to sleep it off. You know that Krddls can't stand to drink, much less drink *flnnx*—and that topped off with a smoke of the hellish *krmml* weed. Here, let me pour you a mug of *flnnx*, oops, sorry about your sleeve. When it dries you can scrape it off with a knife. Here's to your health and may your tubeliners never fail you when the *kpnnz* hordes are on your tail.

No, sorry, never heard your name before. Too many good men come and go and the good ones die early, aye! Me? You never heard of me. Just call me Old Sarge, as good a name as any. Good men I say, and the best of them was—well, we'll call him Gentleman Jax. He had another name, but there's a little girl waiting on a planet I could name, a little girl that's waiting and watching the shimmering trails of the deep-spacers when they come, and waiting for a man. So for her sake we'll call him Gentleman Jax, he would have liked that, and she would like that if only she knew, although she must be getting kind of gray or bald by now, and arthritic from all that sitting and waiting but, golly, that's another story and by Orion it's not for me to tell. That's it, help yourself, a large one. Sure the green fumes are normal for good *flnnx*, though you better close your eyes when you drink or you'll be blind in a week, ha-ha!, by the sacred name of the Prophet Mrddl!

Yes, I can tell what you're thinking. What's an old

289

space rat like me doing in a dive like this out here at galaxy's end where the rim stars flicker wanly and the tired photons go slow. I'll tell you what I'm doing, getting drunker than a Planizzian *pfrdffl,* that's what. They say that drink has the power to dim memories and by Cygnus I have some memories that need dimming. I see you looking at those scars on my hands. Each one is a story, matey, aye, and the scars on my back each a story and the scars on my . . . well, that's a different story. Yes, I'll tell you a story, a true one by Mrddl's holy name, though I might change a name or two, that little girl waiting, you know.

You heard tell of the C.C.C.? I can see by the sudden widening of your eyes and the blanching of your space-tanned skin that you have. Well, yours truly, Old Sarge here, was one of the first of the Space Rats of the C.C.C., and my buddy then was the man they know as Gentleman Jax. May Great Kramddl curse his name and blacken the memory of the first day when I first set eyes on him . . .

"Graduating class . . . ten-SHUN!"

The sergeant's stentorian voice bellowed forth, cracking like a whiplash across the expectant ears of the mathematically aligned rows of cadets. With the harsh snap of those fateful words a hundred and three incredibly polished bootheels crashed together with a single snap and the eighty-seven cadets of the graduating class snapped to steel-rigid attention. (It should be explained that some of them were from alien worlds, different numbers of legs, etc.) Not a breath was drawn, not an eyelid twitched a thousandths of a millimeter as Colonel von Thorax stepped forward, glaring down at them all through the glass monocle in front of his glass eye, close-cropped gray hair stiff as barbed wire, black uniform faultlessly cut and smooth, a *krmml* weed cigarette clutched in the steel fingers of his prosthetic left arm, black-gloved fingers of his prosthetic right arm snapping to hatbrim's edge in a perfect salute, motors whining thinly in his prosthetic lungs to power the Brobdingnagian roar of his harshly bellowed command.

"At ease. And listen to me. You are the hand-picked men—and hand-picked things, too, of course—from all the civilized worlds of the galaxy. Six million and forty-three cadets entered the first year of training and most of them washed out in one way or another. Some could not toe the mark. Some were expelled and shot for buggery. Some believed the lying commy pinko crying liberal claims that continuous war and slaughter is not necessary and they were expelled and shot as well. One by one the weaklings fell away through the years, leaving the hard core of the Corps—*you!* The Corpsmen of the first graduating class of the C.C.C.! Ready to spread the benefits of civilization to the stars. Ready at last to find out what the initials C.C.C. stand for!"

A mighty roar went up from the massed throats, a cheer of hoarse masculine enthusiasm that echoed and boomed from the stadium walls. At a signal from von Thorax a switch was thrown and a great shield of imperviomite slid into place above, sealing the stadium from prying eyes and ears and snooping spyish rays. The roaring voices roared on enthusiastically—and many an eardrum was burst that day!—yet were stilled in an instant when the Colonel raised his hand.

"You Corpsmen will not be alone when you push the frontiers of civilization out to the barbaric stars. Oh, no! You will each have a faithful companion by your side. First man, first row—step forward and meet your faithful companion!"

The Corpsman called out stepped forward a smart pace and clicked his heels sharply, said click being echoed in the clack of a thrown wide door and, without conscious intent, every eye in that stadium was drawn in the direction of the dark doorway from which emerged . . .

How to describe it? How to describe the whirlwind that batters you, the storm that engulfs you, the spacewarp that enwraps you? It was as indescribable as any natural force!

It was a creature three meters high at the shoulders, four meters high at the ugly, drooling, tooth-clashing head, a whirlwinded, spacewarped storm that rushed forward on four piston-like legs, great-clawed feet tearing grooves in the untearable surface of the impervitium flooring, a monster born of madness and nightmares that reared up before them and bellowed in a soul-destroying screech.

"There!" Colonel von Thorax bellowed in answer, blood-specked spittle mottling his lips. *"There* is your faithful companion, the mutacamel, mutation of the noble beast of Good Old Earth, symbol and pride of the C.C.C. —the *Combat Camel Corps!* Corpsman, meet your camel!"

The selected Corpsman stepped forward and raised his arm in greeting to this noble beast, which promptly bit the arm off. His shrill screams mingled with the barely stifled gasps of his companions who watched, with more than casual interest, as camel trainers girt with brass-buckled leather harness rushed out and beat the protesting camel with clubs back from whence it had come while a medic clamped a tourniquet on the wounded man's stump and dragged his limp body away.

"That is your first lesson on combat camels," the Colonel cried huskily. "Never raise your arms to them. Your companion, with a newly grafted arm will, I am certain, ha-ha!, remember this little lesson. Next man, next companion!"

Again the thunder of rushing feet and the high-pitched, gurgling, scream-like roar of the combat camel at full charge. This time the Corpsman kept his arm down and the camel bit his head off.

"Can't graft on a head I am afraid," the Colonel leered maliciously at them. "A moment of silence for our departed companion who has gone to the big rocket pad in the sky. That's enough. Ten-SHUN! You will now proceed to the camel-training area, where you will learn to get along with your faithful companions. Never forgetting that they each have a complete set of false teeth made of imperviumite, as well as razor sharp claw caps of this same substance. Dis-MISSED!"

The student barracks of the C.C.C. was well known for its "no frills" or rather "no coddling" decor and comforts. The beds were impervitium slabs—no spine-sapping mattresses here!—and the sheets of thin burlap. No blankets of course, not with the air kept at a healthy 4 degrees centigrade. The rest of the comforts matched so that it was a great surprise to the graduates to find unaccustomed comforts awaiting them upon their return from the ceremonies and training. There was a *shade* on each bare-bulbed reading light and a nice soft 2-centimeter-thick pillow on every bed. Already they were reaping the benefits of all the years of labor.

Now, among all the students, the top student by far was named M———. There are some secrets that must not be told, names that are important to loved ones and neighbors, therefore I shall draw the cloak of anonymity over the true identity of the man known as M———. Suffice to call him "Steel," for that was the nickname of someone who knew him best. "Steel," or Steel as we can call him, had at this time a roommate by the name of L———. Later, much later, L——— was to be called by certain people "Gentleman Jax," so for the purpose of this narrative we shall call him "Gentleman Jax" as well, or perhaps just plain "Jax," or Jax as some people pronounce it. Jax was second only to Steel in scholastic and sporting attainments and the two were the best of chums. They had been roommates for the past year and now they were back in their room with their feet up, basking in the unexpected luxury of the new furnishings, sipping decaffeinated coffee, called koffee, and smoking deeply of the school's own brand of denicotinized cigarettes, called Denikcig by the manufacturer but always referred to, humorously, by the C.C.C. students as "gaspers" or "lungbusters."

"Throw me over a gasper, will you Jax," Steel said, from where he lolled on the bed, hands behind his head, dreaming of what was in store for him now that he would be having his own camel soon. "Ouch!" he chuckled as the pack of "gaspers" caught him in the eye. He drew out one of the slim white forms and tapped it on the wall to ignite it, then drew in a lungful of refreshing smoke. "I still can't believe it . . ." he smoke-ringed.

"Well it's true enough, by Mrddl," Jax smiled. "We're

graduates. Now throw back that pack of lungbusters so I can join you in a draw or two."

Steel complied, but did it so enthusiastically that the pack hit the wall and instantly all the cigarettes ignited and the whole thing burst into flame. A glass of water doused the conflagration but, while it was still fizzling fitfully, a light flashed redly on the comscreen.

"High-priority message," Steel bit out, slamming down the actuator button. Both youths snapped to rigid attention as the screen filled with the stern visage of Colonel von Thorax.

"M———, L———, to my office on the triple." The words fell like leaden weights from his lips. What could it mean?

"What can it mean?" Jax asked as they hurtled down a dropchute at close to the speed of gravity.

"We'll find out quickly enough," Steel ejaculated as they drew up at the "old man's" door and activated the announcer button.

Moved by some hidden mechanism the door swung wide and, not without a certain amount of trepidation, they entered. But what was this? *This!* The Colonel was looking at them and smiling, *smiling,* an expression never before known to cross his iron visage at any time.

"Make yourself comfortable, lads," he indicated, pointing at comfortable chairs that rose out of the floor at the touch of a button. "You'll find 'gaspers' in the arms of these servochairs, as well as Valumian wine or Snaggian beer."

"No koffee?" Jax open-mouthedly expostulated and they all laughed.

"I don't think you really want it," the Colonel susurrated coyly through his artificial larynx. "Drink up, lads, you're Space Rats of the C.C.C. now and your youth is behind you. Now look at that."

That was a three-dimensional image that sprang into being in the air before them at the touch of a button, an image of a spacer like none ever seen before. She was as slender as a swordfish, fine-winged as a bird, solid as a whale and as armed to the teeth as an alligator.

"Holy Kolon," Steel sighed in open-mouthed awe. "Now *that* is what I call a hunk o' rocket!"

"Some of us prefer to call it the *Indefectible*," the Colonel said, not unhumorously.

"Is that *her?* We heard something . . ."

"You heard very little, for we have had this baby under wraps ever since the earliest stage. She has the largest engines ever built, new improved MacPhersons* of the most advanced design, Kelly drive ** gear that has been improved to where you would not recognize it in a month of Thursdays—as well as double-strength Fitzroy projectors† that make the old ones look like a kid's pop-gun. And I've saved the best for last . . ."

"*Nothing* can be better than what you have already told us," Steel broke in.

"That's what *you* think!" the Colonel laughed, not unkindly, with a sound like tearing steel. "The best news is that, Steel, you are going to be Captain of this space-going super-dreadnaught, while lucky Jax is Chief Engineer."

"Lucky Jax would be a lot happier if he was Captain instead of king of the stokehold," he muttered and they all laughed at this joke. All except him because it was no joke.

"Everything is completely automated," the Colonel continued, "so it can be flown by a crew of two. But I must warn you that it has experimental gear aboard so whoever flies her has to volunteer . . ."

"I volunteer!" Steel shouted.

"I have to go to the terlet," Jax said, rising, though he sat again instantly when the ugly blaster leaped from its

* The MacPherson engine was first mentioned in the author's story, *Rocket Rangers of the I.R.T.* (*Spicy-Weird Stories,* 1923).

** Loyal readers first discovered the Kelly drive in the famous book *Hell Hounds of the Coal Sack Cluster* (Slimecreeper Press, Ltd., 1931), also published in the German language as *Teufelhund Nach der Knockwurst Exspres*. Translated into Italian by Re Umberto; unpublished in Italy to date.

† A media breakthrough was made when the Fitzroy projector first appeared in *Female Space Zombies of Venus* in 1936 in *True Story Confessions*.

holster to the Colonel's hand. "Ha-ha, just a joke, I volunteer, sure."

"I knew I could count on you lads. The C.C.C. breeds *men*. Camels too, of course. So here is what you do. At 0304 hours tomorrow you two in the *Indefectible* will crack ether headed out Cygnus way. In the direction of a *certain* planet."

"Let me guess, if I can, that is," Steel said grimly through tight-clenched teeth. "You don't mean to give us a crack at the larshnik-loaded world of Biru-2, do you?"

"I do. This is the larshnik's prime base, the seat of operation of all their drug and gambling traffic, where the white-slavers offload and the queer green is printed, site of the *flnnx* distilleries and lair of the pirate hordes."

"If you want action, that sounds like *it!*" Steel grimaced.

"You are not just whistling through your back teeth," the Colonel agreed. "If I were younger and had a few less replaceable parts, this is the kind of opportunity I would leap at . . ."

"You can be Chief Engineer," Jax hinted.

"Shut up," the Colonel implied. "Good luck, gentlemen, for the honor of the C.C.C. rides with you."

"But not the camels?" Steel asked.

"Maybe next time. There are, well, adjustment problems. We have lost four more graduates since we have been sitting here. Maybe we'll even change animals. Make it the C.D.C."

"With combat *dogs?*" Jax asked.

"Either that or donkeys. Or dugongs. But it is my worry, not yours. All you guys have to do is get out there and crack Biru-2 wide open. I know you can do it."

If the stern-faced Corpsmen had any doubts, they kept them to themselves, for that is the way of the Corps. They did what had to be done and the next morning, at exactly 0304:00 hours, the mighty bulk of the *Indefectible* hurled itself into space. The roaring MacPherson engines poured quintillions of ergs of energy into the reactor drive until they were safely out of the gravity field of mother Earth. Jax labored over his engines, shoveling the radioactive *transvestite* into the gaping maw of the hungry furnace, until Steel signaled from the bridge that it was "change-over" time. Then they changed over to the space-eating Kelly drive. Steel jammed home the button that activated the drive and the great ship leaped starward at seven times the speed of light.* Since the drive was fully automatic Jax freshened up in the fresher, while his clothes were automatically washed in the washer, then proceeded to the bridge.

"Really," Steel said, his eyebrows climbing up his forehead. "I didn't know you went in for polkadot jockstraps."

"It was the only thing I had clean. The washer dissolved the rest of my clothes."

"Don't worry about it. It's the larshniks of Biru-2 who have to worry! We hit atmosphere in exactly seventeen minutes and I have been thinking about what to do when that happens."

"Well I certainly hope *someone* has! I haven't had time to draw a deep breath, much less think."

"Don't worry, old pal, we are in this together. The way I figure it we have two choices. We can blast right in, guns roaring, or we can slip in by stealth."

"Oh, you really *have* been thinking, haven't you."

"I'll ignore that because you are tired. Strong as we are I think the land-based batteries are stronger. So I suggest we slip in without being noticed."

"Isn't that a little hard when you are flying in a thirty million ton spacer?"

"Normally, yes. But do you see this button here marked *invisibility?* While you were loading the fuel they explained this to me. It is a new invention, never used in action before, that will render us invisible and impervious to detection by any of their detection instruments."

"Now that's more like it. Fifteen minutes to go, we should be getting mighty close. Turn on the old invisibility ray . . ."

---

* When the inventor, Patsy Kelly, was asked how ships could move at seven times the speed of light when the limiting velocity of matter, according to Einstein, was the speed of light, he responded in his droll Goidelic way, with a shrug, "Well—sure and I guess Einstein was wrong."

"Don't!!"

"Done. Now what's your problem."

"Nothing really. Except the experimental invisibility device is not expected to last more than thirteen minutes before it burns out."

Unhappily, this proved to be the case. One hundred miles above the barren, blasted surface of Biru-2 the good old *Indefectible* popped into existence.

In the minutest fraction of a millisecond the mighty spacesonar and superadar had locked grimly onto the invading ship while the sublights flickered their secret signals, waiting for the correct response that would reveal the invader as one of theirs.

"I'll send a signal, stall them, these larshniks aren't too bright," Steel laughed. He thumbed on the microphone, switched to the interstellar emergency frequency, then bit out the rasping words in a sordid voice. "Agent X-9 to prime base. Had a firefight with the patrol, shot up my code books, but I got all the ———— ————s, ha-ha! Am coming home with a load of 800,000 long tons of the hellish *krmml* weed."

The larshnik response was instantaneous. From the gaping, pitted orifices of thousands of giant blaster cannon there vomited force ravening rays of energy that strained the very fabric of space itself. These coruscating forces blasted into the impregnable screens of the old *Indefectible,* which, sadly, was destined not to get much older, and instantly punched their way through and splashed coruscatingly from the very hull of the ship itself. Mere matter could not stand against such forces unlocked in the coruscating bowels of the planet itself so that the impregnable imperialite metal walls instantly vaporized into a thin gas which was, in turn, vaporized into the very electrons and protons (and neutrons too) of which it was made.

Mere flesh and blood could not stand against such forces. But in the few seconds it took the coruscating energies to eat through the force screens, hull, vaporized gas and protons, the reckless pair of valiant Corpsmen had hurled themselves headlong into their space armor.

And just in time! The ruin of the once great ship hit the atmosphere and seconds later slammed into the poison soil of Biru-2.

To the casual observer it looked like the end. The once mighty queen of the spaceways would fly no more, for she now consisted of no more than two-hundred pounds of smoking junk. Nor was there any sign of life from the tragic wreck as was evidenced when surface crawlers erupted from a nearby secret hatch concealed in the rock and crawled through the smoking remains with all their detectors detecting at maximum gain. *Report!* the radio signal wailed. *No sign of life to fifteen decimal places!* snapped back the cursing operator of the crawlers before he signaled them to return to base. Their metal cleats clanked viciously across the barren soil and then they were gone. All that remained was the cooling metal wreck hissing with despair as the poison rain poured like tears upon it.

Were these two good friends dead? I thought you would never ask. Unbeknownst to the larshnik technicians just one millisecond before the wreck struck down two massive and almost indestructible suits of space armor had been ejected by coiled steelite springs, sent flying to the very horizon, where they landed behind a concealing spine of rock, which, just by *chance* was the spine of rock into which the secret hatch had been built that concealed the crawlway from which the surface crawlers with their detectors emerged for their fruitless search, to which they returned under control of their cursing operator who, stoned again with hellish *krmml* weed, never noticed the quick flick of the detector needles as the crawlers re-entered the tunnel, this time bearing on their return journey a cargo they had not exited with as the great door slammed shut behind them.

"We've done it! We're inside their defenses," Steel rejoiced. "And no thanks to you, pushing that Mrddl-cursed invisibility button."

"Well, how was I to know," Jax grated. "Anyways, we don't have a ship anymore but we *do* have the element of surprise. They don't know that *we* are here, but we know *they* are here!"

"Good thinking . . . hssst!" he hissed. "Stay low, we're coming to something."

The clanking crawlers rattled into the immense chamber cut into the living stone and now filled with deadly war machines of all description. The only human there, if he could be called human, was the larshnik operator whose soiled fingertips sprang to the gun controls the instant he spotted the intruders but he never stood a chance. Precisely aimed rays from two blasters zeroed in on him and in a millisecond he was no more than a charred fragment of smoking flesh in the chair. Corps justice was striking at last to the larshnik lair.

Justice it was, impersonal and final, impartial and murderous, for there were no "innocents" in this lair of evil. Ravening forces of civilized vengeance struck down all that crossed their path as the two chums rode a death-dealing combat gun through the corridors of infamy.

"This is the big one," Steel grimaced as they came to an immense door of gold-plated impervialite before which a suicide squad committed suicide under the relentless scourge of fire. There was more feeble resistance, smokily, coruscatingly and noisily exterminated, before this last barrier went down and they rode in triumph into the central control, now manned by a single figure at the main panel. Superlarsh himself, secret head of the empire of interstellar crime.

"You have met your destiny," Steel intoned grimly, his weapon fixed unmovingly upon the black-robed figure in the opaque space helmet. "Take off that helmet or you die upon the instant."

His only reply was a slobbered growl of inchoate rage and for a long instant the black-gloved hands trembled over the gun controls. Then, ever so slowly, these same hands raised themselves to clutch at the helmet, to turn it, to lift it slowly off . . .

"By the sacred name of the Prophet Mrddl!" the two Corpsmen gasped in unison, struck speechless by what they saw.

"Yes, so now you know," grated Superlarsh through angry teeth. "But, ha-ha, I'll bet you never suspected."

"You!!" Steel insufflated breaking the frozen silence. "You! *You!!* YOU!!!"

"Yes, me, I, Colonel von Thorax, Commandant of the C.C.C. You never suspected me and, ohh, how I laughed at you all of the time."

"But . . ." Jax stammered. *"Why?"*

"Why? The answer is obvious to any but democratic interstellar swine like you. The only thing the larshniks of the galaxy had to fear was something like the C.C.C., a powerful force impervious to outside bribery or sedition, noble in the cause of righteousness. You could have caused us trouble. Therefore *we* founded the C.C.C. and I have long been head of both organizations. Our recruiters bring in the best that the civilized planets can offer and I see to it that most of them are brutalized, morale destroyed, bodies wasted and spirits crushed so they are no longer a danger. Of course a few always make it through the course no matter how disgusting I make it, every generation has its share of super-masochists, but I see that these are taken care of pretty quickly."

"Like being sent on suicide missions?" Steel asked ironly.

"That's a good way."

"Like the one we were sent on—but it *didn't work!* Say your prayers, you filthy larshnik, for you are about to meet your maker!"

"Maker? Prayers? Are you out of your skull? All larshniks are atheists to the end . . ."

And then it was the end, in a coruscating puff of vapor, dead with those vile words upon his lips, no less than he deserved.

"Now what?" Steel asked.

"This," Jax responded, shooting the gun from his hand and imprisoning him instantly with an unbreakable paralysis ray. "No more second best for me, in the engine room with you on the bridge. This is *my* ball game from here on in."

"Are you mad!" Steel fluttered through paralyzed lips.

"Sane for the first time in my life. The superlarsh is dead, long live the new superlarsh. It's mine, the whole galaxy, *mine*."

"And what about me?"

"I should kill you, but that would be too easy. And you did share your chocolate bars with me. You will be blamed for this entire debacle, for the death of Colonel von Thorax *and* for the disaster here at larshnik prime base. Every man's hand will be against you and you will be an outcast and will flee for your life to the farflung outposts of the galaxy, where you will live in terror."

"Remember the chocolate bars!"

"I do. All I ever got were the stale ones. Now . . . GO!"

You want to know my name? Old Sarge is good enough. My story? Too much for your tender ears, boyo. Just top up the glasses, that's the way, and join me in a toast. At least that much for a poor old man who has seen much in this long lifetime. A toast of bad luck, bad cess I say, may Great Kramddl curse forever the man some know as Gentleman Jax. What, hungry?, not me—no—NO! Not a chocolate bar!!!!!

Fantasy Novels
from
Pocket Books

___ 83217 THE BOOK OF THE DUN COW
Walter Wangerin, Jr. $2.50
*"Far and away the most literate and intelligent
story of the year."*—The New York Times

___ 43131 THE WHITE HART
Nancy Springer $2.50
*"It has everything; a believable fantasy world...
a lovely, poignant book."*
—Marion Zimmer Bradley

___ 82912 BEAUTY Robin McKinley $1.95
*"The most delightful first novel I've read in
years...I was moved and enchanted."*—Peter S.
Beagle, author of THE LAST UNICORN

___ 83281 CHARMED LIFE $2.25
"An outstanding success."—Andre Norton

___ 83294 ARIOSTO
Chelsea Quinn Yarbo $2.25
*"Colorful and exciting...a vivid tapestry come
to life...superb!"*—Andre Norton

___ 82958 THE ORPHAN
Robert Stallman $2.25
*"An exciting blend of love and violence, of
sensitivity and savagery."*—Fritz Leiber